MURDER ON THE CLYDE

An absolutely gripping crime mystery with a massive twist

DANIEL SELLERS

DCI Lola Harris Series Book 3

Joffe Books, London
www.joffebooks.com

First published in Great Britain in 2024

© Daniel Sellers 2024

This book is a work of fiction. Names, characters, businesses, organizations, places and events are either the product of the author's imagination or are used fictitiously. Any resemblance to actual persons, living or dead, events or locales is entirely coincidental. The spelling used is British English except where fidelity to the author's rendering of accent or dialect supersedes this. The right of Daniel Sellers to be identified as author of this work has been asserted in accordance with the Copyright, Designs and Patents Act 1988.

Cover art by Nebojša Zorić

ISBN: 978-1-83526-498-0

For Alex, Ruth and Abigail

AUTHOR'S NOTE

A number of places referred to in this novel are real, as are some institutions. The characters and the events are fictional. For readers unfamiliar with the geography of Glasgow's main waterway, there are maps on my website: www.danielsellers.co.uk

Please follow me on Twitter (@djsellersauthor) and on Instagram (@danielsellersauthor), or by following the hashtag: #WhatWouldLolaHarrisDo?

PROLOGUE

Glasgow Chronicle, *Wednesday 27 November 2019, p. 7*

LATEST CLYDE DEATH: PROMPTS NEW QUESTIONS

by Dougie Latimer, crime desk

Police Scotland have named the young man found dead in the River Clyde on Monday morning. The body of Mark Brodie, originally of Edinburgh, was spotted shortly after 7 a.m. by the Bells footbridge at Pacific Quay. Circumstances have prompted new speculation that a serial attacker is operating on the banks of the Clyde, one who could be responsible for three other deaths in as many years.

According to police, Mr Brodie — who was twenty-four — was seen by an unnamed witness entering the river from its north bank beside the Kingston Bridge, a few minutes before midnight on Sunday evening. Police believe Brodie was walking from the Finnieston area of the city to his home in Cessnock.

A post-mortem has confirmed Brodie drowned following a head injury.

The victim's mother, Mrs Carole Brodie of Wester Hailes in Edinburgh, believes her son was the victim of a deliberate attack. She describes receiving a call from Mark's mobile number around the time of the incident, but could hear only silence.

A Police Scotland spokesperson was quick to deny reports that this incident is part of a series of attacks on young men which have resulted in three deaths and one assault. There is a popular theory that the attacks are the work of the so-called 'Clyde Pusher', though the existence of such a figure is in question.

Continues on p. 23

CHAPTER ONE

Saturday 11 February
10.05 p.m.

Cammy found shelter from the incessant rain and used his phone's torch to count the money. Two twenties and a ten. The sight of the notes and the smooth, slidey feel of them between his fingers gave him a thrill. A sense of relief too. The money meant he could eat well this week, maybe even get a Chinese or Indian for him and his flatmates.

He stayed in the shelter for some minutes, watching the rain batter the walkway by the river.

'A present,' Warren had told him. Then, when Cammy asked him what for: 'Because you're special to me.'

It wasn't the first time Warren had given him cash. He hadn't exactly come to expect it, but he hoped for it all the same.

'You're one of us now,' his pal Tiffany had cackled a few weeks ago when he told her Warren had given him money.

It wasn't payment, whatever she said. It was a present, a sign of affection. And there was nothing wrong with that. Everyone needed affection.

The rain wasn't stopping and he was getting cold, so he hitched up the collar of his denim jacket and hurried out into it, head down, stopping only to ditch his empty can in the recycling bin.

He didn't really mind the rain. It cleaned the city and made the pavements gleam and the dark river sparkle. Everything seemed so bright this evening, though that might be the energy drink; it did make everything sharper, the colours richer, as if your eyes were wider somehow. He bounced along, heading east along the north bank of the river, minding the jakeys and the worst of the puddles.

He felt elated, euphoric even, and his mind was full of grand schemes — and *hope*. Warren was working on a new project, so he'd told him once they'd finished in the car in the dark Tradeston car park. He'd be freer to meet Cammy more often, and maybe even have him over to the house — the big place he owned in the countryside north of the city.

'I'd like that,' Cammy had said, almost in a whisper, worried he'd break the spell.

'I'd love you to be there,' Warren had said, still buckling his belt. 'It's a dream of mine.'

Cammy smiled, tears pricking his eyes.

'Hiya, Cammy,' a voice called from the darkness.

'Is that you, Larissa?' he called back, peering into the gloom.

She came forward from the shelter of one of the new but weedy trees they'd planted down here — part of the idea of turning this urban stretch into a leafy waterside boulevard. She was wearing a fur jacket and holding a brolly over her lovely golden curls.

'You watching yourself, are you?'

'Aye,' he said, still smiling about Warren. He'd tell Larissa about the money, and about what Warren had said, except Warren was so worried about people knowing — and Cammy tried to be loyal. 'You?'

'Aye, no bad.' Larissa was older than him by some years. Thirty even, though still not as old as Warren. From a distance she looked like a doll, or the heroine from an old Hollywood film. Closer up, not so much. 'Not exactly busy. The rain puts them off. You away hame?'

'Aye. 'Spect I'll get something to eat on the way.'

'You wanna go up through the town,' Larissa said now.

'How?'

'Mandy said that creep's about again.'

'Really . . . ?'

'You know the one I mean. So you be careful, aye? Young lad like you — it's not safe.'

'Okay.' He beamed to reassure her. 'Better go.'

He hurried on, turning once to see Larissa looking after him, brolly angled so her face was still visible from the road. Even as he watched, a car slowed by the kerb and she turned her attention to that.

That creep's about again.

The one they all knew about, though nothing was ever done. The one everyone called the Clyde Pusher.

Larissa had told him to go through the town. It was good advice, but he'd be fine. He was watchful and fast, and besides, he liked walking by the river. It was so big and dark and, tonight, alive with drumming rain.

And then he saw him.

Across the road, a figure stood in the arch of a doorway of one of the older buildings facing the river. Tall and broad, surely a man. He was all in black, down to his gloved hands, and he wore a hood that concealed his face. Cammy felt sure it was the Clyde Pusher; this was how he was said to dress, and he seemed transfixed by the river.

Cammy stopped and hung back, feeling safe on the other side of the road in the shadows of the trees. He watched the figure and experienced a sensation he'd never had before. The Pusher might be responsible for all sorts of horrible things, but he had no idea Cammy was there, and that gave Cammy *power*.

He studied the figure as he might have studied a slug as a wee boy. One he could stamp on.

Standing there, watching, he had an idea. If the Pusher moved, he could go after him. Could track him. Maybe even take photos or a video he could put online, tagging the police and the TV news, of course. He'd be a hero!

Excitement ran like static round the inside of his ribcage and his fingers tingled.

But what if the Pusher went to attack someone while Cammy was tailing him? Well, then he'd call out, warn the victim. The victim would thank him. Maybe together they'd wrestle the Pusher to the ground!

Warren would be so proud when he told him.

Now the man was on the move. Out of the doorway and moving east, keeping close to the buildings, a shadow slipping between shadows.

Cammy followed on the other side of the road, trying to look chilled, bobbing his head as if he was listening to Lady Gaga. He activated the video setting of his camera app and pointed it. He tried to zoom in, to lighten the setting, but it was no good. He needed to get closer.

He hurried, eyes moving between his phone and the figure over the road. But then, suddenly, *somehow*, the figure was gone.

Cammy stopped and looked about, nervous. There was no traffic just now. A tall guy in a light-coloured hoodie had been walking this way, but he'd passed by and was already some distance behind him. Cammy was alone, by the wide, rain-troubled river, and somewhere a killer was hiding.

Ahead was a junction with traffic lights and one of the bridges. He hurried towards it, pins and needles in his hands and arms, eyes darting, his plan to video the Pusher forgotten. He just wanted to get home.

He stopped in the shelter of a tree and checked his phone.

When he looked up, he nearly dropped it — because the Pusher was only a few metres away, on this side of the road, right by the edge of the river. And he was looking right this way.

Cammy shrank deeper into the shadow of the tree, choked with fear. He could see the Pusher's masked face beneath the hood . . . could see his eyes.

And now the Pusher was tearing this way. One black-gloved hand came up, and in it was what looked like a lump of wood.

Cammy held his nerve as the Pusher flew by his hiding place, and saw he was following the guy in the pale hoodie who'd passed by a minute ago. The Pusher reached the man beside the river railings and brought the wood down hard on the back of his head.

Cammy opened his mouth to scream a warning, but nothing came out.

It was too late anyway.

CHAPTER TWO

10.19 p.m.

Ella had her phone out again and Lola stifled a groan. This was serious business to Ella, so she told herself to behave and made a polite face.

'The first principle,' Ella read loudly over the noise of the cocktail bar, 'is to acknowledge your feelings about your ex.' She eyed her two companions in turn to check they'd taken it in. 'The second is to "let those emotions flow".'

'*Jeezo*,' Lola muttered. 'Are they having a laugh?'

'It makes sense!' Ella said, eyes wide.

'Oh, I know it does. Nothing new, though, is it?'

'Miss Cynical,' teased Sorcha, the woman on Lola's right, but at the same time dropping her a wink of solidarity.

'Sorry, Ella,' Lola said. 'Just ignore me.'

They were in a swish new place in Brunswick Street in the Merchant City, all white and silver and full of light, with mirrors and crystal chandeliers everywhere. Smartly dressed waiters served expensive wine, cocktails you'd never heard of and fancy tapas. Ella's choice. Lola would have settled for a quieter, more traditional place. Vroni's wine bar, perhaps, or Sloans — authentically Victorian and cosily atmospheric. Still, it was nice to go somewhere new.

'Keep reading, Ella,' Sorcha urged. 'It's interesting.' She caught Lola's eye again and Lola looked quickly away before either of them cracked up.

Ella took a sip of her espresso martini and squinted at her phone for the next of her 'top tips for getting over a failed relationship'. She was forever searching for guidance that might help heal her broken heart. Lola didn't want, or need, guidance to get over Joe — so she'd told herself. She'd signed up with a counsellor but knew it wasn't for her when he suggested that, as Lola was now in 'middle life', she might consider pursuing fulfilment in 'non-relationship domains'. She'd swiftly cancelled the rest of the planned sessions. There were no doubt better counsellors out there, but she didn't have the energy for the search.

Ella read out some further 'top tips', and Lola nodded along without paying attention.

Ella would be fine, of course. Still in her twenties, she was clever, darkly attractive and incredibly sweet. Lola had no doubt she'd find a man she liked — once she'd got over the oaf of a second-division footballer she'd just split from . . .

Sorcha was a woman closer to Lola's own heart, as well as being of a similar age. Like Lola, she'd heard every pearl of relationship wisdom going and could beat anyone in the cynicism stakes. Sorcha had emerged from a bruising marriage to a controlling bully-boy executive. She'd be okay too, Lola had no doubt — especially once the divorce settlement came through. She'd already promised the members of the club an all-expenses-paid trip to Rome for the weekend as a treat when that happened. Sorcha had *no* intention of entering another relationship any time soon, and wanted the world to know it.

It was Sorcha who'd set up the Covid Divorce Club, a group of people whose relationships had ended during the pandemic. She and Ella were neighbours. Lola had been recruited thanks to her sister, who'd been at university with Sorcha. They'd begun to meet on Zoom, consoling each other as they dealt with the trauma of change. The end of the pandemic had meant they could meet in person and eat and drink themselves cheerful. Latterly the women had been joined by Tom, a friend of a friend of Ella's. He'd split from his boyfriend of a decade right at the start of lockdown. Despite his protestations to the contrary, Lola suspected Tom was having a whale of a time as a single man, and seemed to be making the most of every dating app he could download onto his phone. He was outside just now, on the phone to a friend who was having some kind of crisis — a long-winded one, it seemed. He finally reappeared, soaked from the rain, as Ella prepared to read another piece of relationship advice:

'"Even at your lowest ebb",' she read, her voice cracking with emotion, '"it's important to remember this: *the heart will go on*."'

Sorcha burst out in gales of laughter and Lola joined in.

'Come off it, Ella,' Sorcha cried. 'Does it honestly say that?'

'Never a truer word written,' Tom said and flung out his arms, DiCaprio-style, crying, '*I'm the King of the World!*'

'You're all horrible,' Ella said, dropping her phone on the table. But now she was laughing too.

They were paying the bill when Tom turned to Lola and said, with heavy meaning, '*So . . . ?*'

The two women eyed her with interest, and she recognised this was an ambush.

'"So" what?' she said innocently.

'Are you gonna meet Sorcha's pal?' Tom said.

'Och, I don't know.' She gave it a moment's contemplation, eyeing Sorcha, anxious not to upset her. 'I haven't made my mind up.'

'You should!' cried Ella.

'Barry's lovely,' Sorcha said. 'I mean, I don't know him *that* well, but he's a really nice guy.'

'He looks nice in the photos,' Tom pointed out. 'In a clever way.'

Barry did sound — and look — mildly promising. He was an engineering lecturer at the university. He liked old films, wanted to travel more, and enjoyed good food and wine. A recommendation from a friend, especially a discerning one like Sorcha, had to be worth more than picking a profile online, at any rate. Since announcing her intention to dip her toe into the dating pool, Lola had heard endless horror stories of fake profiles, creepy blokes and awkward — even dangerous — dates. She'd gone out with two men so far. With the first she'd gone to a café in Shawlands and he'd cried about his divorce for half the time. Her overriding memory was of snotty tissues. The second had been with a very handsome man called Hughie. He was smart, witty and astonishingly attractive, with lovely light-green eyes. Wealthy too, with a 'bolt-hole' in Argyll, where he was building a boat. The trouble with Hughie was that he was younger than her by some years, only in his late thirties. That, and the fact he'd been eager to the point of pushy — asking to drive her home from dinner, wanting to see her again soon, to pick her up at her house. She'd asked herself repeatedly why someone so young and attractive would be interested in her — and alarm bells had started to chime.

'You're coming to mine on Wednesday evening, aren't you?' Sorcha said now. 'For my birthday thing? I wasn't planning to invite Barry, but I could. You never know. You might hit it off.'

'Please don't invite him,' Lola said, pained. 'I need to do this in my own time.' She saw her new pals' well-meaning faces, and felt she owed them an explanation. 'Truth is, like I said, I'm not sure how I'd be — how I'd come across. I'm worried he'll be lovely and warm and open, and I'll just sit there, not engaging. I'm still not sleeping and it doesn't exactly make me fun to be around.'

'Never know till you try,' Sorcha said. 'See it as an experiment.'

'Not fair on him, though, is it?'

Sorcha exchanged a look with Tom, then the pair of them pulled faces.

'Dating's a tough gig,' Sorcha said. 'Barry's a grown-up. He'd cope. Anyway, you're always great company, Lola. Just be yourself.'

* * *

10.34 p.m.

They emerged from the bar into bucketing rain. Ella and Sorcha were heading to the West End on the Subway so said hurried goodbyes and splashed off, umbrellas up, in the direction of St Enoch Square.

'You can't queue for a cab in this,' Tom said as he and Lola sheltered in the doorway of the bar, surveying the widening puddles. 'You'll look like you've been in the river! Why don't I give you a lift?'

'To the Southside? But you're Anniesland. Isn't that a right pain?'

'I don't mind. Anyway, it's an excuse to grab a McD's on the way back.'

She studied his face and saw he meant the offer. 'If you're sure, that'd be great. Where are you parked?'

'Q-Park in Candleriggs. Race you.'

It was only a couple of streets away, but they were soaked by the time they reached Tom's Mini Cooper in the multi-storey. Rain dripped off Lola's dark fringe and the vanity mirror in the sun visor showed green eyes smeared with mascara. 'I look like I've had a hard night,' she said.

'Och, you're grand.'

Tom's short blond hair was plastered to his scalp. He was a handsome lad, with a thin, chiselled face and prominent nose. A scar on his chin gave him a noble, slightly war-wounded look. Lola liked him, finding him open-minded and generous, but direct, with a cutting sense of humour. His intensely blue eyes held a mischievous twinkle.

'Just to warn you, I'm a shit driver,' he said with a snigger, as he drove down the ramp and out onto the cobbles of Albion Street. 'This could be the longest fifteen minutes of your life!'

True to his word, he plonked them neatly in the wrong lane at the lights by the Tron.

'Don't panic, just indicate when the lights change,' Lola told him in a soothing voice, craning her neck to watch the traffic through the rain-smeared windows.

She directed him down the Saltmarket, keeping him right as they approached Glasgow Green, starting to wish she'd gone for a cab after all.

'I'm hardly ever south of the river,' he said, breathless with nerves. 'It's like "there be dragons".'

'No — *this lane*!'

They'd come to the lights at Clyde Street. Ahead lay one of the broad Victorian bridges spanning the river. The lights turned green and Tom sped up — before quickly slowing again.

'Something's going on,' he murmured, peering off to one side.

Lola followed his line of sight. Despite the lashing rain, a small crowd had gathered on the pavement on the other side of the bridge, right by the parapet, all looking down into the river.

'And look who it is,' he murmured in dismay, seeming to spot someone he knew. 'Mighta known she'd be here.'

'Pull in,' Lola said.

'It's double yellows,' he said.

'Doesn't matter. Pull in.'

He stopped, ramming the Mini's front left tyre into the kerb.

Lola got out. Tom too, and they made their way across the four lanes, hunched against the rain.

'What's happened?' Lola asked a woman in a red jacket sheltering under a big umbrella.

'Someone's went into the river,' the woman told her.

'Not long since,' said another woman, Red Jacket's pal. 'We were watching him but he's disappeared. He was over there, to the left.'

She pointed across the expanse of dark water. The river didn't so much flow through the city centre as lie like a quiet pool. It was about a hundred metres wide at this point, and its banks were dark, overhung with leafless foliage.

'That lifeboat's a fat lot of use, eh?' Red Jacket said, pointing at the orange craft suspended from a metal frame linked to the south bank of the river beside the college building.

'I telt ye,' the second woman chided. 'It's for the students to learn on. It's not a real lifeboat.'

'Has someone called for help?' Lola asked.

'She did,' Red Jacket said, indicating a tall, older woman in a dark leather trench coat standing by the parapet.

Tom was talking to the tall woman. Lola guessed she was the person he'd recognised. She went over.

'Have you called for help?' Lola said, interrupting their conversation.

The woman in the trench coat gave Lola the once-over. 'This your pal?' she asked Tom.

'Aye, this is Lola,' Tom said. 'Lola, meet my Auntie Brenda.'

'Hi,' Lola repeated. 'Did you call 999?'

'I did.'

'How long ago?'

The woman pushed out her lips and thought about it. 'Matter of minutes. They're sending a car and an ambulance. They said they'd alert Fire and Rescue to send the body boat along from Anderston.'

Lola nodded, recognising the grim moniker most of the city's residents gave the familiar rescue vessel. She relaxed a little, reassured there was little more she could do. Auntie

Brenda was taller than Lola by some inches. Her wide cheekbones gave her a Slavic look, and her hair, though wet, stood out in spikes. It was hard to tell in this light, but the spikes looked purple. One of her eyebrows was pierced with a silver barbell. There was something oddly familiar about her . . .

'Did you see him go into the water?' Lola asked, eyes on the dark, rain-pitted river. It looked icy cold.

'Not me. I happened by and this lot—' she indicated the little group — 'were causing a fuss, so I stuck my nose in. I saw him briefly but then he vanished. Goner by now, I reckon.' She took out an e-cigarette and drew deeply on it.

'Well, let's hope not,' Lola said.

'Not the first and won't be the last,' Auntie Brenda said, through a cloud of cherry-scented vapour.

Blue lights caught Lola's attention and she moved to the pavement's edge to flag the car down.

'Good evening, DCI Harris,' a dry, familiar voice said.

'Inspector Brown,' Lola said crisply.

Inspector Michelle Brown, known for her dry and no-nonsense manner, stepped onto the pavement, followed by a young male sergeant, and made a beeline for the parapet.

'Which one of you is Brenda Cheney?' she asked loudly of the crowd — which was growing fast, drawn like insects by the blue lights.

Auntie Brenda made herself known.

A paramedic car came next, then a second cop car.

Lola caught Tom's attention. 'Your Auntie often down here, is she?' she asked.

'All the time,' he said. 'This was her patch, you see. She never let go.' He saw Lola's expression change. 'Oh no, not that! She's — she *was* — a social worker. She kept an eye on, you know, the women who work down here — got quite close to some of them, likes to make sure they're all right. She worries about the young ones. I mean, some of them are *really* young.'

Lola glanced back at the crowd. Michelle Brown had moved on from Auntie Brenda and was talking to Red Jacket and her friend. As Lola watched, Auntie Brenda stepped away from the crowd, eyes apparently fixed on something — or someone — at the other end of the bridge. Stashing her e-cigarette in her trench coat pocket, she stumped away in that direction, and with unexpected speed.

'There she goes,' Tom mused. 'Spotted one of her pals, no doubt.'

'Her pals?'

'That's what she calls the girls.' He laughed. 'Honestly, they must be bloody sick of her.'

Lola stepped off the pavement into the road to get a better view, but Brenda was already across the bridge and out of sight.

'No need for you to hang around, DCI Harris,' Michelle Brown said.

'Just on my way,' Lola said politely.

Michelle nodded.

She glanced over the inspector's shoulder and saw the body boat making its ominous progress this way, ready to fish another poor victim from the river.

'Hope you find him,' Lola said, looking the inspector coolly in the eye. 'I'll check in in a day or two, if that's all right with you.'

'Suit yourself.'

Lola smiled. 'You know me, Michelle. I get curious.'

* * *

11.20 p.m.

They'd only just set off when Tom threw on the Mini's brakes and swerved back into the pavement.

'There she is!' he said.

He had his window down and shouted, 'Auntie Brenda! Do you want a lift home?'

Brenda, e-cig in her mouth, was coming back onto the bridge from the south bank. She'd jumped at Tom's cry but now seemed distracted.

'Y'all right?'

Brenda crossed to their side of the road.

Lola got out and came round to meet the woman. 'Saw you run off,' she said.

'Aye, well . . . Saw a young pal of mine. I haven't seen him in a few days. He didn't want to hang around.'

The woman peered back the way she'd come, as if scanning the night for the mystery friend.

'Something wrong, Brenda?' Lola asked.

The woman looked back at her and her expression had changed. She remained wary, but there was a new defensiveness now, as if she resented Lola's questioning.

Lola glanced back across the bridge to where her colleagues had taken efficient charge. She looked back at Tom's auntie. 'This friend of yours,' she probed gently. 'What's he called?'

Brenda took her time. 'Cameron,' she said at last, but still evasive, so that Lola wasn't sure she believed her. 'Goes by Cammy. That's the name he gave me, anyway.' She sniffed and blinked rapidly. 'He's a good boy. God love him, he really is.'

CHAPTER THREE

Monday 13 February
12.19 p.m.

'The Pathfinder meeting is in my room in ten minutes,' Detective Superintendent Elaine Walsh said, passing Lola's desk. She gave Lola a dry look. 'In case you'd forgotten . . .'

'I hadn't,' Lola said, then made a regretful face. 'Only, the thing is—'

'Oh, here we go. Excuses at the ready? May I remind you that the Pathfinder isn't optional.'

'It's the Scotstoun case,' Lola said, laying it on. 'I need to try and get a hold of Kevin Millar again. I'm *inches* from getting him to go on record.'

Elaine narrowed her eyes and the temperature in the office seemed to drop. This was the second of these meetings Lola had wormed her way out of. She was conscious of others watching — the two sergeants, and DC Kirstie Campbell, who'd just returned from the coffee machine.

'I can't risk losing the chance of a statement,' Lola went on. 'I'll catch up on anything I've missed. Promise.'

'Yes, you will,' Elaine said and strode away, shaking her head.

Lola prised open a can of Hyperdrive energy drink and took a mouthful. Elaine hadn't been explicit, but Lola guessed she was as pissed off as the rest of them about the subdivision being roped in as one of seven 'Pathfinder' teams trying out a new career development system that was linked to your calendar and powered by artificial intelligence. It sent you endless requests to 'reflect and learn' after each meeting. So far everyone had found it pointless and irritating — and counter-productive, because it encouraged you not to put meetings in your calendar at all.

'Anything I can help with?' DS Anna Vaughan asked, clearly angling for her own way out of the meeting. DS Aidan Pierce stood behind her, listening in — as he often did, presumably hoping to overhear something he could use against them later.

'Don't think so,' Lola said. 'You go share those reflections of yours.'

She caught Anna's eye and tried not to giggle. Anna was the newest recruit to the team, having transferred from the London Met in the autumn. Her husband was a successful lawyer and they had tonnes of money. It had taken Anna some weeks to settle in and she and Lola had had a sticky start, but they were over it now. She was sharp and dynamic and had been good for Kirstie, bringing her out of her shell a little, even taking her for a night out. As for DS Aidan Pierce, he was still the same sneering menace and very much his own worst enemy — a shame for someone with his sizzling ambition.

The team away to the meeting, Lola logged back into her computer. It was true she needed to get hold of Kevin Millar, a witness on the Scotstoun fire-raising case, but right now she had other fish to fry.

She took another mouthful of her syrupy drink and found what she was looking for within two minutes: the record of a man seen in trouble in the Clyde late on Saturday evening. Michelle Brown's sergeant had logged it, noting names and contact details of witnesses. She read:

> *Report made to 999 at 22.39 following sighting of unidentified male in the River Clyde, 50–100 m west of the Albert Bridge. Witness claimed individual first spotted in water approx. 22.35. Individual was in difficulty but was not heard to make any noise. Appeared to be moving slowly westwards, possibly carried by the current rather than swimming that way. Attending officers Insp. Brown and Serg. McTavish arrived at scene 22.47, by which time individual no longer visible.*
>
> *Individual described as: white male, late twenties/early thirties, short dark hair, wearing light jacket, possibly with hood. Height unknown.*
>
> *Fire & Rescue service notified by 999 operator, boat patrolled the area until midnight.*
>
> *CCTV recordings examined. Result nil.*

A further note, made on the following afternoon by a constable on duty at that time read:

> *Spoke to Fire & Rescue 13.42. Still no sign of individual spotted in river. They will continue to patrol, though suggested that the individual might have made it to safety under own steam.*

Another note — the most recent, and made by the same duty constable — was intriguing:

> *DS L. Gray notified as per agreed protocol.*

Lola sat up. *DS L. Gray? Agreed protocol?* What agreed protocol?

She clicked out of the report and searched the name, finding a Detective Sergeant Lachlan Gray who worked out of the Glasgow City Centre subdivision.

She noted his details on her pad, then read over the names of the witnesses in the initial report. There were three in total, all women, including Brenda Cheney, whom she assumed was Tom's auntie.

Next she logged into the National Missing Persons Application. The NMPA listed missing persons by date and location. She scrolled through the latest reports, focusing on men reported missing in Glasgow over the weekend.

First was for a thirty-year-old called Benny McGhee of Yoker. He was described as balding and overweight. According to a note, he'd gone missing before, always returning to his mum's flat four or five days later.

Next was John Paul (or 'J.P.') McCrae, age twenty-eight, missing since Saturday evening, having failed to return home to the flat he shared with his partner in Garnethill, following a night out with a friend. McCrae's partner said not returning home was unusual behaviour, and that there'd been no sign anything was wrong. The description given included mention of short brown hair, and he'd likely been wearing a light-coloured hoodie. That sounded more likely.

Third was Mitch Keegan, but he was fifty-two, described as obese, alcoholic and vulnerable. Another non-starter, in Lola's opinion.

With a guilty glance about the office, Lola made a discreet note of the name and contact number of John Paul McCrae's partner. Then hesitated.

What was she doing? This wasn't her case. As much as she wanted to know, it wasn't her business either, apart from the fact she'd been there on the bridge. More to the point, it could be news to McCrae's partner that a man matching his boyfriend's description had been spotted in the river. Information that would frighten him unnecessarily — and drop Lola in the stew.

There was another, more reasonable, course of action available to her, and one she could justify. She lifted the receiver.

As DS Lachlan Gray's number rang, she spotted movement at the other end of the office. Anna Vaughan had emerged from Elaine's room and was talking on the phone, nodding away, grim-faced. She was looking Lola's way as she talked.

The call was answered. 'DS Gray,' a quiet, flat voice said.

'Oh, hello,' Lola said pleasantly. She gave her own name and rank.

'Can I help?' the voice asked robotically.

'I hope so,' Lola breezed. 'Matter of a body in the river on Saturday evening. I understand you're already aware of it.' Silence at the other end of the line. 'There was a report of a man in difficulty in the Clyde, west of the Albert Bridge.'

'Can I ask what your interest is?'

Lola took a breath. 'I was there,' she said.

'Okay . . .'

'I happened to be passing, you see,' she said, brightening her tone to mask how unnerved she felt by Gray's apparent lack of interest. 'I'd been in town and I was there just after he'd been spotted in the water. I stopped to find out what was going on.'

'But you didn't see anything?'

'No, but . . . well, I talked to a couple of the people there. I made notes in case an operational statement was needed, but . . .' She swallowed. 'I saw your name on the report. It said you'd been informed as part of an "agreed protocol".'

'Mm?'

'And, well, I wondered what that was about, you being CID. For a detective to be informed of routine incidents—'

'You think it's routine for people to land up in the Clyde?'

'Well, no . . .' She decided to ignore the snark. 'I didn't think that. I thought it might be part of something bigger, that's all. I know there've been other deaths connected to the river.'

This wasn't going the way she'd hoped. She should have planned this better. Should have waited till she was more awake. She took another quick swig of her energy drink.

'Look, I don't want to waste anyone's time,' she said, forcing a pleasant smile into her voice. 'I just wanted to let you know I'd been there.'

'And now you have.'

She realised Anna was at her shoulder, mobile in her hand, looking twitchy.

'I have to go,' Lola told Gray.

'Righty-ho.' She heard the phone click off at the other end.

'Everything all right?' she said, turning to Anna.

'It's Kevin Millar,' Anna said.

Their key witness in the fire-raising case.

'What about him? You gonnae tell me he's turned up dead or something?' She saw Anna's expression. 'Oh, you're kidding me . . .'

''Fraid not, boss. Hit-and-run in Clydebank. Whoever did it reversed over him a couple of times to make sure.'

CHAPTER FOUR

12.27 p.m.

The flat was on the top floor of a Victorian tenement block in Dennistoun. By the time Brenda reached the third landing, she was so out of puff she had to stop and prop herself against the grimy green and white tiles, eyes closed as she wheezed and sweated.

She was getting too old for this. At sixty-four she should be spending her days visiting friends, going round gardens and galleries. Except that was no life. Not to her, at any rate. Brenda Cheney was a woman who needed purpose, who thrived on it. If only her body would oblige.

A few minutes' rest and she was climbing again. She rang the doorbell, taking in the three names penned on the makeshift door plate. Three of them in one flat. Three boys who'd all grown up in care, then been punted out into the world to try and survive.

She heard footsteps approaching across a wooden floor, then the door creaked open, the security chain on. It was dark inside and she had to squint to make out the pale face with suspicious eyes that peered out of the gap.

'I'm Brenda,' she managed when no welcome was forthcoming. 'I'm here to see Cammy. Is he in?'

'Who are you?' the voice said.

'A friend of his.'

She could feel him appraising her appearance. Had he never seen someone in their sixties with an eyebrow piercing before?

'He's no' here.'

'Oh dear. I've made a wasted journey in that case. What's your name, love?'

The suspicious eyes narrowed even more. 'Declan.'

From what she could see he had a similar build to Cammy: small, thin, prominent cheekbones. Similar colouring too: pale skin, dark hair. Could they be related? It was possible.

'It's nice to meet you, Declan. Did Cammy say when he'd be back?'

'Nuh. Reckon he's with his . . . pal.'

'Oh, right.' She groaned inwardly. 'That'd be Warren, would it?'

'Aye.'

'When did you last see him?'

'Can't remember.'

He made to close the door, so she got her Doc Marten in the gap.

'It's just — Cammy's my pal, see, and I worry about him. Do you have a number for him?'

The eyes in the gap widened. 'You're his friend but you don't know his phone number?'

'No. No, I don't.' Resigned to defeat, she withdrew her boot from the door.

'I'll tell him you called,' Declan said.

'Please do. Or maybe I could write out a wee message and you could—'

But the door had already banged shut.

* * *

1.05 p.m.

'Not seen him,' the young woman said, taking a deep drag on Brenda's offered e-cigarette then handing it back to her.

'Since when, Tiffany?' Brenda asked. 'Only, it's important. I've a message for him.'

'What sorta message?'

They were down by the Clyde, on the new prom south of the river, sitting on a bench in the freezing drizzle. People hurried past, making for the Squiggly Bridge over the river to the shops and cafés of the city centre. If they noticed Brenda and the much younger, stick-thin Tiffany, they didn't let on.

'Personal stuff,' Brenda said, 'but it's important. Look—' she made to get up and go — 'if you don't want to help me, just say. I'm sick of wasting my time, and—'

'Saw him Sunday.'

'Where? What time?'

Tiffany thought about it, brow furrowing, nose wrinkling. 'Down by the Sheriff Court,' she said at last, craning her neck and nodding east along the riverbank. 'Afternoon, I reckon.'

'And how was he?'

More nose wrinkling. 'All right. Hungover, if you ask me.'

'Did you talk to him?'

'A wee bit.' Her eyes dropped, a sure sign of evasion in Brenda's mind.

'*And?*'

'*And* nothing.'

Brenda bit her tongue and went into her bag for a notepad and biro. She wrote quickly then tore off the page.

'You see him again, you give him this, okay? You tell him to call me.'

The girl shoved the note in her jacket pocket then looked Brenda in the eye. 'Give us another go of your vape,' she said.

CHAPTER FIVE

1.20 p.m.

Kevin Millar had been run down and killed around 5.25 that morning on a road near the cemetery in Clydebank. It was less than three miles from the site of the fire-raising Millar had provided evidence on.

'Anything on the CCTV?' she asked Jane Thomas, the L-Division detective inspector who was dealing with the incident. They were in the street, a few paces from a tent protecting the crime scene. Millar's remains had already been scraped up and taken away. A group of locals stood behind a cordon. Lola kept her face turned away from them.

'We've got analogue video of Millar leaving the high flats he stayed in just after five, then a bit later walking up Argyle Way,' DI Thomas said. 'He cuts through the cemetery, and we see him emerge into Drumry Road. Nothing after that. As for a vehicle, we've got a white van pelting down from the A82, sun visors down, plates unreadable — caked with mud by the look of it. We lose sight of it at Drumry Road but then pick it up six minutes later on South Street, a clear dent in the front bumper.' Lola winced. 'We've asked Glasgow colleagues to see if they can track it after that.'

Lola nodded.

'He was the witness on the Scotstoun fire, wasn't he?' Thomas asked.

'Who told you that?'

'Och, everyone knows. It's the talk of the Clydebank steamie. Did you get him to sign a statement?'

'No.'

'Ah.'

Lola gave a rueful smile. 'I'd best get back to base,' she said. *And back to square one.*

* * *

2.12 p.m.

'Where does this leave us?' said an antsy-sounding Elaine Walsh.

'Up the Clyde without a paddle?' Lola suggested.

She faced the superintendent, Anna Vaughan at her side, feeling oddly guilty, as if she'd personally flattened Kevin Millar. 'Seems our Kevin just wasn't very discreet.'

Elaine looked like thunder. Her usually tidy bob was ruffled and her mouth was pinched and lined. She was getting it in the neck from above, Lola knew, and the media were jumping up and down for developments. A crime on such a grand scale, involving the destruction by fire of three enormous warehouses, had to be easy to solve, surely? The trouble was, wilful fire-raising was a nightmare to investigate, with evidence often literally going up in smoke.

This crime was no common-or-garden insurance scam either. Glasgow City Council had owned the warehouses and sold the site to a developer of high-spec apartments. The council had put out a tender for a contractor to demolish the warehouses and clear the site. It was a big job, worth the best part of half a million. Four companies had bid for the work, and McGregor Demolition believed they were in the running for it — seemingly on the basis of a nod and a wink. When

Jamie McGregor's company didn't win the tender, his wrath was felt across the city. Nowhere more so than in the City Chambers, where there were strong words and very red faces.

McGregor had been given three weeks to challenge the decision, but the very next weekend the warehouses went up in flames. It just so happened that McGregor Demolition was the city's on-call contractor for emergencies that weekend. Once the flames were out, McGregor's men flattened and cleared the site. Then billed the council for half a million, plus VAT.

The council knew it was a deliberate act, the fire service and police too: it had been set using petrol and wooden pallets, and explosives had then brought the roof down. The challenge would be to prove it. Lola got landed with the case.

And then Kevin Millar came by, with his story about a conversation overheard in a bar in Clydebank. He and an unnamed friend had heard Jamie McGregor telling two pals he was going to 'torch the site to kingdom come' that weekend. But to go on record, to give a statement and sign it, he wanted two things: police protection and a change of identity, and certain criminal charges he was facing to be dropped.

Lola was not in the business of having any charges dropped — certainly not ones relating to the download and storage of images of child sexual exploitation. However, she'd sensed Millar was malleable, and set about trying to persuade him to make — and sign — a statement.

But now he was dead.

'Let's try and see the positives,' Elaine said, sounding strained. 'Millar's friend from the bar might come forward. He might think he's next. If he doesn't, well, maybe we move the focus of our investigation.'

'From fire-raising to murder?' Lola asked.

Lola liked the thought of McGregor, a charming thug of a man, being hauled in on a murder charge. She wondered if he might then confess to wilful fire-raising in a plea bargain.

They threw a few ideas around, Anna scribbling notes.

Elaine got up and stood behind her chair, hands on the headrest — her favourite dismissal.

'Hang back a moment, would you, Lola?' she said. 'Thank you, Anna.'

'Sure thing,' Anna fired back at her, all golden smiles.

'Boss?' Lola said when they were alone.

'Make sure you're here at five, will you?'

'At five?' She stole a glance at the clock on Elaine's wall. 'Is there something specific . . . ?'

'Yes,' Elaine said, her smile not quite reaching her eyes. 'There is. A chat with a couple of colleagues. It'll be five or thereabouts. I'll call you in.'

CHAPTER SIX

2.34 p.m.

Brenda had waited by the sheriff's court for over an hour, sheltering under a tree as the rain battered the river behind her. She'd vaped and cursed quietly to herself before finally accepting her plan had come to nothing. Driven by the urge to pee, she'd given up and headed for the Hook and Line behind the St Enoch Centre.

'Usual, hen?' the barman said when she came through the door, damp and breathless.

'Thanks, Vinnie.'

She went to the loo and collected her port on the way back, then spotted her old colleague Ivan Parry in his usual corner. A few of them from the old days still came in here — it had been their regular haunt when the Social Work department had its offices in this part of town. Younger than Brenda by more than a decade, Ivan had retired early with stress, brought on in part by the job but also by the drawn-out death of his wife Lynne from cancer a decade ago. He was here all the time since retiring — not, he insisted, because he was lonely, but because he enjoyed seeing old faces. He drank in moderation, interspersing beer with soft drinks. In the mornings he went to his local gym, where he swam, then made his way into town, ending up here. He kept fit but walked with a stick while he waited for a hip or knee operation — Brenda could never remember which, and didn't ask for fear of exposing the fact she hadn't listened. At some point in the evening Ivan would move on to another bar. He seemed happy, but Brenda didn't envy him what she considered a purposeless existence. He moved his coat and walking stick as Brenda squeezed in beside him.

'And how's my favourite social warrior?' he asked kindly, and laced his long fingers together on the table edge, smiling faintly so that he resembled a priest ready to hear the concerns of a troubled parishioner.

'Worn out and worried,' she said and took a sip of her port.

The port was thick, syrupy like strong medicine, and sharply woody, and she felt immediately better. She closed her eyes and got her breath back. When she opened them again, Ivan was eyeing her beadily.

'Still intent on rescuing those young lassies?' he asked her now.

She gave him a hard look. 'You don't expect me to give it up, do you? Someone's got to look out for them. 'Specially the ones just out of care. It breaks my heart.'

'But you still object to the idea of a controlled zone?'

She glared at him. Not this again. Not today.

'Even though that's what they want?' He tilted his head and raised his eyebrows.

They'd had it out before: the same old argument, with Ivan reminding her that the women were adults (not all of them, she reminded him — not by anyone's measure), and that they didn't need, or want, to be saved.

She huffed and scowled, wishing she hadn't sat with him now. But too late. She took out her e-cig and, one eye on the bar to make sure she wasn't seen, snuck a drag, then blew the vapour out, up in the direction of the air vent over their heads.

'I do worry about you,' Ivan said after a minute or two. 'You care to your own detriment.'

'It's not the girls this time,' she told him, eyes on her port. 'It's that young lad.'

'Ah, yes! Young Callum.'

'*Cameron*,' she corrected irritably. 'At least try to remember his name. He worries me. He's got this so-called boyfriend now. An older man.' Her breathing quickened with her rage. 'No one's allowed to meet him because he's so bloody "rich and important".'

'Sounds a familiar tale. He's the boy we took the armchair to, isn't he? Crammed in the back of my little car. I only saw him to say hello to but he seemed the switched-on sort. Not in the least vulnerable.'

'*Of course* he's vulnerable! He grew up in care. Just because he puts on a show of being worldly doesn't mean he is. The older man has given him money more than once. "Presents." But that's not what's worrying me right now. Some chap fell into the river near the Albert Bridge on Saturday night. I saw him in the water. Then who should I spot but Cammy — loitering about at the other end of the bridge. Went to talk to him and he was . . . Something had frightened him. Badly.'

Ivan frowned.

She went on: 'He seemed nervy, you know? I said, "Did you see something?" And I knew I was right because he ran off. I've been looking for him since.'

He watched her, blinking slowly, the calmest of calm counsellors.

'Why do you feel so responsible for him?' he enquired kindly.

'There's nobody else. Besides, I like him.'

'You're not his mother, Brenda.'

She glared at him and he recoiled, knowing he'd hit a nerve — *the* nerve.

'I don't know what to do.' Tears welled up. She went into her bag for a Kleenex. 'I went down to Centre 44 and mentioned him to one of the caseworkers. She didn't know him, but she said she'll alert the detached team when they're out on a night. If someone can just tell me he's safe . . .'

'The young are often more resilient than we give them credit for,' Ivan said softly, turning his pint, eyes on the foam up the sides of the glass.

'You think?' She blew her nose. 'Aye, well, maybe.'

Was Cammy resilient? She hadn't given it much thought, but he must be, mustn't he? He'd survived the care system and the lonely life of a care leaver. But a superficial resilience didn't mean he wasn't vulnerable — a child in a young man's body, and prey to anyone who wanted to exploit him.

He was only a child the first time she'd met him, three years ago. She'd still been working then, bussing about the city as a justice social worker, keeping tabs on an ever-growing list of clients. She'd gone to visit Tiffany Charleton, newly handed a community payback order following a conviction for vandalism, but apparently unfussed about the requirements of the order and in need of strong encouragement. Tiffany stayed with her mum in one of the high flats in Cowcaddens, and on this occasion had a gang of mates round, smoking and drinking and blasting music out of their phones. Brenda had spotted the boy sitting among them, sipping a coke and looking out of place. She'd met Tiffany in the quiet of the kitchen and talked some sense into her. Then, as she was leaving, she'd found the boy in the hallway waiting for the lift. They'd ridden down together.

'When did you last eat?' Brenda had asked, clocking his stick-thin wrists and knobbly collarbone.

'This morning.'

'You need a good feed,' she'd said.

He'd shrugged, eyes down.

'There's a café over the road. My treat.'

Over an all-day breakfast, he'd opened up about a period in foster care after his mum died of an overdose when he was six, and about the various care homes he'd lived in after that. About his alcoholic father who'd tried to spring him from care a few times — before dying in a car accident. About the shared accommodation he'd found himself in since leaving care a week after his sixteenth birthday. And about the social worker who was supposed to be helping him find a training course and a job. Cammy wanted to be a chef, but someone, somewhere, had decided it was to be a life of 'business admin' for him. Which was a joke, given he was severely dyslexic. He was a sweet boy, funny, self-deprecating, though erratic in his thought processes.

Since that breakfast she'd met him a few times, coming across him at Tiffany's place or down by the river among his 'friends'. After she'd retired she continued to go down there, and bought him food whenever he'd let her. She'd asked for his phone number a few times. 'So I can check on you from time to time,' she'd explained when he wanted to know why. But he'd never given it to her, telling her to follow him 'on Insta' instead.

Brenda didn't do social media, and wasn't about to start.

He seemed to be spending more and more time at the riverside. She worried about him and told him so — worried that he'd start using drugs, or feel pressured to sell sex to men who saw him as a mere object.

'I'll be fine,' he'd assured her. And besides, he had someone else looking out for him now. A boyfriend. An older man with a posh car. One who had to be careful who he was seen with. Who even gave him money.

Brenda could have wept.

Ivan eased himself up to go to the bar. He asked if she wanted another port.

'No, I'm away home after this,' she told him, swigging the last of the glass in front of her.

She was getting up to go when her phone began to ring. A withheld number.

'Hello?' she answered, finger in one ear to block out the music in the bar. 'Who's this please?'

'It's me,' a small voice said.

'Cammy? Oh, Cammy, love—'

'You need to stop looking for me. I know you've been to the flat and been talking to people. It's dangerous.'

'Cammy? I only—'

'It's dangerous for both of us! Look, the night the guy went into the river. *I saw him. The one who pushed him in.*'

'What . . . ?'

'He saw me too.'

'Cammy—'

'He saw me, Brenda. I reckon he saw me filming him. It's dangerous. So just leave it, will you?'

'What do you—'

But he'd hung up, leaving Brenda reeling.

CHAPTER SEVEN

5.12 p.m.

Lola read emails while she waited for Elaine to call her in. There was someone in with her right now: a statuesque woman with wavy blonde and auburn hair and a plum-coloured suit who'd arrived with an air of great importance. Now, a stocky man with a red, stress-ridden face and grey hair, wearing a black suit, appeared in the office and marched in the direction of Elaine's room. He rapped quickly on the door and slipped inside.

Something was up, she realised, and her stomach did a somersault.

Suspecting she'd need her wits about her, she opened another can of Hyperdrive. This one was a new flavour — blackcurrant and something called 'acai' that she'd meant to google but hadn't yet. She sipped it and grimaced. It was exactly like all the others she'd tried: a revolting syrup of sweetened chemicals.

She disliked the drinks, and hated that she'd come to rely on them to get her through the day. The fact was, she wasn't sleeping well at all. It had started just after she'd finally given up on Joe, the man she'd been in love with for thirty years.

Some nights she went without any sleep at all. She'd gone to the doctor, sobbing wretchedly, and been prescribed sleeping tablets. They were effective, but left her groggy the next day, with a metallic taste in her mouth that was like blood. Three months later, she was getting some sleep with the help of antihistamines — five hours a night if she was lucky — and keeping herself awake in the day with the help of fizzy chemicals.

'Lola?' Elaine called from down the office. 'We're ready for you.'

She got dismally to her feet.

* * *

5.23 p.m.

Elaine got the introductions out of the way. The man was Detective Superintendent Angus Wilde of City Centre subdivision. The woman in the plum suit was Melda Brodick, the newly seconded senior lead of Corporate Comms for Glasgow. Her substantive post was with the council but by all accounts she'd already made her mark in Police Scotland, demanding a series of fast changes and restructuring her team. Right now she looked as if she was only just containing her fury. There was something very *film noir* about her, Lola thought, as if she might pull out a pistol at any moment.

Wilde looked hangdog and exhausted. Easily as tired as Lola.

'This is an informal meeting,' Elaine said, in spite of the stiff atmosphere in the room. 'It won't be minuted.' She looked distinctly uncomfortable.

'Okay . . .' Lola said, tensing.

'The reason we want to talk to you,' Elaine went on, 'is that earlier today you accessed a report of a man who was seen in the river on Saturday evening.'

Lola stared. She'd known the system would record what she looked at, but so what? She had nothing to hide. She cleared her throat.

'That's right. I was there. I met some of the witnesses. I wanted to know if he'd been saved.'

'Then you called DS Lachlan Gray,' Elaine said.

'Yes, I did.' So the sneaky shit had ratted on her. 'There was a note on the report. I wanted to understand why CID needed to be informed of what was probably an accident.' She eyeballed Wilde. 'Not that he gave anything away.'

Wilde said, 'You then looked at details of men reported missing over the weekend.'

Brodick, the Comms woman, was watching her with one finely drawn eyebrow arched.

'You looked specifically at the name of the next of kin of one individual,' Wilde continued. 'A John Paul McCrae.'

Lola's mouth went dry as she anticipated the question that was coming next.

'Did you perhaps contact Mr McCrae's next of kin, DCI Harris?'

'No,' Lola said. It came out in a croak that made her sound as if she was lying. She sat up. 'Of course not! I was curious, that's all. I'm a *detective*. Look. What's this about?'

'Lola . . .' Elaine warned softly.

Lola glared.

'What's going on here?' she demanded, barely containing her rage now. 'If I've stumbled on something sensitive, then I'd like to understand more.'

Wilde and Elaine exchanged glances, then the two of them looked at Brodick, as if to give her a cue.

Lola waited, fists clenched in her lap.

'DCI Harris,' Brodick said, crossing and uncrossing her legs. 'What do you know about the Clyde Pusher?'

'The urban legend?' Lola looked from Brodick to Elaine, who looked antsy. 'You about to tell me it's legit?'

'No, I am not.'

The plum suit looked expensive, as did the hair, beautifully waved and coloured russet and gold. Lola had trained as a hairdresser as a teenager. She knew an expensive cut-and-colour when she saw one, and wondered — not for the first time — how much her Corporate Comms colleagues were earning. More than her, she assumed.

'According to the debunked legend,' the woman said coolly, 'the Clyde Pusher is said to attack young men, hitting them over the head and pushing them into the river to drown. He's supposed to have been doing it for the last seven years and is thought responsible for the deaths of as many as seven — now possibly eight — men. It's nonsense. A fantasy spun by people with too much time on their hands and *no* thought at all to the feelings of families who have lost a loved one. It's the subject of podcasts and articles in conspiracy journals. The idea is that there's a serial killer at work in Glasgow, the most prolific since Bible John. But it's unevidenced supposition, based on fragments of assumptions here and there, and a *lot* of bad will.'

'But CID are keeping tabs "just in case"?' Lola asked, looking at Angus Wilde, who sat, eyes down, seemingly happy for his Comms colleague to take the lead.

'There is a partnership agreement in place,' Brodick said, 'in line with the council's community safety strategy.'

There would be.

Brodick went smoothly on: 'Detective Sergeant Lachlan Gray in Detective Superintendent Wilde's subdivision is the lead officer, linking with communication officials in my team. All river-related incidents are reported in to DS Gray, who maintains a record and examines evidence for patterns. Thus far, *no* patterns have been identified.'

'What about the number of victims who were gay?'

'It's a sleazy part of town.'

Lola raised her eyebrows, momentarily gobsmacked. 'Is that right?' she managed.

'I mean, their sexuality isn't relevant. To raise it could be . . . offensive.'

'Really?'

She could go to town right now, could tear the woman's arguments to shreds, except she didn't have the energy. 'So what's the official line?' she asked instead.

Brodick said, 'There is no evidence that the Clyde Pusher exists. All available evidence has been examined and nothing indicates otherwise.'

'I see.' She looked at Elaine, who was unreadable.

'You do see the risk of non-containment, don't you, DCI Harris?' Brodick asked, adopting a schoolteacher tone. 'The slightest hint that we are taking an urban legend seriously risks giving credibility to the conspiracy theories. Because such speculation is . . . *beneath our notice*.'

'What are you saying to me?' She addressed the question to the three of them, but her eyes rested on Elaine, her line manager.

'Leave it alone, Lola,' Elaine said. 'No good can come of getting involved.'

'Right. Don't I have a right to know what happened to the man who was in the river?'

'Only as much as anyone else in this city,' Elaine said. 'Do we have an understanding, Lola? Anyone asks you about this business, say you'd prefer not to comment, or refer them to Melda and her team. And don't, whatever you do, mention that a report was filed with CID. Understand?'

'Oh yes,' Lola murmured, quiet as a mouse to mask the fury building inside her. 'I understand.'

* * *

6.20 p.m.

'Everything okay, boss?' Anna Vaughan asked, as Lola stomped past on her way back to her desk.

'Mm,' Lola grunted.

'I've had a call from Jamie McGregor's solicitor.' Anna put on an airy tone: 'He and his client will "consent" to a meeting first thing tomorrow morning, at his client's place of business.'

'Fine. Let's play it carefully for now. Agree a time and email me the details.'

'Boss.'

She checked her personal phone and found a message from Hughie, the handsome but too-young — and too-eager — man she'd gone on a date with, asking how she was doing. She ignored it.

She'd had a WhatsApp message from Tom, but not using the Covid Divorce Club's group. He'd texted her direct:

Can we have a chat tonight if poss? My Auntie Brenda's after some advice. It's to do with her friend and what happened at the river. She doesn't want to talk to the police but I persuaded her to talk to you. Ta xxx

Lola glanced along the office in the direction of Elaine's room. Elaine was chatting to Angus Wilde in the corridor, while Brodick lingered nearby, glaring this way.

Lola went into her phone and typed:

Would love to talk. Why don't I give you a call after eight?

She locked eyes with Brodick, smiled nicely and pressed SEND.

CHAPTER EIGHT

9.10 p.m.

Lola was late. She'd fallen asleep on the settee, but woke with a jolt of adrenaline to find it was five to nine. She phoned Tom as she buckled herself into the Audi, but he said not to worry: Brenda was delayed too, which was normal for her.

Being late was absolutely *not* normal for Lola. She cursed herself and drummed her nails on the steering wheel as each set of lights turned against her. She felt stunned with tiredness but had a stash of Hyperdrive in the footwell of the passenger seat. At the lights at Mosspark Boulevard, she opened a can and took a sip.

'I'm so sorry,' she said when Tom let her in to his first-floor new-build flat. 'Is your auntie here?'

'Just arrived. She's in the living room. Have you eaten?' He took her jacket.

'Aye, I had a plate of pasta, but thanks.'

'Come through. Oh, leave your shoes on. The place is a midden.'

'Hello, Brenda,' Lola said, moving into Tom's living room.

'Evening.' A curt nod and a glare from the woman perched on the edge of one of the two armchairs. It was warm in the room but Brenda was clearly intent on keeping her trench coat on.

'Now, ladies — drinks?' Tom said.

'Coffee, please,' Lola said. 'Black and strong.'

Brenda declined with a shake of her head.

Lola sat down at one end of a long settee. The room was pristine and tidily minimalist, furnished expensively in a mid-century style — not a 'midden' by anyone's standards.

'Did you have to come far?' Lola asked to break the ice.

'Not too far.' She cleared her throat. 'Stay just off Garscube Road.'

'Still quite a trek, then.'

Brenda shrugged. 'Hopped on a bus. Free now I've got my pass.' She took an e-cigarette out of one of her coat's big pockets. 'Do you mind?'

'Not at all,' Lola said. 'How is it you're related to Tom? I don't think he said.'

'His dad was my wee brother.' She took a drag on the e-cig and exhaled the vapour.

Was. Yes, Tom had said his dad had passed away. She recalled his mum was remarried and living in Tenerife, or one of the other Canaries.

Tom was back with Lola's coffee in a smoked-glass mug. She took it from him, but her eyes remained on the purple spikes of the woman's hair. She'd had a flash of recognition by the river on Saturday night. There was a myth — one Lola didn't especially subscribe to — that the style a woman had when she was thirty-five was the one she'd maintain for the rest of her life. Brenda must be in her mid-sixties, she calculated, which could mean . . .

'I think we've met before,' Lola said, unable to stop herself smiling at the coincidence.

'Aye. On Saturday just gone.'

'I don't mean that. Did you used to stay in Cessnock?'

Brenda eyed her suspiciously. 'I did. But not for a number of years.'

'And you used to go to Hair by Marie-Claire on Paisley Road West.'

The woman's eyebrows crept up. 'So I did . . .'

'I worked there in the early nineties,' Lola told her. 'I was a junior stylist. I used to wash your hair ready for Marie-Claire.'

'Get away!' Tom cried, looking from one to the other of them.

Brenda gaped too, suspicion gone. '*Lola* . . .' she murmured. Her face brightened a little. 'Marie-Claire had high hopes for you. She said you had good technique, but . . . But you weren't always good at listening to instructions.'

'Sounds about right. It's nice to see you again, Brenda.' She meant it. 'You'd gone back to college, hadn't you? Training for social work?'

'That's right. Found myself on my own and no qualifications. Decided I needed my life to mean something.'

'I take it you qualified.'

'I did. Finished up my career as a criminal justice social worker.'

'Important job,' she said. From what Lola knew of the role, criminal justice social workers had a tough time, supporting people released from jail, overseeing others who'd been handed community payback orders and keeping others out of prison.

'You had a wee boy, didn't you?' She pictured the child, age seven or eight and causing mayhem in the salon while his mum's colour took.

'Your memory's good.' Brenda's face darkened. 'We don't talk anymore,' Brenda said. 'He . . .' She cleared her throat. 'It's his choice.'

'I'm sorry.'

'It's how things go. Nothing you can do.'

Tom was looking uncomfortable, unconsciously fingering the scar on his chin. Brenda's son would be his cousin. Lola made a mental note to ask him what had happened.

'You wanted Lola's advice,' Tom reminded his aunt now.

The woman was back in the moment. 'So I did.'

'What can I do for you, Brenda?'

'It's about a young friend of mine,' she began, clearing her throat again. 'He's in some trouble. Nothing he's done. But I think . . . I think he's in danger.'

Lola leaned in, cradling her coffee. 'This friend. Is it the young lad you saw on Saturday night. The one you said was "a good boy"?'

'That's him.'

'You mentioned his name.'

'He's called Cammy — Cameron Leavey.'

'How old is he?'

'Nineteen.'

'And is it something to do with what happened at the river — and the man who was in the water?'

'That's right.' Brenda looked impressed that Lola had joined the dots. 'It was no accident.' She looked Lola hard in the eye. 'He was pushed in. Cammy saw who did it. It was the Clyde Pusher.'

Lola's skin seemed to tighten all over her body.

'You know who I'm talking about, don't you?'

Lola nodded.

'Cammy phoned me. Told me not to look for him. He's worried the Clyde Pusher saw him.'

'Where is Cammy now, Brenda?'

'Missing,' Tom said.

Brenda explained her efforts to locate Cammy and about his desperate phone call where he claimed to be in danger.

'He's not *actually* missing, then,' Lola pointed out. 'He's lying low. That's not "missing" in the sense of "missing persons".'

'He's in *danger*,' the woman growled. 'I want to find him.'

'What exactly did he say to you?'

Brenda relayed the phone call.

'He'd heard the stories about the Clyde Pusher, then?' Lola said.

'Everybody knows about the Pusher,' Tom cut in.

'Do they?' Lola asked. 'I'm not sure they do. Or if they do they don't know the details — or they think it's plain nonsense.'

'Loads of folk believe in it,' Tom protested. 'You should talk to my pal Stuey. He's out on the scene all the time and he's got *all* the gossip. There's a campaign too — some of the families have got together, the families of his victims. They've got a group on Facebook. There are sometimes articles in the *Gouger*. I think there's a podcast too.'

'The working lassies know about him,' Brenda said. 'Ask any of them. The Pusher's no urban legend to them. He's as real as you or me.'

'Who are Cammy's friends?' Lola asked her.

'He hangs around with Tiffany Charleton. And there's a woman called Larissa. Larissa McKechnie. She mothers him. Or tries to. She's plenty of problems of her own, poor lass.'

'Have you talked to them?'

'I've tried. Tiffany's keeping her mouth shut and Larissa says she hasn't seen him since Saturday.' Her voice darkened as she said, 'There's another possibility . . .'

'Oh?'

'He's got this *boyfriend*.' She said the word with some distaste. 'An older man, name of Warren.'

'Is Warren his first name or surname?'

'Good question. I don't know.'

'You haven't met him?'

'No. He's . . . I think he's grooming the boy. Gives him money. Gifts. Cammy's obsessed, but I don't think he knows much more about him than I do.'

'Does he live in Glasgow, do you know?'

Brenda frowned for a moment. 'I think he has a house outside the city. Somewhere to the north. Cammy told me he's never been there. There are "good reasons", apparently.'

'Can you help?' Tom asked Lola now.

Lola sipped her coffee and thought about it. She could talk to the boy's flatmates, and maybe have a look at his belongings — unofficially, of course, and only if they let her in. It was risky professionally too. If Elaine found out she was even digging lightly around the edges of the business by the river, she'd skin her alive. She heard the super's words again: *Leave it alone, Lola. No good can come of getting involved.*

'There must be something you can do,' Brenda implored.

'Let me think about it,' she said. 'But this thing you've told me, Brenda — that he witnessed a crime and he believes himself in danger. I'd like you to report it.'

'I've told you, haven't I?'

'Not officially, you haven't. There needs to be a record.'

Brenda's eyes narrowed.

'You want to help Cammy, don't you?'

Brenda nodded.

'Then call 101 and tell them what you've told me. Make sure you mention that it might be connected to the man who went into the river on Saturday night.'

The woman made a grumbling noise but Lola took it as assent.

'I've made a note of my mobile number too, in case you need it. But, Brenda, please don't mention that we've spoken. If you do, I can't help you anymore. Do you hear me?'

* * *

10.05 p.m.

Back in her car, she checked her phone and saw a text message from Sorcha from the Covid Divorce Club. Barry the academic had been on at her. *Want me to tell him you've been busy — or is it a definite no? He's a nice guy, he really is!*

Lola typed back: *I'll text him, but you might want to hint that I'm not impressed by impatient blokes!*

She added a smiley face to soften it.

There was a voicemail too. A message from DC Kirstie Campbell. She listened on speakerphone.

'Thought you'd like to know, boss. The body of a twenty-eight-year-old male was pulled from the Clyde earlier today. They think it sank but resurfaced due to gases. It came up down by the Armadillo. Identified as a John Paul McCrae. Pretty messy head wound by the sound of it.'

CHAPTER NINE

11.39 p.m.

Cammy hurried past the boarded-up shops and ducked into the doorway between the convenience store and bookies, both of which were closed and shuttered for the night. He stole one glance back down the road to double-check he hadn't been followed and unlocked the door, frozen fingers trembling.

He raced up the four flights and let himself into the flat, turning to close and bolt the storm doors before locking the inner door and setting the security chain.

There was noise from the kitchen, and the smell of weed.

'Hi,' he said, taking one of his flatmates by surprise.

'Cam!' Finlay cried from his chair at the kitchen table, mouth open. He didn't get up because his girlfriend Erin, possibly very stoned, was on his lap, her arms draped round his neck and her head sagging. 'Where you been?'

'Out.'

Finlay shouted at his phone to lower the volume of the music.

Cammy put his bag on the counter and grabbed a clean-enough glass from the draining board and filled it with water. He drained it in two gulps.

'Want a beer?' Finlay asked, nodding to the stash of cans on the table.

'Not staying.'

'How no?'

Erin lifted her head and studied him in confusion, hair plastered to her face.

'Just came to get my stuff.'

'Your *stuff*?'

'Aye. My box an' that.'

Finlay's mouth opened in shock. He knew what that meant.

'I'm in trouble, man. That creep — the Pusher. He was here when I came back earlier. He was over the road, just inside the cemetery, watching me through the railings.'

'You serious?'

'Totally.'

'You think he followed you here?'

'He wasn't just passing, was he?' he snapped.

Finlay began to unpeel Erin from his body so that he could get up. She groaned and stretched, making way.

'Is Dec in?' Cammy asked.

'In his room. Haven't seen him since I got back, though. I knocked and I could hear his music playing, but he never answered. I noticed he finally took the bin out though — it was stinking like something had died in it. So where you gonnae go? To Warren's place?'

'Not sure,' he said evasively. He'd tried Warren, who'd rejected his call. After that he'd only got the answerphone. 'Maybe, maybe not.' He chewed his lip and went over the list in his head of everything he had to take. Bathroom stuff. One or two old DVDs. Well, just his favourite ones maybe.

'Want me to come with you for protection?'

'I'll be fine. I'm fast, remember?'

In his room he threw clothes into a holdall, then retrieved a handful of DVDs from the cluttered living room and added them to the pile. Last, but most important, was his box — the shoebox he'd had since he was tiny. The one that contained *everything*. Photos of his birth mum, a letter she'd written him when she'd given him up, photos of the foster carers who had him till he was three, and the next family who'd looked after him, until their own son went off the rails and Cammy ended up in a children's home aged nine. There were drawings in there, an autograph book with signatures of his carers in the home, and all the other stuff: pebbles from the beach at Millport, a St Christopher's medal on a chain that might have belonged to his mum's father, Cammy's granddad. He took a pillowcase from the pile of laundry at the foot of his bed and slid the box inside it before putting it carefully on top of the clothes and DVDs.

Finlay knocked on the door.

''M'in.'

'Me and Erin're off to hers. So I'll see you around.'

''Kay.'

'Take care, man.'

He nodded.

Minutes later, he checked he had his phone and money, and he was ready.

'Dec?' he called, knocking on his other flatmate's bedroom door. 'You there?'

Music played softly from within.

'Dec, man, it's me. Can I come in? Only, I'm heading off — for a wee while, anyway.'

He listened some more. No answer.

Finlay must have got it wrong. Dec was out somewhere. He'd left music playing by mistake. But Cammy wanted to check; Finlay was just a flatmate but Dec was his pal.

He turned the door handle and peered in. Light from the hallway cut across Dec's bedroom and fell onto his bed.

Dec was lying there. Except something was wrong.

'*Dec?*'

Cammy scrabbled for the light switch then stood frozen as he took in the scene before him. Dec's still body, and Dec's blood on the wall over the bed, some of it splattering the ceiling.

CHAPTER TEN

Tuesday 14 February
1.30 a.m.

Brenda was in bed but wide awake, which wasn't unusual. She lay in darkness, and thought about Gavin, the son she hadn't seen for so many years now. His memory often visited her in the small hours, and she'd try to focus on better times — the times when they'd got on, were close even. But inevitably her efforts failed and she remembered the arguing, his bellowing, her pleading. And then he'd hit her — just once, but she recalled every second of it: the swing of his arm, the flying fist, the sickening thud as he made contact with the side of her chin. And then she was on the floor, on her back, an upturned beetle thrashing feebly at the air.

He'd be thirty-eight now. Married, maybe. He'd been engaged to a nice enough girl. She wondered if there were children. Her grandchildren.

If there were, she'd never see them.

Despair was a miserable ache in every muscle.

There was nothing for it but to get up. To have light. Strong tea. The radio. She reached out and turned on her lamp — and at that same moment the door buzzer sounded, making her jump.

She looked at the time on the radio by her bed.

Who would possibly . . . ?

Only one person, surely.

'It's Cammy,' his voice said tinnily through the intercom. 'Can I come in?'

'Of course! Second floor,' she told him, and pressed the door release.

He was up the stairs in seconds and throwing himself at her.

'What's wrong?' she cried, holding him tight. 'What's the matter?'

'I didn't know where else to go,' he sobbed.

'You're here now.' She leaned over and pushed the door closed. 'You're here now. And you're safe.' She took his face in her hands, tears in her own eyes now. 'Tell me what's happened.'

CHAPTER ELEVEN

3.32 a.m.

Lola was in a cave deep under the earth: a tiny, dark chamber, with miles of rock on all sides. Joe, her ex, was down here, trapped in another cave in the same system. The only way to reach him was to squeeze through a narrow crack that was flooded and pitch black. Knowing she had no choice, she held her breath and dived, inching through freezing black water only to become quickly encased by rock on all sides, unable to move. Water flooded her mouth and nose—

She woke up and jumped from the bed, gasping for air and scrabbling for her bedside light, knocking over a glass of water in the process.

Anxiety galvanised her like electricity and she had to walk about the house, turning all the lights on, waving her arms and breathing deeply to prove to her brain that she was free and safe. She'd had nightmares before, but this was a new one. Never before had she found herself *buried alive*.

She made tea and sat at her kitchen table, shaken, rubbing her face as she recovered. There'd be no more sleep tonight.

For God's sake . . .

Enough was enough. This couldn't continue. But what could she do? If she went back to the doctor, he'd only give her more tablets.

Her sister Frankie had a friend who swore by hypnotherapy, and had used it to give up smoking and to get over a fear of flying. The friend had gone to someone in Hamilton who was renowned for helping cure any number of phobias and neuroses. She googled 'hypnotherapist Hamilton' but the search returned a number of names and none rang a bell. Stoned with weariness, she gave up.

Some minutes later, a second mug of tea made, she took out her diary and made notes for her meeting with Brenda Cheney later in the day, and how they might go about finding Cammy, wherever he might be hiding.

If the boy had seen the Pusher, then he was right to be frightened. Even thinking about it made Lola shiver — especially now she knew the name of the man whose body had been pulled from the river. She googled John Paul McCrae but nothing came up under 'news'. In the office the previous day, she'd taken a note of McCrae's next of kin, and their contact details, and leafed through her notepad now. His partner's name was Will Aitchison. There was a mobile phone number and an address for a flat in Garnethill, at the north edge of the city centre. She wondered how Mr Aitchison had taken the news. Wondered, too, whether her colleagues had explained there was a possible witness to the attack . . .

She stopped herself. Not her case. Not her business.

But curiosity got the better of her and she googled Aitchison's name. There were a few. She found a LinkedIn profile for a likely candidate, a comms manager for a charity in Glasgow. She quickly found his Twitter account — the avatar was the same. Lola wasn't on Twitter, nor any other social media platform, but from time to time she liked to scroll through it and read about the latest cultural outrage.

And here was something. Will Aitchison had tweeted a thread in tribute to his deceased partner. Each tweet was accompanied by photos of Will and John Paul at different stages of their relationship.

> *WILL AITCHISON @WaitchisonGla44 13 Feb*
> *Friends, my worst fears have come true. JP's body was found in the River Clyde earlier today. We had six precious years together and I will never forget him, nor what we had together. 1/4*

> *WILL AITCHISON @WaitchisonGla44 13 Feb*
> *Police think he went into the river on Saturday evening, 11 Feb between 22.00 and 23.00. They are working on the assumption that JP either took his own life or fell into the river by accident. 2/4*

> *WILL AITCHISON @WaitchisonGla44 13 Feb*
> *I'm certain he didn't kill himself. JP was happy. He was starting a new job in two weeks. He wasn't drunk and he never took drugs. 3/4*

> *WILL AITCHISON @WaitchisonGla44 13 Feb I need to know what happened. Anyone with information about JP's movements on Saturday evening, please contact Police Scotland on 101 and also DM me on here. Somebody knows what happened. Ends. 4/4*

She took screenshots of the tweet thread, then went back into Google and the search she'd begun last night after returning from Tom's for everything relating to 'Clyde Pusher'.

There were hundreds, possibly thousands of results. Making the search more specific helped. The top result was a link to a podcast called *Proving the Pusher*, which claimed to be 'an examination of an urban legend that might be all too real'. There was one series with ten episodes from a couple of years ago. A note on the webpage said that a second series was in production now. The podcast appeared to be the work of one man, Donovan Murphy. She would listen to a few episodes on her phone and then, if it seemed promising, try to contact him.

There were news stories going back eight years, including one on the BBC website. It was short: a call for information from the family of a man whose body had been pulled from the Clyde one Sunday morning. A police spokesperson was quoted, dismissing the suggestion.

The *Chronicle* had mentioned the Clyde Pusher as one of 'Glasgow's most terrifying urban legends' in an unserious listicle for Hallowe'en written by her old sparring partner Shuna Frain. The Pusher appeared at number five, between a story about gangsters being rounded up, shot and buried in the foundations of the Kingston Bridge in the sixties, and the legend of the Gorbals Vampire.

> *AT NUMBER FIVE is the sinister tale of the hooded attacker dubbed the Clyde Pusher, believed responsible for clobbering lone young men and pitching them into the river to perish. Authorities have dismissed the stories as fantasy, but victims' families beg to differ. Talk to the handful of men and women who say they've witnessed the Pusher going about his dark business, and you might suspend your disbelief. There are some frightened people in this city, who wouldn't venture anywhere near our city's main waterway after dark . . .*

There were whole threads on internet forums dedicated to the story, some incoherent and descending into online fights between people with opposing theories. Lola skimmed them with growing confusion. Victims' names changed and the dates weren't clear; no one seemed sure which stretch of the river they were talking about, with some talking about the newly developed Pacific Quay, others about Glasgow Green, nearly three miles east of there; and there was disagreement about whether the young male victims were selling sex or 'innocently' passing by when the Pusher got them.

One person seemed convinced the Pusher was an alien, who could come and go using powers of teleportation.

The *Gouger* appeared more grounded and useful. The magazine, which had begun as a kitchen-table publishing enterprise by a couple of friends who wanted to lay bare corruption and crime in Glasgow, had grown into a flourishing enterprise, and a new edition went on sale weekly in convenience stories and petrol stations. It was renowned for plain talking and exposing the city's underbelly and was a particular source of gossip about gang activities.

Lola found several stories about the Pusher on the *Gouger*'s website, including one sensationally headlined 'The Night the Clyde Pusher Phoned Our Mam'. The stories were behind a paywall, but a subscription was cheap. She bookmarked the page.

Next she found a Facebook group called 'Clyde Pusher Families'. It was set to private, but showed as having forty-eight members. This must be the group Tom had referred to. Lola wasn't on Facebook and didn't like the idea of joining up.

Just then her phone began to buzz on the table beside her, making her start.

An unknown number. She checked the time — 4.12 a.m. Whoever it was, it wasn't going to be good news . . .

She answered.

'Oh, thank God you're there! It's Brenda Cheney here.'

'Brenda? Are you all right?'

'*I* am,' the woman said, her voice shaking. 'But Cammy's not. Could you come round? I'm afraid it's an emergency.'

CHAPTER TWELVE

4.45 a.m.

Brenda came to the door of her tenement flat in her dressing gown, her face puffy and her eyes bloodshot. She looked as tired as Lola felt. But there was something else in her expression — she seemed shaken. Frightened too.

'This is Cammy,' she said, leading the way into the untidy and dark living room. 'Cammy,' she said now, with forced brightness, 'this is the lady.'

'Hi,' the boy whispered, barely making eye contact from his corner of the settee.

'Hello, Cammy,' Lola said.

'Sit anywhere,' Brenda told her.

Cameron Leavey was a thin, folded creature. He was hugging a cushion, watching her with big, miserable eyes.

Lola still didn't understand fully why she was here, except that the frightened boy had something he needed to confide.

'Cammy found something,' Brenda said, and lowered herself awkwardly, with a pained gasp, into a chair. 'Didn't you, Cammy?'

His eyes dropped to the cushion and he gave a tiny nod.

'Well, I'm all ears,' Lola said.

As she watched, his face crumpled and he began to sob, pushing his fists into his eye sockets and heaving with misery.

She looked to Brenda to explain.

The woman took a deep breath and began. 'He went home last night — didn't you, Cammy? — to fetch a few things. Says he was planning on coming here because someone had followed him to the flat earlier in the day. I'd given him my address long since in case he ever needed it, you know?'

'Someone followed you?' Lola asked sharply. 'Who?'

'The one he saw down at the river,' Brenda said cryptically.

The boy managed a feeble nod.

'So he went back to his flat just before midnight . . . and found one of his flatmates — his friend Declan — dead in his bed. Blood everywhere, God help him.'

Lola turned to the boy, electrified by horror and disbelief. 'Is this true?'

'It's true,' Brenda said, answering for him. 'He showed me photos on his phone.'

On cue, the boy took his phone out and tapped it awake before holding it out to Lola. She didn't take it from him, but looked at the image on the screen: a brightly lit single bed, pale limbs sprawled, and dark red everywhere, soaking the sheets and sprayed up the wall behind the bed.

'Brenda, please tell me you've reported this,' Lola said, just about keeping the panic from her voice.

'I phoned 999.'

'Right. And when was that?'

'About three.'

'And you told them what Cammy had found — and gave them the right address?'

'Of course!'

'And you told them who you were, didn't you?'

Brenda gave her a defiant look before saying, quietly, 'No, I did not.'

'Oh, Brenda . . .'

'Cammy asked me not to. I wasn't about to break his trust. I ask you not to break mine.'

They watched each other, Lola trying to control her impatience. It was hard when she was so dizzy from lack of sleep.

'Cammy,' Lola said, making herself sound calmer and more reasonable than she felt, 'you need to talk to the police without delay. You're a crucial witness.'

'You're polis, aren't you?' he said, looking confused and panicky, his gaze flicking to Brenda.

'I am, but this won't be my case. It *can't* be.' She turned to Brenda. 'You've put me in a very difficult position here.'

'He's frightened!' Brenda said. 'Can't you see that? He thinks whoever killed his friend made a mistake — that he meant to kill *him*!' She turned to the boy. 'Tell her about the man's face. Tell her about his eyes. Tell her what—'

'Woah,' Lola cried, hand up. 'Stop right there! That's not how this works at all. I'm not here officially. You save those details for my colleagues.'

The boy began sobbing.

'Look at the state of him,' Brenda hissed.

Lola closed her eyes. *Patience. Practicalities. Do what you can to save the situation.*

'Do you have coffee?' she said now.

'Yes.'

'Well, I'd like some. Black, please. And while you make it, I'll chat to Cammy here.'

Brenda looked disgruntled, but eased herself upright and left the room.

'Right, young man,' Lola began. 'Let's get a few things straight here.'

* * *

5.12 a.m.

'What's your friend's name?' she asked him. 'The one you found.'

'Dec.' He sniffed and cuffed away another tear. 'Declan Bailey.'

'That must have been a terrible shock for you.' She left a pause, in case he wanted to fill it. He didn't, so she went on: 'You'll be as keen as I am to find who did this to him.'

He nodded. Then he reached down the side of the chair and retrieved a metallic-blue cylinder. She recognised it as a can of Hyperdrive. He popped the ring and slurped from it.

'Like that stuff, do you?'

He nodded.

'It's saved my bacon these past few weeks. What's your favourite flavour?'

'This one,' he said quietly, and rotated the can for her to see. 'Blue raspberry.'

'Right.' It was the one Lola liked least of all. 'I like the tropical peach myself,' she told him.

'Not tried it.'

'You should.'

He took another swig.

'Cammy,' she said kindly, 'the best way to help find whoever did this to Declan is to talk to my colleagues.' She saw him tense up. 'All they'll want to know is details of when you found him, and whether you touched anything, that kind of thing. They'll want to know about the man who followed you home.'

He mumbled something.

'What was that?'

'I said, what if they think I did it?'

'Did you?'

'Of course not!' Tears welled again.

She leaned forward. 'Declan was your friend, wasn't he?'

He nodded miserably. 'We were in the same home together.'

'Look, I'm not going to lie to you. They'll probably be interested in why you ran and didn't call them right away. They might even seem cross about it, but believe me — *their priority is to find Declan's killer.*'

He lifted his chin and met her gaze. 'It was his eyes. They were—'

'*Don't* tell me any details,' she snapped, in spite of her urge to know exactly what he'd seen and why he was so frightened. 'If you tell me, I become a witness too. I need to stay apart from this as best I can.'

'Couldn't you stay?' he asked.

'What do you mean?'

'If the polis come to talk to me here, could you stay?'

Brenda had reappeared in the doorway, Lola's coffee in hand. 'Fine by me if they want to interview him here,' Brenda said to Lola.

'I want a brief too,' the boy said.

'What on earth for?' Brenda asked, mystified.

'You shouldn't need a solicitor at this stage,' Lola told him. 'They'll want to interview you as a witness. If they want to take you in for further questioning, they'll explain your right to legal representation then.'

She didn't say so, but she had already thought of a solicitor who'd be a perfect fit for this bright but troubled young man. One who'd defend his rights with angry fervour.

'I'll need witness protection, won't I?' he said now, seeming cheered by the thought. 'They'll have to house me somewhere he can't get at me.'

'We'll see.' She rose from her seat. 'Now, give me five minutes and I'll call in from my car. Look after that coffee for me, Brenda. I'm going to need it.'

CHAPTER THIRTEEN

5.59 a.m.

'I'm DC Janey Carstairs,' the young woman told Lola as she reached the top of the steps.

'DCI Lola Harris, Glasgow South West,' Lola told her from Brenda's doorway. 'I'm not here in any official capacity.'

'Command and Control explained,' Carstairs said. 'You're a friend of the family.'

'Something like that.'

Carstairs was small and well built with short, dyed-blonde hair and a shiny red face. She had the lively and eager look of lots of young detectives. It wouldn't last.

'And this,' she said, turning towards the stairs and the sound of approaching footsteps, 'is DS Lachlan Gray.'

Lola winced. *Lachlan Gray!*

Had they made the connection between the death of Declan Bailey and the Pusher already? In which case, was he here to 'contain' things?

Gray appeared at the turn of the stairs and gazed blankly up at the two of them. He was slim and wiry looking, but his face was drawn and bone-pale, cadaverous even. His cropped fair hair only exacerbated the corpse-like appearance. On he came, steadily climbing. How old was he? Surely not yet forty. Lola wondered if he was ill.

'This is DCI Harris,' Carstairs told him brightly.

He held Lola's gaze and nodded, but said nothing.

'DS Gray,' Lola said, making him narrow his eyes. He wasn't happy to see her. She wondered how quickly he'd begin attempts to send her on her way.

'The witness is Cameron Leavey,' she told the pair of them quietly once they were inside the hallway. 'He's afraid he'll be a suspect and also that the killer might come back for him. He believes he was the intended target. Beyond that I don't know any more.'

'We'll take things from here, DCI Harris,' Gray said breezily now. 'No need for you to stay.'

As quick as that . . .

'He's a reluctant witness,' Lola told him. 'He won't talk to you unless I'm there. I relayed that to Control and Command. Maybe they failed to tell you.'

Gray glared. 'Where is he?'

'This way.'

In the living room she introduced them to Brenda, now dressed in black slacks and a long-sleeved top.

Cammy perched on the edge of the settee, head down, eyeing the newcomers nervously from under his fringe.

'Cameron Leavey?' Gray said.

The boy mumbled a reply.

Gray introduced himself and Carstairs. He caught Lola's eye and nodded questioningly towards Brenda.

'Ms Cheney is going to stay too,' Lola said, and smiled.

The newcomers found seats and Lola sat too, settling down to listen.

Gray led. He explained that they were going to ask Cammy questions, as he was a key witness. He invited Cammy to explain what had happened the night before, asking him to provide, or estimate, times, and what he saw. Then he had Cammy hand over his phone so he and Carstairs could see the photographs the boy had taken of Declan Bailey's bedroom and body. The boy seemed twitchy and Lola guessed he had personal photos and text messages on his phone. Ones he wouldn't want anyone to see.

'Why do you think the attacker was targeting you?' Carstairs asked.

'He followed me, didn't he?'

'What do you mean?'

'He was inside the cemetery, watching me through the fence, when I went home in the afternoon. He'd followed me there, or found out where I lived, or something.'

'I'm sorry,' Gray said, 'you're saying someone's been following you?' He and Carstairs exchanged looks.

'Since I saw him at the river! I saw him, didn't I?'

'At the river?' Carstairs murmured, looking shifty.

Cammy threw himself back in the settee in frustration.

Lola said, eyes on Gray, 'Cammy claims he saw someone attack and push another man into the river on Saturday evening. The attacker saw Cammy there.'

'And he must have recognised me,' Cammy said. 'He knew where I lived and he went there to wait for me, except I spotted him and did a runner. I should have warned Dec and Fin,' he gabbled on. 'He must have got into the flat and thought Dec was me . . . We look a bit alike, see?'

Gray sat very still, eyes focused on a corner of the room as if he was thinking hard.

Carstairs remained silent too, watching the sergeant for a cue.

Lola watched and waited and tried to anticipate Gray's next move.

At last he sat up straight and took a long, furious breath in through his nose so that his nostrils narrowed. His pale bony head swivelled towards Lola. He said crisply, 'I'd like a word.'

She rose without answering and went ahead of him into Brenda's hallway, then turned, arms folded, ready for whatever was coming. Curious too.

Gray was nervous. His eyes flicked about and he kept licking his lips. 'I think you should go now and leave this to us,' he said, avoiding eye contact.

'Oh?'

He glanced behind him at the door to the living room and lowered his voice even more. 'The kid's mixed up. Probably off his face on drugs. A lot of these rent boys are. We'll take him in. Need to take a proper look at his phone, in any case.'

'Why would you take him in?'

More cagey glances. 'This environment's no good, is it? The old woman's probably put ideas in his head.'

What on earth was going on here? It was mention of the river, wasn't it? The reference to an attacker pushing a man into the water.

'What are you so afraid of?' she asked him quietly.

'"Afraid"?' he said nastily. 'I'm not afraid.'

'Yes you are. Detective Superintendent Wilde's afraid too. And Comms — they're just about shitting themselves. Why? A man — John Paul McCrae — was attacked and pushed into the water the other night. Part of a pattern of attacks no one is allowed to mention. Here's a witness. A witness who's subsequently been menaced.'

'There's no evidence McCrae was attacked.' He swallowed hard. 'And there's no evidence his death is linked to the murder of Declan Bailey.'

Lola stared in almost amused incomprehension. Gray began to look antsy again.

'Look, DCI Harris. We're dealing with it. We'll take care of the kid. Just, *please* — leave it to us.'

She eyed the man with disgust. She hadn't taken to him when they first spoke, now she mistrusted him completely. But they worked in different subdivisions and to pull rank on him would cause a whole lot of grief.

'I'll go,' she told Gray, 'but I want to speak to the boy first.'

'Very well.' He stood aside to let her get to the living room door.

'Cammy,' she said, settling gently on the edge of the settee beside him, 'my colleagues are going to need to take you to the station so they can take a statement.' He looked at her with wide, frightened eyes. She could feel Brenda eyeing her cynically, just waiting for her to let the boy down. 'You'll be fine, Cammy, and I'll check in on you, I promise. But listen, I'm going to contact a solicitor and see if she can meet you there.'

'A brief?' he asked eagerly.

'Aye, if you want. Her name's Robyn McArthur and she's tough as anything. You'll like her. If she's available she'll make sure you're well looked after, but really, you've nothing to worry about.'

Lachlan Gray glared thunderously as she rose to go.

But he looked anxious too. And so he should. Because the cowardly shit had it coming to him. Big time.

CHAPTER FOURTEEN

8.37 a.m.

Lola got to the meeting room early to plan for the team briefing at nine o'clock. She took out a can of tropical peach Hyperdrive and opened it. Even the sickly sweet smell of the juice inside gave her a pep.

Today would be all about the Kevin Millar murder, starting with an interview with Jamie McGregor and his legal team at the office of McGregor Demolitions. Lola would take the lead with Anna's support. The plan was to keep things civil with McGregor while they carefully pieced together a picture of his movements and communications in the days leading up to the attack. If McGregor had ordered the killing, then somewhere that order would have left a trace — most likely a digital one.

The second line of enquiry related to Kevin Millar's own movements on the morning he died. Something had brought him from his flat out into the streets of Clydebank before dawn, but what? They needed to know who had contacted him, and how. He'd known he was a target — he'd asked about witness protection often enough — so it must have been something compelling to persuade him to leave his home, alone. Had it been arranged in advance or had a call been made at dawn? Millar's phone was missing and Lola theorised that it had been removed from the scene deliberately. Later in the day, DS Aidan Pierce, along with one of the constables, would pay a second visit to Millar's mother and sister to collect a promised list of all Millar's friends and associates. It was possible someone among them knew where he'd been going that morning.

Then there was the white van, the third line of enquiry. It had been tracked by CCTV barrelling along the river towards Glasgow. In the later images it had a dent in its front bumper. They were still waiting for the results of a request from the CCTV control centre in Glasgow, and Lola was hopeful. Ahead of the COP26 climate summit in Glasgow in 2021, the cameras in the city centre had been replaced with hi-res digital devices, capable of zooming in and rendering fine detail.

A knock at the door.

'Come in! Oh. Morning, boss.'

'Hiding, are you?' Elaine Walsh said.

'If only,' Lola murmured. She saw the superintendent's expression and felt a zap of anxiety.

Elaine took her time finding a seat across the table. She laced her fingers together and faced Lola with the rueful air of an old friend who's about to deliver well-meant home truths. But she didn't speak.

'I can guess what this is about,' Lola said, eyes on the table before her.

Elaine raised a single eyebrow.

Lola looked at her, endeavouring to look calm. 'Has DS Gray complained?'

'Not officially.'

'Oh?'

'I've had Angus Wilde on the phone, wanting to know why you seem to be leading a one-woman crusade to catch the so-called Clyde Pusher.'

'That's what he said?'

'In effect.'

'A friend called me out in the middle of the night. She was helping a young man who was in crisis. I went. When I found out he'd discovered a murder victim, I phoned it in. What would you have done?'

Elaine frowned, seeming to give it serious thought. 'I wouldn't have waited.'

Lola hesitated, trying to pin down her meaning. Her brain was on a go-slow, despite the Hyperdrive drink. 'Waited . . . ?'

'The boy told the two detectives you got to Brenda Cheney's place at four forty-five. You didn't call it in until five twenty.'

'I had to gain the boy's trust,' Lola said, hating the defensiveness in her tone. 'If I'd turned up and called it in right away, he'd have done a runner.'

Elaine looked sceptical.

'The important thing was that Brenda Cheney had reported the murder. I made sure of that. Look, it wasn't an ideal situation. I did what I thought was right, and maybe I wasn't thinking straight. I'd only had three hours' sleep.'

'I'm not surprised you're not sleeping,' Elaine said, her eyes on the blue metallic can on the table.

'This isn't the reason,' she said, defensive again, and this time with a small twinge of panic at the idea of surrendering her tropical peach pick-me-up. 'There's no caffeine in it. It's plant based.'

'Caffeine comes from plants. Let me see.' Elaine reached for the can.

Lola sat on her instinct to snatch it back from her.

Elaine lifted her specs and peered at the ingredients. 'Ginseng, green tea, taurine — whatever that is. Green coffee extract — what's "green" coffee? Guarana. Oh, and sugar. Fifteen grams per hundred mills — and this is, what? Three hundred mills? So that's forty-five grams of sugar in a can. *Nine teaspoons of sugar?*'

Lola breathed deeply and tried to control her irritation.

'Isn't guarana that stuff that's stronger than caffeine anyway?'

'Is it?'

Elaine put the can down and narrowed her eyes. 'Exactly how many cans of this rubbish are you getting through a day?'

'A couple,' Lola mumbled.

'Don't lie to me.'

'Three or four! I don't know. I haven't been counting.'

Elaine screwed up her mouth and shook her head. 'Water,' she said. 'A coffee first thing and the odd cup of tea, but water's the thing. Otherwise you're just stuffing your body full of chemicals.'

Lola went mutinously quiet. She wanted, intensely, to grab the can and take another syrupy mouthful — except Elaine would no doubt call her out for it.

'If you're not sleeping, you need to talk to someone.'

'I have.'

'Who? Your GP?'

'Aye, of course. He gave me sleeping pills. They didn't help. Well, they made me sleep but I woke up feeling worse.'

Elaine's expression changed to one of sympathy. She asked gently, 'Is it Joe?'

'Of course.' She bit her lip. 'Of course it's Joe.'

'These things take time, Lola. A *long* time.'

'I'm aware of that.'

'Look, I know you're not in a great place right now, but if it helps, you're still doing a great job here. I value you and I'll support you if you need help. I'm here if you ever want to talk. Or if you ever want to do anything — come out to the house, if you like. I'll teach you to throw a pot, if you like.' Elaine had a big old manse near Lennoxtown, north of Glasgow, and had recently installed a kiln in an outhouse. Lola suspected a ceramics-related retirement plan was being put in place.

'Thanks,' Lola said. 'So, what did you say to Angus Wilde, by the way?'

'That I'd have a word.'

Lola nodded.

'He'd like you to "keep your nose out", to quote him.'

'They don't want to connect it with what Cameron Leavey saw at the river, do they? The moment he mentioned the river, the sergeant tried to throw me out. Elaine, that boy saw a man *attacked* — the man *died*. Then the attacker appeared outside the boy's flat. A few hours later his flatmate was *murdered in his bed*.'

'And they're investigating that murder.' Elaine's face darkened. '*They* are.' She leaned forward. 'And *you* are not. Do you understand?'

'Aye, okay.'

'Say it.'

'I understand.'

'Okay. Now, have a good meeting. And good luck with Jamie McGregor.'

CHAPTER FIFTEEN

11.59 a.m.

'That was weird, wasn't it?' Lola said to DS Anna Vaughan when they were back in the car behind the prefab offices of McGregor Demolitions in Yoker.

'Just a bit,' Anna said.

Jamie McGregor had been on his best behaviour. In previous interviews there'd been a barely concealed aggression beneath the superficial charm, but today Lola had found him humble and cooperative.

His solicitors were from Glasgow's most expensive firm, a partner and two associates. Ranged around the board table in funereal suits, they gave an impression of yearning to help. They'd already had McGregor produce a printed schedule of his movements for the past week, and it seemed there'd be no problem in the police accessing McGregor's personal phone, a work phone, a tablet or his laptop. Lola asked for phone records for every device registered to the company. 'Fine,' McGregor had responded. 'As I've said, I want to help find who killed that lad.'

Of course, a clever criminal would conceal his tracks using every means available to him, including the use of 'burner' devices.

'Take him at face value,' Lola told Anna now, 'and you'd think he was a pillar of the community.'

'He definitely takes care of himself,' the sergeant mused, a little coyly.

Lola rolled her eyes. Anna set a lot of store on appearance. Her hair was beautifully cut and her nails were pristine. She was open about the fact she paid for botox and fillers.

Lola put the Audi in gear and was approaching the car park exit when her personal phone began to ring. It was Robyn McArthur, the solicitor.

She got out of the car and pressed answer.

'They let Cammy go,' Robyn said. 'He's gone back to Brenda's for a rest. I think he'll stay there a few days.'

'That's good. Everything all right?'

The briefest of silences, then the solicitor said, 'You couldn't stop by the office, could you? Only there are one or two things you might like to hear.'

CHAPTER SIXTEEN

12.32 p.m.

Lola dropped Anna off at Helen Street before ducking onto the motorway for the ten-minute hop to Robyn's office. A hop it was supposed to be, but they were doing something to the M8 at Cowcaddens and she found herself snarled up in an intractable jam.

Someone behind her honked a horn — pointlessly, because nothing was moving. She turned off her engine and messaged Robyn to say she was running late then spotted yet another message from Hughie, the man she'd gone on a date with, the one with the house and boat in Argyll.

When can I see you again? he'd texted. *Was fun last time. Be good to do it again.*

She groaned. She'd fancied him: he was funny, good-looking, well built in a stocky way. He'd had good hair too, nicely styled. But he'd been so pushy about coming back to hers, first offering her a lift and asking all about her house, her neighbours. He'd even asked her the name of her street. It might have been keenness, but in her job she had to be alert. What did she really know about this man? He'd said he was a surveyor with his own business. He'd been married and then divorced. It might be true and it might not.

Almost without thinking, she reached for her bag and pulled out a can of Hyperdrive. She considered it in her hand, and felt a momentary twinge of guilt as Elaine's words replayed in her mind — before she told the voice to shut up, and opened it.

A refreshing sip later, she gave herself a mental shake and typed a reply:

Yes it was fun. I'm pretty busy at the mo. Maybe in a week or two?

Closing the app, she remembered Sorcha's friend Barry, who was impatiently awaiting her call. It felt a bit mean to chat to Hughie without even a hello to the needy Barry — besides, she needed to keep Sorcha off her back.

After checking the traffic again, she found Barry's number and wrote a message:

Hi. It's Lola, Sorcha's friend. Sorcha said we might enjoy a coffee together. Am southside. Let me know when might suit. L.

She read it over, then, with a tingle of apprehension, pressed send — just as the traffic jam around her began to ease.

CHAPTER SEVENTEEN

12.56 p.m.

'Thank you for stepping in like that,' Lola said, once she was sitting in Robyn's office on the third floor of a converted warehouse.

'You're welcome. And if you're wondering, I clocked up just over two hours. Actually, I've knocked fifty quid off the hourly rate because I enjoyed going head to head with that knob of a sergeant.'

'Appreciate it.'

In a fit of generosity, Lola had agreed to pay Robyn's costs for attending Cammy's police interview. In fact, it was less generosity than a bid to assuage her guilt at leaving the boy at the mercy of the icy Lachlan Gray. Robyn was a criminal law solicitor she'd come across during the Lovers' Lane murder investigation during the autumn of the previous year. Lola had been impressed with her feisty commitment to her tricky client, as well as her pragmatism and good humour. She was a smart woman in her forties with closely cropped, shiny black hair and a natty dress sense. Today she had on a cream shirt and gold tweed waistcoat that matched her trousers.

'He's a sweet kid,' Robyn said, flicking on a bean-to-cup coffee machine. 'I'm glad he's gone to Brenda's. I can't help thinking . . .'

'Can't help thinking what?'

'That he might be right about being in danger. This is off the record, right?'

'As far as either of us is concerned, I'm not even here.'

Robyn paused while the coffee machine ground the beans then chugged out their coffee, at the same time filling the room with comforting aroma.

She passed Lola her cup then sat. Lola sipped her coffee. It was rich and bitter and very welcome.

'The man Cammy saw across from his flat — he's convinced it's the same person he saw at the river. He believes it sincerely. And I think I believe him too. But your colleague — DS Gray? — he didn't want to know.'

'What happened?'

'It was pretty straightforward to start with. I got to Stewart Street and made them give me fifteen minutes alone with Cammy before they interviewed him. Brenda waited in reception the whole time. They had his other flatmate there, in another room. Finlay Robson — they'd picked him up at his girlfriend's mum's in the early hours. DS Gray did the heavy-handed thing, as if he knew Cammy killed Declan Bailey and he was just waiting for a confession. I'd warned Cammy they might do that, so he was ready. He was very calm and reasonable. I was proud of him.'

Lola was too.

'He described the man's face . . .'

'Go on.' Cammy had tried to describe it to Lola in the early hours of the morning, but she'd stopped him, unwilling to become party to any information before it was recorded officially.

Robyn flicked through several pages of her pad and read, 'Quote: "The man was all in black, with a hood up. And he had a mask on — you know, like a Covid mask, but decorated. It was a skeleton's jaw and teeth."'

Tiny hairs rose on Lola's arms and the back of her neck.

'Gray and Carstairs went over it repeatedly, like they didn't believe him. Cammy said he'd recognise the eyes again.'

'Did he?'

'Gray was *so* dismissive,' Robyn said. 'Kept referring to the distance Cammy must have been from the cemetery railings. There was a road between him and the cemetery, and traffic passing by.'

'But he saw the man close up on Saturday evening. He did tell them that, didn't he?'

Robyn pursed her mouth. 'He tried to.'

'What do you mean? They didn't want to know, or—?'

'They said they were interested in the attack on his friend, and they thanked him for the description of the man he saw inside the cemetery. Cammy said he'd seen a man attacked and pushed into the river by this same individual. That the man had seen Cammy filming him and that that was why he'd come after him.'

'*Filming* him?' Lola asked.

'That's right. And that the man must have followed him home to Dennistoun, got into the flat and killed Declan thinking he was Cammy. He gave your colleagues a motive, and he linked the murder of his friend to another attack only days before . . . but they *just weren't interested.*'

Lola let the words sink in, feeling shaken.

'I didn't know if you'd be able to do anything,' the solicitor said with a rueful smile, 'but I thought you ought to know.'

'Did you ask about witness protection for Cammy?'

'I did.'

'And?'

'Doesn't warrant it, in their view,' Robyn said. '"There's no evidence he's in any immediate danger" and besides, he "has a place to stay".'

'I see.'

Lola rose. Robyn McArthur rose with her. 'Shout if you need me,' she said. 'I'll do what I can.'

'You know, Brenda Cheney's place isn't far from here,' Lola said. 'I might pop in and see how he's doing.'

CHAPTER EIGHTEEN

1.32 p.m.

Climbing the stairs at Brenda's, she saw Elaine had tried to contact her twice, but hadn't left a message. Face burning guiltily, she switched off her phone and tucked it into her bag.

She shouldn't have hired Robyn — shouldn't have gone to see her, either — and she certainly shouldn't be here now. The tiredness must be affecting her judgement. She knew she should focus on the McGregor–Millar case and mind her own business when it came to the deaths of John Paul McCrae and Declan Bailey . . .

But something was badly wrong here, and she wanted — no, *needed* — to find out what.

'Poor lad's asleep,' Brenda said, when she came to the door. She looked as if she'd been sleeping herself. Her purple-spiked hair was flattened on one side. 'Do you really want me to wake him up?'

'Please, Brenda. I don't have long.'

'Go through,' Brenda said, then retreated grumbling down the corridor.

Cammy appeared a couple of minutes later, wearing old-fashioned men's pyjamas that were too big for him. Lola wondered if they'd belonged to Brenda's husband, or to the son who'd chosen to cut her off.

'I wanted to see if you were all right,' Lola said. 'Come and sit down a minute.'

He perched beside her, wariness in his big watchful eyes.

Brenda appeared in the doorway. 'I'll be in the kitchen,' she said.

Alone, Lola said, 'I caught up with Robyn. She says you did really well.'

'She's pretty sick.'

'*Sick?* That's good, is it?'

'Yeah, 'course.'

'She said you told DS Gray about what happened at the river.'

He gave a little shrug and looked at his lap. 'Tried to.'

'Why don't you tell me about it? I'll listen. Tell me everything you remember. Don't leave anything out.'

He watched her for a few moments, eyes narrow, as if assessing why she was asking him about something her colleagues clearly weren't interested in. Then he told his story — about leaving his boyfriend on the south side of the river, then how he'd crossed the river, planning to walk home. How a friend had warned him the Pusher was out and about.

'What friend was that?' Lola asked gently.

He eyed her warily before saying, 'Larissa. I don't know her other name. She's nice.'

Brenda had mentioned the name Larissa to her when they'd met at Tom's flat.

He told her he'd spotted the Pusher standing in the shadows of a doorway on the other side of the road, and that he'd decided to try to watch him. To follow him and, if possible, film him.

'Did you manage to catch anything?'

'Yeah. D'you wanna see?'

'Please.' She held her breath as he readied his phone. He moved next to her and angled the screen.

The video played. It was grainy, kept tilting dizzily, but she could see white railings, the brown expanse of the river, the glow of street lights — and a tall, hooded figure moving close to the buildings across the road from the promenade. The image tilted, then cut out.

'It's only seventeen seconds,' he said. 'Shame the camera's so pants. I need a better phone.'

'What happened then?'

'I lost sight of him. I panicked a bit.' His voice dropped to a whisper. 'Then I saw him again. He'd crossed the road to the same side as me. He was right in front of me, looking my way.'

'Looking at you, you mean?'

'I thought he was, but I was hiding under a tree. He came running right past me. He was after the other guy, you see?' He stopped, and she watched the emotions in his face as he strove for his next words. 'He ran straight up to this other guy. He had something in his hand — a kind of weapon — and he . . . he hit the guy really hard on the back of his head. There was a sort of *smack* and the guy cried out and fell to his knees.' He looked at her hard and there were tears in his eyes. 'I ran away,' he said. 'I didn't even think about trying to help him. I heard the splash as I was running. I looked back and the Pusher was *staring* at me. He'd seen me.' He started to cry. 'I had my phone in my hand, so maybe he knew I'd filmed him.'

Lola sat quietly for what felt like a long time while the boy recovered himself.

At last she said, 'Did you tell DS Gray and DC Carstairs about this?'

He didn't look at her, but nodded.

'That was the right thing to do.'

'They seemed pissed off. *He* did, anyway. He wanted to talk about other stuff. About Dec. I kept trying to tell them about what happened at the river, but . . . but it was like he didn't want to know.'

'What did he look like?' she asked now. 'The attacker.'

His breathing became shallow and quick, as if conjuring up the image caused him physical discomfort.

He spoke in a whisper. 'Scary. He was big, and he was wearing this scary mask over the bottom half of his face. Like a skull. His eyes were weird too.'

'What do you mean?'

'They were all white apart from the black dots. There was no colour at all.'

'You told this to my colleagues too?'

He nodded uncertainly. 'Tried to.'

Lola sat for a moment, then asked, 'Did you know him, Cammy? Did you recognise him?'

He blinked and looked briefly away, eyes on Brenda's mantelpiece, his smooth young brow wrinkled with the effort of concentration. Then he looked back at her and shook his head. 'No.'

'Would you recognise him again?'

He thought about that too.

'Not if he was dressed normally — in the street, you know? But with the mask on, definitely.'

'How old would you say he was?'

He shook his head, bottom lip out. 'Older than me.'

'My age?'

'Maybe. Dunno.'

They sat quietly for a few moments, then Lola said, 'You've been very brave telling me this. I want you to know that. And to know you've done the right thing. Now, that video. Have you posted it online anywhere? Sent it to anyone?'

He shook his head.

'Okay, good. Now, it's important we keep it safe.'

'I won't delete it.'

'I don't mean that. What if your phone got broken or you lost it?'

'I could message it to you.'

'Yes, okay. Why don't you do that?'

She read out her phone number and a WhatsApp message appeared a minute later.

She got up to go, and saw him relax at the idea of being left alone. She still had a concern, though. 'This friend of yours,' she said, smiling as if she was asking out of mere polite interest. 'Warren, isn't it? How long have you known him?'

He shrugged, eyes down, uncomfortable again. 'Not long.'

'Nice, is he?'

Another shrug, but a nod.

'What's he do?'

He glanced up at her, a cynical light in his eye now. He knew what she was up to and wanted her to know it. 'He's a businessman. He's got companies. Loads of people work for him.'

'Do you know his surname? I'm not asking you to tell me it. I'm just interested.'

'Yeah, I know his name.' Defiant now. 'Why?'

'He's older than you, isn't he? And he gives you money.'

'Brenda tell you that, did she?' He was indignant.

'She's worried about you. So am I.'

'There's no need.' Sulky now.

'There are bad people about who can take advantage of people like . . . people who don't know that much about the world.'

'I'm not stupid.'

'I didn't say that.'

His face was red and he looked embarrassed and annoyed. Maybe she'd gone too far, but what she'd said was true. She was concerned for him. He was young and vulnerable, with the kind of naivety that could so easily be exploited.

'I'll go now,' she said, breezy again. 'Look after yourself, Cammy. Sorry I woke you up.'

CHAPTER NINETEEN

3.25 p.m.

Lola was in the canteen at Helen Street for coffee and a scone with Anna and Kirstie when two of the DCs, Marcus McVittie and Jonno Gillies, appeared. She waved them over.

Small talk out of the way, she asked, trying to sound only mildly interested, 'What do you guys know about the Clyde Pusher? Do you think he's real?'

'Aye, he's real,' Jonno said, looking round at his colleagues to check they were in agreement.

'I'm not so sure,' Marcus said, then frowned at her. 'This about the guy who went into the river at the weekend?'

'I was just interested, that's all.' She felt Kirstie's curious grey eyes on her.

'Of course he's real,' Jonno said to Marcus. 'Too many deaths in a concentrated area. Only, no one wants it looked at.'

'Bullshit,' Marcus said. 'It's an urban legend and any talk of a cover-up is just pish — sorry, boss.'

'There was an investigation early on,' Jonno said. 'Don't you remember? A DS in City Centre subdivision was leading it. Ali Arshad. According to a pal of mine, Arshad was convinced something dodgy was going on, but then . . . he got taken off it and put on other cases.'

Kirstie said, 'Statistically the deaths are in line with expected accidental deaths on waterways in the Central Belt.' She saw their stares and flushed. 'I looked it up.'

'What about the fact every single victim was gay?' Jonno said. 'Bit of a coincidence.'

'Were they, though?' Kirstie asked. 'How can you trust information you read online?'

'Look at it this way,' Anna said, putting her coffee cup down. 'In whose interest would it be to cover up a serial murderer? It doesn't make sense. You'd be relying on a whole organisation to connive at it.'

'That happens *all the time*,' Jonno said. 'It's human instinct to close ranks, especially in some organisations. There are countless examples of cover-ups.'

Kirstie said, 'I studied organisational psychology as part of my course at college. People are frightened of getting into trouble, or don't want to cause upset. If there's a negative culture in the organisation, then everyone just goes along with it.'

'It's usually Corporate Comms spinning a line,' Jonno said, and Marcus chuckled. 'Comms are always paranoid about "reputational damage".'

'So, can I ask,' Lola said, eyeballing Jonno, 'just for the sake of argument, if you're so sure the Pusher's real, why haven't *you* acted?'

Jonno took it in the spirit of the question, and thought about it. 'I'd get put back in my box, wouldn't I?' he said. 'And anyway—' he glanced round at his colleagues — 'I've enough to do already, thanks very much!'

They laughed, Lola joining in, though she felt anything but amused.

CHAPTER TWENTY

8.23 p.m.

'It's not that they don't believe him.' Lola was so cross she was at risk of spitting crumbs across the table. 'For some reason they're choosing not to hear it. I very much doubt they even wrote it down.'

She and her sister Frankie were in a pizza place on one of the balconies in the upmarket, art-nouveau Princes Square shopping mall on Buchanan Street. Rain drummed lightly on the glass roof but it was warm and cosy inside. Twinkly lights bathed the atrium in gold. Somehow she'd missed the fact it was Valentine's Day and the place was heaving. There was a special menu, and all about them couples picked over themed pizzas, some bored and focused on their respective phones; others young, spruced up and very much focused on each other and the pleasures of the night to come. Valentine's Day had never had any place in her relationship with Joe. He always spent it with his wife — as he would be again this year.

Don't even go there.
She gave herself a mental shake.

'But why would they dismiss such good evidence?' Frankie said, putting her glass of sparkling water down. 'It doesn't make sense.'

'God knows.' Lola tapped her fork on the table. 'I wish I knew what's going on.'

'You said Comms were in your face. Maybe that's all it is — they just want to stop conspiracy stories getting out.'

'Mm.'

'Is this what tonight's about?' Frankie asked now. 'Our wee walk down by the river later on? If it is, I don't know what you're hoping to find.'

'I want to see where it happened. I want to make sure it all fits in my head. I know from the records where that poor lad went into the river — I want to see if I recognise the location from the boy's video. If I do . . . well, I'll know, won't I?'

'Know what?'

'That I have to do something.'

Frankie raised her eyebrows and sipped her water. 'Lola to the rescue again?'

'Don't, Frankie. This is serious.'

'I'm sorry. Did you want a dessert, by the way?'

'No, but I'd go for a coffee. What about you?'

'Coffee? Aye, maybe, but is that wise, if you're still not sleeping?'

'It's not the coffee that's keeping me awake,' she said. It came out more tersely than she'd meant.

'What, then?'

'It's my nerves, isn't it? All because of *you-know-who*.'

'You're going through a process, that's all.'

'I know that! But why is it so bloody painful? It's like my brain's turned against me.'

'That's because your brain's job is to keep you alive, not make you happy.'

'Meaning what?'

'Meaning you're still in fight-or-flight mode from finally making the break. You need time. Actually, what I think I'm saying is, what you're going through is perfectly normal.'

Lola huffed. 'Give me abnormal any day.'

'It's important to notice your feelings, and try to notice what makes you feel better.'

As it happened, she wasn't feeling too bad right now. She enjoyed Frankie's company — if not always her mild hectoring. In addition, she'd managed an hour of blissful coma-like sleep after getting home from work, only waking when her phone buzzed to remind her of this dinner date with her sister.

'I've arranged to meet a guy,' she told Frankie now.

'The one your friend knows?'

'Aye, Sorcha's pal Barry. I finally texted him today. He replied within the hour and we're meeting for coffee on Sunday.'

'There you go,' Frankie said, smiling that clever smile of hers, 'you can do it.'

Lola made a face. 'We'll see.'

'Oh, I nearly forgot,' Frankie said now, reaching for her bag. 'Here,' she said, pushing a blank-looking CD in a plastic wallet across the table. 'My friend copied it for you.'

'What is it?'

'Sixty minutes of hypnotherapy for sleep by the guy she goes to. Torquil Carruthers is his name and Julie says he's the best there is.'

'I can't lie in bed and listen to someone called Torquil Carruthers.'

'Cynic.'

'Aye, well.' She checked the time. 'Shall we get the bill?'

'And skip the coffee, you mean?'

'No chance!' Lola cried. 'I'll have mine in a takeaway cup.'

* * *

9.22 p.m.

Down by the Clyde it was still drizzling. More of a wet mist than actual rain, but the kind of weather that made you hunch and screw up your eyes and hurry to get inside.

They started at the bottom of Jamaica Street, where elevated train tracks emerged from the mouth of Central Station and spanned the river. From there they walked eastwards on the north bank. The promenade was well lit by white streetlamps. It had been landscaped, with raised flowerbeds, benches and boxy beech trees still clad in last autumn's dead leaves. An illuminated billboard among the beeches depicted a yellow emoji-style grinning face and beneath it the words: *Glasgow is safe and sound!* It was a slogan the council had adopted to persuade residents the city was a veritable crime-free utopia. Lola found it meaningless and patronising, if not a little sinister.

'Oh, I think this is the place,' she said, stopping and looking around. 'From what the boy said, he first saw the Pusher somewhere along there.' She pointed. 'Beyond the cathedral, standing in a doorway of one of the flats.'

'Good vantage point,' Frankie said.

'He says the Pusher started walking east, keeping close to the buildings, and that's when he had the idea of filming him.'

They walked on, crossing at a junction, and then finding themselves on a lonelier stretch of the river, the traffic having veered north-east at the junction.

'I think it was on this section of Clyde Street,' Lola said, looking around. 'Want to see the film?'

She went into WhatsApp and found Cammy's video. She played it for Frankie, while studying the shaky image to check her bearings. Yes, this was the place all right. In the film, the Pusher crept along the edge of the hoardings then past an abandoned building.

'And that's where John Paul McCrae went into the river,' Lola said, pointing further along the street, almost as far as the Albert Bridge, where she and Tom had stopped on Saturday evening. 'It fits, Frankie. My God.'

'Well, now you know,' Frankie murmured. 'Question is, what the hell can you possibly do about it?'

CHAPTER TWENTY-ONE

10.41 p.m.

'Why have I got that sinking feeling?' Elaine said when she answered the door of the former manse. 'And you didn't even bring me a box of chocolates!'

'Happy Valentine's,' Lola mumbled, and followed her boss through the warren of a house. All the way here she'd been practising how to say it, and reminding herself of the bottom line: a young man had witnessed a murder and could be in grave danger himself — yet their colleagues had chosen to look the other way. It must be put right.

That didn't help the jitters, though.

'Lucky for you I was nowhere near bed,' Elaine said when they were in her study at the back of the house. 'I'm waiting for a batch of pots to cool. If you're still here in twenty minutes you can help me take them out — if I haven't thrown you out on your ear by then.' She shot Lola a look, then pointed to one of two armchairs. Lola sat.

'I've done something,' she began with composure. 'You'll be angry with me but you'll let me explain and then you'll see that I had no choice. And then I think you'll help me to do the right thing.'

'Oh God,' Elaine groaned. 'Am I going to need coffee?'
'Probably,' Lola said.

She was calmer by the time Elaine returned from the kitchen with two steaming mugs — hand potted. How the woman had the time, Lola had no idea. She had teenage kids, to boot.

'Is it to do with the young lad whose flatmate was murdered?' Elaine said, facing her from the other armchair.

Lola nodded.

'Right, tell me the worst.'

Lola came clean. About calling on Robyn's services, and then visiting her once the boy had been released. About their colleagues' apparent refusal to hear anything about the river attack. Then — worst of all — about her return visit to Brenda's to talk to the boy and hear the description of the attack from his own lips.

Elaine listened blank-faced.

'And I asked him to email the video to me,' she confessed lastly.

Elaine closed her eyes and put a hand despairingly to her forehead. She remained like that for thirty long seconds.

'And tonight I went down to the Clyde,' Lola went carefully on. 'I checked the location. It all fits.'

Her boss's eyes opened.

'Is he sincere?' Elaine said.

'He believes everything he's saying.'

Elaine nodded. She had faith in Lola's instincts. She always had done, despite Lola's sometimes unconventional approach.

'Show me the video,' she said.

She rose and Elaine stood beside her. Lola angled her phone and the two of them watched the seventeen-second clip.

'That proves nothing,' Elaine said. 'That figure could be anyone.'

'I know,' Lola agreed. 'But it's another part of the jigsaw. Why wouldn't Gray and Carstairs take him seriously? It can't just be the comms angle. A man died in the river on Saturday night. Another young man was butchered in his bed, and there's a valid reason to investigate a link!'

A timer went off on Elaine's phone. 'The pots are ready,' she said. 'Help me take them out and then we can decide what to do.'

* * *

11.13 p.m.

Armed with torches, they made their way to the bottom of Elaine's garden, where the kiln sat in a shed beyond a small orchard. An owl hooted nearby and over them stars glittered between clouds. It felt surreal, as if she'd stepped into a rustic night-time idyll.

'You'll need these,' Elaine told her, and handed her a pair of oven gloves. 'Mind your arms when you're reaching inside. We'll line the pots along here.'

'Do you sell many?' Lola asked.

'I do! There's a gallery in Balfron that shifts ten to fifteen every month. But that's not why I do it.'

She didn't need to explain. Lola could imagine it was a satisfying hobby, a good way to relieve stress.

The twelve pots were glazed green, blue and pink by turn. Lola lined them in alternating colours and felt soothed.

'Are you managing to stay off those toxic energy drinks?'

'I'm trying.'

'I've a present for you inside. Remind me.'

They worked for a few minutes in companionable silence, then Elaine beamed. 'There, I think that's us.'

'What now?' Lola asked.

'Now we go back to the house and I'll tell you what I'm going to do.'

Back in the study they retook their chairs.

'I don't think there's any point in my speaking to Angus Wilde,' Elaine said. 'He's tired, he's under huge personal strain — you know his wife's disabled, don't you? It's something horrible and degenerative. I think he'll palm me off. And I think his Communications sidekick will help him.'

'Melda Brodick, you mean?'

'The very same. She's a controlling individual. Single-minded and, frankly, unhelpful. No, I'm thinking of going straight to the top. Your good friend Clive Reid is paying us a visit tomorrow. I might just beg five minutes of his precious time.'

'The assistant chief constable? Will you tell him about me?'

'Yes, but I'll be putting your concerns to him as though they're mine.' She put a hand up to stop Lola speaking. 'I happen to agree with you that something very strange is happening. There's got to be a reason behind it. I think we have a right to know what that is.'

Lola managed to sustain a poker face, though she couldn't believe Elaine's boldness. Clive Reid had a fearsome reputation for authoritarian pronouncements and weighing heavily on those parts of the force he considered weren't up to scratch. He also happened to be uncle to DS Aidan Pierce. Last year, Pierce had done everything in his power to make her life hell, including putting in a grievance for bullying against her, and made repeated reference to his influential relative . . . Only for ACC Reid to track Lola down and make it plain that he had the measure of his delinquent, narcissistic nephew. He'd asked her to personally oversee Pierce's professional improvement plan. Humbled, Pierce had given every impression of falling meekly into line, though Lola was aware of malevolent currents beneath the surface, and still detected the occasional sneer or smirk when he thought she wasn't looking. Bottom line, she didn't trust him and doubted she ever would.

'What if he doesn't bite?' Lola asked Elaine now.

'Then we've tried. But Lola — if Clive Reid says don't touch this, then that's an order for both of us. No more cosy visits to witnesses on enquiries that we're not running.

I want you to steer clear of anything river-related until I say otherwise. Do I make myself clear?'

'A hundred per cent,' Lola said.

She got up to go.

'Just a moment,' Elaine said at the door. 'Your present.'

She was gone for a minute, then returned with a purple box in her hands.

'For you.'

Lola took it.

'Tea bags,' Elaine said, all smiles. 'A blend designed to reduce stress and aid sleep. I don't know if they'll work, but you should give them a try.'

CHAPTER TWENTY-TWO

Wednesday 15 February
11.45 a.m.

Shuna Frain, news editor of the *Daily Chronicle*, answered the door to her roomy tenement flat in Queen's Park. 'Get parked okay?' she asked Lola, a wicked glint in her eye. 'It is a bit of a squeeze down there, isn't it?'

Lola fixed a smile, knowing full well what Shuna was referring to. Last autumn, Lola had got herself into a literal scrape while 'just happening' to drive past Joe and Marie's place. She'd dented a neighbour's car and word had reached Shuna's ears, though she'd been persuaded at the last minute not to go to print.

'I'm pleased to report your BMW's unharmed,' Lola said now.

'What a relief.' Shuna stood aside to let Lola in. 'Can't wait to hear what I've done to deserve this honour.'

'I'm not here, remember,' Lola told her. 'If anyone asks, you and I haven't spoken in months.'

'Gotcha.' She pointed down the hallway. 'Door at the end on the left.'

'Have you had this done?' Lola said, surveying the gleaming white kitchen. 'Very nice.'

'Last month. A lot of money, but I'm happy with it. Take a pew.' She waved towards a glass table beside twin sash windows that looked out into a quad. 'Coffee?'

'Not for me,' Lola said.

She'd drunk a cup of Elaine's special tea before bed the night before, grimacing at its bitter flavour, then tried to listen to the CD of Torquil Carruthers whispering creepily about how she should let the tension 'leak' from her limbs. He'd spent a long time talking about upper thighs, and she could stand no more than ten minutes. She'd got three hours' sleep at most. So, Hyperdrive it was, and she'd guzzled a guilty can of the stuff on the way here. The garage in Yoker had only had blue raspberry flavour, so she'd had to make do. She recalled it was Cammy Leavey's favourite flavour, though God knows why. To Lola it tasted of bubblegum. But, apart from making the roof of her mouth go oddly numb, it had had the desired effect. She was buzzing and everything seemed nice and vivid.

'So, why all the secret squirrel?' Shuna said, taking a seat across the table, that smirk twitching her lips again. 'Is this about Jamie McGregor and the not-so-mysterious fire?'

'Now, what do you know about that, I wonder?' Jamie McGregor wasn't the reason she was here, but she was happy to play along, especially if Shuna had a titbit or two to share.

'I've heard one or two things. I'm sure you could help me fill in a few gaps. Such as, whether you're actively investigating McGregor in relation to the death of Kevin Millar.'

'And what's the word on the street about that?' Lola said.

Shuna tilted her head. 'Word is, it was a hit job. He paid one of his obedient thugs to help Millar off this mortal coil.'

Lola said, 'And how did this thug draw Millar out of his house at that time of the morning?'

'Not a clue. Millar's phone's missing, isn't it?'

'It is.'

'I'll ask about,' Shuna said. 'You know I'm always happy to do a favour for an old pal.'

They weren't old pals — they really weren't — but Lola smiled nonetheless.

'You're not here about McGregor, are you?' the journalist said now.

'No, I'm not.' She paused. 'Tell me what you know about the Clyde Pusher.'

'The Clyde Pusher?' Deadpan. 'What about him — assuming it's a him?'

'Is he real?'

'I think the accepted wisdom is that he isn't. That's not to say the deaths might not be suspicious. It is strange that most of them were gay. Why are you asking?'

'I'm interested.'

Shuna leaned in, all but licking her lips at the sense of a juicy morsel. 'You're not about to tell me there's a link with McGregor, are you? I mean, I know the warehouses that burned down were on the banks of the Clyde, but surely . . .'

'I'm talking about a young man who ended up in the river on Saturday just gone,' Lola said. 'A few folk are saying it was the work of the Pusher.'

'And are these folk off their heads on booze or drugs, by any chance?'

'Not all of them.'

Shuna's eyes narrowed. 'Are you talking about the chap who does the podcast? What's his name — Donovan Murphy? Lola, he talks a load of mince. I wouldn't be surprised if he announced the world was flat.'

Donovan Murphy did appear to have some eccentric ideas. So far Lola had listened to two episodes of a ten-episode series called *Proving the Pusher* and been disappointed. The format was off-putting, consisting of the host's tedious and paranoid-sounding monologues, interspersed with segments where Murphy chatted to a woman called Ophelia, who sounded sedated but had plenty of theories of her own. There were repeated pleas to 'subscribe' and, so far, very few actual facts.

'The *Gouger*'s done a few articles too,' Lola said.

'Well, Jack Everett's usually on the money,' Shuna said. 'He knows how to dig for a story, at least. Oh, and there's always Dougie,' she murmured now. 'Yes . . . I'd forgotten about him.'

'Who is he?'

'Dougie Latimer. He was a crime reporter at the *Chronicle*. Retired last year. I'm sure he was cooking up a comprehensive piece on the Pusher a while ago. Before Covid, certainly. "Myth or Reality?" — that sort of thing. He talked to one or two of the families. We spiked it, though. Someone wasn't happy. Order came down from on high. I've got Dougie's email address. Let me drop him a line and see if he'd be up for a quiet chat.'

'That would be helpful, Shuna.'

'You know me. Helpful's my middle name. Now, how about a bit of *quid pro quo*? What exactly is bothering you?'

'I think the Pusher's real,' Lola said simply.

'Why?'

'There's a witness. A decent one.'

'Is that so?' A cat-like smile curled Shuna's lips and her eyes gleamed.

'I've talked to him and I think he's reliable. Only, nobody except me seems in the slightest bit interested.'

'Say,' Shuna said, beaming. 'Why don't I put the kettle on after all?'

* * *

12.12 p.m.

'John Paul McCrae,' Shuna murmured, making a note then asking Lola to confirm the spelling.

'The partner referred to him as "JP" in his tweets. Partner's name is Will Aitchison. I think there's a chance he'd talk to you.'

'Is there an official cause of death?' Shuna asked.

'I haven't seen one — not officially — but he was fished out of the river. There might be reference to a head injury.'

'An *accidental* head injury?'

Lola bit her lip. 'Hard to say.'

'And—' a sceptical glance now — 'this witness of yours . . .'

'Isn't on record.'

Shuna peered hard into Lola's face, as if trying to read even deeper inside her mind. 'Would I be right in thinking that any official statement about McCrae's death would be *unlikely* to make reference to an attacker at all . . . ?'

'Put it this way: I'd be surprised if it did.'

'Blimey.' Shuna sat back in her chair, looking more stunned than Lola had ever seen her. 'I mean — *wow!*'

They sat in an electrified silence, as if they were both waiting for a bomb to drop. 'So . . .' Shuna began slowly, 'if I were to write a piece that hinted at the possibility of an attacker — an attacker with an MO similar to that of the fabled Pusher — then am I right in thinking you would be interested to see what kind of stir it made?'

'Very interested,' Lola said.

Shuna nodded, and gave her cat's smile again.

'In that case,' she said, all but purring, 'I think we understand each other very well.'

CHAPTER TWENTY-THREE

12.51 p.m.

Back in her car outside Shuna's, Lola checked her messages.

Elaine Walsh had left her a voicemail. The super's voice was low and uncomfortable. 'Lola, Clive Reid's agreed to see me privately for fifteen minutes after our main meeting. That'll be around four. I think it would be good if you were nearby in case he wants you to . . . join the conversation.'

With a tingle of apprehension, Lola typed an email, telling Elaine she'd make sure she was around.

She checked the time and saw she was running late for her next meeting. She popped another can of blue raspberry Hyperdrive, and took a sip, wincing at the taste, then calculated the quickest way to the city's east end.

* * *

1.21 p.m.

Predictably, DC Kirstie Campbell had got there ahead of time; Lola had never known her to be late for anything. The constable bounced to her feet when Lola came into the reception and led the way upstairs to the operations centre for Glasgow's public space CCTV system.

'This is Shannon Grant,' Kirstie said once they were in the control room. 'Shannon's the supervisor on duty today.'

'Pleased to meet you,' Grant said, stepping forward to vigorously shake Lola's hand.

She was tall and ruddy-faced, with short blonde hair and lively light-blue eyes, and wearing a formal grey suit.

'How do you like our new set-up?' she asked, swinging her arm in a wide arc as if casting a spell to reveal the wonder that was the bank of screens that crowded the desk and filled two walls.

'Very impressive,' Lola said. 'Nicer than before.'

'Isn't it? I don't normally dress this smart, by the way,' she said, as if feeling the need to apologise. 'We've got council bigwigs coming down for a look around. They're meeting downstairs right now and I'll have to break off if they appear.'

'No problem,' Lola said.

There were three other people working at the monitors: two men — one big, the other skinny, both with beards and glasses — and one mousy-looking older woman in a black cardigan. The three of them watched their supervisor and her guests with mild blinking interest, before turning back to their screens. Lola knew the staff here were employees of the council, rather than of Police Scotland. This operation was a partnership of the council and the police, and came under the oversight of the council's community safety strategy. Framed posters on the walls proclaimed that Glasgow was 'safe and sound', and that sinister yellow emoji grinned out at them.

State of the art it may be, but Lola couldn't have faced a job here, with no natural light and taunted by two-dimensional images of the outside world everywhere you looked.

'Come up this end,' Grant told them. 'I've got the captures you're after. I'll take you through them. Grab yourselves chairs and wheel them over.'

For the next half-hour they watched clip after clip, taken from different vantage points showing the progress of the white van they believed had run over and killed Kevin Millar in Clydebank in the early hours of Monday morning. They watched it leave Clydebank along Glasgow Road before turning onto South Street, which hugged the river. The images were fuzzy, taken from analogue cameras which offered poor detail and only fuzz when you zoomed in. As the van approached the city, though, joining the Expressway, the images suddenly cleared. These digital images provided an almost godlike ability to identify and track individuals. Even retrospective footage allowed you to zoom in close and capture intense detail.

'This is quite a good image,' Grant told them, wiggling her mouse and tap-tapping at her keyboard, and suddenly they had a close-up of the front of the van. They could make out the dent in its front bumper, and a patch of something red. The registration plate was smeared — deliberately, Lola had no doubt — with mud, but she could make out a D at the start, and then the top of either a 6, 8 or 0. The windscreen reflected a streetlight, so was opaque, but there were gloved hands on the steering wheel.

'Can you move it on slowly?' Lola asked.

Grant moved the mouse and the van moved steadily forward, into the frame, its windscreen clearing a little to reveal two arms, and — yes, a chin.

'I think this is the best image we have of a face,' Grant said. 'Shall we keep going?'

Lola nodded.

The van left the Expressway at Anderston, going south towards the river again, then left along the Broomielaw, a seedy area known as 'the Drag'. It was moving fast, and shot a red light at the bottom of Union Street before disappearing under the railway tracks south of Central Station.

The next camera showed its progress along Clyde Street, east of the station, and another camera picked it up at the junction, where the one-way system forced it to veer northeast towards King Street. The lights changed and the van plunged on.

'The camera's out on the next section of the river,' Shannon Grant explained, making Lola start. 'Don't worry—' she smiled in reassurance — 'I pick it up again after it crosses the Albert Bridge.'

'The camera's out?' It was the exact spot where Cammy Leavey had seen the Pusher attack J.P. McCrae.

'Two cameras, in fact. It can happen. A power surge could have knocked them out — though it's more likely it was vandalism. Then it can take weeks to get the engineers out.'

Lola sat in a state of agonised tension as the supervisor took them diligently along the rest of the van's route southeast out of the city centre towards Rutherglen, where it disappeared into a warren of residential streets. She wracked her exhausted brain for a way to turn the conversation back to Clyde Street and what had happened there on Saturday evening — to confirm that the attack on J.P. McCrae had not been recorded.

'You'd need to get on to Lanarkshire if you want to try and see where it went after Rutherglen,' Grant said.

Lola cleared her throat. 'Those cameras on that wee section of Clyde Street — how long have they been like that, out of interest?'

Grant frowned. 'Quilan?' she called out, making the bigger of the two bearded men jump. He swivelled his chair to his boss and waited, eyes wide and anxious. 'The Clyde Street cameras.' She read out a couple of codes. 'When did they go down?'

Quilan frowned at the ceiling while he thought about it. 'Couple of weeks, I'd say.' He mumbled something to his male colleague beside him, who nodded, seeming to agree.

'As I say,' Grant told Lola and Kirstie ruefully, 'these things take time. Is there a reason you're particularly interested in that stretch? It can't be more than a couple of hundred yards and the van didn't even go that way.'

'No particular reason,' Lola said, and managed a smile. She felt Kirstie's inquisitive grey eyes on her face. 'Are there other cameras that might capture activity there, even at a distance, or from one of the other streets — from the Saltmarket, maybe?'

Grant pushed out her bottom lip as she ruminated. She tapped at her keyboard and brought up a map of the streets by the river.

'There's a camera there,' she said, pointing at the bottom of the Saltmarket, just north of the Albert Bridge. 'I'll go into it live and see.'

Moments later they were looking at the view of the north end of the Albert Bridge, and the east end of Clyde Street, the river beyond it. It revealed a long triangle of Clyde Street, providing a view perhaps halfway along the unsurveilled stretch. A blond sandstone Victorian building blocked the rest of the view.

Back into the map, Grant zoomed in on the junction where the Victoria Bridge, west of the Albert Bridge, met Clyde Street. The place where, one Friday night a decade earlier, a police helicopter had fallen from the sky and crashed into the Clutha Vaults pub, killing ten people and injuring dozens more.

'There's a camera here.' She touched the screen, indicating the building at the corner of Stockwell Street.

More tapping of keys, and they were gazing down on the busy junction in real time. She zoomed and swivelled, revealing a good, if partial, view of the road. 'How's that?' she said, eyes on Lola.

'Better,' Lola murmured.

'I'll track back to catch the van and add it into the record,' Grant said.

'Thanks.'

Lola was distracted. She couldn't think how she could ask to see footage from Saturday evening — a good thirty-six hours before the van had passed through — without raising questions.

The door at the far end of the room opened and Lola heard voices.

'Excuse me,' Shannon Grant said, getting up quickly. 'Visitors. Give me a few minutes.'

'Boss,' Kirstie murmured when it was just the two of them, 'that stretch of road — do you think something significant happened there?'

'I do,' Lola replied grimly. 'But not on Monday morning, and it was nothing to do with Kevin Millar and that bloody van.'

* * *

2.13 p.m.

The visitors seemed rapt by the operations centre, and Shannon Grant wasn't going to be free any time soon. She cast Lola a nervous look across the room and mouthed, 'Sorry . . .'

Lola waved back to say it was okay.

'Let's go,' she said to Kirstie.

They were edging past the group of visitors when a falsely smiling voice said, 'Afternoon, DCI Harris' — and Lola's heart missed a beat.

She hadn't spotted her among the group, but it was Melda Brodick from Corporate Comms. She wore a beautiful sapphire suit and her hair was immaculate, as usual.

'Here on a case?' Brodick enquired, stepping forward.

'Of course,' Lola said. Not that it was any of the woman's business.

Brodick's eyes darted to the far end of the room where Lola and Kirstie had been sitting. She returned her gaze to Lola and eyed her suspiciously.

A man stepped away from the group and joined them. He was tall, in his mid-fifties, with long white hair pulled stiffly back over his scalp and tied in a ponytail. He was dressed in black, in a shirt with no collar and splayed sleeves like a kimono. He looked lithe and his irises were strikingly pale, so that his pupils were emphatic black dots. 'Who is this, Melda?' he enquired, beaming grimly at Lola and Kirstie.

Brodick, wrong-footed, cleared her throat. 'This is DCI Harris and her colleague, whose name I sadly don't know.' She smiled daggers at Kirstie.

Kirstie introduced herself.

'Councillor Caleb Munn,' the man said and gripped Lola's hand in a bony vice. The name rang a distant bell in Lola's mind. 'I chair the Glasgow City Community Safety and Neighbourhood Wellbeing Partnership.'

'Very good,' Lola remarked, little the wiser. Then, sensing Brodick's watchful gaze, 'This place comes under your watch, then.'

'It does,' Munn said, beaming a rictus smile that reminded Lola alarmingly of the grinning emojis on posters all over the room. 'It's a key vehicle in our efforts to reassure the public that their city is, indeed, safe and sound.'

'And to fight crime itself, surely?' Lola said pleasantly.

Munn winced with irritation, but then a camera flashed, taking Lola by surprise. The councillor turned as though instinctively towards the lens, and put out his arms to draw Brodick close on one side and Lola on the other into a cheery pose. Lola managed a smile. She noticed Kirstie had neatly sidestepped the impromptu photoshoot.

'We have to go,' Lola told Munn and Brodick. 'Nice to meet you, Councillor.'

She nodded to Kirstie, who looked relieved at the chance to get away.

Shannon Grant was near the door with a guest. Lola tapped her on the shoulder. 'Sorry to interrupt. Thanks for your help,' she said. 'Do you happen to have a mobile number in case I think of anything else?'

'Of course!' The supervisor gave Lola a card.

Pressing the button to release the door, she glanced back and caught Brodick and Munn, his white head close to her golden one, observing her with some displeasure.

CHAPTER TWENTY-FOUR

3.25 p.m.

Back at base, DS Anna Vaughan and DC Jonno Gillies took Lola through the post-mortem report on Kevin Millar.

'You were there, weren't you, Jonno?' Lola asked.

'It wasn't pretty,' he said, looking peaky. 'Never thought I was squeamish till I seen that. His skull was cracked open like an egg.'

She let the image sink in for a few seconds before returning to the report.

'Cannabis, alcohol, but no other substances,' she murmured. She scanned the next two pages before passing it back to Jonno. 'This tells us nothing.'

'Sorry, boss.'

DS Aidan Pierce joined them in the meeting room to give an update on the telecoms evidence, such as it was.

He was antsy and pale — though not as pale as poor Jonno — and pinched around the mouth. Not a hair was out of place, though, and he could have stepped out of a high-end catalogue. And all because a certain revered — and feared — uncle was in the building.

Pierce cleared his throat for the second or third time and once again straightened the plump knot of his fancy tie before finishing his report. 'It's likely Millar was not in possession of a burner phone and that any message he did receive to summon him from his home on Monday morning was to his personal phone. I've applied for a warrant to access his voicemail and text messages. Any particular message platforms that might have been used are probably a lost cause — they're encrypted and the tech companies will never release data.'

Lola thanked him for his work; it was never his work that was the problem.

She filled them in on her and Kirstie's trip to the CCTV operations centre and how she'd asked Kirstie to get on to Lanarkshire division about the van's progress through their patch.

The meeting over, she returned to her desk and logged into her email, but not before checking her phone and finding a text from Sorcha's friend Barry.

Sorcha says you're coming to hers tonight. I'll be there too! Will be great to meet you in person. B.

She was going to Sorcha's party tonight only out of politeness. As much as she enjoyed her, Ella's and Tom's company, big parties weren't at the top of her wish list just now. The thought of having to fend off an eager suitor was almost intolerable.

She typed a message to Sorcha: *Barry's texted to say he's coming tonight. I don't know if I'm ready. Not in a public situation like that. Would you mind if I called off?*

Three waving dots appeared immediately.

Yes I would bloody mind!!! And honest, B asked to come. I could hardly say no! PLEASE come Lola. Not the same without you. X

FFS, Lola wrote back. *OK.*

Thx x

She stole a glance down the office towards Elaine's room and saw the light inside was off. She and Reid must still be in the strategic meeting in one of the rooms downstairs.

She opened a can of Hyperdrive — tropical peach, from the stash in her drawer — and took a discreet swig, then occupied herself with googling Councillor Caleb Munn.

Munn's page on the council's website was brief, providing contact details, a register of his interests (of which there were many, including directorships of several companies and a number of public board roles) and a note that he had taken over the chairing role of Glasgow's Community Safety and Neighbourhood Wellbeing Partnership in November 2018. In his photo he was stiffly posed, with a tight smile on his lips. His too-pale eyes and tied-back white hair gave him a sinister look.

He had a Wikipedia entry too, with a fuller history. He was sixty and had grown up in Irvine on the west coast. He and a friend had started their own software company in the nineties and sold it for two hundred million pounds in the early 2000s. He'd been married but was now divorced, and the marriage had produced a son. He had a flat in Glasgow and a house near the Ayrshire coast. There were houses, too, in Florida and Paris. The entry said Munn was a lay preacher in the Church of the Sacred Light in Ayr, part of a Christian denomination that had grown out of Methodism in North America in the early twentieth century — and suddenly Lola recalled where she'd heard Munn's name before.

She returned to her Google search of Munn's name and filtered it for news stories. Yes, there were a number of articles referring to the fact Munn had led, and personally bankrolled, a campaign for Scotland to reject the UK parliament's Marriage (Same Sex Couples) Act — the so-called equal marriage bill — in 2013. He'd bought a fleet of 'battle buses' that he and fellow campaigners then drove around Scotland, including the islands — *especially* the islands — with speakers blaring out what they called their 'families first' message to communities. The campaign asked citizens to lobby their MPs and MSPs to reject the bill. But the bill wasn't subject to a referendum, and the campaign was always going to fail.

Piecing together dates from the news stories and from Wikipedia, it seemed that after his one-man referendum,

Munn had decided to dedicate himself to public service, joining the boards of several public bodies and charities before standing as an independent Member of the Scottish Parliament in 2016, but missing out on election by a handful of votes. He'd stood for Glasgow City Council in 2017 as an independent and was elected as a councillor for a ward in the city's east end, campaigning against litter and antisocial behaviour, and for fixing potholes. According to what Lola read, he seemed to be popular with constituents, championing and even funding, via his own charitable foundation, a number of causes, and he'd been re-elected in 2022 with an even bigger share of the vote. The latest council was a coalition, and Munn had gone in with the larger party, using it to bolster his own position. He was, it seemed, personally responsible for the city's latest branding — the endless websites, email signatures and fliers declaring the city 'safe and sound', along with that leering emoji that was on billboards, buses and buildings all over the city.

The doors from the stairwell opened behind her. She clicked smartly out of Google and turned to see Elaine and a serious-looking Clive Reid in uniform, hard on her heels.

'DCI Harris, would you join us?' Elaine called across.

'Of course.'

She nearly grabbed her can of Hyperdrive to bring it into the meeting with her, then decided against it.

CHAPTER TWENTY-FIVE

4.15 p.m.

'Have a seat, DCI Harris,' Reid said when Lola had closed the door behind her, pointing to one of two seats.

She risked a glance at Elaine, who wore her best poker face.

Reid sat, crossed his legs, narrowed his eyes and peered hard at Lola. He was a lithe man in his late fifties, nearly bald but for a band of closely cut ginger-white hair round the base of his head.

'Detective Superintendent Walsh has explained the situation you have . . . uh . . . *discovered* yourself in,' Reid said in his slow, serious way, fixing her with his sharp green eyes.

Lola inclined her head and swallowed, feeling butterflies in her stomach. She glanced at Elaine once more, but Elaine remained impassive, her eyes on the senior officer in the room. They'd clearly agreed that the ACC would take the lead.

'I see that you understand the gravity, and the sensitivity, of the situation, and I would like to thank you for your discretion and for seeking advice before taking any further steps.'

She accepted the compliment at face value, but braced herself for a telling off in some form.

'What do you think we should do, sir?' Lola asked.

Reid watched her for a few moments.

'I have some thoughts,' he said. 'I would rather like to hear yours first, however. Given free rein, what would you do, DCI Harris?'

Lola had several ideas — too many! — and hadn't yet put them in order. She thought fast.

'I think I'd start with John Paul McCrae and the investigation into his death,' she said. 'I'd find out if there's a note on his file of a potential witness to the attack. Then I'd ask his partner if he'd been made aware of the fact. If there is no note, or if the partner hasn't been informed, then that would be absurd. I'd challenge Detective Superintendent Wilde on the question.'

Reid and Elaine exchanged a look that Lola couldn't quite translate.

'Then I'd ask why Corporate Comms are so interested in shutting down any questions about the Clyde Pusher.' Reid was concentrating hard on her words. 'The reasoning they give — that they want to avoid talk of urban legends — just doesn't hold water in the face of the evidence. And *then*—' getting into her stride now — 'I'd look into the strange fact that two city centre cameras on a stretch of the river between the Victoria and Albert Bridges have been out of service for several weeks, creating a dead zone. The same stretch where a masked individual was seen attacking a man four nights ago. Seen, *but not filmed.*'

This was news to both Reid and Elaine, and she enjoyed watching them absorb it.

'I'd seek video captures from two cameras at each end of this "dead zone" to see if they managed to catch sight of the attacker. In addition, I'd arrange to take a witness statement from Cameron Leavey, the young man who claims he saw the attacker at the river and then near his flat on the afternoon of the day his flatmate was murdered. I'd forensically analyse the film Mr Leavey took, and I'd register him as a witness in need of protection, on the basis of the fact that the attacker appears to know his identity.'

Reid cleared his throat, ready to speak, but Lola was on a roll — and enjoying herself.

'I'd talk to Centre 44, the service that supports women who sell sex on the streets. I'd ask them to talk to the women they work with and ask if any of them has information about the Clyde Pusher. We don't listen to them enough. Maybe we should start. Sorry, sir, I cut across you.'

He accepted the apology. 'I can tell you've thought a lot about this, DCI Harris.'

'I have, sir. It could be worthy of a dedicated task force, wouldn't you say? What with all the families who believe their sons were victims of the Pusher.'

He fell quiet, and rubbed his bottom lip with a knuckle. He looked to Elaine, as if she might wish to add her own thoughts. Lola suspected she had plenty, but she seemed keen to defer to the big boss.

'I rather think,' the ACC said eventually, 'that I need some time to decide what to do.'

Lola was happy with the active verb. He was going to do *something*. Or at least *consider* doing something . . .

'You will need to back off for now,' he said. 'Do nothing more. No digging, no talking. Try to put it out of your mind. Can you do that?'

'Yes, sir. Thank you.'

He turned to Elaine. 'Would you give us five minutes alone?' he asked her.

Elaine rose, expression neutral but apparently unfazed, and left the room.

Reid shifted in his chair and crossed his legs, as if to signal a change of topic.

'My nephew,' he said. 'I know you're going to share your formal report with me, but how is he coming on?'

She'd already prepared an answer that was diplomatic but honest enough.

'He's attending the meetings, sir. He's responding to challenges adequately enough. I hope we'll see some positive change.'

'*Can* he change?'

She took her time. 'We can all change if we want to, sir.'

He looked irritated. 'That's the kind of meaningless response I hear in too many meetings. I don't welcome it.'

'Sorry, sir.' She felt her face heat up. 'Aidan can change if we help him. I think he's lacking maturity, and that's a shame because his poor relationships with some people are going to hold him back.'

'That's a more constructive answer.'

'Sir.'

He got up and studied her carefully for a moment. Flushed and mortified, she steeled herself for what might be coming next.

'What are you working on at the moment — officially, I mean?'

'A fire-raising case and a murder that's probably linked to it.'

'The case involving the demolition people?'

'That's right, sir.'

'Invested, are you?'

'Sir?'

'What I'm asking is, would you be disappointed if you were taken away from that case and, say, put on another?'

She flushed again, but this time it came with a buzz of excitement. 'Not disappointed at all, sir.'

He nodded.

'That'll be all, then,' he said, and reached for the door.

CHAPTER TWENTY-SIX

5.47 p.m.

Warren finally called Cammy while he was chopping peppers for omelettes for himself and Brenda. He was distracted — trying hard to get the vision of Dec's body and blood out of his mind — so that he jumped when the phone rang and nearly dropped the knife.

Brenda was in the kitchen with him, emptying the dishwasher, so he dismissed the call with a panicked jab of his finger. The last thing he wanted was another lecture from Brenda, even if she meant well.

'Everything all right?' she asked him, closing a cupboard door.

'Yeah,' he said, hearing his voice squeak with nerves. He swiped his phone off the counter. 'I . . . I need to go to the toilet, that's all.'

'You finished those veggies?'

'Aye. I just need to grate the cheese then I'll start cooking.'

He slid out of the kitchen and into the bathroom along the hall. There he turned on the sink tap to create a cover in case Brenda chose to listen in, and rang Warren's number.

'You're there!' Cammy half-yelped when he answered. 'Where've you been?'

'Listen,' Warren said nastily, 'I don't know what you've done, but you have to stop ringing and texting me all the time. It's not fucking *on*.'

'But I need to talk to you!'

'You know how busy I am. You can't just expect me to drop everything because you need help getting yourself out of the shit. That's not how this works. *Christ . . .*'

In all the months he'd known Warren, Cammy had never heard him talk like this. He stared at his own reflection in the mirror over the sink, his mouth an O, his eyes wide. A picture of shock and shame. He quickly turned away, to face the other wall. 'But—'

'"But" *nothing*. Don't call me. I'll call you. That's what we agreed.' He muttered something Cammy didn't catch. But it sounded like, *Should've withheld my number.*

'I need to see you,' Cammy jabbered out.

'Well, you can't. Especially if the police are involved. You kids are . . .'

'*What?*' The word came out in a pitiful squeak.

'Nothing. Look, I'm busy. I'm stressed out of my fucking mind with work. I don't have time for this.'

'They asked about you,' Cammy said, voice suddenly cold, surprising even him.

'What?' Warren's voice was different now.

'The polis. I witnessed an attack then I found a dead body! They wanted to know where I'd been. I said I was with you.'

It was a lie, but Warren didn't know that.

'What did you tell them?' Quieter now. Tense.

'I said you were my boyfriend.' He faced himself in the mirror again and saw a different person this time. A confident one. A cool, calculating one. Someone who wasn't going to be palmed off.

Warren's silence was gratifying. Cammy was back in the care home — the one in Maryhill where he'd spent most of his teenage years. He was in the hallway, at the bottom of the curving staircase, face to face with Paul, the worst of the carers. It was because of Zeb, only a year younger than Cammy but much smaller, and with a learning difficulty that meant he had problems spitting out his words and got frustrated. Sometimes, when the words finally came out, they weren't the ones people wanted to hear. That afternoon, after an hour of goading, he'd called Paul the carer a 'dirty pig' and Paul had hit him. Had belted him with the back of his hand so hard Zeb had fallen, striking his head against the wall. Paul panicked and threatened the others, demanding they tell the warden it was Zeb's fault. It had happened fast and Cammy saw it all. He'd been terrified at first, then a cold hardness came over him.

'I saw what you did,' Cammy had told Paul, ever so calmly.

'And?' Paul stood taller, squaring his shoulders.

'Zeb's right,' Cammy told him. 'You are a pig. And a bully.'

Paul's eyes grew very big, his nostrils widened like dark tunnels and his top lip curled back.

'Do it to me,' Cammy half whispered to him. 'Hit me too.'

That was all it had taken for Paul to back off. He'd left the hallway and gone for a smoke in the yard, leaving him and Zeb eyeballing each other, as if unable to understand what had just happened.

Next day, Paul was gone. There was no explanation and no investigation they heard about. But everyone — staff and boys — knew what had happened, and what Cammy had done. They didn't have to say anything. He could tell by the way they looked at him. The way they . . . deferred.

'They asked me your surname,' Cammy said to Warren now.

Warren sounded frightened when he spoke now. 'You don't know my surname.'

'Then they asked me your car registration,' Cammy told him.

'You're lying.'

Slowly, clearly, Cammy recited the registration.

'*Fuck!*' A scream of fury that hurt Cammy's ear.

'Don't worry, I said I didn't know it,' Cammy said now. 'They asked where you dropped me off. I reckon they were going to look on CCTV.'

More indistinct cursing.

'I didn't tell them that either,' he said, glaring at his own reflection.

'What do you want?' Warren said, sounding defeated.

'Meet me.'

He listened to Warren breathing hard, in and out of his nostrils. 'Where?' he snapped at last.

Cammy told him a place and a time.

Then he hung up without saying goodbye, and burst into tears.

* * *

6.46 p.m.

'Who were you talking to?' Brenda asked when they'd finished their omelettes.

'No one.' Cammy lowered his eyes.

'Don't lie. I heard you,' she went on. 'You were shouting at one point.'

'You don't need to worry about it,' he told her crossly.

'What you mean is, it's none of my business.'

That's right, he wanted to say, *so get out of my face*. But he didn't. He liked Brenda. She was annoying at times, but she meant well. More like an auntie than a friend — or so he imagined. He'd never had an auntie, nor parents, nor grandparents, nor cousins. He felt sorry for her too. She had a son who didn't want to know her, which was sad. He sank down in the chair, shoulders sagging, eyes fixed miserably on the empty plate.

'I hope you told him where to go,' she murmured.

He looked up.

'It *was* Warren, wasn't it?' she said. 'Yes. Thought so.'

'It's fine.'

'So you won't see him anymore?' She scanned his face, reading him. 'Oh, Cammy, please. He's bad for you,' she said. 'These men, they're—'

'You haven't met him! You don't know him.'

She flinched as if he'd slapped her. It took her a moment, then she said, 'And do you? Do *you* know him? Really?'

'What d'you mean?'

'Do you even know his surname? Where he lives, where he works? Do you know how old he is?'

'Yeah . . .' He squirmed. 'Course I do!'

She didn't believe him.

'He gives you money every time, doesn't he?'

He hesitated and she clocked it. His face burned.

'A lot?'

'None of your business.' He wanted to cry.

'Do you know what grooming is?' she said.

Her words soaked him like cold water. He couldn't speak.

'Because it looks a lot like this, let me tell you! An older man, a pretty young lad. Wee presents. Money. It's called "love bombing". It's always on his terms and he gives zero commitment.' He gaped at her, but on she went: 'And then one day it's, "Oh, I need to get this other guy off my back over something. Why don't you help me out by giving him a blow job?" And before you know it, you're doing tricks for him, and then he starts helping himself to a cut of your money, or maybe the punters pay him and he just drives you there, like delivering a parcel.'

'It's not like that at all! It's *not*!'

But his pal Tiffany's voice taunted him: *You're one of us now, Cammy.*

'You're calling me a rent boy?' he said.

'No!' she snapped. 'You're not. But this Warren — that's what he's trying to turn you into. I've seen it a hundred times. He's exploiting you. It's *abuse*.'

He jumped up, knocking his chair over and bashing the edge of the table with his knee so that the plates and cutlery clattered.

'I'm not a victim!' he cried. 'You don't know a thing about it.'

'Is that right?' There was a catch in her voice that stopped him.

'Anyway, he's not my boyfriend. I know he doesn't want that. I'm not stupid.' She was looking at him with such pathetic appeal, such hope, it gave him butterflies.

'I'm an adult,' he told her. 'You're not my mum. I know you want to help, but I can sort things on my own. What do you think I've done all my life?'

'Cammy, sit down! Why don't we—'

'No.' He shoved the chair back under the table and reached for his plate and glass, to take them to the kitchen. He held out a hand for hers and she passed them to him.

'Please,' she appealed. 'Promise me you'll stay away from him.'

'No. I'm seeing him tonight.'

Nothing for a moment, as she absorbed the news. Then she lifted her chin and her expression cooled and hardened. 'For the money? For whatever present he brings you tonight?'

He stared, mouth open, feeling his lips quiver, and tried to reach for words he couldn't muster.

'It's worked hasn't it?' she near-taunted him. 'His plan's worked a treat. The money's like a drug and now you're hooked. What next?'

'No . . .' He was breathless with shock. 'I . . . It's—'

'It's what?' Brenda asked.

'It's none of your fucking business!' He threw the plates and glasses onto the table and lurched for the door.

CHAPTER TWENTY-SEVEN

7.40 p.m.

'Usual please, love,' Brenda said, arriving at the bar of the Hook and Line. She was breathless and upset following the argument with Cammy. After he'd stormed out of the flat she'd tried phoning him but got no reply, which had left her frantic.

Her former colleague Ivan was in his usual spot, with a lemonade in front of him. He waved to say to come and join him. She nearly declined, but then decided that would be rude. The man had nothing and nobody in his life, and there but for the grace of God and all that . . .

'Been here long?' she asked him, and eased herself into the seat beside him.

'An hour,' he said. 'Anita and Desi were in earlier.' Old colleagues, still working for social services. 'Nice to see them. You look all in.'

'I am.' She shrugged off her coat.

He started to ask what was wrong and she deflected, asking about his health. He talked mildly, looking on the bright side, counting his blessings — the kind of meaningless upbeat nonsense she always found depressing and unhelpful.

'Is it that young friend of yours again?' he asked eventually. 'Callum?'

'*Cammy*,' she snapped, making him flinch. 'His name's *Cammy*.'

Ivan began to stammer out an apology.

'I'm sorry,' she groaned. 'I didn't mean to bite your head off. I'm out of sorts.'

He inclined his head.

'He's staying at mine,' she told him after a bit.

'Is he?' He raised a sceptical eyebrow.

'He's a friend, not a service user. He's in trouble, Ivan. I'm trying to do what I can. We argued,' she went on, continuing to give vent to the thoughts that jostled for space in her brain. 'I'm so worried about him. God, listen to me. You'd think he was my own flesh and blood.'

She took a sip of port and felt calmer.

'What did you argue about?' Ivan pressed gently.

'His so-called "love life",' she said, tossing her head in disdain.

'Ah.'

She turned on him, rage rising. 'It's that older man. The one who's grooming him.'

Ivan went quiet. He'd often accused her, if gently, of caring too much.

'He was insisting on going to meet him but I told him it wasn't safe! His flatmate was killed, for God's sake.'

'Killed?' Ivan's eyes widened.

'Yes. The lad was murdered in his bed. That's why Cammy's staying at mine.'

'My God!'

'I'm too old for this.' She shook her head. 'It brings it all back, and it's just too much.'

'I'm sorry.' He put a hand on her arm. He meant well but it felt oppressive. *Re*pressive too — when she needed to release her emotions, not contain them.

She shook herself free and turned to face him. 'Do you know — can you *imagine* how it feels to be rejected by your own son? To be called a failed mother? To be blamed for what he's chosen to become? Can you?'

Ivan listened, eyes tracking across her face.

'It's eight years since I've spoken to Gavin. Eight years since he told me he wanted me off his back and — and out of his life.'

She was talking loudly now and some of the other punters were beginning to look round but, frankly, she didn't care.

'I've no idea where he is or what he's doing.' She fumbled open her purse and fished out a photograph. 'There,' she said. 'A born angel.'

Ivan looked, then passed the photograph back to her. She studied it: Gavin, age six in his primary-two uniform, one morning in August thirty years ago. His eyes — his dad's pale-green eyes — tilted slightly as he smiled, gap-toothed, for the camera. She found herself melting and rejected the feeling, shoving the picture back into her purse, away where it belonged.

'Nothing is so broken it can't be mended,' Ivan said gently. 'Have you thought about looking for him?'

'Of course I bloody have,' she snapped, irritated by the sentiment. 'I tried to for a year. Then I got a letter. It was because I'd thrown his father out, that's what he wrote. My fault. Everything stemmed back to that.'

She'd finished her port. She stared at the red spot at the bottom of the glass, like blood from the prick of a needle. She thought about the letter from Gavin, and about another letter — the one that rested, folded in her handbag. The one from the hospital. She put it from her mind.

'How about another of those?' Ivan asked.

She breathed in and out. 'Go on, then,' she said. 'Just the one.'

CHAPTER TWENTY-EIGHT

7.57 p.m.

Shuna Frain called Lola while she was driving to Sorcha's party, and she answered on hands-free.

Shuna explained that she'd spoken to Will Aitchison, J.P. McCrae's other half, and that he'd not held back about his displeasure with the police's efforts thus far. She'd written a piece that would be on the *Chronicle*'s website this evening and in the following morning's print edition.

'Remember, I never gave you the tip-off,' Lola told her, fingers tingling with apprehension.

'Of course!' the journalist retorted. 'Oh, and there's one other thing. I emailed Dougie Latimer, my old crime desk colleague — the one who was working on a story about the Pusher? He got back within minutes. Quote, unquote: thank God someone's finally taking this seriously. Upshot is, he'd love to talk to you. I'll text you his number.'

* * *

8.56 p.m.

Lola had expected to hate every minute of the party. She found events with strangers uncomfortable and had planned to stay no more than an hour. In fact, she was enjoying herself immensely. Sorcha's sister had a high-end catering business, and well-turned-out teenagers served some of the nicest party food Lola had ever tasted. Booze flowed, but she was driving so stuck to soft drinks. There were at least fifty guests, but the house in classy Dowanhill was huge, with three levels and rooms and new staircases everywhere you turned. Sorcha's expensive personal tastes were reflected in the house's fine furnishings. There was high-end paper on the walls and arty sculptures on little tables, and everything was beautifully lit with lots of red, green and gold. Artistic, but cosy too.

She'd spent most of her time with Tom and Ella from the Covid Divorce Club, but also enjoyed chatting to Sorcha's brother and his wife, and some of her neighbours, including a BBC TV presenter and a self-effacing but amusing woman who wrote literary fiction and had just won a prestigious award.

Sorcha floated effortlessly from guest to guest, clearly in her element. She introduced people to others she thought they might get on with, oiling the introductions with flattering words. Some way into the party, she came Lola's way with a handsome, intellectual-looking, if nervy, man following anxiously in her wake. Lola recognised him and steeled herself.

'Lola, this is Barry,' Sorcha said, all coy smiles. 'Barry, meet Lola. I believe you're already in touch.'

Dropping Lola a meaningful but mischievous wink, she floated away, leaving them together by a bookcase.

Barry was medium height with narrow shoulders, good-looking in an academic way, with floppy blond hair and red plastic glasses. His linen jacket was baggy, as were his trousers, as if someone had picked them out with the intention he'd grow into them. How old was he? Younger than her, she thought. Forty-two, forty-three? He was nervous to the point of giddy.

'Feels like cheating, this, doesn't it?' he said, stammering. 'We're meeting on Sunday as it is. Better not use up all our conversation topics, eh? Ha! Maybe you'll cancel on me after we've spoken.'

'I'm sure we'll do fine,' she said kindly, studying his face. His eyes were strikingly blue and tilted slightly at the corners. He had good teeth too, white and even. She saw them every time he licked his lips.

'Sorcha said you're in the police.'

'Aye, that's right.'

'A detective, she said! Wow. Better watch myself.'

'Mm.' Her interest was waning fast, but she told herself to make an effort.

'How do you know Sorcha?' she said.

'Oh, everybody knows Sorcha.'

'So it seems.' She looked about her and sipped her sparkling water.

'We were neighbours when I had a flat opposite here,' he said. 'I've a place down by the river now — one of the new apartments. I'm an engineer, by the way.'

'An engineer!' She beamed. 'But you're at the university, aren't you?'

'I am. I lecture, but I worked in Saudi for years. And Oman. Very interesting places.'

He told her about building a dam to serve a housing development. Told her about it at length. She caught Tom's eye as he passed her with fresh drinks. He suppressed a giggle.

It went on for at least twenty minutes. Lola made the right noises, but deliberately didn't encourage him. This was miserable. A slow death. How could she possibly contemplate going on a date with this sweet but boring man? Joe had been a lot of things — but he wasn't boring. Never that.

A wave of sadness swelled inside her and she did her best to suppress it before it reached her face.

'Oh God, sorry,' Barry said, suddenly aghast. 'I've been going on. I'm so sorry.' He lifted a hand to his mouth. It was trembling.

'It's okay,' she said, and touched his wrist. 'I can see you love your work.'

'I do.' His expression darkened. 'I don't need to drone on about it for hours, though, do I? *God*, I'm such an idiot. This is what comes of living on your own for so long.'

A view Lola didn't subscribe to — not that she said so.

Barry was in full self-flagellation mode now, actually beating his forehead with the heel of his hand.

'Please don't cancel Sunday,' he said with stricken eyes. 'I'm not normally like this. Honest. I'll make every effort. I really like you.'

'Listen,' she began, 'it's—'

'Please — I think you're amazing. The things you do. Sorcha's told me so much. And I think . . . I think you're really attractive.' He was nearly crying now. 'Please just give me a chance.'

'It's fine,' she said, forcing a smile. 'I'm happy to go for a coffee.'

'Really?' The relief on his face was remarkable, if not a little unsettling. 'Thank you so much.' He made to touch her, to embrace her maybe, then decided against it.

'Two o'clock on Sunday at Moyra Jane's,' she said, to reassure him.

He nodded, repeatedly, and seemed lost for words.

'Thank you,' he said.

Then he was gone, weaving through the crowd, head down.

Lola closed her eyes and cursed her own niceness. What was she thinking? The man was a wreck.

* * *

10.11 p.m.

Whether it was the atmosphere of the party, or the fizz of the sparkling water she was downing, Lola felt more awake than she had for weeks. Hungry too. Sorcha pounced as she was helping herself to seconds of the trifle, with the news that Barry was smitten.

'Is he?'

Sorcha's face fell. 'But you're not?'

'Jury's out.'

'But he's lovely!'

'I'm sure.'

Sorcha wasn't happy with her. Well, tough. Lola spotted Tom on his own and made a beeline.

She'd been trying to get him on his own all evening to ask him about Brenda's son.

'Gavin?' he answered cagily. 'Aye, he's my cousin. A few years younger than me, mind.' He looked warily at her. 'What did Brenda tell you?'

'Nothing,' Lola said. 'It's just . . . I thought I touched a nerve the other night. She said they didn't talk and it was his choice. I wondered if that was why she was so keen to help Cammy.'

'Not much gets past you, does it?' Tom said.

'Not a lot, no.'

He took a swig from his bottle of Italian beer. 'Gav went off the rails. Never got back on.'

'Off the rails how?'

'Drugs.' He eyed her carefully, as if even talking about such things might implicate him. 'Stuff I'd never touch with a bargepole. He was selling them, not taking them. He's an idiot but he's not daft. I heard he was working for one of the big dealers in the east end, then he got caught up in some kind of territory war. Shot in the leg. Auntie Brenda thought that might shock some sense into him, but he just got more careful. Went out on his own. Started dealing online. He was arrested five or six years ago, but there wasn't enough evidence.'

'His surname the same as his mum's?' she asked.

'No. He kept his dad's name, MacQuoid. Auntie Brenda tried to help him. She really did . . .'

Lola detected something unspoken. 'But?' she pressed.

'She found out he was pimping young girls.'

'Ah.' And suddenly a few pieces fell neatly, grimly into place.

'She was gutted. I mean, *gutted*. She'd spent her working life trying to help these women help themselves, and then her own son . . . You can imagine, can't you? Hence all her "good works", even though she's retired. Hence why she's so interested in helping that kid.'

'What happened?' Lola said.

'She told him she'd disown him if he didn't stop it. That she'd tell the police what he was doing. He laughed at her. Told her she was a bleeding-heart fool and that the girls know what they're doing and business is business. She told him to get out of her flat, and he went. As far as I know, that was the last time she saw him. That was seven or eight years ago.'

'Your poor auntie. And have you seen or heard from him since then?'

'Nah. I don't want to either. I'm sure he's moved on to something else now, anyway.'

'Like what?'

He cast a glance about the room, checking they weren't overheard. 'Gavin knows about explosives. For demolition — that kind of thing. He works for a number of building companies. Word is, he's involved with a dodgy bastard called Jamie McGregor. D'you know him?'

'Heard of him,' she said, hoping her sudden start at the name hadn't shown. 'It's a small world.'

'Nasty bastard, apparently. You know those warehouses down at Scotstoun — the ones that went on fire? It was McGregor who was behind that. Something to do with a contract he reckoned should have been his.'

Lola chose her words very carefully. 'Do you believe Gavin was involved in the fire?'

'Who knows?'

'You said "word is" he's involved with McGregor. Whose word?'

He eyed her with alarm now, as if realising he'd implicated himself as well as his cousin. 'Look, it was gossip. And Brenda doesn't know anything about it. Look, it was nothing. I mean—'

'Tom, if you know anything about that fire, then you need to tell me about it. Not here, not now. Tomorrow.'

'Oh fuck . . . You're working on that case, aren't you?'

Lola said nothing.

'Look, I—'

She put a hand up. Her phone was ringing, and caller ID told her she had to answer it.

'Don't say any more,' she said to Tom, then put her phone to her ear. 'DCI Harris speaking . . . Hello, Assistant Chief Constable Reid.'

CHAPTER TWENTY-NINE

10.22 p.m.

It was dry but freezing cold with stars visible over the city. The kind of cold that made your muscles lock round your bones so hard they hurt.

South of the river, away from the shelter of city offices, the pavements glittered and frost formed on the windows of the cars parked in the forecourt of the dealership. Cammy hunched his denim jacket more tightly round his shoulders, put his head down and hurried under the motorway flyover, following the curve of West Street towards Shields Road Subway station.

He'd told Warren half past, but the Jaguar was there already, in the layby outside the Victorian school that was now a visitor attraction. The car's engine hummed and its twin exhausts breathed poisonous fumes into the frozen air.

He approached the passenger side and the window came silently down. He peered into the darkness and saw the glint of Warren's glasses.

'Get in,' the voice said.

He obeyed.

It was warm in the car. A hot bubble in the freezing night. Warren didn't look at him. Cammy studied his profile, noting the lift of his chin, the tight set of his lips, the flare of his nostrils. The knuckles of the hand that gripped the steering wheel were sharp points.

He was furious.

Well, good.

The steel of anger was in Cammy again.

'I mean nothing to you, do I?' Cammy said quietly, conversationally, still watching Warren's profile.

A sharp glance. 'The fuck are you talking about?'

'I was in trouble and you didn't give a shit.' His emotions were in turmoil but his voice held steady, and he was glad.

'I'm here now, aren't I?'

'Only because I threatened to tell the police your car reg.'

Warren muttered something.

'What?' Cammy asked.

'I said you're a blackmailing shit.'

Cammy shrugged. Fair enough.

'My friend says you've been grooming me,' he said. 'That you're planning to feed me to punters for money — and that you'll take a cut.'

Warren stared. Shocked or caught out? He couldn't tell. It was hard to see his expression in the car's dim interior. Warren was handsome, if old. He'd told Cammy he was thirty-five, but Cammy didn't believe him, suspecting he was forty at least. He was slim but nicely muscled, his body tanned and only lightly hairy. But his skin crinkled at the corners of his mouth and eyes, and his hands were a giveaway. He must be older than he said, because he was rich. Really rich, going by the evidence of the Jaguar. You didn't get Jaguar-rich till you were much older.

Brenda had been right when she taunted Cammy about Warren's surname and profession. He knew neither. He had taken note of the car's registration, to try to find out more about the man he liked to think of as his boyfriend. There was a website where you could check when a car's MOT was due. He'd put the registration number into that, and it had come up with the make, model and colour of the Jaguar, giving information about the date it was registered, its engine size and some other details. But it didn't give the owner's name, nor his address. A dead end.

'Well,' Cammy said, 'is it true?'

'No. No, of course not. It's . . .' He went quiet for several seconds. Then he reached out and gripped Cammy's neck lightly. 'I like you, Cammy. A lot. But, as I've said before, I'm busy. I don't have time to have a proper relationship, and . . . and I explained about my work and things. It's difficult for me to be "out". Nobody knows. Nobody, except you. You see, you're the one I trust.'

Cammy felt himself softening like butter, and tightened his resolve.

'You don't like me,' he said simply, 'or trust me. If you did you'd be more open with me. But I don't trust you either. You're a liar.'

'I'm not.'

'Take me to your house.'

'What—'

'I said, take me to your house.'

Warren went very still.

'Let me meet your friends. *Tell me your surname.*'

'Smith,' Warren said.

'Smith?' He laughed. 'Really?'

'Yeah, *really*. Gonna check it, are you?'

'Probably.'

They fell silent. It was almost companionable. Like they were both knackered and couldn't be bothered with conversation or arguing anymore.

After a minute or two, Warren sighed. 'I'll take you home, but not tonight. Another time.'

'Why not tonight?'

'Because I want an early night. I want to be on my own. Is that so strange?'

'Are you married?'

'*What?*' He laughed, but too readily. 'Where did that come from?'

'There's a mark on your ring finger.' Cammy held up his left hand to show the spot. 'I saw it before, but I never said anything.'

Warren gave a half-amused, half-exasperated groan. 'You're wrong. Look, I did wear a ring there, but not anymore. Please can we stop this? We're friends, you and me. We have an arrangement.'

'"An arrangement"?'

'Yes. An arrangement. We're not in a relationship. We meet and have fun and I give you presents.'

'You pay me.'

'Because *I want to.*'

'Because of the power it gives you, you mean.'

Warren seemed to contemplate it at least. 'No,' he said, but sounded unconvinced. 'Not that.'

More silence. Warren's hand came over and landed gently on Cammy's knee. It felt nice. Reassuring, seductive, but confusing too. 'I've been looking forward to seeing you,' he said.

'I've got nowhere to live,' Cammy said, suddenly near to tears. 'I can't go back to my flat and I walked out of my friend's place tonight. I'm basically homeless.'

He left a gap for Warren to fill, but he chose not to. He was dimly aware, from within his funk of self-pity, of a low, dark vehicle passing by, perhaps even slowing as it passed, then moving on.

'If I can't stay at yours, then . . . I thought maybe you'd pay for me to stay in a hotel.'

'You did, did you?' Warren removed his hand from Cammy's knee and sat up.

'As part of the "arrangement".'

'How much do you want?'

'I just—'

'How much? Five hundred? Six hundred? Name your price. That's what your threats are about.'

Cammy stared, amazed. He meant it. Warren really meant it! He was prepared to pay for silence. The thought of money seduced him more than any promise of affection. It meant so many things. Safety, nice food, comfort, independence . . .

'A thousand,' he said, hearing a crack of shame in his voice. 'And I want it now. In cash. Can you get it?'

Warren's eyes burned into him through the darkness. 'I can get it.'

Then he turned, pressed the ignition, yanked the steering wheel and screeched in a U-turn towards Shields Road.

A little way along Shields Road, a dark car started its engine and prepared to follow.

CHAPTER THIRTY

10.29 p.m.

The party was too noisy, so Lola had told Reid she'd go out to her car and ring him back from there.

She took a few minutes to compose herself — and to try to put Tom's revelation about his dodgy cousin out of her mind, though it wasn't working. He'd told her something that could be critical to the case. She had to act and Tom would be a witness — and that would likely put paid to their friendship . . .

She nearly opened a can of Hyperdrive but stopped herself. Besides, it was the last of the stash she kept in the car. She'd save it for an emergency. She dialled Reid's number.

'DCI Harris,' Reid said, formal as ever. 'Thank you for phoning back. Did I catch you at an event?'

'A friend's party,' she told him, putting on a smile so that her distress over Tom wouldn't reveal itself in her voice. 'I was just leaving, as it happens.'

'Is now an appropriate time to talk?' he said.

'Perfectly, sir. I'm in my car. We won't be overheard.' She'd taken a pad and now held a pen over it, trying to keep calm for whatever Reid was about to say — good or bad.

'I've had a busy evening, DCI Harris, and I believe I may have upset one or two people along the way. Well, so be it. I paid a visit to Superintendent Angus Wilde of City Centre division at his home. We spoke at length. I enquired about the investigation into the death of John Paul McCrae, and into certain other river deaths over the past few years — specifically those that have been laid at the door of the so-called Clyde Pusher.'

Lola held her breath and wished she could read the man's tone better.

'I think it's fair to say he didn't appreciate the questions. He referred me to a Corporate Communications colleague of his, a Ms Brodick — a suggestion I did not receive kindly, let me tell you.'

Lola could imagine.

'DCI Harris, your sense that things, shall we say, do not "add up" is, I think, valid. I got the distinct impression that a hypothesis has been locked in, and any evidence is being tested against that — and rejected if it doesn't fit. The hypothesis appears to be that there is no Clyde Pusher, that these are unlinked deaths. They were either accidental or suicide. The Pusher theory seems to be simply taboo. I do not understand why, but I would very much like to. I said as much, at which point the conversation became, shall we say, strained, and I'm afraid your name was mentioned.'

Lola winced. 'Sir.'

'Detective Superintendent Wilde suggested you were inappropriately invested in the death of John Paul McCrae — most probably because you were at the scene shortly after the young man was spotted in the river. I ended the conversation there because I had another appointment to keep. The appointment was at the Glasgow CCTV operations centre, where I met with the supervisor on duty, a Shannon Grant.'

Lola felt a tingle of excitement.

'In line with your suggestion, I asked to review footage between ten p.m. and eleven p.m. on the evening of the eleventh of February, showing the stretch of Clyde Street between the Victoria and Albert Bridges. You were quite right: the two cameras on that part of the road are not working, and haven't been for some weeks. I asked to see footage taken by the cameras on Stockwell Street and the Saltmarket, which should by rights provide partial views of the area in question.' A pause, during which Lola didn't breathe. 'DCI Harris, for sixteen hours, starting at four p.m. on the Saturday, both of those cameras were angled *away* from Clyde Street. The one at the bottom of the Saltmarket was angled towards the bridge and a corner of Glasgow Green. The one on Stockwell Street was turned in *towards a blank wall* . . .'

'My God . . .'

'Indeed. Hardly a coincidence.'

'Someone must have changed the settings. They can tell who from their login, surely?'

'If only it were that easy,' Reid murmured.

Lola saw herself back at the operations centre with Kirstie and Shannon Grant, with screens before them, keyboards and mice on desks, and every machine open and available to be used.

'At that point I telephoned Detective Superintendent Wilde,' Reid said now, a grim note in his voice now. 'He was aware that the cameras were out on that part of Clyde Street, but he was not aware that other cameras might have been tampered with.

'DCI Harris, none of this proves that the Clyde Pusher is real. But it does suggest there is something suspect about the death of John Paul McCrae.'

'How can I help, sir?' she said, every fibre tingling.

'I don't want your help,' Reid said. 'I want you to lead this thing.'

'Sir . . .'

'You made a very sensible suggestion earlier today, DCI Harris. In the morning, with your permission — and Elaine Walsh's — I am going to go back to Superintendent Wilde to inform him you'll be setting up a task force to investigate the death of John Paul McCrae and every other death that has been attributed to the Clyde Pusher over the years. You'll be provided with as many resources as you need in terms of staffing and budget, and you will have full access to every record relating to river deaths. Now, I said I would proceed only with your permission. Do I have it?'

A task force? She thought quickly, tried to envisage how she might execute such a huge undertaking. Tried but struggled. She was dragging herself through her working days, fuelled by sugar and chemicals. It was a big risk to take on something of this importance — and potential high profile. But what choice did she really have? If she said no, who else would do the job? No one, probably. It might be shelved once more.

'You do, sir,' she said in a small voice. 'Of course. And thank you. Your confidence in me — it means everything.'

CHAPTER THIRTY-ONE

10.34 p.m.

Something was bothering Warren, Cammy could tell — and not just the fact Cammy had demanded money from him. He was checking his mirrors at the lights and breathing faster.

'What's wrong?' Cammy asked.

'Guy behind us.' Warren licked his lips and swallowed.

'What about him?' He turned and strained to see through the small rear window. A low black car hunkered close behind them. It looked like an old car that had been souped up. Sounded like it too, the way its exhaust coughed and spluttered.

'He was parked up by the bridge. He came out as we passed. Drove fast up behind us. I don't fucking like it.'

'Maybe it's just how he drives.'

Warren wasn't persuaded, and kept checking his mirrors as he turned left. 'Can he get any fucking closer?'

The car chugged noisily on their tail. There were speed-bumps and Warren had to go slowly over them because the Jaguar's chassis was so low and it was easy to scrape it. His speed — or lack of it — seemed to infuriate the driver of the black car, which revved its engine and swerved from side to side.

'Why doesn't he just go past?' Cammy asked.

'Because he's a prick and he wants to make a point,' Warren said.

They were talking as if there'd been no argument, no shouting, no threats or blackmail. It was weird.

'He's hanging back now,' Cammy said, craning his neck again.

'No he isn't.' Warren sounded panicked now, and that alarmed Cammy.

Warren sped up, but there were more red lights ahead. The car was gaining on them. Warren braked but the black car kept coming — and smashed into the back of the Jaguar, hammering it forward.

'*Jesus Fucking Christ!*' Warren screamed.

'Don't get out!' Cammy begged.

'What's he doing? He's reversing! *Shit!*'

Heart racing, Cammy looked for other cars, other people. But this was a side road and there was no one about. A horrible realisation dawned . . .

'*Fuck!*' Warren screamed, and the car smashed into the back of the Jaguar again. Harder this time, sending it skidding several metres.

'He wants you!' Warren screamed, face contorted with fear and rage. 'It's you he's after, you fucking *Jonah*.'

'What? *No!*'

But he was right, wasn't he?

'It's your fault. *Get out!*'

Screeching tyres as the car reversed behind them.

'Warren, no! Please—'

'I said, *get out of my fucking car!*'

The black car was some way behind them, but its full beams blazed.

Cammy whimpered and scrabbled for the door handle, hearing the furiously revving engine.

He half fell out of the car into the freezing night air. He stumbled to his feet and ran for the pavement, then turned and screamed as the black car smacked hard into the back of the Jaguar, this time sending it careering across the junction at an angle and into the corner of a building.

The Jaguar's front end concertinaed. The black car reversed again, and Cammy saw its front was unscathed. It had bars instead of a bumper, like something built for battle.

Cammy pressed his back against the fence that ran beside the railway, hands to his mouth as if to keep the horror from escaping. He watched as Warren's door came open and Warren's foot appeared, and wanted to yell at him to watch out — to run. But the words wouldn't come.

Warren was out of the Jaguar now, holding himself as if he was hurt, and limped a step or two towards the road. There was blood on his face and he was lifting a hand to his temple when the black car began to rev again.

Cammy screamed, '*Watch out!*' but the black car was fast.

It struck Warren's legs, buckling him so that he folded and his head smacked into the bonnet.

The car was reversing again and Warren was a bent and feeble figure lying on the road. He lifted his head and opened his mouth. Blood ran out of it.

'Oh God . . .' Cammy's knees were jelly and he was at risk of folding himself.

It took all his strength to tense his muscles, to lock his joints, and to focus his eyes and brain. He had one chance, and seconds to take it.

CHAPTER THIRTY-TWO

Thursday 16 February
11.22 a.m.

'Are you well, DCI Harris?' ACC Clive Reid asked when Lola arrived in the reception at Stewart Street police office, City Centre division's HQ.

Reid wasn't given to pleasantries and she suspected the question was from genuine concern.

'Quite well, thank you, sir,' she said, fixing a smile.

She was tired, having slept badly again, and suspected she looked as drained and bleary-eyed as she felt. She'd woken just after four and, after some tossing and turning, abandoned all hope of sleep. There'd been no nightmares this time, thank God, just a physical and mental restlessness that animated her limbs and brain and wouldn't let her settle. She'd got up, made tea and spent a couple of hours writing handover notes for whoever would take over the lead on the Scotstoun/Millar case. Then she noted down questions she hoped to answer quickly in the Pusher enquiry.

'I've booked a room upstairs,' Reid said. 'This way.'

Lola followed.

At half past they were due to meet Detective Superintendent Angus Wilde ahead of a wider meeting with a number of Wilde's detectives, including the chilly DS Lachlan Gray.

'I assume everything went to plan with the handover of the Scotstoun enquiry this morning?' Reid asked as they passed down a corridor.

'Yes, sir.'

On hearing of Lola's temporary new role, Elaine Walsh had immediately sought to transfer responsibility for the Scotstoun fire-raising case — and the murder of Kevin Millar — to the Major Investigations Team, or MIT. Graeme Izatt, who had only recently been moved from CID to MIT, had been landed with the case. He seemed less than delighted about it when he appeared in Elaine's office.

Among her handover notes, Lola had included a suggestion that Izatt should seek out Gavin MacQuoid, following a tip-off to the effect that he was in Jamie McGregor's employment. All morning she'd been expecting a call or message from Tom with a panicked retraction or a plea to ignore what he'd told her. But so far, nothing.

She'd had a worried phone call from Brenda, though, saying Cammy had walked out after a row and not come back to the flat. Mentally Lola added a question about Cammy's whereabouts to the top of her list of questions.

They reached the meeting room.

'You'll be answerable to Superintendent Wilde, not me,' Reid said, taking a seat. 'It's important he has his place, for a number of reasons, not least morale. He will report to me. You and I will have no official communication.' He lifted an eyebrow, and she hoped she was reading accurately between the lines: *politics* . . .

'I'll ease the handover just now,' Reid said, 'and then I'll take my leave. You and Superintendent Wilde will present the plan for the task force to the rest of the team.'

She nodded.

'Superintendent Walsh has given permission for you to bring across two colleagues from South West division, I understand.'

'Yes. DS Anna Vaughan and DC Kirstie Campbell, sir.'

'You'll be busy. A live case combined with a complex cold one. Eight deaths in seven years — that's a lot to investigate. If you find evidence of a serial attacker, you'll need effective comms. Ms Brodick will be on hand to provide that help.'

Lola groaned to herself but hoped she masked it. 'Very good, sir.'

A rap at the door. Reid answered and Detective Superintendent Wilde came scowling into the room.

'Angus,' Reid said, indicating a vacant chair and beaming. 'I believe you've met DCI Lola Harris — the head of your new task force.'

Wilde sat heavily, cleared his throat and eyeballed his new team member. Lola tried not to wriggle under his gaze.

If looks could kill, she'd be splattered halfway up the wall.

* * *

12.03 p.m.

In the end it was amicable enough. Wilde was unhappy but cowed, taking comfort in the pragmatic, pinning down reporting timescales and agreeing the availability of resources.

'Daily updates, then,' Reid told the other man. 'Six p.m. or thereabouts and I'll call you. No more than fifteen minutes unless something crops up.' He smiled coolly.

He turned to Lola. 'Best of luck, DCI Harris. If there's something to find, I have every faith you'll be the one to do it.'

He stood and left. Wilde, seemingly unable to look at Lola, lifted the phone on the table and dialled an extension. 'Melda, that's us ready,' he muttered, sounding sick. 'Room six.'

Meanwhile Lola tapped out a text message to Anna waiting in the car park with Kirstie, telling them it was time.

Gotcha boss, Anna typed back immediately.

Lola relaxed, knowing she'd feel better with her team in place. Who knew, she might even begin to enjoy herself.

CHAPTER THIRTY-THREE

12.15 p.m.

The atmosphere crackled with unvented irritation. Lola smiled and breezed through her agenda, glad of the adrenaline that was keeping her going. She smiled most generously of all for Melda Brodick, who looked fit to explode, and for DS Lachlan Gray, whose presence was somewhat chilling. DC Janey Carstairs, Gray's cheerful, ruddy-faced sidekick, seemed most open to this sudden new development, and listened intently, nodding almost giddily, as Lola explained her thinking.

'So, there are three interconnected lines of enquiry here,' she said, summing up at last. 'First, the death of John Paul McCrae. We may have a witness to Mr McCrae being attacked. We need to secure a statement from that witness, but his whereabouts are currently unknown. I will lead attempts to find him. In addition, there is evidence that CCTV cameras covering the place where Mr McCrae went into the river have been tampered with, either by vandalism to the cameras themselves or at the operations centre. DS Vaughan, I'd like you to talk to the supervisor there this afternoon. Find out what was tampered with, when and by whom.'

'Boss,' Anna said.

'Second, the murder of Declan Bailey, which might have been a consequence of Cameron Leavey witnessing the attack on Mr McCrae. DS Gray here is already working on that enquiry. I would like a presentation of what we know later this afternoon, please, DS Gray. Say, at five thirty, here?'

Gray lowered his too-pale eyes and scratched out a neat little note.

'Third,' Lola carried breezily on, 'there is a longer, more complicated piece of work: to establish whether there is a link between a number of deaths of young men in the Clyde going back seven years. I would like DC Campbell and DC Carstairs to spend today and tomorrow examining the evidence we have to establish whether there is at least an indication of a possible link between some or all of these deaths. If there is, we will open a formal enquiry — potentially a huge piece of work, and one on which I expect we will need to go public, and sooner rather than later.'

She eyeballed Brodick, who scowled back.

'I will meet with the two DCs straight after this meeting to map out a plan for reviewing the available evidence.'

Both Kirstie and Janey Carstairs nodded and looked eager for the task.

'I would hope we might have a good sense of next steps by the end of tomorrow, at which point I'll discuss a plan of action with Superintendent Wilde and Melda. Now—' she clicked her pen — 'any questions?'

The team was apparently stunned into silence, so Lola closed the meeting.

CHAPTER THIRTY-FOUR

12.48 p.m.

Janey Carstairs nipped out for sandwiches for the three of them — Lola's treat — and reappeared with a choice of dubious-looking rolls and change for Lola.

'There are a number of people I want to talk to about the Pusher,' Lola said. 'We'll all be busy, so we'll need to choreograph things tightly.'

She told Kirstie and Janey about the Facebook group for victims' families, about Jack Everett, editor of the *Gouger*, and about Dougie Latimer, the former crime reporter at the *Chronicle*. She didn't mention that Shuna Frain was her link to Latimer.

'There's a story in today's *Chronicle*,' Janey said, in response to which Lola feigned surprise. 'J.P. McCrae's partner's given them an "exclusive interview". He's pretty peed off with us.'

'I'll aim to talk to Mr Aitchison with Anna this afternoon or this evening,' Lola said. She made a note to ask Anna to arrange a time.

She turned another page in her book.

'Looking at the information that's publicly available, I've made a list of the Pusher's supposed victims. I've included dates too, but these change depending on what you read. You can use this as a starting point for trying to pin down some of the details from existing records.' She tore out the page with the list and passed it to Kirstie. 'Could one of you type it up and complete it as best you can? I've a feeling the Facebook group members are going to be key to refining it.'

Kirstie and Janey pored over the names while Lola spoke.

'I've also drafted some questions for us to try to answer as we look at the evidence available.' She passed Kirstie and Janey a printed sheet to look over.

The questions were about what evidence they already had relating to the killings, who had it and how reliable it was, and what gaps there were. She'd also included a question about whether the Pusher was real at all — and if so, why so many people and institutions denied his existence. She already had thoughts about this apparent wilful blindness. Laziness was one explanation, incompetence another, then there was malice. There were other possibilities too, including fear and vanity. From her own point of view, she could imagine turning her face away from reality due to sheer exhaustion.

'It's a big job, boss,' Kirstie said, looking up from the page of questions.

'It is,' Lola agreed. 'And of course, we need to find that missing boy, Cameron Leavey.'

Her heart skipped when she saw on her phone, which was set to silent, that Brenda had tried to call her three times in the past twenty minutes.

CHAPTER THIRTY-FIVE

1.03 p.m.

'Slow down, Brenda,' Lola told the panicking woman. She was still in the meeting room, but alone now. 'Take a deep breath and take your time.'

'It was on the news,' the woman told her, breaths coming hard and fast. 'Just now. A car accident last night — some kind of attack — in the Southside. Darnley Street, they said.'

'Right . . .'

'A fatal attack, they said. One report says a black car drove repeatedly at a *green Jaguar*.'

'A green Jaguar?'

'That's what Warren drives. I've seen it. At a distance, at least. I saw Cammy getting out of it once. I mean, I didn't know it was a Jaguar. I said to him that it looked like Warren drove an expensive car and he said it was a Jaguar. I still haven't heard a thing from Cammy and I'm terrified. What if he was with him? You can check, can't you? Oh God . . .'

The woman's distress was infectious and Lola forced herself to calm her own thoughts.

'I'll check it, Brenda. Try not to worry. There's nothing you can do.'

'Oh please . . . And do call me when you hear anything.'

* * *

1.09 p.m.

Lola found a hot desk and set about logging on. Meantime, she flicked through the BBC news app on her phone. The second-to-top story was about an incident in Glasgow's southside, where a black car had been seen repeatedly ramming into a green Jaguar near the crossroads of Darnley Street and Albert Drive in Pollokshields around 10.45 p.m. the night before. 'Pulverising it', according to one of two unnamed witnesses. A forty-two-year-old man, also unnamed, had been fatally injured in the attack, dying before reaching hospital. It was a short, factual piece with a call for witnesses. She suspected the text had been lifted word for word from the police report.

The location of the attack was in South West subdivision, so she phoned control at Helen Street. Two minutes later, she was talking to a stiff-sounding Inspector Michelle Brown.

Lola told her what she wanted to know, skirting round the why. 'Just the one victim involved, as far as we could tell,' Michelle told her. 'Name of David Warren Maxwell. That's not public, by the way. His father and brother identified him this morning. There's a fiancée who's out of the country, so it's under wraps for now.'

'Any suggestion as to a motive?'

'Not yet. The car that did the ramming was found burnt out at Cathkin Braes this morning. Stolen, according to the owner, who's a fairly shady character. CID are all over it if you want to know more.' She gave Lola the name of the detective inspector in charge of the investigation.

Lola rang off and dialled Brenda.

'It sounds as if it might have been the man Cammy knows as Warren,' she told her. 'So far there's no sign that Cammy was there or involved in any way.'

Brenda burst into tears.

'We need to find him, though. Things have changed, Brenda. I'll come and see you this afternoon. I'll aim to be with you sometime after four. Meantime, I want you to note down any thoughts you have — anything that occurs to you about where Cammy might be. And please stay at home in case he comes back, and ring me ASAP if he does.'

A rap on the door and Lola saw Anna peering in through the tiny window. She waved her in.

'Just spoke to J.P. McCrae's partner, Will Aitchison, boss,' she said. 'He's in and can see us any time this afternoon. The place is only five minutes' walk from here. I'd said we'd be round as soon as. Hope that was all right.'

Lola shot up and reached for her jacket.

CHAPTER THIRTY-SIX

1.27 p.m.

Will Aitchison and John Paul McCrae had shared a second-floor tenement flat on Garnethill. Aitchison was waiting for them when they reached the top of the stairs. He wore a dark trendy tracksuit and gleaming white trainers. His eyes were red and teary, but Lola saw he was very handsome. Mid-twenties, she'd guess.

She introduced herself and Anna.

'Sorry about my appearance,' he said gruffly, as he closed the door and put the chain on. 'Through here.' He had a northern English accent.

Lola heard a radio playing somewhere in the flat — possibly in the bathroom, because she could hear water running as well. They followed the young man into a large living room. Big north-facing windows framed the tower blocks that loomed over this edge of the city centre. One of the windows was open and noise from the motorway rumbled distantly. Aitchison closed it and the sound cut off.

He stood before them, shoulders sagging, gazing miserably about. 'Oh God, this place is a mess. Just let me move this — sorry.' He cleared one of two leather settees, throwing clothes and blankets to one side. He looked suddenly pained and put a hand to his forehead as if to help him think through the social niceties. 'Do you want something to drink? Tea, or . . . ?'

'We're fine,' Lola said. 'Why don't we sit down?'

'Yeah. Yeah, okay.' He sat, but on the edge of the settee opposite them, and leaned forward, chewing his lip. 'He was killed, wasn't he?'

'We're working on that premise.'

He nodded. 'I said so. But—'

The door to the room opened, and a tall, skinny young man with a shaved head came in, eyeing the visitors intently. He had on a red hoodie and cream jeans that emphasised his stick-thin legs.

Aitchison jumped up. 'This is my friend Steve Manners,' he said. 'Steve, these are the police detectives, come about J.P.'

'Hi,' said Steve, wriggling his shoulders in apparent discomfort.

'It was Steve J.P. was visiting on Saturday night,' Aitchison explained.

'Is that right?' Lola said.

'Him and J.P. were really close.'

'Is it all right if I stay?' Steve asked warily.

'Fine by us,' Lola said kindly. 'Won't you sit down?'

Steve perched beside Aitchison.

It didn't matter they were both here for this first interview. Today was in part about public relations — about trust, and putting things right. She'd read Lachlan Gray's notes of the brief interview he and Janey Carstairs had undertaken with Will Aitchison the morning after the body of his partner was pulled from the Clyde. The notes were scant at best and seemed written in haste. She hadn't yet had sight of the statement Cammy had provided when he was interviewed about finding Declan Bailey's body, but she doubted it would include any reference to his witnessing the river attack. She planned to grill Gray hard on the matter later on.

Aitchison murmured, 'Something's changed, hasn't it?'

'What do you mean, Mr Aitchison?'

'Your colleagues who were here before — they just seemed to want me to accept it was an accident, or that J.P. had done it himself. I insisted he'd never do a thing like that, but they — well, *he* — kept pointing out that people did unaccountable things. He asked if J.P. did drugs, and when I said no, he said people didn't always know what was "really going on". He asked what J.P. was doing by the river when it would have made more sense for him to go straight up the Saltmarket. I couldn't tell him. They said there'd be a fatal accident inquiry and that he . . .' He paused, choked. 'That J.P. wasn't the first person to end up in the river, and that he wouldn't be the last.'

Lola swallowed down her disgust. 'I'm so sorry.'

He nodded.

'So what is it, then?' he asked now. 'What's made the difference?'

'We have a possible witness,' Lola said simply.

'A *witness*?' He glanced at his pal, then they both frowned at Lola, waiting. 'Who?' Lola hesitated before answering and he snapped, 'How long have you known about this?'

'A witness claims he saw a masked individual assault a man fitting J.P.'s description on the easternmost section of Clyde Street on Saturday evening. He claims he heard a splash.'

'It was the Pusher, wasn't it?' Aitchison asked. He looked sick. 'You're saying J.P. was killed by the Pusher — the murderer no one thinks is real?'

'We can't say just yet,' Lola said gently.

Aitchison looked utterly shaken. His friend, looking just as sick, pulled him into an embrace.

After a minute, Aitchison disentangled himself and turned back to Lola. 'If this witness saw who did it, then . . .'

'He didn't see his face,' she said. 'But he thinks the assailant might have known who he was. It's possible the attacker followed the witness home and attacked his flatmate.'

Aitchison watched her for several seconds, then said, turning sharply to Steve, 'I was right, *see*?' He wheeled back round to Lola and Anna. 'I said it. I *said* it was bullshit. No way it was an accident or suicide. J.P. was *happy*. He'd just got a new job. *We* were happy. Why . . . Why would your colleagues want to cover up something like that? Oh God—'

He crumpled suddenly, palms flat on his face, rocking with sobs.

Steve clamped a hand on his shoulder and closed his own eyes. 'I talked to your colleagues as well. I knew something wasn't right. But they just didn't want to know.' He shrugged sadly.

Lola said, 'DS Vaughan, or another member of my team, will be in touch with you both, separately, to take new statements. I'm sure you'll understand why we want to start from a fresh page. We'll leave you shortly, but I'd like to ask you something first, Will.'

'Go on.' Wary eyes again.

'Did anything happen before or after J.P. disappeared on Saturday evening? Anything out of the ordinary? It doesn't matter how small it is.'

He thought about it, eyes focused on the rug in the middle of the room. Steve whispered a couple of words, earning a sharp glance and a quick shake of the head.

'No,' he said, eyes not meeting Lola's.

'Are you sure?'

'Yes.'

'Mr Manners?' she said, noting how flushed the thin man's face had become.

'It's okay,' Will Aitchison said to his friend. 'She needs to know.'

Lola waited, eyebrows up, ready for whatever was coming.

'J.P. and I had an "arrangement",' Will said. 'An *open* arrangement. We could see other people, so long as we were careful — if you know what I mean. I played about occasionally, but J.P. was more "active" than me. He used an app to meet other guys.'

'What app?'

'It's called Matey,' Steve said, looking mortified. 'It uses GPS to tell you who's nearby and you can contact people through messages.'

'What are you telling me, Mr Manners?' Lola asked, almost seeing where this was going. 'Was J.P. planning to meet someone the other night when he left you?'

'That's just it — I don't think he was. He said he was going to walk home and hit the hay.'

'There have been stories, though,' Will said. 'There was a rumour going round the city that the Pusher was using Matey to lure his victims.'

'Right.' This had cropped up more than once in Lola's reading about the Pusher, but only as a suggested means of luring victims.

'You do get the occasional weirdo,' Steve said. 'Friends warn friends and word gets around. A guy appeared on the app, firing messages to folk, flattering them, asking to meet. He had photos and he looked nice. One guy went to meet him, down by the river. They pulled him out the water the next day. Drew someone, I think his name was.

'I never knew him, but as I say, words gets round. The guy on the app started contacting more people. Folk reported him to the app, but they don't care, do they? In the end he disappeared.'

'You don't happen to have screenshots of any of this person's messages, do you?'

'Sorry, no.'

'Okay,' Lola said. 'J.P.'s phone is with forensics now. They're trying to get into it. You don't happen to know J.P.'s login or password for the Matey app, do you?'

'His login, yeah. He always just used his email address. Not his password, though. Sorry.'

CHAPTER THIRTY-SEVEN

1.51 p.m.

'How you feeling, Cammy love?' Larissa asked in her soft, kind voice.

She'd woken him up. It was dark in the little bedroom and it took him a moment to work out where he was.

'All right.' His voice was a croak.

'You sure?' she said, head round the door. 'You want a wee cup of tea or anything?'

'No, thanks.'

''Kay.' She hesitated. He couldn't see her face but sensed she was nervous. 'My Chris is on his way over. He'll not be here long. Best to stay in here, eh? Keep quiet. It's best that way.'

He nodded.

'You go back to sleep.' She closed the door and left him.

He'd found Larissa down on the Drag just after one in the morning. He'd spent an hour looking for her, repeatedly trying her mobile number, given him by a slurring Tiffany — who'd clearly been off her face on something. Then he'd spotted Larissa emerging from the tunnel under the railway tracks, striding forward on her towering heels, head down. He'd made her jump, then she stared as he gabbled out that he was in trouble — real trouble. He asked if she'd been serious the time she said she'd help him if ever he needed it. She said she had, and here he was.

She'd brought him home in a cab to this tiny house in Pollok, giving up working for the night, made him a sandwich and given him vodka, then sat up with him while he came to terms with what he'd seen, the fact Warren was probably dead, and the likelihood he, Cammy, had been the intended victim. That idea sent repeated waves of cold horror washing over him, making him shiver and shrink within his own skin each time he remembered. He was in danger and completely alone — and of the two things, being alone was the worst.

'It's like I'm cursed,' he'd told her tearfully, well into his second double vodka. 'First Dec, now Warren.'

He'd fallen asleep on Larissa's couch, curled up with her ginger tom, Alfie, and woken in this box room. He didn't remember her leading him here.

The sound of a doorbell downstairs, then footsteps and voices. The mysterious Chris. He sounded gruff, angry, and Larissa responded in increasingly high and pleading tones. Cammy wanted to get up, to rush downstairs to defend her, but she'd asked him to stay quiet and hidden. He respected her, so defied his better instincts and did as she'd asked.

Blocking out the raised voices downstairs, he steeled himself and went onto the BBC news website on his phone, looking for Scottish news, then stories relating to Glasgow. And there it was: 'Man dies in Pollokshields car attack'.

Oh God . . .

A photo and only a short piece. A mere few lines.

He shut his eyes tight, then opened them. One thing he'd learned growing up in care: you never looked away from the worst possibility. Denial and self-deception only made you more vulnerable.

He opened his eyes and read the story.

A man has died after his car, a Jaguar F-TYPE, was driven into repeatedly by an unknown assailant.

> *The incident happened at the junction of Darnley Street and Albert Drive in East Pollokshields in Glasgow's Southside at 22:42 on Wednesday. Sections of both roads were closed and remain so. Police said the forty-two-year-old male was the only victim of the attack, the motive for which is unknown.*
>
> *A large black car, possibly an Audi, is thought to be the other vehicle involved in the incident. It was witnessed being driven off at speed and has yet to be traced.*
>
> *Police have yet to name the victim.*

The article quoted a police spokesperson asking for witnesses, including any drivers who might have been in the area shortly before or after the time of the attack, in case they had dashcam footage to share.

Cammy was a witness, but no way was he going to the police. They wouldn't believe him, and would probably suspect he was involved in Warren's death — the way that dead-eyed sergeant had suggested he knew more about Dec's death than he was letting on.

He closed the news app and rolled over in the bed, clamping the pillow over his ears to deaden the sound of Larissa and Chris having their row.

He saw Warren's face again, contorted in pain and fear, and blood running down his chin. He opened his eyes and sat up, panting.

Warren had told him his surname was Smith, but he still hadn't found him online. He'd googled 'Warren Smith' in the early hours, finding hundreds of people, including some who were famous one way or another. Narrowing the search to include 'Glasgow' hadn't helped. He'd scanned pages of images, but failed to find the Warren he knew.

So he'd lied.

Well, that had been Warren's choice, but Cammy would learn his real name before long. And then he'd start digging. He'd find out the real reason Warren had needed to conceal his identity.

CHAPTER THIRTY-EIGHT

2.05 p.m.

DI Mairi Marshall, the inspector in charge of the attack on the green Jaguar, was running late but Lola didn't get her apologetic text message till she'd parked up at Helen Street.

It was fine — she was dizzy with tiredness, and had driven here with all her windows down to blast herself alert. A twenty-minute coffee break was more than welcome.

She found a corner of the canteen and texted Mairi Marshall to say where she was, then texted Tom: *It's me. Do you know about an app called Matey?*

He got it and began replying immediately. The text came through. *Aye, course. It's not exactly up your street, Lola. You're best sticking to hetero apps.*

She rolled her eyes and replied, *Heard a rumour the Pusher used it. Didn't you say you had a friend on the scene who had a few theories? Would he know about that?*

Stuey. Yeah, he'd know. Want me to ask if he'll talk to you? came his reply.

Please, Lola typed.

Will get onto it right away!

She went into her personal emails. Frankie had sent an invite to go as her plus-one to some education awards event in Edinburgh. Lola couldn't think of anything worse. She flagged it to reply to later.

She'd also had an email from Sorcha with a selection of photos from her birthday party, including one of Lola and Barry appearing to smile fondly at one another. It gave her the heebie-jeebies and she clicked out of it.

'So sorry I'm late!' a bright anxious voice called across the canteen, making Lola start.

DI Mairi Marshall was threading her way clumsily between the tables, crashing into chairs and sending one flying.

'Can I get you a coffee?' Lola asked when the other woman landed at the table, spilling files and the contents of her handbag. 'Give you a chance to settle?'

'I'm fine, honestly.' Mairi gathered her stuff together and shrugged off her jacket. They were old pals, having joined CID at the same time. Mairi was a good detective but didn't want promotion any time soon. She had a young family and dogs and didn't want any more stress — so she said. She seemed to Lola forever on the verge of meltdown.

'You all right?' Mairi asked Lola now, swiping a stray lock of blonde hair out of her eyes. 'I heard your news. A task force on the Clyde Pusher! Blimey!'

'It's going to be interesting.'

'Angus Wilde's okay,' Mairi said. 'But he's left the building, from what I hear. What do they call it, "quiet quitting"? His wife's health isn't good. You'd think he'd just jack it in and go, but maybe he prefers to work.' She leaned in. 'Isn't there a DS who's a wee bit tricky too? I guess you'll know that by now. Lachlan something. Green? Anyway, you're not here to gossip, are you? You want to know about the car attack in Pollokshields?'

'I do,' Lola said, wondering what Mairi might have been about to reveal, and making a mental note to circle back to the laconic DS Gray.

'So, do you think there's a link between this car thing and what you'll be looking at?'

'I've no proof but I suspect there's a link with one of the attacks, yes.'

'Really?'

'It all depends on who the driver of the Jaguar was.'

Mairi went into her bag and found her notebook then flicked through a few pages.

'Driver was a forty-two-year-old male, name of David Warren Maxwell.' She paused. 'Ring a bell?'

'Possibly,' Lola said, chewing her lip thoughtfully. 'Who was he?'

'He was a property developer and worked for his father's firm, Maxwell Land and Buildings.'

Lola had a sudden image of hoardings round building sites with the name Maxwell stencilled everywhere. 'They're the company that's developing the big site in the Merchant City, aren't they?'

'Yep. Housing, restaurants, offices and some kind of . . . "public plaza". I think that's what they're calling it. They're also going to be developing a section of the south side of the riverbank.'

'Is that right?'

'Turning it into a kind of "Left Bank". Paris come to Glasgow. Can't see it, myself. I mean, make it look like Paris if you want, but it's still going to be pissing with rain.' She saw Lola's expression. 'What have I said?'

'The deaths I'm looking at were all connected to the river. That's where the bodies ended up.'

'Yeah, that's weird, isn't it?'

Lola made a note — *river development* — and circled it. She couldn't begin to imagine what it might mean, but it was worth a look.

'I might want to meet Maxwell's family at some point,' she said.

'Just give me the nod.'

'What else do you know about the victim?' she asked.

'He was — oh yes, this is the juicy bit — he was engaged to be married in a year's time. To the daughter of a Russian businessman — one of those "oligarchs". Her dad owns an airline and a football club somewhere. Worth billions, rather than millions. Rich in a way you can barely imagine. I haven't spoken to her yet — she was in Japan, looking after businesses her dad's family have got there. She's on her way here today. There's a younger Maxwell brother — Patrick. I think he's more gutted about the marriage not happening than the fact his brother's been killed. The fiancée's father — the oligarch — owns half of the Highlands, though you'd never know it. It's all shell companies and trusts, foundations for wildlife and forests.'

'Murky?'

'Very.'

'As murky as David Warren Maxwell's private life too.'

'What do you mean?' Mairi's blue eyes grew wide.

'Come across any suggestion he was bisexual?'

'Can't say so. Why?'

'There's a chance he was in a casual relationship with a nineteen-year-old man called Cameron Leavey. Care-experienced, possibly vulnerable . . . And possibly the target of the attack that killed David Warren Maxwell.'

Mairi positioned her pen. 'I'm all ears.'

Lola explained about Cammy. About the attack on J.P. McCrae he claimed to have witnessed, and the subsequent murder of Declan Bailey. About Cammy's claim to have an older boyfriend called Warren who drove a sporty green Jag.

'Sounds like the same bloke, doesn't it?' Mairi said. 'There's no suggestion anyone else was in the car or anywhere near it. Not yet anyway. We're all over the CCTV, but that area's less well served by CCTV because it's outside the city centre. So where is he now, this Cammy?'

'That's what I'd like to know.'

'Are you going to put out a public call?'

'Maybe. I need a statement from him about the river attack. He has a habit of disappearing then turning up a day or two later. I've officers patrolling the river. Thing is, he's badly frightened.'

'Sounds like he's got reason to be.'

'He's a nice kid. It's a shame.'

'I'll want to talk to him, especially if it turns out his Warren and my David Maxwell are one and the same.'

'Don't worry, I'll shout you when I find him. I might need to talk to his friends or family too, if it comes to it. I expect his involvement with a teenage lad will come as a bit of a surprise.'

'Just a bit.'

'When are you planning to name him?' Lola asked.

'Later today. Nothing grand — a standard press release to all media. I'm sure one or two of the local papers will pick it up.'

They were packing up to go, when Lola asked, as if it were mere small talk, 'What were you going to say about Lachlan Gray?'

'Oh aye, him,' Mairi said, her tone light but hiding something. She made a face. 'Funny guy. Not "funny ha-ha" either.'

'Anything I should know?'

The briefest of pauses. 'Maybe,' she said. 'But you didn't hear it from me. He watches people.'

'"Watches people"? What, like stalking them, you mean?'

'No, not that. I've not seen any proof. It's just rumours.'

'Tell me anyway.'

'He keeps tabs on folk. He *monitors* them.'

Lola opened then closed her mouth. She sat down and gestured for Mairi to rejoin her.

'An officer — a young female, I won't say who — caught him watching her while she was changing to go running. She'd found a wee corner in the gym room and he was standing, half hiding behind a cupboard. She called him out and he vanished. Horrible, isn't it?'

'Just a bit.'

'She confronted him and he denied it. She was on the verge of putting in a complaint but then decided against it. I hope to God he didn't threaten her.'

'That's awful.'

'Oh, he's a creep. But it's the usual story, he's got the odd senior watching out for him. A handful of lads too, ready to back him up.'

An all-too-familiar scenario, in Lola's experience . . .

'I'm sure he'll behave himself while you're around,' Mairi said. 'Your reputation does kind of precede you.'

'Does it?' Lola had never thought about it before. It was oddly reassuring.

'This handful of lads you mentioned,' she said. 'Who are they, out of interest? Just so I can keep a lookout.'

Mairi took her time before answering, seeming almost to steel herself for Lola's likely reaction. 'You know one of them.'

'Oh?' A prickle crept over Lola's shoulders.

Mairi nodded and said quietly, 'Pal of mine spotted Lachlan Gray in a corner of the canteen at Stewart Street just the other afternoon, having a deep-and-meaningful with Aidan Pierce.'

'How very interesting,' Lola said darkly.

* * *

2.37 p.m.

Lola had a text from Anna, saying she was meeting Shannon Grant at the CCTV operations centre at five and would report back ASAP.

She also had a text from Tom to say his pal Stuey would be 'thrilled' to talk to her. He'd sent a phone number. She rang it, recoiling slightly from the evident glee with which Stuey apparently relished her call, and arranged to meet him the next day.

CHAPTER THIRTY-NINE

4.32 p.m.

'So it was him?' Brenda took a long drag of her e-cigarette and settled back into her armchair, taking in the news.

'Sounds like it,' Lola said. 'But, like I say: there's no suggestion Cammy was involved or harmed in the incident.'

Brenda gave her a sceptical look.

'What?' Lola said.

'It's the third death connected to the boy in under a week.'

'I know. At some point finding him is going to become urgent.'

'So for now you're going to do nothing, you mean?' the woman said, growing cross.

'He may turn up once he sees the news. If not, we might need to put out a public call.'

'"A public call" — what's that?'

'A post on social media in the first instance. Or we could mention his name at a press conference and ask him to get in touch.'

'That won't work. Not if he doesn't want to be found.'

'Can you think of anyone who might know where he is, Brenda?'

'Larissa might.'

'Larissa?' Brenda had mentioned the name before.

'Works down on the Drag. She mothers Cammy,' Brenda said. 'Needs mothering herself, really. She's an addict. Had her kids taken off her. Her fella's an abusive shit.'

'And where does she stay?'

'Don't know. Southside somewhere, or over towards Paisley. Crookston, maybe.'

Lola thought as quickly as she could. Her brain was fuzzy, as though connections were misfiring.

'Would you come down to the Drag with me to try and find her?'

'Can do.' She looked sheepish. 'As a matter of fact I was thinking of taking a hike down there later myself. You know, to ask about.'

'I wouldn't want you to put yourself in any danger.'

'Don't worry about me.' She coughed out a dismissive laugh.

'When would be a good time, do you reckon?'

'Nine. Ten, maybe. No earlier.'

By nine Lola had planned to be in her house, in her PJs and ready for bed. Ready — please, God — to sleep, at least for a few hours. The idea of being out in Glasgow at that time of night, stalking the Drag, possibly getting a lead as to Cammy's whereabouts, then having to go there, to bring him in and interview him into the small hours . . . it made her want to weep.

'Tonight, then.' She groaned inwardly as she got to her feet. 'I'll pick you up here at nine thirty.'

'Ring me first,' Brenda said, getting up too. 'I might be out. I sometimes meet old colleagues for a drink. You've got my mobile number, haven't you? Call me at half eight and I'll tell you where I am.' She stopped and frowned hard at Lola. 'Are you all right? You look about ready to drop.'

'Do I?' She tried not to sound defensive and failed. 'I'm tired, that's all.'

'How? Not sleeping?'

'No.'

'Insomnia's hell. I've suffered for years. You lie there, in darkness, knowing everyone around you is fast asleep, and you're there with your horrible thoughts spinning round and round, faster and faster and more of them joining in.'

'That describes it well. Have you seen anyone about it?'

'I've tried everything,' Brenda said. 'Pills, meditation, hot milk, whisky. Nothing works. Some nights I don't even bother going to bed. I just stay up. I read or watch a film. I walk about the town. I get the sleep I need when I need it. Buses are good. I can nod off for twenty minutes and it makes a difference. What about you? Tried anything?'

'Pills. Counselling. Even tried hypnotherapy.'

'Now that's the one thing I never did.'

'Didn't work. The chap had a creepy voice.'

It was oddly comforting to share her pain with a relative stranger like this: a spontaneous support group of two.

'I get to sleep all right,' Lola said now. 'But then dreams wake me up. They're so vivid. I'm trying to find someone, but I never quite manage it. He's always too far away.'

'I'm sorry,' Brenda said with pity. 'If it's any comfort I've had plenty of those dreams myself.'

'Of trying to find someone?'

Brenda nodded.

'Your son?' The words were out before she could stop them and she regretted speaking immediately. Only that morning she'd passed information about Gavin MacQuoid to DCI Izatt. It felt treacherous even to ask the question.

Brenda eyed her carefully for a moment then raised her eyebrows and nodded sadly. She stood, clearing her throat and looking about as if for something she'd lost.

Lola took the hint.

'I'll be on my way,' she said, smiling. 'Thanks for the chat. I'll call you tonight.'

CHAPTER FORTY

5.12 p.m.

'Based on the information that's publicly available,' DC Kirstie Campbell said, handing over a single sheet of A4, 'including all the gossip and speculation, we think we can account for nine attacks in the past seven years.'

Lola scanned down the list she and Janey Carstairs had produced. Her vision was fuzzy — getting worse.

'According to this,' Kirstie went on, 'it looks as if eight deaths have been attributed to the Pusher over the years. One person survived.'

'Alec Bennett,' Lola read aloud. The name was new to her. There was a note beside the name, saying he'd been interviewed in the *Chronicle* about the attack. 'Have you got a copy of the interview?'

'It's listed in the *Chronicle*'s web archive but you can't read it online, even with an account.'

'Call Shuna Frain,' Lola said. 'Tell her I've asked for it.'

'Boss.'

She scanned down the rest of the names, forcing herself to focus, drawing circles and underlining. She recognised several names from her own review of the available information.

> *Richard (Ricky) Linton, 29, civil servant. Date of death: 4 Dec 2016. Assumed to be the first victim. Gay. Head injury. Death by drowning. Found in river by Atlantic Quay, Broomielaw.*

> *Drew Morris, 32, builder. Date of death: c. 30 May 2017. Bisexual, but this was not known by family until after he died. Head injury. Body found among reeds by the Victoria Bridge by north bank (beside Clyde Street).*

> *Alec Bennett, 28, bar manager. Attacked but survived 11 Mar 2018. Bisexual, living with girlfriend at the time. Interview appeared in the Chronicle, 21 Mar 2018. Article archived on the Chronicle's website but not available to read.*

> *Neil Prine, 26, occupation unknown. Date of death: 17 Sept 2018. Sexuality unknown. Little known about circumstances, but body found in river at Renfrew three days later.*

> *Mark Brodie, 24, occupation unknown. Date of death: 24 Nov 2019. Gay, head injury and died by drowning. Found in river at Pacific Quay, next to the BBC. Phone call was placed to Mark's mother from his mobile, assumed at or around the time of the attack.*

> *Unknown victim, 20s. Attacked 1 or 2 Dec 2020. Sexuality unknown. Nationality unknown but had a tattoo in Polish. Body found in river by Victoria Bridge, on mud by the south bank of the river. No information on injury (one forum claims he was strangled).*

> *Michael Mackinnon, 23, PhD student. Attacked 15 or 16 Aug 2021. Gay. Part-time job in a restaurant in Merchant*

City. Found in river, caught underneath Victoria Bridge. Head injury reported. Fatal accident inquiry held.

Khalid Hussain, 23, trainee doctor. Died 10 or 11 Dec 2022. Married to woman. Some speculation he might have been bisexual, but wife denies this, according to internet.

John Paul McCrae, 28, call centre team leader. Died 11 Feb 2023. Gay. Attack possibly witnessed and filmed.

'This is excellent,' she said, still studying the list. 'So we have evidence that *six* of these nine were gay or bisexual, and the other three could be.' She looked up at the two constables. 'I'd call that a pattern, wouldn't you?'

Janey Carstairs lowered her eyes, but the red in her cheeks gave her away.

'You and your colleagues must have noticed a pattern before now,' Lola prompted gently.

'It . . . It wasn't felt it was . . .' She was struggling for words.

'What wasn't "felt"?'

The young woman looked pained. Lola felt irritation swell inside her and made herself swallow it down.

'Who wasn't it "felt" by?'

'DS Gray,' Janey Carstairs muttered. 'And others.'

The girl meant well. She was too obedient, too loyal, but Lola sensed she'd acted without malice.

'What does DS Gray think about gay men?' she asked for the hell of it.

Janey looked up sharply, her lips parting, her cheek going redder than ever. 'I think . . . I mean, I don't know. I'm sure it wasn't that.'

Lola let it go. For now.

'There's another pattern,' Kirstie said now.

'Go on.'

'We don't have any information about where three of the nine were attacked or went into the water. Of the remaining six, three were attacked on the stretch of Clyde Street between the Clutha Vaults pub and Glasgow Green, and the other three were just to the west of the Kingston Bridge on Anderston Quay.'

'Is that so?'

'Prine, Morris and Brodie were all last seen by the Kingston Bridge. Linton and McCrae went into the water on Clyde Street, and Bennett — the only survivor — was attacked there.'

'So it looks as if he has two hunting grounds,' Lola murmured. 'What's the significance of that, I wonder. More importantly, what's the CCTV coverage like round there?'

She fell quiet, thinking about it. Trying to envisage those stretches of the north bank of the Clyde, to visualise the buildings round there, and places someone could hide before ambushing a victim . . .

'Do you want us to start by filling in some of the blanks?' Kirstie asked.

'Yes,' Lola said. 'But we should also focus on the latest three supposed victims,' she said. 'Try and find next-of-kin contacts for Michael Mackinnon and Khalid Hussain and start there. Where are we with Jack Everett and Dougie Latimer?'

These were the contacts Shuna had provided: Jack, the editor of the *Gouger*, and Dougie, her former colleague who'd been researching the Pusher before he was made to focus his attentions elsewhere.

'Mr Everett says he's available whenever we want him,' Kirstie said. 'I've got an address. He volunteered Mr Latimer's name — seems they're pals. He suggested it would make sense to see the two of them together.'

'Good plan. Would you set something up for tomorrow morning for me and Anna?' Lola said. 'First thing, if possible.'

'Yes, boss. Oh, and Yvonne Craigie who runs the Facebook group for the families — she's "more than happy" to help. Says it's about time, *et cetera, et cetera*. I'll find out when she can meet us.'

'Good. It might be an idea to add workplaces and home addresses to this list. Next of kin too, with contact details where we have them. Then print me a few more copies. Hopefully by this time tomorrow we'll have a much fuller picture of what happened — and who it happened to. We might even start to understand why.'

She checked the time. 'I need to see DS Gray about Declan Bailey,' she said. 'Thanks, Kirstie, that'll be everything. Janey, would you mind hanging back for a minute or two?'

CHAPTER FORTY-ONE

5.27 p.m.

'Are you going to tell me what's been going on around here?' Lola asked, making her tone bright and mumsy.

Janey Carstairs cringed — actually *cringed*, clenching her fists, lifting her knees and hunching her shoulders as if to curl into a protective ball.

Lola asked, 'Is it plain old homophobia, laziness or straight-up incompetence? It's okay. You can tell me what you think. No judgement, and it won't go outside these four walls.'

It took her a minute, but the girl began to relax a little, but her face was still pink with embarrassment. 'I've worked in DS Gray's team for six months,' she said. 'I was aware of the reporting protocol. People do call, you know? Families. Journalists. Bloggers. There's a set of lines — I mean, *lines* printed out for us to read out if people call. It's always seemed so . . . well, weird.'

Lola nodded. 'Did you question it?'

'No.' She shifted uncomfortably in her chair. 'Well, once.'

'Go on.'

'The second victim's sister phoned and I spoke to her.'

Lola consulted the list. 'Drew Morris's sister?'

Janey nodded but avoided eye contact. She was ashamed, Lola could tell.

'Her name was Sharon Morris,' the constable said. 'Drew had died in 2017. Sharon said both her parents had passed away recently — they'd asked her not to make a fuss about Drew's death while they were alive. "What happened, happened" — that kind of thing. She suspects they were embarrassed Drew had been gay. But now Sharon wanted to find out what really happened. She'd never believed it was an accident, and she wanted to know what we'd done about it.

'I read out the lines, but—' a cynical laugh — 'she'd heard them before. She said, or words to this effect: "My brother was murdered. I know it and you know it and so do other people. And the person who killed him is still out there." She said she was in touch with one of the other families and that they'd be going to the press.'

'When was this?'

Janey's eyes searched the room. 'Beginning of December,' she said at last. Her tone darkened. 'And then I spoke to DS Gray . . .'

'Oh?'

'He told me not to talk about it to anyone. Then I got called to a meeting.'

'A meeting?'

She nodded. 'That new Corporate Comms woman was there. Melda Brodick. Superintendent Wilde joined us after a bit, but Melda was in charge. She wanted to know what the woman had said, whether she'd identified the other family or who in the press she was talking to. She was really annoyed. So were DS Gray and the super.'

'Annoyed — with you?'

'Not so much that. I think they were annoyed with her — with Sharon Morris. They talked among themselves about someone "paying her a visit", like gangsters or something. Well, maybe not gangsters. Sorry, poor choice of words.'

'Don't apologise,' Lola said. It did sound like gangsters. It sounded *exactly* like gangsters. 'What happened then?'

'I got on with my job. No one mentioned Sharon Morris to me again, and I didn't ask.'

'You felt uncomfortable about it?'

She nodded, eyes down.

A sharp knock at the door made them both jump. DS Lachlan Gray's pale eyes peered in through the diamond-shaped window. Lola thanked Janey and said she could go. Then she called Gray in.

CHAPTER FORTY-TWO

5.41 p.m.

Lachlan Gray set his notepad on the table then pulled out a chair and sat, blinking slowly, his expression blank.

From a folder, Lola took out a copy of the statement Gray and Carstairs had obtained from Cammy Leavey about the death of Declan Bailey, and steeled herself. She'd been here before — several times — with Aidan Pierce. It was never easy to face down a self-satisfied egotist who thought he could do no wrong. But Gray was a different challenge. She had no doubt he was toxic — she'd heard as much from Mairi Marshall at Helen Street — but, unlike Pierce, Gray appeared to have willing patrons, in the form of Detective Superintendent Angus Wilde and Comms director Melda Brodick. It made him dangerous. It even crossed her mind he might be covertly recording the meeting. She must stay cool, stick to the script she had in her head and keep things as short as possible. She wanted nothing more than to get home and get her head down — to take what scraps of sleep she might hope to snatch.

'Declan Bailey,' she said. 'In a nutshell, please.'

'Investigation proceeding at pace,' Gray said, his pale eyes focused somewhere over Lola's right shoulder. 'The key will be forensic evidence and IB have scoured the place. I'm waiting for a report. Bailey was at home alone at the time and must have let his attacker in.'

'But he was found dead in his bed, wasn't he? Why would he go back to bed with an attacker in the house?'

'My theory is that the attacker said he was there to visit one of the other tenants, or perhaps to carry out work for the housing association. Bailey let him in then went back to bed. According to his flatmates—' one of whom was Cammy Leavey, Lola reminded herself — 'he often stayed up at night playing video games, then slept in the daytime. So he was probably asleep when the attacker found him in his room and proceeded to stab him in the face and neck then slit his throat.'

'You're suggesting the attacker was hiding in the flat for quite some time, then?'

Gray shrugged.

'You don't suspect either flatmate?'

'Not at this time,' he said in a near whisper. She realised he was one of those people who spoke more softly the more angry they were.

'Any witnesses?'

His gaze slid away over her shoulder again, making her want to take a glance behind her.

'One of the flatmates, Cameron Leavey,' he said blandly. 'He claims a man followed him home and was observing the flat from the cemetery over the road.'

'He gave you a description, didn't he?'

'He did.' Softer still.

'And he claimed he'd seen this individual once before, didn't he?'

A slow blink. 'He did.'

'In fact, DS Gray, he claimed it was the same individual he'd seen attack J.P. McCrae at the river on the evening of Saturday the eleventh of February.'

'So he claimed.'

'And yet there's no note at all in this statement—' she tapped the pages on the table before her — 'about anything that had happened at the river.'

No response.

'I know he told you about what he saw there, DS Gray.'

More blinking.

'When we find him, you'll take another statement from Cameron Leavey. It will be an accurate record. Do you understand me?'

They battled on for some minutes, Gray murmuring bland responses to Lola's increasingly pointed questions. She realised she disliked him intensely — and mistrusted him too. He'd be a burden on the investigation. But how to handle that? Her gut instinct was to bin him fast, but Clive Reid had been keen to keep Detective Superintendent Wilde on side, and he clearly valued the sergeant. The best course of action was probably to box him in to clear tasks and monitor him like a hawk, as much as she disliked the idea.

'Is that us?' he asked at last, and for the first time a smile — no, a smirk — touched his thin lips. It was the same smirk Pierce had worn more than once.

'Nearly,' she said, blood suddenly ice in her veins. 'Why the cover-up, DS Gray? Time to talk.'

His strange eyes flitted briefly back to her face before finding renewed interest in the wall.

'For years you have *proactively ignored* an increasingly evident pattern in a series of deaths. Why?'

He muttered something.

'Sorry, what did you say?'

'I said,' he sneered, nice and loud this time, eyes wide and sharp discoloured teeth showing under his curled top lip, 'there is no pattern. It's a fabrication by attention seekers.'

'You don't believe that.' She stared, horrified. 'You can't, surely?'

'It's the truth.' He stood and snatched up his pad. 'Our city is *safe and sound.*'

Gray reached for the door.

'By whose measure?' she demanded, but he'd gone.

* * *

6.20 p.m.

Anna Vaughan was coming quickly along the corridor when Lola emerged from the meeting room a few minutes after Gray's departure.

'Oh good, you're there!' the sergeant said, looking and sounding frazzled. 'I'm just back from the CCTV operations centre.'

'Come in here,' Lola said, and led the way back into the meeting room. 'What happened?'

Anna sat, then hesitated, eyes on Lola's face. 'Are you okay, boss? Only, you don't look very well.'

'I'm fine. Tell me what's wrong.'

Anna eyed her dubiously for a moment, then began: 'The cameras on the east section of Clyde Street — the ones that have been out for the past three weeks — they were vandalised. An engineer finally went out this morning. Looks like they were *shot* at — an air rifle could have done it. But the other two cameras — the ones on Stockwell Street and the Saltmarket — they were definitely moved remotely from the operations centre.'

'Is that right?'

'Shannon Grant was giving me the timings when she got an "urgent" phone call. Someone higher up telling her not to speak to us without lawyers present.'

'*What?*'

'She was mortified. I asked who'd called but she said she wasn't allowed to tell me. They'll see us, but at a time to suit them and their lawyers.'

'They're a public service. Why do they need lawyers?'

Anna shrugged and made a face.

'Push back. Demand a meeting tomorrow — by five p.m. at the latest. Lawyers don't scare me.'

'Boss.'

'And now I'm going home to sleep.'

CHAPTER FORTY-THREE

7.01 p.m.

Brenda showed the scruffy, angry-faced detective and his slickly pristine sidekick into her living room. 'Is this about Cammy?' she asked, voice catching as she readied herself for bad news.

'Who's Cammy?'

'Cameron Leavey. He's—'

'Never heard of him,' the man said, off-hand, taking in the living room with a sneer on his lips.

'Then why're you here?'

'We're here, Miss Cheney, about your son, Gavin MacQuoid.'

Her heart skipped a beat. She put a steadying hand on the mantelpiece. 'What about him?'

'We want to know where he is. We're hoping you can tell us.'

Reeling, she bought time asking them to repeat their names.

'DCI Izatt,' the big man growled, 'and this is DS Pierce. Now, Mrs Cheney — your son?'

'I don't know where he is and that's the truth.' The sob in her own voice took her by surprise. 'I haven't seen or spoken to him for eight years. What's he done?'

'Never you mind.' Then, with false, almost sarcastic politeness, 'May we sit down?'

She nodded, but remained standing herself. Her e-cigarette was in her cardigan pocket and she took a much-needed drag. Her heart raced with the nicotine but there was relief too.

They wanted to know what contact she'd had with Gavin and didn't believe her when she said it had been eight years. The sergeant, who was particularly snide, wanted to know what she'd done to alienate her own son, then asked, tauntingly, whether she knew he was a criminal. Of course she knew. It was her life's regret. But that didn't change the fact she hadn't seen or spoken to Gavin for nearly a decade. They demanded names of Gavin's old friends. She gave them a couple she could remember, beyond which she couldn't help them anymore and they prepared to go.

'Aren't you going to tell me anything?' she half wailed, following them into the hallway. 'Don't you owe me that?'

'Ask your nephew,' DCI Izatt said, reaching for the door. 'He seems to know a lot more than you.'

'*Tom?*' She stared, mouth open, shaken. 'What does Tom know?'

'As I say, ask him.'

CHAPTER FORTY-FOUR

8.44 p.m.

Lola had slept, deeply and without dreaming, for ninety blissful minutes. She lay in the dark, warm and listless, but not anxious. She might manage more sleep, given the chance. Except she had to get up. Had to phone Brenda and arrange to meet her so the two of them could stake out the river for signs of Cammy — and if not Cammy, then Larissa, who might or might not be harbouring him.

There were texts on her phone from her sister and from Anna Vaughan. She saw, too, that Tom had called and left her a message. She had no time to read or listen, so dressed quickly and called Brenda as she hunted for her car keys.

Brenda answered with a snapped, 'Hello?' It sounded as if she was in a pub.

'Brenda, it's Lola Harris. I'm on my way. Tell me where you are and I'll pick you up.'

'Don't bother. I don't need your help.'

'Why? Has Cammy come back?' Silence — or rather, just the noise of the pub. 'Brenda? What's wrong?'

'You don't know? I've had your lot round at mine asking about my son. Somebody Izatt and an arsehole of a sergeant.'

She caught her own reflection in the hall mirror. She looked as sick as she felt. 'I see.'

'Tom asked for your help with Cammy,' Brenda spat, 'but you used his trust to wheedle information out of him. He's in *bits*. How dare you? You're a bully.'

Now she knew why Tom had called her . . . She shut her eyes so she didn't have to look at her own reflection.

'Brenda, please—'

'Coming over to mine today,' the woman went on, 'all friendly, asking all sorts of questions. A front, wasn't it?'

'Brenda, please! It wasn't like that.'

'I don't believe you.'

Then don't. 'I'm sorry you're upset,' she said glumly. 'But we need to find Cammy. He could be in danger. Can we try to put it to one side, for his sake?'

'I'll find Cammy,' Brenda said. 'You suit yourself.'

* * *

9.03 p.m.

Traffic on the M77 was gridlocked, for no apparent reason, so she tried Tom again from her hands-free. He'd been engaged the first time she tried him but now he answered, saying grimly, 'Yeah?'

'It's Lola.'

'I know who it is.'

A van indicated so she stood on her brake to let it in.

'What do you want to say to me, Tom?'

More silence, then: 'Did you have to send those guys round to see Auntie Brenda? Couldn't they have phoned? Couldn't *you* have phoned? You just decided to set the dogs on her. She's old! She's not well.'

'I could have handled it better,' she said. 'I'm sorry.'

'Yeah, you could.'

More silence.

She didn't generally mind silences. They could allow pressure to ease.

'She's fucking raging at me.' His voice faltered and he sounded teary.

Oh God . . .

'Tom, I took over a major investigation today,' she said, while he sniffed at the other end of the line. 'I had to hand over everything I was working on. You told me something last night that I couldn't ignore. I tried to do the right thing. Please believe me when I say that. I wasn't being devious. When I asked you about Gavin, I was genuinely interested in what had happened to him . . .'

'Well, it's done now, isn't it?'

She braked to let a couple more cars enter her lane.

'I called her but she told me to get lost.'

'Then do as she says.'

'I *can't*. We said we'd go down to the river to try and find Cammy. He's missing and he could be in danger. Do you know where Brenda goes, Tom? Somewhere she drinks with old colleagues.'

Silence.

'Tom, please.'

'The Hook and Line,' he said. 'It's behind the St Enoch Centre. But I didn't tell you that, d'you hear me?'

CHAPTER FORTY-FIVE

9.06 p.m.

A photo of Warren had appeared on the BBC news website at tea-time. In the picture he was smiling, looking so handsome, so happy, and next to his face, the words: *Fatal car attack victim named.*

It was the name that was the problem.

Cammy had read the news story in Larissa's kitchen, having to prop his phone on one of the foil cartons of their Chinese takeaway because his hands were trembling too much to hold it.

'Is it him?' Larissa had asked him, coming round the table and rubbing a hand on his back.

He nodded, then shifted the screen so she could read it too.

'"David Warren Maxwell",' she said, then read on a few lines. '"Engaged to—" oh my God — "daughter of . . . of a Russian billionaire"?' She gasped. 'That's how come he drove a Jag, then.'

He sat very still, blinking as the news sank in.

'You should go and see his folks,' Larissa said, moving from his side and taking her plate to the sink. 'Tell them you want money to keep schtum.'

He stared at her. His instinct was to be righteous and offended, to say he didn't want money. But he did. In fact, he needed it.

She saw his face. 'I'm being serious. He was your boyfriend. You're entitled to something. We could both go. I'll say I'm your solicitor or something. Or your big sister, anyway.'

'You could get a cut,' he said.

'That's what I was thinking.'

He went to the bedroom after that and read the story again, then cried a bit.

He slept and felt better when he woke. In fact he felt better than he had in days. In weeks. He felt stronger and free — rootless, but in a good way.

'You're not going out, are you?' Larissa said when he came into the living room. She was fixing her hair in the mirror over the fireplace. 'Cammy, you can't! The Pusher's still out there. Stay here. You could stream a film on my box.'

'I'm not scared. At first thought I must be cursed, with people dying all around me. But then I realised something.'

'What are you talking about?'

He thought of the words to say it.

'It's never me, is it?' he said, smiling. 'He can't get me. Something's keeping me safe.'

She looked horrified. 'Cammy, no . . .'

'It's okay. Really, it is! And do you see what it means? It means *I*'m the only one who can get *him*.'

CHAPTER FORTY-SIX

9.08 p.m.

'Then let me come with you,' Ivan insisted, when Brenda said she was heading for the river as soon as she'd finished her drink. 'It's dark and freezing cold. It's not safe — whatever you say.'

She eyed him, then nodded to the handle of his walking stick, poking up beside their table. 'Aye, and much good you'd be in a crisis!'

'Well, there is that.' He looked at his hands, seeming hurt.

'Sorry,' she mumbled.

'I'm happy to help,' he said quietly.

She sipped her port and considered it. He'd slow her down, no denying it, but the company would be welcome — provided he didn't start lecturing her about tolerance zones and decriminalising the men who paid the women for sex. She was still upset from the phone call with the DCI. It just went to show: you couldn't trust anyone.

'All right,' she said. 'You can come. Get your coat on.'

CHAPTER FORTY-SEVEN

9.27 p.m.

Yes, Brenda had been at the Hook and Line, the barman told Lola. She'd left ten minutes ago with a friend of hers. No, he didn't know where they were headed.

Back in the car, she drove as slowly as she could along the two-mile north bank of the Clyde, between Glasgow Green in the east to the Scottish Exhibition Campus in the west, hunched close to the wheel as she peered about for any sign of Brenda or the boy.

At the SEC she turned round and drove back the way she came, briefly foiled in her bid to stick to the river by the one-way system at the Clutha Vaults. She paid special attention to shadowy places: doorways, the dark expanse under the railway lines coming south out of Central Station, and under the monstrous piles of the Kingston Bridge that carried the motorway over the river. The evening was unusually dry, if cold, and she drove with her windows down to get a better view. But two return trips revealed nothing.

She turned north off the Broomielaw into York Street and parked up in a space. This street and the ones that ran parallel to it comprised part of the Drag, but right now it was deserted. Glass office buildings loomed darkly on all sides. She listened to the ranting voicemail Tom had left her earlier then deleted it. Trust Izatt to barge in and upset everyone. She groaned, but the milk was spilled.

She cracked open her last can of Hyperdrive and took a swig. She'd promised herself this would be her last can, so she meant to enjoy it. Another mouthful and she clicked into her text messages and read DS Anna Vaughan's first.

Meeting with Jack Everett (Gouger) and Dougie Latimer (ex-Chronicle) fixed for you and me 9 a.m. tomorrow at Everett's place. Any prob-lems, let me know.

A follow-up text gave the address of a flat in Battlefield.

See you there, Lola replied.

She realised someone was standing by the car. A tall, thin, scantily clad woman. She seemed edgy, checking up and down the street, then bent, peering into the car.

Lola rolled down her window.

'What you looking for?' the woman asked.

'Nothing,' Lola said sharply, shocked as she realised the woman was offering her sex.

'You sure?' She was very young — twenty at most — and gauntly thin with bad skin poorly concealed by powdery make-up.

'I'm sure. Are you all right? You must be freezing.'

The girl was already backing off, stepping towards the river.

Lola got out of the car. The girl spun sharply round and faced her, eyes wide and wary.

'Can I talk to you?' Lola called, and the girl's expression shifted quickly from fear to scorn.

'You from the church or something?'

'What? No! I'm looking for someone. A friend.'

'Not looking very hard, sat in your car on your phone!'

'Fair point . . .'

'Who's your friend?' She came a step closer. She had simply styled shoulder-length hair and beautiful eyes, heavily defined to emphasise their almond shape.

'Cammy Leavey.'

The girl frowned.

'D'you know him?' Lola said.

The young woman's eyes roved the dark street as if to place him. 'Tiffany's wee pal? Young skinny lad?'

'That sounds like him. When did you last see him?'

'Not sure. Who are you?'

'A friend.'

'Social worker?'

'No. Police.'

The girl's chin went defiantly up and she folded her arms and brought her shoulders together.

'What's your name?' Lola tried.

'Doesn't matter.'

'Look, I want to help him. He's not in trouble, but he could be in danger.'

That seemed to get through, but the girl quickly recovered herself. 'Cammy can look after himself.'

'You do know him, then?'

She shrugged and looked miffed to be caught out.

'You're not Larissa, are you?'

'*Larissa?*' She laughed. 'Larissa's ancient. At least thirty-five, whatever she says.'

'I'd like to talk to her. Do you know where she is? It's to help Cammy.'

That got through, Lola could tell. The woman looked at her shoes, red stilettos, and scuffed the heels a bit. 'I saw her earlier.'

'Where?'

She hooked her head to indicate the direction of the river.

'Can you take me to her?'

'I said I saw her earlier. Doesn't mean she'll still be there.'

'Have you got a number for her?'

'No. She was on the south bank, other side of the Squiggly Bridge.'

'When was this?'

The girl checked her phone. 'Half an hour ago, I reckon.'

'Thank you. Tell me your name. Just so I know who helped me.'

'Amanda,' she said, a smile touching her lips for the first time. 'Most people call me Mandy.'

'Well, thank you, Mandy. I'm very grateful.'

CHAPTER FORTY-EIGHT

9.42 p.m.

'Shield me,' Brenda said sharply, turning her face as a car passed them on the Broomielaw.

'What's wrong?'

'Someone I don't want to see, that's all.'

Ivan turned his body and Brenda leaned close to him. Anyone passing might think they were a couple enjoying a cuddle on a chilly night.

A few moments passed and she peered past Ivan's shoulder. Yes, it was her, the chief inspector. She'd appeared from one of the streets of offices running north from the river and hurried across the dual carriageway, heading for the curving footbridge. Even at this distance she could see DCI Harris looked a mess. Her expression was harassed, her short dark hair disarranged as though she'd just woken up. Well, Brenda hoped she was unhappy. She'd lied to her — to Tom too. Those cosy questions had all been an act. She watched as the woman crossed the bridge to the south bank.

'All right now?' Ivan asked as she relaxed a bit.

'Aye, I'm all right.' She sucked hard at the e-cigarette and blew a cloud into the cold night air.

'This way?' He pointed with his stick.

'No. I think we'll start along here.' She waved towards the motorway bridge.

'How?' He seemed dismayed.

'Look, you offered to come! If you don't want to go any further, you can go back to the pub.'

'All right, all right.' He gave her a wee smile. 'After you.'

She led the way to the concrete piles of the bridge.

'This is where the old bus station was, isn't it?' he said.

'Aye, up there.' She peered about, eyes like lasers scanning, scanning.

They moved on, as far as the new blocks of flats. There was something on at the Arena. Booming music filled the air. In an hour or so this area would be swarming with people leaving the venue, walking into town. Cabs and buses would block the roads.

'This is no good,' she snapped suddenly.

'So now she realises!' Ivan chuckled, but he was breathless. They'd walked about a mile so far, and him with his bad knee. Well, tough. It was up to him to bloody well keep up.

Back east along the Broomielaw they came to the Squiggly Bridge. Brenda lurked among the ratty beeches and peered about for the chief inspector but saw no sign of her.

'Come on.'

They crossed the bridge, Brenda marching ahead, Ivan shuffling after. He wanted to stand in the middle and look up and down the water, at the lights. She waited on the south bank, vaping and muttering curses at his slowness.

She led him impatiently east along the newly landscaped quays and Carlton Place. Past the Sheriff Court, she turned onto the Victoria Bridge and began to cross the river. Part way across she realised Ivan was no longer moving. She stopped, ready to bark at him to call it a night and get back to his beer, when she saw him at the parapet, leaning on his stick, looking north and along Clyde Street, where the old railway line crossed the river. It was on that strip of the bank that Cammy had seen J.P. McCrae be attacked.

'*Look*,' he hissed, and his eyes were wide and frightened.

The north bank appeared deserted, but for one tall, hooded figure — male, surely, at that height — moving steadily westward. He was in dark clothes and his hands were gloved.

'My God,' Brenda whispered. Her face was trembling and her hands tingled as if the blood was leaving them. 'Is it him?'

'Hard to know,' Ivan said.

'He's coming this way.' She looked about. The place was deserted.

'He's stopped,' Ivan whispered.

He was right. The figure had stopped — and then he turned. Turned *this way*, looking diagonally across the water. With gloved hands he gripped the top bar of the white railings and looked *right at them*.

'Oh God.' A squeak of fear. Of terror. 'Oh Ivan.'

The bottom half of the figure's face was wrong — skeletal. And then she remembered the mask Cammy had described. Bones and teeth, he'd said. He was wearing glasses, but strange ones, or some kind of reflective visor.

'He knows we've seen him,' she managed to say. 'What do we do?'

'I don't know.' Ivan sounded gruff. Frightened too.

Suddenly the figure stepped back from the railings and was off, taking great strides away from them, east along Clyde Street, under the railway bridge in the direction of the Albert Bridge and Glasgow Green.

* * *

10.34 p.m.

'I'll call the police,' she said, and scrambled in her bag for her phone.

Then, her attention caught by something, she stopped and gazed back along the bridge towards to the south bank

— and there was Cammy, as slight as a teenage girl, but tall as a grown man, standing in a pool of streetlight at the south end of the bridge, watching them like a curious, frightened child.

'Oh, Cammy!' she called. She forgot the phone and hurried towards him, leaving Ivan behind.

'What are you doing here?' Cammy asked when she arrived and pulled him into a rough embrace.

'Looking for you. We saw him. We saw the Pusher — just now!'

'What?' His eyes seemed to sharpen.

'A man in a hood and mask. He saw us looking at him but he didn't care and then he disappeared.'

Cammy became quickly agitated, his breathing fast and shallow. 'Show me where.'

'Right *there*.' She jabbed a finger. 'We both saw him. I need to call the police.'

'They won't give a shit,' he said, eyes scanning the north bank. 'Which way did he go?'

'Greetings, young man,' Ivan said, approaching slowly on his stick.

Cammy ignored him, and growled to Brenda, 'He killed Warren.'

'What do you mean?'

'But Warren wasn't even his name. It was David. He lied to me. I was with him. I'd just got out of the car and now he's dead!'

'Oh, my poor love.' She grabbed him again and hugged him to her. 'You need to come home with me. You could be in danger.'

'So you can tell me how to live my life? I don't want to.'

'Oh, Cammy, please don't be like that! The police want to talk to you. We can talk to them together. We'll make them believe us.'

The boy pulled away, eyes scanning the river.

'Where did he go?' he demanded.

'Headed for the Green, I'd say,' Ivan said.

And suddenly the boy was off.

'Cammy, no!'

He slowed for a moment and turned, feet scuffing the pavement. 'I'm going to stop him,' he yelled back to her. 'I'm the only one who can!'

He had something in his hand, Brenda saw, and her breath caught in her throat. Then he was away, into the night. Her last glimpse of him: he was tearing over the bridge, heading for Clyde Street, towards the shadowy expanse of Glasgow Green.

CHAPTER FORTY-NINE

Friday 17 February
8.42 a.m.

Battlefield wasn't far from Lola's house but the traffic was always heavy at this time of day, so she set off in plenty of time. Anna called and she answered, hands-free, at the lights in Shawlands.

'It's Melda, boss. She's freaking out.'

'Oh?'

'About the CCTV operations centre. She says Councillor Caleb Munn has been on to top brass this morning, screaming about data protection and saying we have to back off right away. Melda says we need to contain things "at all costs" and she's setting up a meeting for you, her and Superintendent Wilde at ten this morning. I told her you have a full morning to buy you time. Whose side is she on, anyway?'

'Data protection? Ridiculous.' She was blinking and dizzy with tiredness, and craving a Hyperdrive. She hoped Jack Everett would have coffee.

'What do you want me to say, boss?'

'Make them wait. Tell them one o'clock.'

* * *

9.05 a.m.

'What do I think?' Jack Everett tilted his head, pushed out his bottom lip and rocked back in his chair. 'It's my considered view there's a serial killer at work. One nobody seems to want to acknowledge, let alone catch.' He turned to eye his pal Dougie Latimer beside him. 'Dougie?'

Dougie Latimer nodded thoughtfully, eyes like slits. 'Couldn't put it clearer if I tried,' he murmured.

Jack, editor of the *Gouger*, the gossipy Glasgow newspaper that specialised in reporting on underworld crime, was a round little man in his fifties with a big head and no neck. He was a Londoner and still sounded the part, despite having lived in Glasgow for thirty years. They were in his flat, crammed round his kitchen table: Lola, Anna and the two men. There was a strong smell of last night's Indian takeaway. Upstairs someone was drilling. Dougie, recently retired from the crime desk at the *Chronicle*, was older, neat, wire thin and tanned the colour of mahogany. He was just back from three months at his place on the Costa del Sol. The pristine Pringle sweater vest gave him away as a golfer.

'And as for proof?' Lola asked Jack.

'I'd say we have evidence rather than proof.' He knitted his plump fingers on the table before him. 'The stories I've published are the tip of the iceberg. Say, twenty per cent of the material we've gathered. The rest I've held back. Some of it's circumstantial, some speculative. And some of it's sensitive and the families don't want me to publish it. There are more witnesses than you'd expect. There are photos too, and at least one video, though it's fairly poor quality. But despite all that, *no one wants to know.*'

'No one in the police, you mean?'

'Exactly.'

Dougie Latimer made a groaning noise. 'Brick wall every time.'

'Could you be wrong?' Lola asked.

'Yes,' Jack said. 'Neither of us is pig-headed enough to claim only we can see the truth. Of course we could be wrong. But . . . we haven't seen any evidence that we are. Not yet.'

Lola described the task force she would lead, that she intended to examine all the evidence available and speak to as many people as she could, with a view to possibly opening an official enquiry into the deaths.

'We'd be happy to help,' Jack said.

Anna took out copies of the list of possible Pusher victims from a plastic wallet. She drew their attention to a couple of gaps.

The men took the sheets, Dougie taking a few moments to find his glasses first.

'Looks about right,' Jack murmured, then caught himself. He leaned into his pal, and seemed to point at a name halfway down the list. Lola didn't catch his murmured words. Dougie seemed to assent.

'As DS Vaughan says, we'd welcome any corrections you could give us.'

Jack frowned at the page again. Drilling reverberated from upstairs. It reminded Lola of the dentist's.

Jack cleared his throat. 'The unknown chap who might or might not be Polish.'

'What about him?'

'We know his name — or we think we know it. He was Czech, but his mother was Polish, which explains the Polish tattoo.'

He shifted in his chair and reached down to his side.

'Everything we've learned is in here,' he said, bringing up a Lidl bag and lifting out a lever arch file. It was fat and stuffed with paper and dividers. Corners of ratty-looking plastic wallets poked out here and there. Lola had to restrain herself from reaching for it. 'It's everything Dougie and I have uncovered over the years — individually or working together. All of it was shared with one or other of us in confidence or for specific use in a story. The families have given

Dougie and me permission to share information with one another.'

The unspoken implication was clear.

'You could go back to the families and ask if you can share it with us. Surely?'

'We could,' Jack agreed, eyes on Dougie. 'Have you been in touch with Yvonne Craigie? She of the Facebook families group?'

'We're seeing her tomorrow.'

'She might be a quicker route to some of the families, though of course not all of them are in her group.' He appraised Anna's matrix again, then nodded, as if to lock in his statement.

'What exactly do you think you can achieve?' Dougie Latimer asked now, with heavy scepticism.

'I want to find out if the Clyde Pusher exists,' Lola said, laying down her notepad. 'I can't do that without the families' help. I want to meet them. I want to take new, detailed statements about what happened to their loved ones.'

From what she could see, the statements taken by DS Ali Arshad, who'd investigated the first deaths, were detailed and comprehensive. After Neil Prine's death they became cursory, lacking in detail, if not downright full of holes. She'd sent an email first thing to Arshad at his new workplace, but got an out-of-office reply saying he was on leave, due back on Monday.

'I'd be interested in any new leads or contacts they might wish to share. Then I want to look at everything together, to analyse what we know and to find workable theories we can test. If I find reason to believe the Pusher is real I'll say so, publicly,' she said firmly, looking from Jack to Dougie and back again. 'Then I'll do my best to catch him.'

'You're very optimistic,' Jack said.

'Am I?'

'Your seniors won't want to listen. They'll pressure you. You'll find yourself rejecting the evidence of your own eyes and ears — to coin a phrase.'

She raised her eyebrows.

Jack shrugged. 'You'll start to wonder if it's worth the hassle. You'll find yourself wishing you were working on something else, and then, perhaps, an opportunity will come along and all this evidence — along with your fine intentions — will go into a folder like this.' He patted the stuffed file before him and smiled sadly. 'And the file will go on a shelf.'

Lola didn't speak for a few moments. At her side she could feel Anna writhing and trying to contain her anger.

'You might be right,' Lola said, reasonably enough. 'I might fail. But the way you talk, anyone would think you had money on it. I prefer to hope. Otherwise, what's the point?'

'I apologise.' Jack had the grace to look embarrassed. 'But you've got to understand the history. At some point you'll hit a wall too.'

'Tell me about this wall.' She folded her arms. 'I'm all ears.'

'There's a narrative,' he said. 'A script, if you like. It's in stone and nobody deviates from it.'

'"Suggestions there's a serial attacker are all nonsense"?' Lola said.

'Exactly.'

'But *why*?'

Jack thought about it. 'If I were as optimistic as you, I might say it's the result of well-intentioned people thinking they're doing the right thing. There's a community safety strategy.' He turned to Dougie. 'What's its full name? I can never remember.'

Dougie went into a notepad and squinted. 'The Community Safety and Neighbourhood Wellbeing Partnership Strategic Plan.'

'It was first published in 2015,' Jack said, 'and refreshed, hurriedly, at the end of 2018. It seems it was dreamed up by one of these arm's-length, multi-agency committees, and it's chaired by a particularly unsavoury individual who happens to be a city councillor.'

'Caleb Munn?' Lola said.

'Know him, do you?' He spoke drily, an eyebrow raised.

'I've met him. Why, what's the deal?'

'The council did some research a few years ago,' Jack said, sitting back in his chair, settling in for the tale. 'Its findings chimed with other, international research. It said that fear of crime affects people's mental wellbeing more than crime itself. Makes sense. If you're terrified of where you live and the people around you, you're going to be living on your nerves. So that's where this so-called strategic plan focuses its main actions: on trying to reduce people's fear. There's been a concerted effort to get all the public services — health centres, social services, education — talking about "safe and thriving communities". There's a communications plan attached to the strategy, and you'll have seen that bloody awful grinning face all over the city with the slogan: "Glasgow is safe and sound." If you look at the committee's minutes, all they bang on about is "Metric 01A", which says, "Fear of crime is reduced." The main indicator is a survey they carry out once a year, and which costs *tens of thousands*. Each year so far they've published a shiny report about how everything's great and getting better. *Actual* crime statistics are reported in what they call a "statistical annex", which isn't published.'

Lola stole a glance at Anna. Her eyes were wide and her nostrils flared.

'Let me get this straight,' Lola said, containing her own rage. 'You're saying the council and other agencies, including the police, are spinning crime statistics? As far as they're concerned, the fear of crime is going down, so that's a win?'

'Exactly.'

'It's true that some crime is reducing,' she said, 'but other types are getting worse year on year. Some of our communities aren't safe. That's a fact.'

'You don't need to tell us that,' Jack snorted.

She sat back, taking a moment to gather her thoughts, which were by now clamouring.

'So you think that's why the Clyde Pusher theory is being suppressed?'

'Yes.'

'You realise how far-fetched that sounds?'

Jack turned to his pal. 'Tell them what happened to you.'

'I had a story ready to go in December 2019,' the retired reporter said, eyes narrow again. 'It was a month or so after Mark Brodie was pulled from the river down at the BBC. His mum is the one who'd received the strange phone call. She and Mark's brothers weren't happy with the police. She felt they didn't believe her and she was talking about putting in a complaint. I spent time with her. I was there at her council flat in Wester Hailes when she got a visit from a detective sergeant from Glasgow. She asked me to stay and said I was "a friend of the family". He hadn't a clue who I was. This detective started off all deferential and concerned. Then he said his colleagues had learned she was planning to make a complaint. He said that could interfere with the investigation into her son's death. At that point, I couldn't help myself and I asked for an explanation. He said that "several unhelpful individuals" — those were his words — were in the business of spinning a conspiracy that there was an attacker targeting gay men in Glasgow. That there was no evidence of this and that it was upsetting some very influential people. If she pursued the complaint, she might find her son Mark's reputation "tarnished" publicly.'

'"Tarnished publicly"?' Anna asked sharply.

'What was this sergeant's name?' Lola asked.

'Lachlan Gray,' Dougie said sourly. 'Know him?'

'Yes,' she said.

'I was biting my tongue pretty hard,' the ex-reporter said now. 'I asked what he meant as calmly as I could. He said, "Your Mark had some very interesting images on his phone." That he'd seen them but he was inclined to be discreet because the impact of their becoming public could add to his loved ones' distress.'

'What happened?' She felt cold with shock.

'Mrs Brodie was upset. Panicking, you know? I asked to see evidence of these images. The detective refused. I said I would advise Mrs Brodie to hire a solicitor and that this solicitor would request to see the images. At which point he became . . . edgy. I told him who I was. Then it was his turn to panic and he left. I was so shocked, I went straight back to Glasgow and spoke to my editor. He called Legal and we discussed what to do. At which point things took an even darker turn.'

Lola steeled herself.

'The *Chronicle* is owned by the Reverb Group, a public limited company. One individual owns fifty-one per cent of the shares.'

He paused and Lola waited.

'His name is Lawrie Trimble. He got on to Reverb's CEO that morning. In the middle of the meeting, the CEO called the office and demanded to speak to my editor. He left the room to take the call. He came back a few minutes later. Bone-white, I think you could say. He said we were being accused of spinning conspiracy theories and thus failing to meet basic journalistic standards. My editor had been instructed to cease all reporting on the Clyde Pusher "conspiracy" or lose his job. I believe — though I have no evidence to the effect — he might have been threatened with more than that.'

Dougie Latimer sat back and rubbed his face with his hands. He looked tired and suddenly quite frail.

'Our editor has a mortgage, a family and enough stress on his plate. I understand why he did what he did. I didn't agree with it. I tried to take my story elsewhere, but no one would touch it. And so I retired to play golf in the sunshine. And then one day I got an email from this gentleman beside me, and we joined forces.'

'What do you know about this Lawrie Trimble?' Lola asked.

The men exchanged quick glances. Jack shrugged, happy to defer to Dougie.

'He made his money in software in the early 2000s,' Dougie said. He named the company. Lola hadn't heard of it. 'His business partner was Caleb Munn.'

Lola stared. She looked at Anna, then back at the two men. 'You're saying . . .'

'That a pal of the city councillor with responsibility for community safety managed to stop the city's biggest paper reporting on the crime of murder.'

The drilling from upstairs reached a new intensity.

'*Why?*' Lola said. 'No one — not even the most fanatical political spin merchant would *cover up murder*.'

'They might,' Jack said, 'if they had a personal interest.'

'If they were the killer, you mean?' Lola said with a laugh.

'Not that, no.'

'Then what?'

'Are you speaking to Munn?'

'Today, as it happens.'

'Weigh in on him. He's a nasty piece of work — a dangerous one, too — and you might come away with nothing. If you do, come back to us. We might be able to persuade someone to help fill in some of the gaps. Whether she'll go on the record or not, it's hard to say.'

'Who is she?'

'Lips are sealed for now, sorry.'

Time was getting on. Jack and Dougie promised to seek their contacts' permission to hand over their data.

'Who is it?' Anna asked the men as they were preparing to leave. 'The Pusher? You must have some idea.'

'None,' Jack said. 'Honest truth. The man must be a psychopath, driven by some compulsion. Probably someone who hates gays — possibly because he's gay himself but can't admit it. Talk to a shrink. Ask for one of these forensic profiles you can get.'

'Do you think the river has any kind of significance?' she asked.

The two men looked at one another.

'Can't see why,' Jack said with a shrug. 'The river's a dead thing, isn't it? Useless nowadays.' He saw her face and explained: 'It used to be a channel for bringing goods into the heart of the city. Now it's just an obstacle you need to cross.

The council keeps trying to gentrify the walkways, but it's never going to be Paris or Rome. At least the Pusher's making use of it — the Clyde is now a resource for killers.

'What I do know is this,' he went on, leaning forward, finger stabbing the tabletop. 'Not one of the Pusher's crimes has been captured on CCTV — or if it has, the footage doesn't exist. He either knows how to avoid being recorded, or knows how to wipe the tapes. He either works there or knows someone who does. And again, you know who's in charge of that whole operation.'

CHAPTER FIFTY

10.40 a.m.

'Email from Kirstie,' Anna said, eyes on her phone as they emerged from Jack Everett's tenement block. 'She's seen Gregor Mackinnon, Michael's dad, and right now she's on her way to talk to Saeeda Hussain, widow of Khalid. She'll fill us in later. There's a message from Janey, as well,' Anna said. 'Says she's about to go talk to a Ms Brenda Cheney. Ms Cheney and a friend claim they spotted the Pusher on Clyde Street late last night. She rang it in last night and a duty sergeant called to see her and the friend later on. The sergeant passed it across to us this morning.'

'Call Janey back,' Lola said quickly. 'Ask where she is and tell her I'll come along, but not to tell Brenda beforehand.'

'Boss.'

'Meanwhile, can you and Kirstie try to find out everything you can about Caleb Munn? Also take a look at that Trimble guy. Don't breathe a word to DS Gray. I don't know what he's up to, but I want him off the case ASAP.'

* * *

11.12 a.m.

'I've nothing to say to you,' Brenda said, breathing hard.

'This is murder, Brenda,' Lola said, walking into the flat. 'You have to put your anger aside and tell us what you saw.'

The woman glowered.

'You want the Pusher caught, don't you? Every minute he's still out there another young man is at risk. It could be Cammy next.'

Brenda took a drag of her e-cigarette then, furious-eyed, turned and led the way into her living room.

Janey Carstairs asked questions and Lola chipped in when she needed to, enquiring in particular about the friend she had been with, Mr Parry.

'He's pretty much an invalid, but he insisted on coming with me. I thought he was a fool, but I'm rather glad he was there now. Another witness, see?'

'Did Cammy say he'd seen the man too?' she asked when Brenda had finished.

She pushed out her bottom lip. 'I'm sure he hadn't. He seemed surprised and took after him. He—' She caught herself.

'He what, Brenda?'

The woman closed her eyes in regret and said quietly, 'I think he had a knife.'

'Who? The Pusher or Cammy?'

'Cammy.'

'Did he show it to you?'

She shook her head. 'He had it in his hand as he ran off. At least I think it was a knife.' She looked sick from the revelation.

'I'm going to leave you now,' Lola said. 'DC Carstairs here will take a full statement from you. Tell her everything you remember about the man's appearance.'

Brenda nodded.

'Quick word?' Lola said to Janey Carstairs, and the constable followed her into the hallway. 'Get hold of Ivan Parry,' she said quietly. 'We're looking for a full statement. I'm interested in timings and exactly where the man was standing. Right, I'm off back to base.'

CHAPTER FIFTY-ONE

11.45 a.m.

'You need to eat something,' Larissa pleaded, sounding as if she was about to cry.

'I'm not hungry,' Cammy told her from the kitchen table. 'I'll eat when I want to.' Then he saw the hurt on her face. 'Sorry.' He let his head droop onto his arms on the table.

It was true, he wasn't a bit hungry. He'd had chips and gravy at nineish last night and nothing since. His mind and body had one preoccupation: the shit who'd killed Dec, Warren and any number of others.

Not that he cared about Warren, because *fuck him*.

Warren . . .

Suddenly he was crying — painful, pealing sobs that wracked him and made his ribs hurt. Larissa was round his side of the table in a second, her thin arms tugging at his shoulders. He let her hold him. She smelled of soap and body lotion. Like him, she was only just up, but while she'd been out working, earning money, he'd spent the night roaming the streets, a blade tucked up his sleeve, waiting to execute a killer.

Except he hadn't found him. Once again he'd failed. People were dead because of him. If he couldn't make the killer pay, what right did he have to survive?

'You poor, poor lamb,' Larissa cooed.

He'd told her about it, here at this table when she'd come in just before 5 a.m. He'd been working his way through a bottle of her vodka. She didn't even mind. She'd joined him in a drink and they'd smoked her cigarettes till six, when tiredness finally overcame them.

'You need some help,' she said now, pulling out of the embrace so she could look him in the eyes.

'Help from who? Don't say the polis.'

'Cammy, love, you can't stay here long-term. Chris won't wear it. I'm sorry, but you knew that. There was a woman polis out on the Drag last night. Mandy talked to her. She said she seemed worried about you. Mandy thought she was genuine.'

'Mandy's an idiot.'

'No she's not! And neither am I, so will you listen to me?'

He blinked. 'What was she like, the woman?'

'I don't know. Older, Mandy said. Mandy said she was kind to her. Said she went off across the Squiggly Bridge, like she really meant to find you.'

He sat up, thinking about it. Wondering if she was the same detective he'd met at Brenda's. He'd liked her. She had a friendly, open face and kind, dark green eyes that sparkled as she listened to you.

'They'll arrest me.'

'Maybe,' Larissa said. 'But they'll let you go. They'll know you're telling the truth. Cammy, you're the victim here. You *need help*.'

CHAPTER FIFTY-TWO

12.25 p.m.

Lola met Kirstie in a corner of the canteen over bowls of lentil soup.

'Khalid Hussain was walking home from a late shift at the Royal Infirmary,' Kirstie said. 'He was too late for trains and there were no cabs because it was December and everyone was going home from Christmas parties. Home was in Pollokshields, so the route makes sense: he'd have come down the High Street to the Tron, then down the Saltmarket to the river. That's where he was attacked.'

'She thinks it was random?' Lola asked, tearing a granary bread roll.

'Completely. She was adamant: Khalid wasn't gay or bisexual.'

'She would say that.'

'She had a friend with her,' Kirstie said. 'Irfan Abbas. He's gay, a dancer. He grew up with Khalid — they were best friends. He swears it too. He says he fancied Khalid for years and even tried it on. He said Khalid was "as straight as they come".'

'So the attacker — the Pusher, if it was him — saw a man walking alone and went for him. Does that make it a mistake, or is he becoming less selective? Does it no longer matter to him who he kills?' She mopped soup from the bottom of her bowl with a piece of bread roll and ate it, thinking about what it might mean. 'You spoke to Michael Mackinnon's dad as well, didn't you?'

'He's very unhappy. Believes we've failed him and his son. He thinks the whole investigation into his son's death was prejudiced by DS Gray. He called him a "supercilious creep".'

It seemed a fair judgement to Lola but she said nothing.

'He's angry. Talking about suing.'

'Well, that's up to him,' Lola said, but with a twinge of sympathy. 'Did either of them mention getting a phone call about the time their relatives died?'

'No, boss. But looking at the records, the victims had their phones on them when they were brought out of the river. Maybe Mark Brodie's phone simply fell onto the pavement during the attack, and the attacker took the opportunity to use it to play a cruel trick.'

'You could be right.'

She checked the time on her own phone.

'I'm seeing Superintendent Wilde in fifteen minutes,' she told Kirstie. 'Would you mind leaving me? I need to get my thoughts focused.'

CHAPTER FIFTY-THREE

1.01 p.m.

They met in Wilde's office on the third floor. Wilde looked angry — though less furious than Melda Brodick sitting beside him, bug-eyed with rage.

'Sit down, please, DCI Harris,' Wilde started.

Lola sat and smiled pleasantly at Brodick.

'I can't overstate the sensitivity required in the line of enquiry you seem intent on pursuing,' Wilde began. It sounded rehearsed. Lola could see he was nervous.

'Which particular line of enquiry would that be, sir?' she asked.

'The involvement of colleagues at the CCTV operations centre,' he said.

Lola raised an eyebrow. 'Are they strictly our colleagues, sir? Council employees, I would have thought. I know the centre is managed within a partnership, but the folk there aren't on the payroll, are they?'

'Partnership is critical in delivering outcomes across our shared strategic agenda,' Wilde said.

Lola paused, trying not to laugh at the spray of jargon. 'Sorry, sir. Could you explain?'

He went puce and looked to his colleague.

'We value our critical partnership with the council,' Brodick said. 'It's key to achieving our strategic vision.'

'You mean: don't piss them off?'

Brodick narrowed her eyes and pushed out her lips. She despised Lola and Lola was fine with that.

'I don't see the problem,' Lola said now. 'That place is indicated in a murder enquiry. A *major* enquiry going back several years. It provides a public service and it has to be accountable. This is about Councillor Munn, isn't it? Him and that metric of his. "Reducing fear of crime"? Let's say the garden's rosy and suddenly it is?'

Brodick took a breath as if to speak but Lola cut her off.

'I've talked to Dougie Latimer today. Know the name? He was a crime reporter at the *Chronicle*. He had a big story about the Pusher ready to go, but he was gagged. Just so happens a pal of Munn's — guy named Trimble — is the *Chronicle*'s majority shareholder.'

Wilde's eyebrows lifted a millimetre. News to him, then.

'That . . . *ludicrous*!' Brodick spluttered, eyes on Wilde as if to demand support. 'Offensive and slanderous if spoken outside this room.'

'You're in with Munn, aren't you?' Lola asked her calmly.

It was Brodick's turn to go red. 'Implying what, exactly?'

'You tell me. You seem very concerned to protect him from any criticism, that's all.'

'DCI Harris,' Wilde warned.

Brodick flushed, which was nice to see.

'The community safety strategy is a key framework for delivery,' Brodick said, high-pitched and defensive. 'Councillor Munn is the kingpin. He's the *brand*!'

'The "brand"?' Lola said, trying not to laugh. 'The brand that's about telling people to look the other way? That grieving families should disbelieve evidence about how their relatives died?'

Fast footsteps sounded outside the meeting room and there was a rap at the door.

Before Wilde could speak the door opened and Councillor Caleb Munn slipped inside and closed the door behind him, then eyeballed them and grinned his rictus grin.

'*Caleb!*' Brodick cooed, rising.

Munn ignored her. He faced Lola, blinking fast, the pupils of his strange pale eyes like black holes.

'You're trying to undermine our city's integrity as a safe place,' he said, coming uncomfortably close to her. She could feel his breath on her face.

'We weren't expecting you, Caleb,' Wilde said, getting up and neatly blocking him.

'Oh?' Munn raised an eyebrow at Brodick, who looked away, her face inscrutable. It occurred to Lola that Brodick had tipped him off that the meeting was taking place. Had she invited him to turn up?

'Won't you have a seat?' Wilde said now.

He manoeuvred Munn into a chair, but all the time he eyeballed Lola, blinking away. The pink tip of his tongue came out and wetted his lips.

Lola maintained a blank expression of polite expectation.

'Caleb, we know you're upset,' Wilde said calmly.

Munn rounded on him, sitting on the edge of his seat. His breath was coming in little gasps. Was he unwell, Lola wondered? He was unhinged, certainly.

'You might like to instruct this individual to back off, Wilde,' Munn said. 'She answers to you, doesn't she? You've got to tell *her*—' he jabbed a finger in Lola's direction — 'to leave this alone. Everything is quite fine here!'

Brodick was gazing contemptuously at Lola over Munn's shoulder, as if Lola was responsible for the man's state of upset. Lola raised a single eyebrow back at her and Brodick's eyes narrowed.

Wilde said, 'Caleb, we're treading very carefully. We're mindful of the sensitivities of the outcomes of the strategic plan.'

Brodick said smoothly, 'Everything will be managed to reduce alarm and to maintain relations with all stakeholders.'

'Meaning what?' Lola demanded of her, causing the woman to bridle.

'Meaning that any disruption will be minimised, in order to protect work programme schedules.'

'I don't understand anything you're saying,' Lola said. 'I'm sorry, I don't. It's just words and then more words.'

'DCI Harris . . .' Wilde began.

'Sorry, sir, but all I'm hearing is mince. "Outcomes", "stakeholders", "delivery partnerships". When it boils down to it, it's just about fooling poor people in dangerous neighbourhoods into being less afraid of the criminal gangs roaming the streets.' She heard her voice starting to rise. 'You're talking about covering up *murder* to make a committee look good!'

Wilde looked panicked, Brodick furious, while Munn began to tremble.

'Am I right?' she demanded of Munn. 'Or is there something else going on? Something behind all the smoke and mirrors.'

'You're on very thin ice, miss,' Munn spat. 'Tell her, Wilde! Tell her she's on thin ice!'

Lola said, 'Come on, what's really going on?'

Wilde was eyeing Lola with a kind of curious alarm, as if he'd finally realised she was onto something, while at the same time wishing the earth would swallow him up.

Munn was about to speak but Brodick hushed him.

'Let him speak,' Lola snapped at her.

'I . . . I don't have to listen to this,' Munn gabbled out, starting to rise. He turned on the superintendent. 'This is your responsibility, Wilde.'

'Nothing and no one is off limits, Caleb,' Wilde said steadily.

Lola stared at her boss with cautious hope.

'You or your committee have nothing to hide, have you?' Wilde went on. 'Because the way you're reacting, Caleb, I'm asking myself questions.'

Munn made as if to speak but couldn't. Brodick was at his back, glaring daggers at Wilde now. She was protecting

Munn, Lola realised. Protecting not his ego but his emotional wellbeing.

She recalled Jack Everett's words. He'd said Munn was hard but could be pushed; and that if it didn't work, someone else — he'd talked about a "she" — might be willing to fill in some gaps. And suddenly an idea occurred to her.

'You knew one of the victims, didn't you?' Lola said. 'Which one was it?'

The horror on the man's face told her she was right.

'Angus!' Brodick hissed at Wilde, who looked as panicked as the Comms director.

'Caleb,' Wilde began, 'if there's something we should know . . .'

Munn got to his feet again. His white face seemed to sag off its bones.

'I've had enough of this,' he managed to roar as he scrabbled for the door handle. '*Enough!*'

CHAPTER FIFTY-FOUR

1.50 p.m.

Ivan Parry had volunteered to come to Stewart Street to give his statement, so once Lola had calmed down after the confrontation with Munn, she went to join him and Janey Carstairs in the interview room. Janey was just writing down the last sentence of Parry's statement.

'Thank you for coming in, Mr Parry,' Lola said, eyes on the man's walking stick as she took a seat. 'We could have come to you. Saved you the trip.'

'Oh, it's no trouble at all,' the man said, leaning forward, elbows on the table, fingers knitted. He was excited to be here, Lola realised, and felt a brief pang of pity. 'I told your colleague here—' he nodded to Janey — 'anything that gets me out of the flat is welcome. And I need to exercise the limbs.'

He was in his early fifties, Lola estimated, but dressed much older in a beige anorak and slacks, like the stereotype of a pensioner. Brenda had described him as an invalid but he looked well enough to Lola, despite the stick he walked with.

'I'm waiting for a knee op,' he said, as if reading her mind. 'Pavements are fine if I take my time. Stairs are a different matter.'

He'd been in the army as a young man, he explained. 'It takes its toll on your joints. Of course, lots of rugby at a boarding school probably didn't help either. Very ageing, rugby.'

'May I?' Lola said, hand out for the pages that constituted the man's statement. She read through it, but the words swam a bit, despite Janey's neatly rounded handwriting. She blinked her dry eyes, and managed to note Parry's address in Finnieston.

'The man's face,' Lola said to Parry, reading over his description of the individual he and Brenda had spotted across the river. 'Could you see his eyes?'

'His eyes? Oh . . .' He appeared puzzled and gazed about the room as if his memories were pasted to the walls. 'His eyes. He . . . I couldn't see them. No, that's right! He was wearing glasses, but big ones, reflective almost.'

It chimed with what Brenda had told them.

Lola handed the pages back to Janey with a look the constable understood. She added a note at the end of the statement.

'How long have you known Brenda Cheney?' Lola asked, conversationally.

'Oh, a good many years! Fifteen or more. Yes, that's right. We worked together. I took early retirement, for medical reasons. My wife, you see. She was ill. She . . . died.'

'I'm sorry.'

'The stress of that. I wonder sometimes if I should have gone back afterwards. Something to fill the days.' His face crumpled but he regained control. 'Lynnie was everything to me.'

'Did you have children?'

'No. Sadly.'

'You met Cameron Leavey, Ms Cheney's young friend, down by the river last night. Had you met him before?'

'No, and I'd hardly call last night a meeting.'

'You'd heard Brenda talk about him before, though?'

'He's one of her protégés. She cares very deeply, especially for the younger ones. The boy seemed keyed up.'

Lola looked to Janey, who signalled with a nod that she had nothing further to ask.

'Can one of my officers give you a lift somewhere, Mr Parry?'

'No! But thank you. In any case, it's all downhill from here — as they say!' He chuckled at his own joke.

CHAPTER FIFTY-FIVE

2.37 p.m.

Shannon Grant, supervisor of the CCTV operations centre, welcomed Lola and Anna in the main reception. She'd just had a call from Councillor Munn's PA, she explained, a little awkwardly, assuring her the 'data protection issue' had been clarified and that she should cooperate with the enquiry. She looked and sounded relieved.

They followed her into a meeting room on the ground floor.

'I'll start with the bad news,' the supervisor said. 'What you've got to understand is that our human-eye-to-camera ratio is low, to put it mildly. At most you'd find one supervisor and three officers in here — that's it — and they're responsible for monitoring images from over four hundred cameras. Calls from your colleagues can come in at any time and we have to switch the screens to view a particular street or shopping arcade or stairwell within seconds. We go between computer terminals. Friday and Saturday nights are a nightmare every week. Then there are football matches. An Old Firm game on a Saturday — I'm sure you can imagine.'

Lola could. 'So, at any one time,' she said, summing up, '*anyone* who's on duty could have access to any of the terminals?'

'Exactly that.' Grant's face darkened. 'I can tell you, however,' she began, 'that the cameras at the bottom of Stockwell Street and the Saltmarket were moved at 2.21 on Saturday afternoon. I reviewed the footage myself and the time they were turned away — but there's no way of knowing precisely who moved them.'

'Who was on duty then?'

'I was. So was Pauline Knox, along with Quilan MacDonald and Walter Clark.'

So one of those three people — four if you counted Grant — had tampered with those cameras. To help the Pusher, either willingly or under duress? Or worse? If the person who moved the cameras was the Pusher, and if the Pusher was male, then it was MacDonald or Clark.

They needed to interview the four, starting with the men — and fast.

'Who's on duty just now?' she asked.

'Pauline's here along with two other officers, Danny and Craig. Walter Clark's on night shift; he's due in at eight. He'll probably be here at quarter to. He's so conscientious.' She shifted in her chair, eyes down, as if she was stalling for time. 'I'm sure he'd be happy to help.'

'And Quilan MacDonald?'

The supervisor looked up sheepishly and bit her lip. 'Quil's been off sick the last two days,' she said. 'He didn't even phone, just texted to say he was ill and couldn't come in. In all the years he's worked here, I've never known him not come in before.'

* * *

3.05 p.m.

Shannon Grant gave them contact details for Quilan MacDonald and Walter Clark. She didn't seem surprised that they weren't interested in talking to Pauline Knox yet, even though she was on site.

'You think it's Quil, don't you?' she asked, no longer able to contain herself.

'We can't say,' Lola said.

'He's such a docile guy.' She seemed pained by the idea. 'I mean he's big, but he's a softy. Gentle. I should probably tell you he's autistic — he might panic when you talk to him. Of course, neurodiversity can be a superpower in a job like this. All that information in front of you, having to spot minute anomalies, patterns.'

'You like him, don't you?'

Grant nodded and looked utterly miserable. 'He was in trouble once before,' she said quietly now. 'I don't know the details, but . . . I expect you'll be about to find out about that, won't you?'

'I expect so,' Lola said. She gave Anna a meaningful look. Anna nodded to say she'd get on to it.

Lola asked Grant to review footage from cameras in streets and public areas around Clyde Street in the hours before and after the attack, looking for evidence of anyone who might be the Pusher and to isolate clips for Lola and her team to examine. Grant said she'd see to the task herself.

Lola reminded the supervisor to keep the contents of their discussion confidential, then asked if she and Anna could use the meeting room for a few more minutes on their own.

'Priority Quilan MacDonald?' Anna asked when they were alone, perched coiled and ready on the edge of her seat.

'Yes. Go there with a constable and bring him in. We'd better bring Clark in too. We can talk to Pauline Knox after we've interviewed the men. If there's something to corroborate she might be able to help.'

She sat back, thinking, still pushing against the wall of weariness.

'Was there something else, boss?' Anna said, studying her with concern.

'We've been working on this case less than forty-eight hours — no time at all — and we've already got two names, one of whom seems indicated. This is all it would have taken: someone to take a good look at the evidence and ask a few sticky questions. This could have been solved years ago, but instead people looked away. They didn't want to know. And more young men died. Munn must be behind the cover-up and I want to know why.'

She checked the time on her phone.

'I'll see you back at HQ. Wait for me before interviewing either of the suspects. Meantime, I'm meeting a man in a bar.'

CHAPTER FIFTY-SIX

3.30 p.m.

Tom's friend Stuey had said the Lo Rent Bar in Miller Street would be quiet at this time, and it was. Apart from two women and the barman, they were the only people in the dark basement.

Stuey was in his thirties, short, tubby and very friendly with a sharply trimmed goatee. He was a travel agent, he told Lola, and began trying to sell her the idea of a Mediterranean cruise.

'I don't have a lot of time,' she said.

'Oh! No bother.' Stuey became immediately very serious. 'What do you want to know?'

'Tom said you had theories about the Clyde Pusher.'

'I suppose I do . . . You think he's real, then?'

'I think he could be. Do you?'

'Of course he is. I thought the official line was that it was a load of nonsense.'

'Do you know who he is?'

'Not that, no.'

'Tom seemed to think you had ideas.'

'Maybe I do.'

He was being cagey now and Lola had no patience.

'Look, Stuey, I need all the gen. Nothing shocks me. Don't be embarrassed, just spill, okay?'

He seemed to relax.

'He was all over the apps for a while. Creepy guy. Called himself "Glasgow Fox". Nice profile pic, but probably nicked off the internet. Dark, handsome, flirty. Messaging anyone and everyone. The younger guys aren't taken in by that crap. They can spot a fake profile a mile off. But you get someone who's older, or a bit desperate, or just plain drunk, and they're easy prey.'

'When was this?'

'Few years back — 2016, 2017, something like that. And he wasn't on there long. He caught a victim that way. Might have been more than one.'

'Who?'

'Young lad called Drew Morris. You know the name?'

She nodded. Morris's was the second name on the list of potential victims of the Pusher.

'Nice lad. I met him once. Friend of a friend of a friend. Word is he was going to meet this guy at the guy's place by the river — and that was that. Word got round pretty quick about Glasgow Fox, let me tell you. He was online again the next night, chatting up guys. Folk told him to go fuck himself. That the polis were on to him.'

'Who reported it?'

'Oh, a couple of people. Gave statements, but it didn't come to anything. Folk tried reporting the profile to the developers as well, saying he might be a killer, but what do they care? Then he disappeared. No one saw him again. I mean, he might have come back with another profile. Frightening.'

'Did anyone get screenshots — anything like that?'

Stuey brightened. 'Like this, you mean?' He brought his phone out to show her.

He flicked through his photos until he found a screenshot of a profile from the Matey app and turned the screen to Lola. *Glasgow Fox, 36*, she read. The profile showed a young George

Clooney–esque man in a white shirt posing for the camera. The pose was slightly self-mocking, as was the man's smile. It was an appealing image, and one she imagined would work well.

Stuey flicked to the next image. This showed a two-way conversation in alternate colours. 'That's a convo my pal Vic had with Glasgow Fox,' he said. 'Glasgow Fox's chat's down the left side.'

Lola read.

—*U horny?*

—Aye a bit

—Where r u?

—Glas. Where u?

—G1. Can accommodate. Wanna meet?

—Mebbe. What u offerin?

—Good time 4 u.

—Lolol. That mean I'm gonna end up in the Clyde like Drew Morris?

'Vic took the screenshot just before Glasgow Fox and the chat disappeared. Touched a nerve, eh?'

'Was that the last anyone heard from him?' Lola asked.

'No, he was back a week or two later, new profile name, new photo. Same chat every time: "G1, can accommodate" and "Good time for you", but with a number "4".'

She gave Stuey back his phone.

'You're telling me,' she said after a moment, 'that it was well known on the gay scene in Glasgow that a murderer was trying to trap young men using a dating app? And people reported this?'

'Aye. To you lot and to the app's developers.' He eyed her. 'You seem shocked.'

'I am.'

'No one wanted to know,' he said. 'Lot of hard work — and who cares if it's gays getting killed anyway?'

'Could you send me these screenshots?'

'Aye, course.'

'Thanks. And I'm sorry no one listened. I'm going to do my best to make up for it.'

CHAPTER FIFTY-SEVEN

4.21 p.m.

Jack Everett had left Lola in the kitchen while he went to phone the woman who he claimed could fill in the gaps about Munn's behaviour, repeating as he went that he was promising nothing.

She checked her email and saw that Kirstie had sent her a scanned image of the interview Alec Bennett, thought to be the Pusher's only surviving victim, had given to the *Chronicle* — 'courtesy of Shuna Frain,' Kirstie had noted.

She began to scan the article, which included a photograph of a handsome but mournful-looking redhead, when Jack Everett returned from the other room.

'She's happy to talk to you,' he said, sounding relieved.
'Great! Maybe you could tell me a bit about her.'
'Her name's Rona Prine. Rona without an H.'

He spelled the surname, but Lola had already recognised it.

'She's the mother of one of the victims,' Jack said.
'Neil Prine,' Lola read aloud, consulting the list of victims, 'aged twenty-six, body found in the river at Renfrew.

Date of death assumed to be the seventeenth of September, 2018.' She looked up. 'And the connection to Munn?'

'Rona Prine and Caleb Munn were married. They divorced in the early 2000s. Neil was their son.'

* * *

4.38 p.m.

Before phoning Rona Prine from her car, Lola called Kirstie for an update. It was getting dark and rain clouds hung low in the sky.

'Walter Clark's at Stewart Street,' Kirstie told her. 'Anna says he's in a bit of a state but he's cooperating . . .'

'What about Quilan MacDonald?' Lola asked, sensing a 'but' before it came.

'Missing from home, boss. He lives with his mum and she hasn't seen or heard from him since yesterday morning. I'd say she's pretty worried. I'm outside the house in the car just now.'

'Put a "Wanted Missing" marker on PNC for him,' she told Kirstie.

It meant that if he was stopped and checked out by any officer, they'd know he was wanted. 'Put a note to arrest him as a suspect and have him brought to Stewart Street. Ask the mum for a list of any friends or family he might be with. Any places he likes to go.'

'Already got a couple of names, boss. A couple of photos too.'

'Thanks, Kirstie.'

Something wasn't right here. She could sense it. The idea that Quilan MacDonald was their man — it was too easy.

CHAPTER FIFTY-EIGHT

5.34 p.m.

'You want to talk about my son,' Rona Prine said.

'That's right, Ms Prine. About how Neil died — and about his father's reaction to his death.'

Rona Prine was a slender woman of sixty or so with finely cut and coloured hair and expensive clothes. They sat in the conservatory of her Clarkston villa, a conservatory so grand it nearly constituted another wing of the house. It was possibly original, with intricate ironwork, and had been beautifully restored. Rain pattered on the glass over their heads.

'I see. And it's Rona, please. Have you talked to Caleb?'

'Yes. About . . . other matters. Not about Neil. Jack Everett explained the link and I took him up on his offer to talk to you direct.'

'We haven't been together since Neil was four,' Rona said. 'I finished it. He was a controlling man, steeped in his religious piety. He had a terrible temper and could be quite violent, as I discovered. He had no respect for me or for any woman. He didn't want to divorce, on grounds of offending God. I threatened to go to the police and tell them he'd assaulted me on several occasions. That frightened him. I said, sign the divorce papers, give me this house and my son, and I'll leave you alone. He did as I asked. He had to. I had a witness to one of the assaults. My sister was here. She saw it. She took me to the hospital to check my arm wasn't broken, so there were medical records too.'

'I'm sorry.'

'We were married a total of six years. He came crawling back — oh, in the late nineties, it must have been. He wanted to see Neil. He was starting a business and he hoped one day Neil might work for him. I agreed to his seeing Neil once a month. Neil went to stay at the house in Ayrshire and he seemed to look forward to the weekends. He would have been eight or nine years old. I wasn't very happy about him going along to Caleb's church. Fanatical bunch. Narrow-minded. But I let it slide.

'Neil was thirteen when Caleb came here to see me. He turned up one evening. Neil was away with the school. A skiing trip, I think. He said he was worried Neil didn't seem interested in things boys "ought to be interested in". I said, "What on earth are you talking about?" and he said he thought Neil might grow up "homosexual" — that was the word he used. He said it was because he hadn't had a father in his life — and that was my fault.' She threw out her hands in a despairing gesture. 'He said his church would make him leave if they found out. He wanted Neil to go live with him and that he'd "make a man of him". Caleb talked about psychiatrists, about "staging interventions". I said, "If Neil's gay, then it's a fact of nature and a done deal" and I threatened him not to torture the boy with his peculiar religious ideas. Certainly not to involve his church friends. I said I might reconsider Neil's contact with his father — it was an informal arrangement, after all. Caleb pushed back, so I reminded him about my threat to go to the police — at which point he left.'

Lola asked, 'Was Neil in contact with his father at the time of his death?'

'Yes, but he was an adult by then, so it was his choice. He explained it was important for him to know his father. To try to understand him.'

'Would you tell me about Neil's death?'

She nodded, then took time to gather herself. She cleared her throat.

'Neil was living in the city centre, in a flat by the river, just beside the cathedral. He was working for a software company, designing graphics, animating things. I didn't really understand what he did, but he was doing well and he'd been promoted. I thought he might take after his father and set up his own company. He had a new boyfriend at the time he died — which was in the September of 2018 — a man called Evan, a university lecturer with a place in Hyndland. Caleb didn't know about this, by the way. Neil had been at Evan's house the night before he was found. He'd left Evan's around ten thirty. He didn't make it home — the security system at the flats hadn't registered his key fob, and there was a camera on the door too. Your colleagues found footage of him walking down Finnieston Street in the direction of the river, then he turned east to walk along Lancefield Quay towards Anderston Quay and the Kingston Bridge. This was about eleven. After that, nothing.' She went quiet for another few moments. 'His body was spotted in the water at Renfrew the next morning by one of the men who operate the foot ferry.'

'What happened next?' Lola asked gently.

'Your colleagues came to the house.' She swallowed and took another moment. 'I went with them to identify Neil . . . I asked them to notify Caleb. A post-mortem found Neil had drowned, but that he'd had a head injury too. Two detectives came to see me. Two men.'

'Do you remember their names?'

'The detective sergeant's surname was Arshad,' the woman said. 'He was helpful — at first. He opened an enquiry, appealed for witnesses, took statements from poor Evan and from a woman who said she'd heard a man cry out beside the Kingston Bridge.

'Then they went to see Neil's father. Caleb came round here, rigid with anger. He said Neil must have had an accident, that people were "suggesting things". I asked him what he meant, and he said the detectives wanted to link the incident to three previous attacks over the preceding couple of years. He said those attacks were thought to be perpetrated by a man who attacked gay men. Caleb said it couldn't have been the same attacker, because Neil wasn't gay. I was so stunned I didn't know what to say. I told him about Evan. I thought he was going to hit me, but he didn't. Instead he became very quiet and nasty. He accused me of perverting Neil, or "encouraging him" to be gay as a way of destroying Caleb. I asked him to leave.

'Caleb had been elected to the city council by then. He lived in Ayrshire but he's always had a flat in Glasgow, which meant he was eligible to stand. Two months after Neil's death he was elected chair of the community safety committee. I forget its title — something long and ridiculous. And then Sergeant Arshad stopped taking my calls. When I finally got hold of him to ask what was happening, he said he'd been moved to another case. He gave me a new contact name, a DS Gray — but he wouldn't take my calls. He wouldn't talk to me at all until I turned up at his office. He was very unhappy about it but he took me to a meeting room. He sort of stared through me. I asked what was happening about the investigation into my son's death. He said there was no evidence Neil's death was anything other than accidental. I couldn't believe what I was hearing. After that I wrote to the chief constable. The reply came from someone else. A Superintendent Wilde. Said the case had been closed.

'I contacted Caleb. I said, wasn't there something he could do, given his committee role? He just repeated the line I'd had from the police. No evidence of foul play. He'd told me this already, he said. Neil died accidentally. Neil was not gay.

'I went into a state of shock. I talked to a lawyer. He helped me make a complaint. The complaint was dismissed, though at least Mr Wilde had the good grace to come and see me. He said that rumours of someone attacking gay men were exactly that — rumours. That in line with some refreshed crime strategy or other — the one my ex-husband was personally responsible for — the police's focus was now on reassuring the public the streets were safe. Then he hinted that I was at risk of making myself liable for wasting police time.'

She paused, eyes down, allowing Lola time to absorb her words.

'You're saying he preferred to hush up your son's murder rather than acknowledge he was gay?'

'That's right.' She met Lola's gaze once more. 'I'm not making excuses, but something happened to him. Years ago, when he was a child himself, at boarding school. It changed him in . . . a number of ways. But that's his business. I tried to push your colleagues about Neil's death, but they became harder to engage with. In the end, I'm afraid I . . . I'm afraid I gave up. I gave up on my own dead son.' She swallowed and tears began to well.

'You can help us now.'

'I'll do anything,' the woman said. 'Anything at all.'

* * *

6.40 p.m.

Lola called Superintendent Angus Wilde from the car. She was still shaken by what she'd heard, and was uncertain, in her tired state, as to whether she would hold it together on the call.

It was probably a good thing that Wilde didn't answer. Instead she left a message, telling him she needed to talk to him about Munn and the Clyde Pusher cover-up. Now.

CHAPTER FIFTY-NINE

7.09 p.m.

Walter Clark denied tampering with any CCTV equipment. On that subject he was open and vehement and more than a little offended.

His manner changed when they asked about Quilan MacDonald. Then he became strained and evasive, telling them he felt 'mortified' to be answering questions about someone he considered, if not a pal, then a trusted colleague.

'What do you mean, "acting strange"?' Lola asked him, when he volunteered that much.

'I dunno. Jumpy. Guilty. Oh God, I don't mean . . . he's a good lad, is Quil. He follows the rules! He *likes* rules. He's a stickler. He's reliable. He'll spend hours going through footage if your lot make a request, and he spends ages making notes in the book, you know — where we record any footage we've shared. What's this all about, anyway?'

The questioning became circular, and Lola knew it was time to close. She was inclined to believe Clark had done nothing and knew nothing either.

She left Anna to finish off and let the man go and bumped into Kirstie on her way into the office.

'Any word on MacDonald?'

'Talked to two friends and a cousin. No sign of him. We've got the warrant. Want me to put out a call to all officers?'

Before she could answer, Kirstie's phone began to ring. She checked the number. 'It's his mum, boss.'

Lola gave the constable the nod to answer, then chewed her lip listening to Kirstie's side of the conversation with growing alarm.

'She's just had a call,' Kirstie explained, coming off the phone. 'From her son's mobile but silent. She says she could hear someone breathing. Laughing too, she thinks.'

They watched each other, processing the news.

Lola's phone began to ring. She grabbed it, heart in her mouth in case it was Wilde. But it was a number she didn't recognise.

It was DI Mairi Marshall, who was investigating the attack on Cammy and Warren.

'I've just had a call from Genevieve Maxwell,' the DI said. 'David Warren Maxwell's mother. The Russian fiancée has just arrived at their place in Bearsden. I'm heading out there now. I know it's late, but I wondered if you wanted to join me.'

CHAPTER SIXTY

8.31 p.m.

Inchallan was a vast, floodlit construction of stone and glass, with wings firing off at right angles, some held up by stilts where the ground slipped away towards a river that ran noisily and unseen somewhere in the dark woods. It was built in the grounds of a ruined castle at the end of a long drive, and from the road you would never know the house was there.

Lola and Mairi approached the main entrance to be met by Genevieve Maxwell, a thin, slightly stooped but otherwise well-preserved woman in her sixties. She was dressed in black and seemed irritated and distracted at the same time, as if they'd interrupted her trying to find something she'd lost.

'You know the way,' she murmured to Mairi, closing the door, then following as the DI marched towards the far end of a wood-floored hallway.

'I'm sorry about your son,' Lola said, as they made their way towards the back of the house and began to walk down a flight of open stairs.

'Thank you,' the woman muttered back. They were in another wing of the house now, one with glass for walls on one side. They came to more stairs. 'We go down again here.'

Finally they arrived in a living area, with settees and armchairs spread about. There was glass on three sides, with views of the floodlit woodland, and Lola realised this room was in one of the stilted wings. Two men rose to meet them: an older man, tall with thick grey hair and an angry, hawk-like expression, and a stocky, younger man who looked frankly sick.

'Mr Maxwell,' Mairi said, acknowledging the older man. 'Mr Maxwell,' to the younger. David Maxwell's brother, Lola guessed.

A slender woman in her thirties rose from an armchair. She was dark and beautiful with perfect make-up. She was dressed all in black and her perfectly straight black hair came almost to her waist.

'I am Oksana Baranova,' the woman said. 'David and I were to be married.'

'I'm very sorry for your loss,' Mairi said. Then she turned to Lola and introduced her to the family.

A few minutes later, drinks refused, they were sitting on the settees, facing one another.

This visit was ostensibly a courtesy, given the arrival of David Maxwell's fiancée, but the family had questions, principally Genevieve, the mother, and Patrick, the brother.

Mairi did her best to answer, but could tell them little more than she apparently already had.

'When will we know something?' the older woman asked, turning her anguished face on Lola, as if she might have the answer. 'When will we know if this was deliberate — personal, I mean.'

'Of course it was deliberate,' her husband growled. 'It wasn't an accident.'

'I know that, Leo,' his wife spat at him, and got up and went to one of the windows. 'I meant, *why*.'

Leo Maxwell said to Lola, 'My wife's afraid the attack on David was linked to our business. She's frightened that whoever did it might not be finished.'

The woman at the window wailed.

'Mum's afraid for my kids,' the younger man said. 'I've three. All under the age of five.' He spoke to his mother: 'Mum, the children are safe. Eloise is going to take them to her parents'. Anyway, this isn't to do with us. It was to do with David.'

'What do you mean by that?' Oksana spat.

He looked embarrassed.

'Would you care to explain what you mean, Mr Maxwell?' Lola pressed him.

'David had a number of . . . other interests,' Patrick Maxwell said, shifty now, as if he wished he hadn't spoken.

Lola exchanged glances with Mairi. 'It's okay if you prefer not to talk here,' she said quickly.

He looked relieved, but his eyes stayed on Lola. He was burning to speak, she knew it.

At Lola's nod, Mairi moved the conversation quickly on, asking Oksana what contact she'd had with her fiancé in the day or two leading up to his death. They had spoken twice, Oksana told her, via FaceTime on both occasions. David had seemed cheerful, if anxious about the project he was managing: the redevelopment of a section of the south bank of the river on behalf of his father's firm.

'Anxious in what way?' Lola asked gently.

'Nothing in particular,' the woman replied tersely. 'The quantity of problems he had to deal with, that is all.'

'Did David spend a lot of time down at the river development?' Lola asked, eyes on Leo Maxwell.

'It was his project,' the man answered gruffly. 'There are offices there. Portakabins. I believe he was there most weekdays. He had been for the past year.'

'Did David ever mention a young man called Cameron, or Cammy, Leavey?'

Leo and Genevieve exchanged puzzled glances.

'Not to me,' Oksana said with a shrug.

'Who is he?' Genevieve asked.

Lola turned to David's brother, who didn't return her gaze.

'Patrick?' she prompted.

'Never heard of him,' the man said, eyes down. 'But Davey knew a lot of people.'

The silence was oppressive.

'Miss . . . Harris,' Genevieve Maxwell said distractedly. 'We've told you we don't know this person. Perhaps you'd be kind enough to tell us who he is.'

'I can't do that just yet,' Lola said.

The older woman's voice became brittle. 'Then I'm afraid we're at a loss as to how we can help you.' She turned to her husband with an exasperated wave of a hand.

Mairi spoke. 'I will have more questions for Ms Baranova. They can wait until tomorrow. Perhaps you'd give me a note of where you plan to be.'

The Russian woman told Mairi her plans. Meanwhile, Lola observed the dynamic between Patrick Maxwell and his parents. There were questioning glances, cues, warnings . . .

Mairi put away her notebook, signalled to Lola that she was done and the two of them got up to go.

'My card,' Lola said to Patrick Maxwell before they followed Genevieve back through the house.

He took it gingerly, face flushing.

'Any time at all,' she told him quietly.

* * *

10.49 p.m.

Wilde sent a text message as Lola was going to bed, saying he'd talk to her the next day, Saturday. He suggested they meet at his home at midday. She messaged back to say fine, and he sent her his address.

A few minutes later, halfway up the stairs armed with a cup of Elaine's disgusting insomniac's tea, Patrick Maxwell called. She put the mug on the stairs then sat and answered.

The man sounded breathless, like someone committing treason. 'David never mentioned Cameron Leavey,' he said, 'but I think I've met him.'

'Oh?'

'At the site on the south bank of the river, one afternoon two weeks ago.' She heard him swallow and blow air through his lips as if he was struggling to remain composed. 'I was there, Davey wasn't. I came out of one of the offices and there was this kid standing there at the gate. I said, "Can I help you?" and he asked for Warren. I said I didn't know anyone of that name — who was he, a builder? He said Warren ran the place, then I realised who he meant. He meant Davey. Warren is — *was* — Davey's middle name. I didn't let on. I asked the kid who he was. He didn't want to tell me. I said I couldn't help him if he didn't tell me his name. He said it was Cameron. He was anxious as anything, looking past me, trying to see into the offices. I asked him what he wanted. He said it didn't matter. Then . . . Then I saw he was upset. Teary.'

'Thank you for telling me this,' Lola said. 'What happened then?'

'Oh, he left. I didn't know what to do. In the end I decided to mention it to Davey. He was offhand with me, dismissive. I asked who the kid was. He said, how the hell should he know? I asked if he was buying . . . buying drugs. He said no and not to worry my head about it.' He took a breath. 'Is that what it was? Is the kid a dealer?'

'I don't believe so, Mr Maxwell.'

'Then what?'

She gazed down her stairwell into the dark hallway below and tried to decide what was best to say. The man on the other end of the line had lost his brother. A brother he'd clearly loved. He was in the pits of grief. To tell him what she knew might worsen his misery and reveal his brother to have lied to him. But not to tell . . . That might be worse.

'I believe he was David's lover,' Lola told him. 'That's certainly how Cameron understood the situation.'

Silence. Then a weak, 'What?'

'Did you have any inkling?'

'About what? That Davey . . . That Davey liked *blokes*? No, of course not. That's . . .'

He began sobbing.

After a few seconds he spoke again. His voice was clearer now. 'It explains a few things,' he said. 'My God.'

'I'd ask you not to share this information more widely,' she said gently. 'It could be important to the investigation into David's death. And to another investigation as well.'

'Okay.'

As he recovered he had questions, and they came thick and fast. He wanted to know who Cameron Leavey was, how his brother had met him and whether he was involved in his brother's death.

Lola answered what she could, but ultimately slowed him to a halt, with the promise that DI Mairi Marshall would talk to him in more detail at a later date.

Emotionally drained, the foul tea now cool enough to drink, Lola took herself to bed.

CHAPTER SIXTY-ONE

Saturday 18 February
10.02 a.m.

'I've been looking for the Pusher since the beginning,' Yvonne Craigie, founder of the Facebook group, told Lola and Anna. 'Of course, nobody called him the Pusher.'

They were in the tiny living room of her modern flat in Thornliebank, a little to the south of Pollok Park. Mrs Craigie was sixty-something, spry and slightly prickly in blue jeans and a white long-sleeved top. She'd met them at the door with a look of cool scepticism, as if she was ready to be disappointed once again. Lola took it as a challenge.

'My nephew Ricky was the first,' she went on, eyes on a photograph on the mantelpiece over an electric fire. It was a portrait of a nice-looking young man with blond hair and glasses. 'Died just before Christmas, 2016. Police said it was an accident but we didn't buy it. He had this *dent* in the side of his head! I talked to doctors. No way did he do that falling in. Besides, I know this sounds awful, but Ricky was camp, you know? Visibly gay, which made him a target. I just knew he'd been attacked. His mum, my sister, was ill. Dying. She passed in the February. I promised her on her deathbed that I'd find out who killed her boy.'

She began to tear up and snatched for a tissue from a box and blew her nose.

Yvonne had been a primary school teacher, she told them. She'd taken retirement a couple of years early in the summer of 2016, the same time as her husband, Hugh. Hugh had died during the pandemic. No, not from Covid, but from a heart attack while walking in Rouken Glen Park one evening.

'It's just me here now. No husband, no sister, no nephew. Just me and this unexpected vocation: to band the families together and catch a killer most folk think doesn't even exist. More coffee?'

They both declined.

'You wanted to know who I've got in the group?' she said. 'I can tell you. I wrote a post on the group's page yesterday morning. I've had quite a few replies already and they're all positive. No objections.'

She changed her glasses and studied the list of victims once more.

'Going by date order, then, there's Drew Morris's sister and her husband, and one of Drew's cousins. A friend or two, I think.

'Alec Bennett's a member. He's the only known survivor. He chips in occasionally, but he went quiet after a couple of the other members started laying into him about what he remembered and why he wasn't doing more, which was hardly fair. He'd spoken to the press and let them print his photograph, for goodness' sake! I put *quite* a strongly worded post up that evening!

'Next on your list is Neil Prine. I know the name, of course, but his family have never engaged.

'Mark Brodie's two brothers joined the group. They've never written a post, but one of them replies to other people's posts from time to time.

'Michael Mackinnon's dad and uncle are members. So are a couple of his friends. There are a few other folk too — some of the victims' friends, ex-colleagues, people's second cousins, that sort of thing. I started off vetting every one of them but it was tricky and it upset people. I'm sure some of them are just snoopers, or people who think they're helping.'

She lowered the paper in her hand. 'Are you going to help? Genuinely, I mean? Are you going to take us seriously?'

'We are, Yvonne,' Lola said.

'You believe there's a killer, then? That someone murdered these men?' She flicked the paper.

'That's what we believe.'

The woman's face and body language changed. She seemed to catch herself and took a moment to recalibrate her thoughts and feelings. She put a hand to her lips. 'Then you're serious!'

'Yes,' Lola said.

'*Thank God!*' the woman said quietly. 'Thank God. You have no idea what this means. After all these years of *trying* and getting nowhere! I've been to my MP, my MSPs too. They've written letters, but ultimately it's for the police. Even the procurator fiscal doesn't want to know.'

'Things will change now,' Lola said. 'I can't promise we'll catch the killer, but I'm very close to making a public statement that the Clyde Pusher is real.'

'There's been another one, you know. His name's John Paul McCrae. Is that why things have changed?'

'In a way.'

'You mean somebody saw it happen, don't you? There was a witness!'

Lola remained poker faced. 'Yvonne, I'd like your help to organise a meeting for the families,' Lola said now. 'I can provide a room on Monday.'

'Monday?' Her red-edged eyes grew wide.

'Yes. Do you think that's too soon?'

'No! How could it be? We've been waiting for this moment for years. I'll start right away.'

* * *

11.16 a.m.

They'd agreed Lola would drive Anna to a café she knew in Clarkston — a place she could check emails and wait while Lola went to see Superintendent Wilde. Driving there, Anna called Kirstie for an update. Lola could tell from the sergeant's tone that something had happened.

Anna finished the call and took a moment to collect her thoughts. 'Not good news, boss. Body of an unidentified male's been found in the mud on the south bank of the river between the Albert and Victoria Bridges. Age estimated as mid-thirties, been dead about twelve hours. Officer who was first on the scene says he looks like Quilan MacDonald as per the photo attached to the misper report.'

Lola swallowed. 'Any sign of how he died?'

'Looks like multiple head injuries. His clothes are dry. Looks like he didn't go into the river, so it's possible he was killed elsewhere and dumped there. They'll have the body ready for ID early afternoon.'

CHAPTER SIXTY-TWO

12.10 p.m.

Detective Superintendent Angus Wilde looked sick.

'Munn's played a lot of people,' Lola said, managing to withhold the words, *including you*.

'His son . . .' Wilde said, for the third or fourth time.

They were in IKEA armchairs in Angus and Cynthia Wilde's pine 'garden room', which sat at the foot of the extensive lawn behind their house in Barrhead. A frail Cynthia Wilde had seemed less than pleased that her husband's colleague had descended on his precious day off. Now, swaddled in a coat, scarf and oversized hat, she was making painful-looking efforts to cut back ornamental grasses, while keeping a beady and disapproving watch. Lola reminded herself the woman was ill — she must be generous.

'I've tried to piece together a timeline,' she said. 'From what I can tell, in the weeks after Neil died, Munn lobbied hard to take over the community safety committee. Once there, he pushed for a fast refresh of the city's crime strategy. A panel oversaw the rewrite. You were on that panel, sir.'

He looked mortified. And so he should. Lola had reread the strategy before coming here. The vision in the refreshed plan talked first and foremost about 'reducing fear of crime'. The first actions were all about communications, and the strategy's success was in large part indicated by survey responses about how scared the public said they felt, as well as how much crime they perceived took place in their communities. Pointless and demeaning, in Lola's view.

'And after the strategy was published,' Wilde went on miserably, 'the committee took responsibility for its implementation and the prioritisation of resources. Caleb made it clear we shouldn't be spending time and money investigating the river deaths.'

'So had the deaths been considered as a series before that, sir?'

He nodded. 'A DS called Ali Arshad was in charge. Munn had me ascertain what evidence Arshad had gathered. So much of it was circumstantial or anecdotal. Witnesses were reluctant, or unconvincing. We were talking about drug users down by the river, women out selling sex, a couple of drunks. They'd have struggled to convince a jury. I . . . I moved Ali off the case. But I did manage to persuade Munn we needed to continue to gather reports, so we had a point of contact for any future cases. Someone who could take a look, make a note and . . . deflect attention. I suggested Lachlan Gray. Munn asked to meet him and agreed he was the man for the job.'

The job. To cover up serial murders.

'Don't you think it might be best if DS Gray was removed from the task force now, sir?'

He looked uncomfortable, but nodded.

'What happened to Dougie Latimer's story for the *Chronicle*?' she asked now. 'The editor was about to publish it when it got pulled.'

'Munn got wind of it. He was livid. He wanted us to arrest the editor. Obviously that wasn't going to happen. Instead I believe Munn used his personal network to get it pulled.'

'The Clyde Pusher is real, sir. My evidence is circumstantial and anecdotal but it's coherent, and I believe there's more evidence out there — Jack Everett and Dougie Latimer have a folder full of it.'

He eyed her with that sick expression still on his face.

'Sir, I want to go public.'

He stared, then closed his eyes. He looked wearier than Lola had ever felt.

'It's time, sir. The deaths are clearly linked. We need to call for information and witnesses and have staff ready to take statements. We'll need Corporate Comms onside.'

'Monday,' Wilde said, biting his lip. 'We can't do anything before then. We'll meet Melda first thing Monday morning and make a plan.'

'You should know that I plan to pay Munn a visit later today, sir.'

'What for?'

'He needs to know he's been found out,' she said. 'Only fair he should know, wouldn't you say?'

'He'll be on to me straight away,' Wilde said. 'He might go higher.'

'He might, sir. But if his interference becomes public then so does his son's sexuality. I think there's a chance he'll go to ground.'

Wilde looked unconvinced.

She left him in his garden room, said a few brief words to a pinch-faced Cynthia Wilde and returned to her car.

Driving to the café where she'd left Anna, her mind remained troubled. What Wilde had disclosed shocked her. At best the actions he'd taken, the decisions he'd made, were unethical. At worst they'd allowed a killer to remain free to kill again.

CHAPTER SIXTY-THREE

1.35 p.m.

First thing that morning Lola had received a winsomely polite text from Barry, checking she was still okay to meet the next day. Heart sinking at even reading his words, she'd put it firmly out of her mind. Now, as Anna drove them to Ayrshire, she forced herself to write the reply she knew she had to send.

So sorry but I have to cancel, she typed. *I'm in the middle of a major case and am working all hours. Maybe we can do it again some time. All best wishes. Lola.*

It felt mean. Dismissive and insensitive. It was true she was working all hours, but it was also true she'd have made time for another man, one she actually liked. Fancied, even a smidgen.

She read it over, groaned inwardly, and pressed send.

That grisly task performed, she typed an email to Dr Enid Burrows, the forensic psychologist at the university, begging a consultation ahead of a likely request for a full profile of a suspected serial murderer. Burrows' help had been critical in identifying the killer in the Pollok Park murder in the autumn and Lola was keen to get her views on the Pusher.

A wave of tiredness came over her and her vision swam, so she put her phone away and watched the road unfold before them.

'You okay, boss?'

'Just sleepy.'

'We'll be another twenty minutes,' Anna said, eyes on the GPS display. 'Have a snooze.'

'Best if I stay awake and try to sleep at night.'

'Are you having trouble sleeping? Only, I've noticed you looking tired lately. I saw you using those energy drinks too. Sorry,' she said, clocking Lola's side-eye. 'It's just — insomnia's like "my thing",' she rattled on. 'I mean, it *was*. I struggled for years.'

'Really?' Lola gazed in some astonishment. Anna was a picture of optimal health: a willowy, dewy-skinned honey-blonde with good teeth. She had buckets of energy and never seemed anything but level-headed and emotionally content.

'I guess it was a low-level stress thing. Nick was panicking about not being made partner in his firm and we'd thrown everything into a house we couldn't afford. I was in a state about whether we should be starting a family or holding off. My mum was going on at me about my body clock and how hard it had been for my sister. I'd lie awake, sometimes for the whole night, in a cold sweat, then have to go to work and I was like a zombie. Honestly, I shouldn't have been driving.'

'So what did you do?' Lola asked.

'I tried *everything*. Pills, CBT, hypnotherapy, Indian head massage, reflexology — it got pretty expensive. They all helped to an extent and in different ways, but nothing hit the mark. And then I started wild swimming. You know, in the ponds at Hampstead Heath? Freezing cold water — it sounds horrific, but it's incredible. It's intense, so your mind becomes really focused on the here and now — it's just you and the freezing water and the dopamine floods your brain. It does something to your circulation too and that helps your immune system. I went the first time one evening in September with a girlfriend. That night I slept for ten hours.

The next night too. By the Sunday I was getting twitchy so I drove up to the Heath in the afternoon and went in the Ladies' pond on my own. I've done it ever since!' She said, laughing, 'I don't have insomnia anymore.'

'Do you do it here — since you moved to Scotland, I mean?'

'God, yeah! I joined a group before I even arrived. We go to the White Loch three or four times a week.'

'The White Loch? I don't know where that is.'

'We passed it twenty minutes ago. It's a couple of miles off the motorway after Newton Mearns. It's dreamy on a moonlit night!'

Lola hadn't swum since she was a teenager, had barely dunked herself in the pool on holiday. She didn't even have a costume.

'Why don't you give it a go? You could come with me.'

Lola made half-hearted noises, but she was intrigued. The thought of swimming in freezing water didn't appeal, but the hope it offered did.

Her phone pinged. Dr Burrows had replied. She planned to be in her office on Sunday afternoon to take care of some marking. She suggested Lola might call to speak to her at three thirty.

She had a text message too, from Barry in reply to hers. She clicked into it and winced.

I understand, he'd written. *Sorry not to see you. Please let me know if things change. I like you a lot. B.*

CHAPTER SIXTY-FOUR

2.25 p.m.

Munn's home was a white 1920s villa at the end of a long driveway, hemmed in by woods a mile or two from the coast south of Ayr. Councillor Munn wasn't at home, his housekeeper, a round-faced woman in her fifties, told them. Shown their warrant cards, she began to fret and told them they'd find him at a charity event at a local golf club.

'Think she'll ring and warn him?' Anna asked as they walked back to the car.

'Probably,' Lola said. 'I rather hope she will. Noise him up nicely for us.'

It was a short drive to the golf club, another art deco building. They heard the boom of someone talking through a sound system. The car park was rammed so they parked on the grass verge then went inside.

Munn was on the stage in a large function room, seated, perhaps waiting to speak after a man in a crumpled suit currently at the lectern. The man talking urged the hundred or so people to buy up the remaining raffle tickets ahead of a big draw.

Lola led Anna through the crowd, eyes on Munn, who finally looked her way. The panic on his face was gratifying. His jaw looked tight and his bottom lip trembled.

Lola reached the front of the throng, folded her arms and stared unblinking at the frightened man on the stage.

Munn looked away, fixing a fake smile as he appeared to pay full attention to the speaker. The fists in his lap tightened, knuckles shining white.

The man with the microphone finished speaking and turned to Munn, who made a quick gesture that looked to say no, he didn't wish to say anything.

The speeches over, the crowd dispersed, retaking their seats. No one appeared to have registered the presence of the detectives, apart from Munn — who now made a beeline.

'What do you want?' he hissed.

'To talk to you about your son, Mr Munn,' Lola said loudly, over the music.

His pale eyes popped, but he quickly recovered.

'Not here.'

'Wherever suits, sir,' Lola said nicely.

He looked quickly about, then turned and snarled, 'This way.'

He took them through a curtain and down a corridor to an office. Once inside he closed the door. 'You have no business tracking me down like this. I have *nothing* to say to you.'

'That's a shame, sir,' Lola said. 'It means I'll have to arrest you.'

His face contorted. 'On what grounds?' he shrieked.

Lola shrugged. 'How about: attempting to pervert the course of justice. To be honest, I doubt it's police charges you should be worrying about. More reputational damage, I expect. That, and *everything* coming out into the public domain.'

Munn's chin rose. His pale eyes were wide and hunted.

'We know you pressured Superintendent Wilde to kill the investigation into the river deaths,' Lola said mildly. 'You preferred your own son's killer to go free rather than have it known Neil was gay.'

'Neil . . . My son was *not* a homosexual! His death was an *accident*!'

'You don't believe that. Neither did the pathologist, nor any of the officers who wanted to investigate his death — until you stopped them.'

He frowned, blinking fast, as if he was having trouble understanding what Lola was saying to him.

'Investigations into the previous deaths stopped too,' she said. 'And any attempt to investigate the ones after came to nothing.'

'Coincidence!' he cried. 'Accidents, that's all!'

'All of them gay men of similar age, all with head injuries, all found drowned in the Clyde. A pattern, but one you refused to see — or let others see.'

He'd begun to sway.

'You might want to sit down,' Lola said. She gave Anna a little nod and the sergeant rose, took Munn firmly by the elbow, dragged out a chair and manoeuvred him into it.

'I have some questions for you,' Lola said when he was sitting.

'I've nothing to say.' He watched her with nervy defiance.

'We'll see about that. Did you tamper with CCTV equipment at the operations centre, or do you know who did?'

'What? Tamper with—?'

'Did you cause cameras to move so they wouldn't record a particular area at any time?'

He looked genuinely shocked. '*No!*'

'Do you know who is killing these men — who killed your son?'

She saw it had stung him deep inside. He recoiled, wincing, and his fists clenched and unclenched on the table.

'Mr Munn?'

'No,' he said in that strangled whisper.

She stole a look at Anna, who was impassive apart from her eyes. She believed him too, then.

'That's all for now,' she said, getting up. 'You'll be hearing from our colleagues in due course.'

He gaped at her.

'You engineered the cover-up of a crime, Mr Munn,' Lola said. 'You lied to all those families. More young men died. People need to know what you did — and why you did it.'

* * *

3.14 p.m.

About to climb back into the passenger seat of the car, Lola took a last look at the golf club, from where 1970s music now emanated.

Someone was watching them from a window: a woman with red-gold hair, face close to the pane, hands cupped against the glass. Lola strained to get a better look and the person seemed to take fright and withdraw.

'Of all the golf clubs, in all the world,' she muttered, doing up her belt.

'Boss?' Anna asked.

'Someone watching us leave,' she said. 'I can't be sure, but it looked for all the world like a certain comms professional.'

'What would she be doing here?' Anna asked, aghast.

'A very good question.'

Once they were on the road, she listened to two voicemails.

The first was from Yvonne Craigie. So far seven family members had offered to come to a meeting at short notice. Between them, and adding Yvonne herself, they represented four of the victims. She asked Lola to confirm the date, time and venue and said she'd get people there, come hell or high water. Alec Bennett, the sole survivor, had sent Yvonne a private message to say he'd talk to the police, but preferred to do so one to one. She read out Bennett's number.

The second voicemail was from Kirstie.

Quilan MacDonald's mother had positively identified her son's body. Kirstie described her as 'confused' and 'barely making sense'. The woman's sister, Quilan's aunt, had gone with her to the mortuary.

Separately Kirstie had found a record of the 'trouble' Quilan MacDonald had found himself in, as referred to by Shannon Grant. Nine years ago he'd been arrested over a dispute with his mother's neighbours. He'd threatened the husband of the family with a baseball bat, then begun battering in their front door and, when that didn't work, smashed in one of their windows. He'd been convicted of threatening and abusive behaviour and vandalism, and given a payback order involving unpaid work in the community as well as attending an anger management group.

She called Kirstie back.

'If MacDonald had a payback order,' she said, 'someone must have supervised it. Find out who. They might know something that can help us.'

She hung up and focused on the road, her heart seeming to race as fast as the white lines under them.

CHAPTER SIXTY-FIVE

Sunday 19 February
1.45 p.m.

Lola should have been on her date with Barry just now. Instead she was in another café with a different man. This one the only known survivor of an attack by the Pusher.

Alec Bennett had suggested this place. 'Let's keep it informal,' he'd said, slightly breathless on the phone. 'Just a chat, you know? I'm not sure my mental health will stand everything being raked up again, but I do want to help.'

She was installed in a booth at the back of the trendy west end establishment, and spotted him when he came in, recognising him from the photo alongside the *Chronicle* interview. Tall, slim and good-looking with dark red hair and a trimmed beard, he looked horribly nervous.

She waited while he ordered a sparkling water and made small talk to put him at ease until it arrived.

'I read the interview you gave to the *Chronicle*,' she said at last.

'Oh yeah? I thought it might make a difference. Much good it did me. Got called a faggot on Twitter. Someone else told me they wished I'd died in the attack. I asked them to take the interview off the website, which they did.'

Lola commiserated. Alec shrugged.

'Tell me about the attack in your own words,' she said.

He told her it had happened around ten thirty on a Sunday night in March 2018. He'd been running a bar on Stockwell Street back then. That evening, business was slow, so he'd locked up and left early. It wasn't raining, so he'd decided to walk home to the flat he shared with his girlfriend in the Gorbals. He walked his usual way, heading down Stockwell Street to the river then along Clyde Street, under the disused railway line, then across the river at Glasgow Green. He'd realised someone was going the same way, but on the other side of the road: a hooded figure, keeping pace with him.

'Next thing, he was coming across the road, *running*. I saw he had a brick-shaped thing in his hand. I froze at first, then I bombed it, but he caught up with me and brought that thing down, just here.' He turned his head and touched a hairless patch behind his left ear. 'I fell to the ground and he was on me, arms round my middle, pulling me upright and walking me to the railings. The side of my head felt wet. I don't know what happened next, but I managed to twist round and get his arms off me. He'd dropped the brick and he tripped backwards over it — and I ran. Ran so fast. I got to the bridge and I saw an ambulance coming down the Saltmarket. No blue lights or anything. It was heading for the bridge. My vision was going so I just threw myself at it. It stopped. A paramedic got out and started talking to me and then I blacked out. That's all I remember.'

They'd taken him to hospital. A duty sergeant came to see him there, then a detective came a few days later. 'DS Arshad. He told me I might have been attacked by the same person who'd already attacked and killed two guys. He took a statement. We even went down there together a few days later, to Clyde Street. I showed him the place where the attacker had come from. They put out an appeal for witnesses, but no one came forward. The CCTV cameras had been vandalised. I guess that probably happens quite a lot, doesn't it?'

'You said you showed DS Arshad "the place where the attacker had come from". What did you mean?'

'He came out of the alley.'

'The alley?'

'There's an alleyway or a lane between the old railway line arches and the building next to it. You can cut through to the car park at the northern end.'

Lola took out her phone and went into the maps app, scrolling till she found Clyde Street. She turned the phone so Alec could get a look.

'That's it,' he said. 'Merchant Lane.' He scrolled. 'And there's Bridgegate, where it comes out at the top.'

Lola studied the map. The lane was crooked, bending in the middle. From one end you wouldn't be able to see the other.

'There's nothing up the alley, right enough,' Alec said.

'I don't recall any mention of the alley in your original statement,' Lola said now.

'I didn't really realise till later, when I went down there with DS Arshad.'

'In that case I'm sure there'll be a note added to your file.'

'He definitely made a note. He even drew a wee map in his notebook. He was good. We kept in touch even though he wasn't making a lot of progress. Then he got taken off the case. No one wanted to talk to me after that. I heard he'd moved to London. I contacted him. He couldn't talk to me about the case anymore, he said. He was sorry I wasn't having any luck with anyone here.'

Lola explained that she was running a new investigation and that tomorrow she hoped to make an announcement that the so-called Pusher deaths were being formally linked and investigated as the work of a serial murderer.

He stared, mouth open, for several seconds.

'You do think he's real then? The Pusher?'

'I do. Don't you?'

'I don't know.' He looked at his hands and she saw emotion working in his face. 'Sorry, this is quite unsettling for me. Part of me wants it all out in the open. Another part . . .' He shuddered visibly. 'I just don't understand it.'

'What do you mean?'

'All the men he's killed were gay, weren't they?'

She chose her words carefully. 'Where we know the victims' sexuality, then yes, all the victims were gay men.'

'I'm bisexual,' he said, 'but I was living with Cara at the time. How did he know to come for me? I hadn't been with a guy for over five years. I wasn't on any dating apps and I hadn't been in a gay bar for two or three years. Most people meeting me would take me for straight. So why did he pick me?'

* * *

3.12 p.m.

Shannon Grant had tried to call her. Lola rang her back from her car.

'I've spent at least ten hours reviewing footage from the streets around Clyde Street from eight p.m. on Saturday evening till midnight,' the supervisor told her. 'Unless I've missed something, there's no one fitting the description of the individual you're looking for. He's either got magic powers or a secret route in and out of the area. I'm sorry.'

CHAPTER SIXTY-SIX

11.07 a.m.

Dr Enid Burrows was one of those people who always looked the same, from decade to decade. She'd had the same hairstyle and clothes as long as Lola had known her, dressing like an austere librarian from the 1950s, complete with Alice band and frizzy grey hair.

They met in her office, seated in low bucket seats under looming bookshelves. Lola angled her chair to avoid looking at the skull Dr Burrows kept on a shelf behind her desk. A pot with ivy grew next to it and tendrils had worked their way inside the skull and sprouted through its eye sockets and grinning jaw. There was something unsettling about how shiny and healthy the ivy looked.

'I read your email,' Dr Burrows said, straightening her dark wool skirt. 'I was dimly aware of the Clyde Pusher legend. So, you think it's real?'

'I do. We're going to make a statement about an investigation later today.'

'And you'd like me to help you begin to understand the motivation, the possible background, of an individual who would act in this way?'

'If you can.'

The doctor peered at a notebook through the bottom halves of her glasses while Lola readied a pen. 'You realise, of course, that you could be looking for someone in the grip of delusion. Someone who does not operate according to the same rules as other people.'

'You mean he could be insane.'

'I wouldn't use that term, per se. He could merely be operating according to an understanding of the world or a set of values that seem alien to you and me. On the basis of the information you've provided about the victims and their manner of death, and completely without prejudice, I can suggest the following:

'You're looking for a male, older than his victims, I'd say, but young enough to remain athletic, between the ages of thirty and fifty perhaps. He's likely to be white and to have anger issues, but ones he has taught himself to manage and hide. He enjoys the attacks. He plans them, he strategises and he has tactics, using boltholes, alleyways like the one you say you found yesterday. In everyday life he's likely to be pleasant, to have acquaintances rather than friends. He uses these acquaintances to assist him. I expect he's manipulative, especially of those who are vulnerable.

'Two matters interest me particularly: sexuality and geography.

'Sexuality first: it seems glaringly obvious to me that this is a case of internalised homophobia. I imagine the man is gay and has lived life as a heterosexual. He may even have been married. He might still be married, and there might be children. His occupation would be interesting if that is the case. How does he account for his whereabouts to his partner? On the whole, however, I'd expect him to be single now, perhaps divorced. Something triggered the killings. Something happened that probably humiliated, hurt or frightened him badly. I'd expect he had taken an opportunity to explore his sexuality, perhaps met someone — and that it went horribly wrong. Perhaps he was blackmailed or threatened.'

'By the first victim, you mean?' Lola asked.

'I don't think so. If he killed the person who humiliated him, it would have been immediate and done in anger — a lashing out. Your first victim, Mr Linton — his death was the first in a series and is all of a pattern. It was as calmly planned as the subsequent crimes.'

'So what do you recommend?'

'Go to places where gay men meet. Bars, online forums or apps that they use. Interview people. Someone might know who he is.'

'I've already spoken to a couple of friends. It seems the Pusher might have used an app to try to lure people, but then he seemed to disappear.'

Dr Burrows nodded slowly. 'It may have worked for a time. But perhaps he feared being tracked. Once he got a taste for killing, perhaps he started selecting victims by sight — he literally waited until he saw a man on his own who he thought was gay . . . and attacked.'

'You mentioned geography,' Lola prompted.

'He knows the city. The river and the area around it especially. I suspect he lives or works near the river. If he does, it's reasonable to suggest he would be known there. He wouldn't seem out of place, if you know what I mean. I'm interested in the two "hotspots" where he appears to have committed his crimes. There may be some significance to those. Perhaps there are places he hides, or perhaps he accesses them through alleyways that aren't overlooked.'

'Again, what should I think about?'

'Interview people who live and work near the river, systematically.'

'What about work? If he's in the age bracket you suggest then he's probably still working.'

Dr Burrows took her time before answering, eyes away in a corner of the room as she considered.

'He might work across an area,' she said at last. 'Or across a community, out and about, meeting people, visiting places. The same places. Perhaps he sells, or has a "round".' She looked Lola in the eye and added, 'I hesitate to suggest this, but . . . you should consider the possibility he might be a police officer.'

CHAPTER SIXTY-SEVEN

4.31 p.m.

Town wasn't busy and Lola managed to park on King Street. From there she walked back to Bridgegate and found the north opening of Merchant Lane, between two bars.

She made her way gingerly over a mat of discarded cigarette ends and other litter that clogged the cobbles. The lane turned where it met the wall that carried the disused railway line and she got her first glimpse of Clyde Street and the river. She emerged from the south end and looked both ways along Clyde Street, her skin prickling as she thought of the Pusher using this same passage to stalk his victims.

She turned and made her way back up the dirty lane. As she rounded the turn, a hooded figure coming the other way made her jump. He jumped too, face lifting from his phone to stare open-mouthed.

'Cammy?' she said. 'Cameron Leavey?'

But he was already running, dirt flying from his shoes as he went.

'Wait!' she cried, and took off after him.

She emerged into Bridgegate to see his lithe figure darting through the car park over the road.

He was too fast for her. She gave up.

Catching her breath, she gazed around, wondering if the Pusher drove and, if so, where he parked.

She considered the two bars flanking the lane's entrance. The one on the left, Gail's, was closed, its windows shuttered. The one on the right, the Spinning Jenny, looked open though anything but welcoming. Bracing herself, she went in.

The bar was dark and it took her a moment to make out there were people inside, perhaps a dozen of them, hunched round tables. A bored-looking man with a ratty moustache was wiping up drippings from the bar.

'Help you?' he asked, sounding sceptical.

'A lemonade, please. Diet.'

'Only ordinary.'

'That'll do, thanks.'

He poured.

'You looking for some'dy?'

'A friend of mine got attacked near here. A while back.'

'Sorry to hear, but it happens.'

'Aye, well. A witness thought he saw the attacker come out of the alley here. You ever seen anything?'

He was eyeing her with great suspicion now. 'You polis?'

'Aye. But I'm just asking about—'

'What's she want, Malky?' a gruff female voice called from the shadows.

'Friend got attacked,' Malky the barman called back. 'Attacker was in the lane here.'

'That the gay lad who went into the river a week ago?' the woman asked her. She was big, wearing a dirty-looking lemon-coloured jumper and her hair was badly dyed and needed a wash as well as a cut.

'Do you know anything about it?' Lola asked.

'Naw. How would I?'

Lola realised she was very drunk.

'Loadsa folk cut through there,' said an older man sitting along from her and wearing a flat cap. 'There is a fella who hangs about. Seen him coming and going from Gail's next door. Uses the back door. He's got his own key. Always has his hood up.'

'Oh?' She felt a rush of adrenalin.

'I seen him an' aw,' Lemon Jumper said. 'Has his head down.'

'This is important,' Lola said, approaching their table, but aware that everyone else in the place was listening in, including Malky behind the bar. 'It has to do with murder.'

'Whit?' Lemon Jumper squeaked. 'You serious?'

'I am. I'd like you to give statements to my colleagues about this man. Will you do that for me?'

'I'm not giving no statement,' Lemon Jumper cried. 'Fuck's sake.'

'I will,' Flat Cap said.

'Will you give me your name?' she said. 'I'll make a note of it in my phone.'

'I seen him, too,' another woman, much older, said. 'He scared me. I'd be happy if you took him away.'

Lola took their names and thanked them.

'Has the place next door shut down?'

'Naw,' Malky said. 'Gail's away to Lanzarote. Always goes this time a' year. She's due back any day now.'

'You don't have a number for her, do you?'

Malky gave her a look. 'Aye, go on, then.' He wasn't happy about it but he went into his phone and read out Gail's phone number.

'Thanks so much, everyone,' Lola said, ready to go.

'Do you not want your lemonade?' Malky said. 'You've paid for it.'

'You drink it for me,' she said.

Outside it was starting to get dark. The place felt bleak, lonely. A wind had picked up and litter blew in spirals. She looked across at the pub next door. There was an inset doorway giving onto the lane, possibly the doorway through which the Pusher had emerged and crept down the lane, out onto the riverside, there to stalk his victims.

Eyes still on the doorway, she rang the number Malky had given her. Gail, away in Lanzarote, didn't answer, so Lola left her a message, asking her to call back as soon as she could.

CHAPTER SIXTY-EIGHT

9.57 p.m.

Cammy stole back to the river, keeping to the shadows, extra vigilant in case the inspector was still around, though some hours had passed. He traversed streets and circled the car parks beside King Street, watching from afar, keeping close to walls. Always ready to run.

She wasn't here.

What had she been doing anyway? Looking for him or for the Pusher? He'd had the fright of his life in the lane. Had she realised that was the way the Pusher used to cut through from the town to the riverside? But she'd been on her own. What did she think she could possibly do if she came face to face with the killer? He doubted she was armed . . .

Cammy was, though — armed and ready. And not a bit frightened.

He'd found a spot beside the river from which to watch and wait. Here, evergreen bushes sprouted up from the riverbank, overhanging the pavement and creating a curtain from behind which he could keep a close eye on the mouth of the lane.

He'd chased about Glasgow Green on Thursday night for hours, growing tired and cold and thoroughly demoralised. He'd even started to doubt the story Brenda and her friend had told about seeing the Pusher. Except Brenda was sensible and reliable.

He missed her, but he couldn't go and see her. Not yet. Not until he'd done the job he needed to do.

He'd been down here much of Friday and Saturday night too, roaming, creeping between shadows, and waiting here behind the bushes until he shivered.

He might be disappointed again tonight. But he'd made a pact with himself to be here every night until he'd fulfilled his mission.

The scuff of a step alerted him, and there — *miracle!* — across the street was the man he'd seen just over a week ago, moving quickly, close to the building, head down and face invisible under his hood. It was the Pusher, he was sure. There was something in the way he walked, the way he held his arms and kept his face turned to the wall.

Every molecule of Cammy's body vibrated. Adrenalin made everything brighter, clearer, and somehow slowed things down too.

It was going to be easy.

The Pusher came on, approaching the southern entrance of the lane now. If he turned into the lane, Cammy would dart silently across the road and then creep in after him. When he reached the turn, he would sprint after him, knife held high, blade tilted down and ready.

The Pusher reached the lane and slipped into it. Cammy moved out from behind the foliage and stepped into the road.

A taxi tooted hard, making him fall back, and now another car was coming.

Shit!

The traffic moved on and he scampered across the road and into the lane.

He ran, quietly as he could, over the muddy, uneven cobbles to the point where the lane turned — and there was the Pusher, making his way silently towards the lane's north opening, between the two bars.

Cammy hung back but kept pace, then the Pusher stopped and stepped to the right. Something flashed in his gloved right hand. A key. He pushed it into a lock and slipped through a door, closing it behind him.

Cammy crept up to the building and examined the door. It was plain wood, no glass. He moved forward to the lane's end and rounded the corner. The pub, Gail's, was closed down. The frosted windows were in darkness. And yet the Pusher had gone inside.

Cammy's skin prickled with realisation.

He'd found the Pusher's lair.

CHAPTER SIXTY-NINE

10.20 p.m.

Brenda Cheney sat in her dimly lit living room, TV and radio off, and only a second glass of port to keep her company.

Cammy wasn't coming back here. She knew that now. Had accepted it. Brenda was just another person on his list of people not to trust — people who said they'd help him, but then let him down.

She knew how it was to feel let down, to not know who to trust. But she was old and battle-hardened. He was just a boy. A boy who'd grown up in difficult circumstances, who'd learned to mistrust and run away when things got really bad.

She'd tried to look for him after that brief encounter on Thursday evening. Had gone out Friday night too, down to the river, repeatedly walking the four sides of the river that lay between the Albert and Victoria Bridges, looking, always looking. She walked back towards town along the river's north bank, looking for Larissa, finding her at last just after midnight.

'Aye, I know Cammy. Course I know him,' Larissa had told her, curling one of her blonde locks round a finger so Brenda knew she was nervous. 'But I've not seen him. Not for ages.' Nervous and lying.

'You tell him Brenda's looking for him, will you? Tell him to come home to me. Use those words, you hear?'

Larissa had nodded, but relaxed too quickly as Brenda took her leave.

She'd spent Saturday on the Broomielaw, vaping and drinking coffee from takeaway cups. She'd seen Tiffany and Mandy, out early. They'd answered her evasively.

By Saturday evening she was too tired to go out. Her feet hurt and her spirit was drained. Cammy might come back, but most probably wouldn't. She'd watched a film, feet up, and fell asleep, waking around 4 a.m.

Now it was Sunday and late. She'd done the washing, but spent a lazy day, staying local, and soon it would be time for bed.

She felt exhausted and defeated, like someone accepting her fate was to fade and die. But still her heart ached. Not for Cammy now — he'd gone. Another bird who'd flown away. No, her heart ached for her own boy.

When Tom told her he'd spoken about Gav to the inspector, she'd been furious. Unexpectedly so. She'd spent several hours since then trying to work out why. She'd long since cut off hope she'd see her son again, or that they'd ever be part of one another's lives. The last time they'd met, Gav had been as furious with her as she was with him, and they'd spoken poisonous words, the kind you could never take back.

But time had passed. And now Brenda was ill — not that anyone apart from the doctors knew it. Tom knew where Gav was. If he was working for that demolition man, he must be in Glasgow and nearby . . .

She wanted desperately to see him, perhaps for the last time, and for it to be okay. Equable, with kind words instead of harsh ones. Forgiveness, maybe, and the possibility of peace.

Gav's school photo in her hand — the one she kept with her at all times — she phoned her nephew.

CHAPTER SEVENTY

Monday 20 February
9.06 a.m.

Melda Brodick's draft statement had ripped Lola's knitting to shreds. The Comms director seemed shocked by her response.

'Because it's saying we did everything right,' Lola said. 'It's meaningless and offensive and it lets everyone off the hook.'

She wanted to add that its tone was weaselly and sanctimonious but didn't.

'What do you think it should say, Lola?' Wilde asked, sounding a bit scared. Melda glared at the two of them, eyes big, throat growing pink with rage.

'We should present facts and recognise failings with humility.'

'That's all very well—' Brodick began.

'And we should reference a potentially criminal intervention from a third party that might have hindered a proper investigation.'

'No!' Brodick snapped. 'Angus, you can't sanction this.'
Wilde put a hand up. 'Hold on a moment, Melda.'
'You're just going to throw Caleb to the wolves?'
'"Caleb"?' Lola enquired mildly, eyebrows raised.

Wilde fired her a warning look but it was too late.

'Melda, do you have a personal relationship with Caleb Munn?'

'No, I . . . I know him professionally, of course. I admire him—'

'You "admire" him?'

'Yes.'

'You're a friend of his, aren't you?'

'Lola . . .' Wilde said.

'That's why you were with him at the golf club on Saturday afternoon. Or was that a coincidence?'

Brodick went bright red. She opened then shut her mouth and pouted. Lost for words, for once.

'I happen to know Caleb socially, yes,' she said at last. 'What about it?'

'I didn't know that,' Wilde said, looking alarmed.

'Explains one or two things, doesn't it, sir?' Lola challenged him. 'Like how you got a cushy secondment from the council. An insider in the camp.'

'Angus, please,' Brodick snapped.

'Lola!' Wilde shouted. 'This isn't helping.'

She shut up and folded her arms.

'Please, can we try to be constructive?' Wilde asked. 'Lola, why don't you draft a statement?'

Lola glared at Wilde, who had the decency to look embarrassed, then at Brodick, who glared right back.

'I'll write a statement,' she said, mutinously. 'But whatever we say, I want to pass by the families. This is their moment — finally. If they're happy with the text then I will be too.'

* * *

9.34 a.m.

'Quil and I played video games,' Anthony Tait told Lola. 'He'd come round to mine most times, but sometimes I went to his — if his ma was away at her sister's or the time she was in hospital. Other times we played online. Through the night sometimes.'

Kirstie had got Anthony's name from Quilan MacDonald's mother and tracked him down without much trouble. He'd agreed to come in to Stewart Street and seemed more fascinated than fazed by the gloomy confines of the interview room. She'd got him a can of coke from the canteen at the same time as fetching herself a strong coffee — her third of the morning, and hardly a healthy substitute for tropical peach Hyperdrive, which she still craved like an addict.

Tait was the same age as Quilan, thirty-four, but was gawkily skinny with prominent bones and red curly hair, so that he resembled an overgrown kid. Predictably, he had a job in IT, coding for a big company but home based — something he preferred to office work.

He'd known Quilan since school, saying, 'We were the weird kids.'

Quilan hadn't had many friends and neither had he. Their interest was in computers, aeroplanes and any kind of technology. Video games above all else. He spoke fondly of Quilan's lack of social skills and how he, Anthony, had done the talking when they went to gaming conventions.

'Did the Clyde Pusher get him?' he asked suddenly, fixing his eyes hard on her, as if to scrutinise her for any sign she was lying.

'We don't know the answer to that question yet.'

'Because . . . well, Quil wasn't gay, you see. He liked women, though of course he didn't have the nerve to ask anyone out. Do you think the Pusher thought he was gay? Like he made a mistake? Or was it something else?'

'We don't know.'

He nodded, clearly disappointed with the lack of information.

'When did you see him last?' she asked, after a sip of coffee.

'A week ago. He came round on the Sunday afternoon to play games.'

Sunday. The day after the attack on John Paul McCrae.

'And how was he then?'

Anthony shrugged and looked about the interview room. 'Different, I guess.' He eyed her, then looked at his can of coke, seeming shifty.

'Anthony, if you have information that could help us find out who killed your friend, then you need to tell me everything you know.'

He peered at her, then said nervously, 'He was worried. We talked about it. About what he should do.'

'Go on.'

More silence, more nervous glancing about. 'I don't want to get into trouble.'

'Tell me what Quilan told you.'

He eyed her with a mix of suspicion and misery.

'By telling me, you'll help him,' she pressed.

Still unhappy, he relented. 'He said he'd done something and because of that someone had died.'

'What had he done, Anthony?'

'He'd moved a couple of cameras at work, on one particular street. I don't know which one, but he said down by the river, near Glasgow Green. That night a man was attacked on that street.'

'Did he say why he did it?'

'Someone had asked him to. A friend. I don't know who.'

'Did he tell you anything at all about this friend?'

Anthony shook his head. 'He said it was a "he". He said he'd done things for him before. Moved cameras. And . . . and he'd given him a map showing where all the cameras were in Glasgow.'

'Was this over a number of years, or . . . ?'

'Years, yes.' He was acting shiftily now and Lola realised there was more to come. 'He never told me this until last week, honest. He said this friend was helping him in return, but that he was worried. He'd tried not to think about what his friend could be doing — about why he needed the cameras moving — but deep down he'd started to suspect this friend might be the Clyde Pusher. He said what happened on Saturday proved it.'

'The friend was helping Quilan in return, you said. Did he say what that meant?'

Anthony watched her for a moment. 'The friend said he'd found something on Quil's phone. Bad stuff.'

'What sort of "bad stuff"?'

Eyes down. 'Stuff to do with kids. Except it wasn't true! Quil didn't know anything about it. The friend knew it too, but he said if anyone found out . . . But he'd make sure he'd be okay. He was in a position to help him — that's what he said. He told Quil he needed to help him in return, so Quil did.'

'The friend was blackmailing him, then?'

'That's exactly what I said! I said, this is blackmail. I told him to go to the police, but he was scared. It was the friend who killed him, wasn't it? His friend was the Pusher and Quil helped him without realising it. Then he killed Quil too.'

* * *

10.24 a.m.

Checking her email Lola saw she'd had a reply from DS Ali Arshad of the London Met, back from leave. His reply was curt but willing. He'd be free at 3 p.m. today, he'd written, and given his personal mobile number. Then he'd added a curious question: *Is this on the record?*

CHAPTER SEVENTY-ONE

12.20 p.m.

Tom texted while Lola was in the canteen, asking her to ring him back *about Auntie Brenda*.

'Oh, hi,' he began, sounding sheepish. 'Sorry about all that business before.'

'Water under the bridge,' she said, sitting at a corner table. 'What can I do for you?'

'Brenda's been on to me. Not about the kid this time. It's about Gav, my cousin.'

She took a breath. 'What about him?'

'She wants to see him. She says all the stuff with the kid has made her realise she wants to talk to him. She doesn't know I'm calling you. But it occurred to me you might be able to help find him — if he is working for that Jamie McGregor guy.'

'I can't help you,' she told him. 'And even if I could I probably shouldn't.'

'Oh, okay.' He sounded dejected. 'I wondered about going to see Jamie McGregor myself and being upfront about it. Do you think that'd work?'

'It might,' she said. 'But I'd strongly advise against it.'

'Would you?'

'Jamie McGregor's a nasty piece of work, Tom. If I were you I'd stay well clear.'

* * *

12.43 p.m.

'I think it's good,' Angus Wilde said, lifting his eyes from the A4 page Lola had given him. 'Melda?'

Melda Brodick, beside him, was still reading, lips pursed.

'It's only a draft,' Lola reminded them. 'I want the families to approve it.'

At last the Comms director raised her eyes from the page. She gazed balefully at Lola for a second, then turned to the senior officer in the room. 'I can live with it,' she said.

'Well done,' Wilde said to Lola. 'I think you've got the balance of tone and content just right.'

'Thanks, boss,' she said, and beamed at Brodick.

* * *

1.05 p.m.

No one was late. In fact, Kirstie told her, some of them had been there an hour, so eager were they for the opportunity to be heard.

They sat in a circle, apart from Wilde and Brodick, who were there to observe, and so occupied chairs against the back wall.

The atmosphere was palpably tense. While some people talked in whispers, others watched Lola with wide, sometimes teary eyes. She felt a tug of empathy in her chest. These people had been bereaved in the worst way, then lied to and abandoned.

Kirstie had names and relationships noted on a clipboard and passed it to Lola. She looked at the names and surveyed the faces.

Yvonne Craigie was there, representing her nephew, the first victim, Ricky Linton. She'd brought a friend. The sister of Drew Morris, the second victim, was there with her husband and one of Drew's cousins. Mark Brodie's two brothers were there, looking sick and anxious. Michael Mackinnon's father was there, and next to him was Saeeda Hussain and her friend Irfan Abbas. John Paul McCrae's partner, Will Aitchison, was there along with his friend Steve Manners. Twelve in all.

Missing from the meeting were Rona Prine and Alec Bennett, both of whom had declined to attend, and any family or friends of the Czech man who'd died in December 2020.

She cleared her throat.

'May I start by thanking you all for giving Jack Everett permission to share with us the evidence he's been gathering with your help. We'll be collecting his file of evidence in the next few hours, and I promise you we'll take excellent care of it.

'Now, I expect you will all know by now why you're here. We believe there is a possibility your loved ones were killed and by the same individual. We believe that the serial attacker often referred to as the "Clyde Pusher" is real and still active.'

She fell deliberately silent and surveyed the faces of the people in the room as the news sank in. One of Mark Brodie's brothers put his head in his hands and began to sob.

She went carefully on: 'I recognise this meeting is likely to raise uncomfortable and upsetting emotions.' One eye on Brodick at the back of the room, she said, 'It is clear big mistakes have been made in relation to the investigations into your loved ones' deaths.'

Again she paused.

'At the same time, I'd ask you to try to contain any anger or frustration you might feel for the present. We need to be as productive as we can. I need your help to stop this individual before he kills anyone else.'

Nods went round the circle, though she could see scepticism on some faces, and downright resentment on others.

She explained that they might ask the relatives to provide new statements and received nods in reply.

'I have a question for you now,' she said. 'Do you know or suspect who the attacker might be? No matter how fanciful the idea seems, please share it with us. We're open to all suggestions.'

Michael Mackinnon's father spoke up. 'What she means is, she hasn't a clue who it is,' he said, gruff with anger. 'They want us to solve this thing for them!'

One of Mark Brodie's brothers began to protest but the older man wasn't having it: 'No!' he yelled back. 'She's brought us here so we can be all grateful she's taking us seriously, but she's as clueless as the rest of them. Meantime, my son's still dead and gone.'

'Please don't do this,' Drew Morris's sister wailed, and he looked chastened.

'These are early days,' Lola said, clearly, eyes on him. 'We have a number of leads but we need your help too.'

'Of course we'll help,' Yvonne Craigie said sharply, eyes on Mr Mackinnon.

A murmur travelled round the circle, then subsided.

'I would like to read you something,' Lola said, now she had their attention again. 'It's a statement I would like to make to the media later this afternoon. I want you to hear it first.'

Wilde was watching from under his eyebrows from the back of the room. Brodick glowered beside him.

'We propose to release the following press statement at three p.m. today,' she said, and read:

'Police Scotland is investigating the deaths of a number of young men, between 2016 and the present day, each of which occurred beside the River Clyde in Glasgow City Centre.

'Each case was investigated in line with protocol—' some grumbling met that assertion; she chose to ignore it for now — 'and in one case a fatal accident inquiry ruled on the death. A recent review of these cases, however, has found a possible link between the deaths which suggests suspicious circumstances, and that they could be the work of one individual.

'It is our intention to review each individual case, working with the victims' families and friends and any witnesses to the deaths, with a view to bring the perpetrator to justice.

'The review has also found that opportunities were missed that could have identified criminality and linked the cases before now. This failure may in turn be the subject of an enquiry.

'We are seeking information about an individual who fits the following description: a male of between five feet ten (178 centimetres) and six feet two (188 centimetres), broad shouldered and well built. The individual has been described as wearing a hood and possibly a face mask illustrated with sharp teeth and bones, resembling a skeleton's jaw.

'We ask anyone with information to come forward, by calling the following dedicated phone number.'

She stopped, lowered the A4 page and surveyed the room, braced for any response.

Members of the circle looked at one another as the words sank in. She saw frowns and confusion, but also relief and realisation.

'It's good,' Yvonne Craigie said, loudly and firmly. 'Isn't it?' she demanded of the others. 'They're admitting they failed. They're going to take us seriously.'

'Not an apology, is it?' Michael Mackinnon's father grumbled. Someone else agreed.

'It's as good as,' Yvonne near cried. 'For God's sake, look how far we've come!'

'I'm happy with it,' Drew Morris's sister said, then she turned to Lola and mouthed, 'Thank you.'

'Is the mask since Covid?' one of Mark Brodie's brothers asked. 'I mean, it'd make a good disguise, wouldn't it? No one would bat an eyelid at someone cutting about wearing a mask these days.'

'We don't know,' Lola said. 'So far we have no witness statements that pre-date the pandemic.'

Something snagged briefly in her mind. A mask would be useful to conceal any sort of facial feature you wanted to hide . . .

'My Michael's death wasn't investigated "according to protocol",' Gregor Mackinnon snorted. 'Far from it.'

Lola reviewed the line containing those words.

'I can change it if you like,' she said, drawing looks of astonishment. 'I'd be happy to put, "Each case was investigated." Could you live with that?'

Looking slightly stunned, Gregor Mackinnon's brother nodded. Lola glanced at Wilde, who appeared unmoved, then at Brodick, who looked to be barely containing her own outrage.

Tough.

She returned her attention to the ones she was really here for. The circle of bereaved people.

'Now,' she said, 'does anyone have any questions?'

CHAPTER SEVENTY-TWO

1.57 p.m.

Lola was exhausted from the meeting, her vision seeming to swim. Melda Brodick had stormed over but got a hand in her face.

'Not now, Melda.'

Anna went with her to the canteen and stood in line for coffees while Lola found a seat and checked her phone. Her heart jumped into her mouth when she saw a missed call from Gail Long, proprietor of Gail's, the bar at the north end of Merchant Lane. There was a voice message.

'I don't know what this is about,' a disgruntled, smoky east-end voice said, 'but I'm in Lanzarote the now so this isn't awfy convenient. I know you said there hadn't been a break-in or nothing, so what's the urgency? There's no signal at my place up the valley but I'm down in the town the now. Anyway, maybe you could call me back.'

Steeling herself in anticipation of a failure, Lola rang the number.

'The number you are calling is currently unavailable.'

'For God's sake . . .' She near threw her phone across the table.

'Thought I might see you down here,' said an all-too-familiar voice dripping with sarcasm.

'Hello, Graeme,' she said, finding DCI Izatt standing along from her, dressed like he'd been dragged through bushes. 'Having fun with Jamie McGregor, are you?'

'Coming together, as it happens,' he said with a sour expression, no doubt still smarting from having to take over the Scotstoun case from her earlier in the week.

'Found who ran over Kevin Millar yet?' she asked.

'Not quite. We do have evidence of who ordered it, though. Let's just say an arrest might be imminent.'

'Excellent. Come across Gavin MacQuoid yet, have you?'

'Not in person, no. Met your pal Brenda, though. Bit of character, isn't she?'

'I happen to like her.'

'Takes all sorts, I suppose.' He made a face. 'Well, that son of hers is up to his neck in McGregor's business. *Very* nasty piece of work.'

'She wants to see him,' Lola said. 'Brenda, I mean. They lost contact. It's a sad business, really.'

'She might get her chance before long,' Izatt said with a smirk. 'In court, hopefully. He's a handsome bugger too. Want a look?' He went into a folder.

Anna was on her way over with their coffees. Izatt pulled an A4 sheet out. It had text and a colour photo printed on it.

'Here he is,' Izatt said, and handed it to her.

Lola stared, heart stopped, mouth open.

'D'you know him?' Izatt asked.

She swallowed. 'Oh, I know him.' She was trembling all over. 'He called himself something else. My God . . .'

'You okay, boss?' Anna said, arriving with their drinks and staring at Lola with alarm.

She took the coffee but her hand was shaking and she had to put it down. 'I've met him,' she told Graeme, while Anna stared, uncomprehending. In her mind she saw his handsome face, and photos of him and the boat he was building in Argyll. 'He took me out for a drink. He called himself Hughie. He wanted to come back to the house! I knew . . . I felt something wasn't right, but I never imagined . . . He must have tracked me down on behalf of Jamie McGregor.'

CHAPTER SEVENTY-THREE

3.02 p.m.

Ali Arshad sounded breathless as he hunted 'for a quiet corner'.

She heard a door open and close, then he panted, 'That's me in a wee room. I'm dreading what you're about to tell me, if I'm honest.'

'There's no need,' Lola said calmly, disguising how jangled she still felt following the revelation about Hughie. 'The fact is, your name's come up a few times lately. All the same, you might want to sit down.'

'Go on . . .'

He'd been in London for years, she knew, but his accent was still pure Glaswegian.

She explained about the investigation, and that she'd learned he'd been leading enquiries into the deaths of Ricky Linton and Drew Morris, and the attack on Alec Bennett.

'That's right,' he said.

'Then you were taken off the case.'

'So I was,' he said gloomily.

'Would you tell me what happened?'

'Aye. Though who knows you're talking to me? Does Detective Superintendent Wilde know?'

'Not yet, but he might find out. But please don't worry about that.'

'He's the one who took me off the case. I pushed back. We had a bit of a barney about it. I threatened to blow the whistle.'

'I didn't know that.'

'He made it clear it would do no good. That seniors wouldn't listen to me . . . He told me that I'd find myself back in uniform and even face a disciplinary if I wasn't careful.'

'Superintendent Wilde said that to you?'

'That's right. Him and his pal.'

'His "pal"? Who's that?'

'Councillor Munn. Mr Law and Order himself.'

'I see. No one should have spoken to you that way.'

'I know. I know, and . . .' His voice cracked. 'You know, I've never forgiven myself.'

'What for?'

'For not fighting.'

'I can understand why you didn't.'

'Can you? I can't. I've a cousin who's gay. I kept thinking about him.' His voice rose now. 'Those families never got answers. You know some of them tried to contact me after I was taken off the case? I just said I couldn't talk to them. Can you imagine how they must have felt? And worse than that. So many more men died, didn't they?' He paused. 'This is definitely off the record, isn't it?'

'For now, yes.'

She heard him take a deep breath. 'I did something I shouldn't have done. I'm trusting you by telling you this.'

'Go on.'

'I wrote to the *Chronicle*. I wrote to the guy on the crime desk there. His name's Dougie Latimer. D'you know him?'

'Aye, aye I do.'

'He's a good guy. I wrote and told him what I knew. That there'd been a cover-up. We spoke a couple of times.

Once on the phone. Once in person when I was back in Scotland visiting family. He said he'd see what he could do. But the same thing happened to him, didn't it? He was going to do a story but the plug got pulled.'

She tried to move the conversation on, and asked if he could remember any leads that could be of use to her.

'Everything's in the records,' he said. 'Assuming they haven't been shredded.'

'They haven't. Ali, at any point did you suspect who was committing the crimes?'

Silence again. '*I* didn't,' he said at last, and Lola spotted the emphasis.

'Someone else did, you mean?'

'I talked to a lot of the women down by the river. You know, along the Drag? They had ideas.'

'Any names?'

'Sadly no. I remember hearing one of the women talking about his "boltholes", though.'

'His boltholes?'

'Aye. Places he hid, I think.'

'Who said this?'

'Can't remember. I can't even picture her. But the word always stuck with me, you know? It made me think of a wild animal with a den. Gave me the creeps.'

CHAPTER SEVENTY-FOUR

4.37 p.m.

'I thought you'd passed your test,' Brenda growled at her nephew as he briefly mounted the kerb rounding a tight bend.

'I did!' Tom said. 'Fifth time lucky.'

'Maybe you could take it again, for good measure.'

She was making light because in truth she was sick with nerves. Her insides had been upset since the weekend. She wanted to see Gavin, desperately, but at the same time she dreaded it. The look on his face if he didn't want to see her . . . Her stomach flipped once more at the thought of it. Of course, as Tom had told her repeatedly, he might not even be at McGregor's office. McGregor might deny all knowledge . . .

'How you feeling?' he asked her now.

'I'm all right.'

Things had thawed following his offer to help her find Gavin, but she still nursed a grudge. How could he have been so stupid to blab to the police like that? Well, maybe he'd learned his lesson now. Or would he need to repeat that five times as well?

'This can't be the right way,' she said, peering through the windscreen at the Victorian warehouses that stood between them and the river.

'It is. I looked it up,' Tom said.

He'd got mixed up, Brenda was sure of it. He'd always been disorganised — late for things, misplacing possessions. But he was a good lad. Her brother and his wife had raised him well. Made a better job than she had made with Gavin, and that was a fact.

Butterflies all over again. What if he was there? What if he wasn't?

'Here, see,' Tom said triumphantly now and slowed.

There was a break in the railings and a big sign: *McGregor Demolitions Ltd*.

Tom slowed, indicated and took the Mini through the gates and into a yard. There were prefab buildings and vehicles and machinery ranged around a yard.

'Visitor parking,' Brenda said, pointing at a sign.

They followed the arrows then Tom parked and turned off the engine. He turned to her and said, 'What now?'

'I'm going in,' she said, unbuckling. 'You come with me. Always helps to have a reliable witness.'

He looked unwilling but sheepish too. Hopefully remembering that he could have kept his big mouth shut . . .

'Can I help you?' the receptionist said unpleasantly. She was a sad-looking creature in her forties, wearing an old-fashioned cream blouse.

'I'm here to see Mr McGregor,' Brenda said firmly, to show she meant business.

The receptionist's badly drawn eyebrows went up. She peered dubiously at Tom. 'What about?'

'Private business.'

'You need to tell me your name.'

'Tell him . . .' Brenda said, riled. 'Tell him I'm Gavin MacQuoid's mum.'

'Gavin MacQuoid?' She said it as if the name was new to her.

'He'll know who I mean.'

The woman looked unhappy but picked up a phone and muttered into it.

'He'll be down shortly,' she said a minute later.

'Very well.'

Jamie McGregor, all smiles, took Brenda and Tom into what he called his boardroom and spoke to them standing up. He was all sweetness and light, and did his best to appear thoroughly confused. He was sorry, he said, but he didn't know anyone called Gavin MacQuoid.

'Rubbish. You're lying.'

'Why would I lie?' The smile became strained.

'Because you're a criminal and my son's involved. I know what he's like but I want to see him. Where is he?'

The smile vanished completely.

'Mrs Cheney, perhaps you would like to leave now.'

'I'm not going anywhere.'

'Auntie Brenda,' Tom hissed in her ear.

'Gavin MacQuoid doesn't work here,' McGregor said, nastily now, the smile gone. 'And you are leaving right now.'

'Don't give me that, you cheeky prick.'

Tom began tugging at her upper arm and she shook him off.

'Where's my son?' she said, raising her voice to a shout, hoping the receptionist would hear.

McGregor bared his teeth at Tom. 'Get her out of here.'

'Or what?' Brenda demanded of him. 'You'll call the polis? I'd like to see that!'

The sound of engines and screeching tyres filled their ears. A siren gave a single blast. More tyres, brakes now. McGregor was wide-eyed and panicking. She saw his Adam's apple rise and fall.

Out in reception they heard the buzz of the intercom and fists banging on the door. A man's voice yelled that he was from the police and demanded the door be opened. Someone began rapping on the boardroom door and the receptionist's voice, high and frightened, called out, 'Jamie? *Jamie!*'

'Shit,' McGregor said, face white and sweating, eyes on the door then flashing about the room, as if for a weapon or an escape.

'Sounds like someone's time's up,' Brenda commented mildly.

'Mind your own fucking—'

McGregor was cut off by a loud crack and the sound of splintered wood, followed by the receptionist's pitiful scream.

CHAPTER SEVENTY-FIVE

4.46 p.m.

The statement had gone to the press at 3.30 p.m., marked *for immediate release*. The BBC and STV had it on their respective websites within the hour and the *Chronicle* had already put out a link on social media. At the same time it had gone out on Police Scotland's various social media channels.

Meeting in the corridor, Melda Brodick informed Lola that the *Herald* and the *Scotsman* had already been on to her. 'They're asking for a press conference,' Brodick said. 'I hope you're happy with the response.'

'Delighted.' Lola attempted to smile nicely but decided it was too much effort. 'A press conference in a day or two, I think, don't you? It would be good to get a sense of the public response before we speak to the media.'

Brodick looked askance. 'You know best.'

Lola climbed the stairs to the canteen, but stopped at the door. Aidan Pierce was there, hunched over a table in smirking, whispered communion with his pal Lachlan Gray. Gray was no longer on the task force, and would no doubt have it in for her.

Gray spotted her and murmured something to Pierce, who turned and eyed her with gleaming contempt. Izatt would have told Pierce Lola had gone on a date with a gangster. It didn't matter that she'd instinctively kept him at arm's length. The fact was, it had happened — and oh, how Pierce would enjoy himself with the information.

She turned and left.

Pathetic boys. Sad little lives.

She had bigger problems to deal with. Like serial murder.

She headed for the room where Kirstie, Janey Carstairs and a civilian member of staff were answering phones.

The lines had lit up within minutes of the statement going online. Kirstie and her colleagues would spend the next few hours — until eight on the first day, they'd agreed — taking callers' details and information using a computer form that would filter the information into a database.

Kirstie was between calls and shared a number of promising leads. She'd personally taken two calls from potential witnesses who'd seen a man they believed to be the Pusher, including one who'd seen him making his way down King Street, turning along Bridgegate and disappearing into the lane.

'Janey took a call from the manager of Centre 44,' Kirstie told her now.

'The outreach place?'

'Yes. Her name's Caz Barlow. She said several of the women claim they've come face to face with the Pusher. She wants you to ring her.'

* * *

4.52 p.m.

'That was quick!' Caz Barlow said.

'Time's against us, Ms Barlow. My constable said there are women who claim to have encountered the Pusher.'

'That's right. He's well known down on the Drag. I have to say, I'm glad you're taking him seriously at last. And it's Caz, by the way.'

'I need to talk to these women, Caz. Can you help me with that?'

A little sigh. 'Probably. Depends how, and where. We want them to keep using this service, and trust is key.'

'What do you suggest?'

'It'll take me a day or two, and I can't guarantee they'd be willing. You could meet them here for a drop-in, though I doubt very much they'd want to tell you their names or addresses or make statements.'

'Anything they can tell me would be helpful at this stage.'

'I'm sure.' She added, as an almost throwaway comment, 'Of course, a couple of them claim to know who he is.'

'Really?'

'Oh yes. Might be just talk, but you never know.'

'Did they tell you who?'

'No. One told me he's "one of the do-gooders".'

'The "do-gooders"? What — from a church, or . . . ?'

'No idea.'

'Didn't you encourage them to come to us?'

'Oh, I did!' She sounded indignant. 'Of course I did. But they didn't want to. So I reported it myself at the time. I didn't name any names obviously.'

'What happened after you reported it?' Lola closed her eyes, feeling the downward drag of dismay.

'Nothing. I barely got a thank-you.'

'I see.'

'Oh, there was another thing. I remember someone saying he — the Pusher — had a house near the river.'

'Really?'

'I think she said somewhere near the Kingston Bridge.'

Lola's own phone started to buzz in her bag. She saw the call was from a number in Spain and adrenalin zapped through her.

'I'm sorry but I have to go,' she said. 'One my officers will be in touch about the drop-in. Meantime, please try to remember anything else the women told you.'

CHAPTER SEVENTY-SIX

4.54 p.m.

Cammy had seen a video on YouTube that said the key to success was patience and grit. He'd been here two hours now, circling the car park that occupied the area between Stockwell Street and King Street, occasionally making a detour down to the river, then heading east along Clyde Street a little way, returning to Bridgegate by cutting up through Merchant Lane. Pusher's Alley, as he called it to himself now.

He was coming along Bridgegate from King Street when his patience paid off. He was over the road from the north entrance of Merchant Lane, over from the two bars, when the Pusher appeared, a dark-clothed, hooded man, moving quickly, head down, a black formless sports-style bag over one shoulder.

Cammy froze for a second, then followed, tracking from across the road, keeping pace as the Pusher headed for the Clutha Vaults at the bottom of Stockwell Street.

There were people milling on the corner here, smoking outside the bar. The Pusher melted between them, head down, and no one seemed to see him.

The Pusher was across the junction now, at the north end of the Victoria Bridge, heading across the river. Cammy hurried after him, and crouched, watchful, at the opening of the bridge. The Pusher stalked on, reaching the middle of the bridge, at which point Cammy started after him, phone out as a decoy, head bobbing to imagined Lady Gaga songs.

Traffic came over the bridge towards him. No one would think anything was out of the ordinary, that the boy with the bobbing head was tailing a murderer. He gazed about, adrenalin flooding him with a feeling of near-hysterical glee and invincibility. He missed an oncoming cyclist and had to jump out of the way.

But when he looked again, the Pusher had disappeared.

Cammy stopped dead. He couldn't have got across the bridge so quickly, even sprinting!

The traffic had crossed the bridge now and no more was coming on, the rest held by lights at the southern end. The cyclist had gone on her way. Cammy was alone in the centre of the bridge spanning the deep and dangerous river.

He spun round, breath shallow, heart up in his throat, eyes wide for any information that might help him. It was getting dark already. Shadows formed, even on the bridge. The streetlights seemed oddly dimmed.

Something — a sense of being watched — drew his attention, and he looked across to the pavement on the other side of the bridge.

The Pusher was there, his unseen eyes looking right at Cammy from under his hood.

Cammy's blood went to ice and he began to tremble, his face actually shaking. His right hand went into his left sleeve for the knife, drew it clear — only to drop it. He fell to the ground, scrabbling, catching its handle but sending it skittering further away — as footsteps sped towards him.

He fell back against the bridge's balustrade, whimpering as the Pusher loomed over him.

'No!' he yelped, and at that moment realised the knife's handle was beside his hand. He grabbed it.

The Pusher had him by the shoulders, lifting him to standing.

Cammy writhed and buckled his body, and managed to get the knife ready to strike. He plunged randomly, and heard the Pusher grunt and gasp. He plunged again. The man let go of him, grabbing at his left arm.

Cammy made to bolt, but the Pusher had his collar and dragged him back to him, at the same time twisting the collar so Cammy began to choke. He had a sensation of lifting, and his feet left the pavement.

Oh no. Oh God!

The Pusher was lifting him over the balustrade, and all he could do was thrash and wave the hand that held the knife, stabbing only at air. He'd cry out but he had no breath.

He was high now, his centre of balance higher than the top of the balustrade and the Pusher leaned in closer.

'No, *no!*' he managed.

As the Pusher lifted him, his hood pulled back a little. Just enough to reveal the face beneath. No mask this time. A face. A human being's face. A normal face. One he recognised. Had seen only recently.

Except . . . Except it wasn't possible . . .

Still wrestling to understand, he found himself angled atop the balustrade, his hand catching on its surface, and then—

And then he plunged head first, and the oily black surface of the Clyde rose to meet him.

CHAPTER SEVENTY-SEVEN

4.59 p.m.

'Someone letting himself into my bar?' Gail Long said. 'While it's closed up, you mean? With a *key*? Are you kidding me?'

She was calling from a friend's in Arrecife, Lanzarote's capital, so Lola had called her back to save her friend's bill.

'Who's supposed to have a key, Gail?'

'Me, obviously. My mum's got one, and my brother-in-law Terry. He's got a security company. Hang on a minute — you're saying he didn't set any alarm off either?'

'So it seems.'

'But there's a code. You need to know the code!'

'How can I contact Terry?'

'Through my sister. But Terry's in hospital. Had a heart attack, didn't he? He's been ill for a year and getting worse. Whoever it was, it wasn't him. I'll text you my sister's number.'

'Have you any idea who might have got hold of a key or a copy of one, and who might know the code to your alarm?'

'No.'

'How about one of your regulars?'

'One of . . . Are you kidding me? They're a bunch of oldies. I mean . . .'

'What, Gail? Tell me what you're thinking.'

'There's a couple of oddballs.'

'Names?'

'There's a guy called Yorath. Very quiet. Morose, you know? He spent years in Barlinnie for armed robbery. I don't know his surname. He pays cash. Don't know where he lives, either, come to that. A flat in the town, I think. Maybe in the Calton.'

'You said a *couple* of oddballs.'

'There's a creepy guy, younger than most of the others. His name'll come to me. Unusual. Eric? No. He reckons his leg's bad but it's not. Saw him run for a taxi once.'

'Creepy in what way?'

'Always buttering me up. Comes behind the bar. Wants to help out.'

'Tell me everything you know about him, Gail. Please, this is very important.'

'Oh God, it's him, isn't it? He retired because of stress. Now he spends his days drinking.' Lola heard her clucking her tongue as she searched for his name. 'Some kind of social worker, I think. Worked with criminals. That's it!' she said suddenly. 'I remembered. He got cross with me because I kept calling him Ivor the Engine, like the kids' programme, you know? Only his name isn't Ivor at all. It's Ivan.'

CHAPTER SEVENTY-EIGHT

5.03 p.m.

Brenda watched the scene unfold with a curious feeling of detachment, as if it was on a cinema screen or a stage. Police, some in uniform, some in plain clothes, swarmed into the boardroom, one man — the shabby rude one who'd come to her house — shouting orders before addressing Jamie McGregor and telling him he was under arrest on suspicion of fire-raising and murder. He didn't appear to see Brenda, or if he did he'd chosen to ignore her.

A female officer pushed her and Tom back to a far corner of the boardroom, while McGregor writhed and fought before submitting as his wrists were cuffed.

Such noise, such activity — but over so quickly.

The female officer returned for their names and contact details.

'What for?' Brenda snapped.

'To help us with our enquiries,' the officer said.

'Don't make a fuss, Auntie Brenda,' Tom muttered to her.

The place fell eerily quiet, but for the sound of sobbing. The receptionist who'd received them on arrival was standing by her desk, weeping away, fingers steepled and touching her lips. She let out a little scream when she saw Brenda and Tom emerge from the boardroom.

Through the open front door of the building they could see McGregor being pushed into the back of a police car. The female officer who'd kept them back during the arrest was eyeing the building with a male colleague as if they were about to make their way back inside. They'd want to search the place, for sure, Brenda decided.

'What's going to happen to me?' the receptionist gulped out.

'You'll be fine,' Brenda told her darkly and the woman stared at her, mouth open as if Brenda had spoken in an unknown language. 'Do you know where my son Gavin is?' she asked her now. 'It's too late for pretending. Where is he?'

The receptionist frowned and gazed about her, as if trying to remember where she'd left a file. 'I think he's in Clydebank,' she said.

'Where in Clydebank?'

'Auntie Brenda,' Tom said, and she felt his hand on her arm. 'I really think—'

'Ssh,' she told him, then said pointedly to the secretary, '*Where in Clydebank?*'

'Oh . . .' She became jittery with the need to obey a command. 'I'll write it down.'

Brenda snatched the Post-it from her and read. She'd included a post code.

'Good girl,' Brenda said, then to Tom: 'Come on, you.'

CHAPTER SEVENTY-NINE

5.06 p.m.

Lola had to stop herself interrupting Kirstie's phone call.

At last the constable was free.

'Did you get the name of the social worker who oversaw Quilan MacDonald's payback order?'

'I requested it,' Kirstie said. 'Let me check my email.'

She maximised her email inbox.

'Here,' she said, and read, 'MacDonald had a criminal justice social worker for a twelve-month period, July 2015 to July 2016. Name of Ivan Parry.' She gazed into Lola's face and understood. 'Is he . . . ?'

'I think he is. Where's Anna?'

'Upstairs.'

'Log off here then come up and join us. I'm going to request a sheriff's warrant to enter Parry's place.'

* * *

5.12 p.m.

Anna was in a meeting room, on a video call on her laptop. She looked happy to see Lola and Kirstie.

'Hold on, please, Shannon,' she said to the screen in front of her. 'I'm going to mute you for one moment.' She pressed a key. 'I'm talking to Shannon Grant,' she told Lola and Kirstie. 'One of her officers, Pauline Knox, has found something on the system — it's to do with Quilan MacDonald's death. She was just about to show me some footage.'

'Let's see it,' Lola said.

Anna unmuted the laptop and turned the screen. The CCTV operations centre supervisor appeared on screen against the council's pink corporate background, with the ominous slogan that turned Lola's stomach: *Glasgow is safe and sound.*

Lola reminded Grant they'd met before, and asked her to explain what Pauline Knox had found.

'Pauline liked Quilan,' Grant said. 'We all did, but Pauline was particularly fond of him. His death has upset her more than any of us. As I was explaining to DS Vaughan just now, Pauline came to speak to me earlier to say she'd been doing a bit of detective work, taking a remote tour of some of the cameras around Adelphi Street, looking at footage from Friday night — assuming that's when Quilan was killed.'

'Adelphi Street?' Lola asked. 'Where's that?'

Kirstie said, 'It's the name of the path that runs along the south bank of the river, opposite Clyde Street. Quilan MacDonald's body was found beside it.'

'That path's always been a dead zone,' Grant explained. 'But Pauline found that a camera on Gorbals Street at the south end of Victoria Bridge had turned to point right along the path, so you could see a good way along the riverbank.'

'And it's not normally pointed that way?' Lola asked.

'No. It's angled along the bridge. She checked back and it looks like it was moved from within the operations centre the last time Quilan was in, right at the end of his shift.'

'And is there anything caught on camera?' Lola asked, holding her breath.

'I can show you, if you like.'

Anna changed a setting and the screen switched to a nighttime still of a path, seemingly enhanced to maximise the light.

'Ready?' Grant asked, and the video began to play.

For three or four seconds nothing, then a figure appeared at the bottom of the screen: a man walking along the path, away from the camera. He was big and slightly hunched.

'Pauline swears that's Quilan,' Grant told them, then added after a moment, 'And I think so too.'

They watched the footage as the man made his way along the path, then paused and seemed to look left, into undergrowth. And then, a second or two later, another figure appeared, stepping out of the bushes: another man, but indistinctly seen.

The men seemed to converse. The one who might be Quilan MacDonald appeared to become agitated and waved his arms. The other man moved back into the undergrowth, and MacDonald moved with him, head down. The figures disappeared and nothing happened for several seconds — then a shape suddenly appeared at ground level. One of the men had fallen. He moved, struggling to get up, then the other man was on him, beating him, then rising and dragging the man on the ground into the shadows. It was chilling to watch. Lola's mouth was dry and her fingers tingled.

Nothing for a minute, during which time Grant assured them there was more to come. She fast forwarded, then slowed the footage.

A man emerged from the shadows, pausing to look behind him into the undergrowth. Then, seeming satisfied, he came forward. He was using a walking stick and had the limping gait of an old and unwell man. He came towards the camera along the path, stick jabbing at the ground. Just before he vanished from the bottom of the frame, he looked up and about. Grant paused the film and zoomed in, lightening the image at her end.

'That's the best I can get,' Grant told them. 'I don't recognise him, but maybe you do?'

'I do,' Lola said grimly.

It was Ivan Parry. No doubt about it.

CHAPTER EIGHTY

5.18 p.m.

Freezing water, blackness and choking panic. Hands on him, grabbing, pulling, and a woman's voice urging him to stay calm and breathe.

And then he was on land. Mushy, muddy ground oozing more icy water.

'That's it,' the woman said. 'You're okay now.'

Cammy's arms and legs buckled under him and he fell and rolled on his side. Tussocks of grass stabbed his face.

She stood over him, a thin woman, fists on her hips, panting in visible clouds as she got her own breath back. He saw she was soaking wet too. Her high-viz jacket gleamed yellow under the streetlights.

'You saved me,' he croaked, shivering. His mouth tasted of river: mud and leaves and dead things. He spat a glob of dirty saliva.

'Couldn't just leave you, could I?' She knelt and her face came close. 'What's your name?'

'Cameron,' he said. 'You saw him, didn't you?'

'I did but he ran off.' She was unzipping a pocket high up in her jacket. She took out a phone. 'I'm Louise. I was on my bike. I saw you go into the water and came in after you.'

'You saw him.'

'Yeah, like I said.' She jabbed at her phone and it lit up. 'Thank God this thing's still working.' She dialled a three-digit number and put the phone to her ear. 'What?' she asked him while it rang. 'Why are you laughing?'

He laughed till he started choking again. 'It was the Clyde Pusher,' he managed, and now he was crying as well as laughing. 'He's real. He's really real!'

'You're kidding me . . .'

'Till now I was the only witness. Now I've got a pal.'

He heard a voice answer at the other end of the phone. Heard her say she needed the police and an ambulance—

Then he blacked out.

CHAPTER EIGHTY-ONE

5.36 p.m.

The sheriff's warrant to enter Parry's address came back in record time. If Parry was there, she would arrest him on the evidence of the film alone.

Lola tasked Anna with arranging uniformed backup for the arrest then headed for the third floor and Superintendent Wilde's office.

Janey Carstairs caught her in the corridor. 'If you're looking for Detective Superintendent Wilde, he's not here.'

'Oh?'

The constable's cheeks flushed. 'You haven't heard, have you?' she said.

'Heard what?'

'It's all over the news.'

'*What is?*'

'Councillor Munn has made a statement condemning us, saying we're responsible for Glasgow becoming a "den of iniquity".'

'You're joking.'

Lola took out her phone, went into the BBC app, and read the top headline:

GLASGOW COUNCILLOR BRANDS POLICE 'WOKE WEAKLINGS'

Standing in the corridor, Janey twitching nervously beside her, Lola read:

A prominent city councillor has condemned Police Scotland's efforts to make Glasgow the safest city in the UK.

Councillor Caleb Munn, Independent for Swinton and Broomhouse, made a devastating statement this evening to a group of invited reporters on the steps of Glasgow City Chambers.

Munn, who has oversight of the city's Community Safety and Neighbourhood Wellbeing Partnership Strategic Plan, has accused police of being 'woke weaklings, with a commitment to failing citizens'. He accused police bosses of failing to make the city 'safe and sound' in line with the vision in the Strategic Plan, and of allowing the organisation to become 'riddled with power-hungry juniors with destructive agendas'.

He made specific reference to this afternoon's announcement by Police Scotland that they are opening a new investigation into a series of unexplained deaths along the River Clyde in Glasgow City Centre. Munn said, 'Bosses have lost control of their staff and the tail is well and truly wagging the dog.'

Police Scotland have been approached for comment.

'It's bad, isn't it?' Janey said.

'For Councillor Munn,' Lola murmured. 'So where's Superintendent Wilde? In a bunker with Melda, by any chance?'

'Ah . . .'

'What?'

'Melda's resigned from her secondment and gone back to the council — with immediate effect. She rang Superintendent Wilde five minutes before Councillor Munn made his statement. She was on the steps at City Chambers alongside him. Looks like she's working direct for him now.'

Lola stared at her open-mouthed.

Just then, Kirstie appeared from the stairwell, phone in her hand, quickly followed by Anna.

'There's been another attack, boss,' Kirstie said. 'Woman called it in. She saw a hooded man throw a young lad off the Victoria Bridge. The victim's alive. He told her his name's Cameron Leavey.'

'Is he still on the scene?'

'Yes. Uniforms are there. Paramedics just arrived.'

'Anna and Janey, go there. See he's protected and get what information you can from the woman who called it in. Kirstie, you come with me to Parry's.'

CHAPTER EIGHTY-TWO

5.40 p.m.

'Hello, son,' Brenda said, entering the Portakabin at the back of this deserted builder's yard.

The man in the lumberjack shirt stopped his work and gawped at her with amazement. He blinked as if it might clear his vision, make his mother's spectre vanish.

'I've nothing to say to you,' he said, pulling himself together and going back to his business — frenetically dumping sheaves of paper, like someone packing fast for a clean getaway.

He was pale-faced and sweating. But still handsome. Her handsome boy, but grown older, greyer.

Tom appeared in the doorway behind her, still in a panic.

'Are you mixed up in something?' she asked Gavin.

He didn't answer, just went on lifting papers and dumping them into boxes.

'You are, aren't you?' she pushed.

At last he paused and eyed her. 'Why? Come to gloat?'

'I wanted to see you.'

He seemed to see Tom for the first time. 'And what's *he* doing here?'

'He brought me.' She felt Tom cringe behind her shoulder. 'I missed you, Gavin.'

'That right?'

'It is. And when I heard you were working here, I decided to come and find you.'

He pulled a face, shook his head and, muttering under his breath, went back to his task — but faster, throwing papers and thumping down box lids.

When he saw she wasn't moving, he snapped, 'You've seen me now. Say what you've got to say and then leave me in peace.'

'The police arrested your boss,' she said. 'Broke the door down and took him away, leaving that poor receptionist in bits.' She observed his body language, noted his shoulders rise defensively. 'What's he done, Gavin? Did you help him? Will they come and arrest you too?'

He peered at her. 'Why are you really here?'

She stepped closer to the desk where he was working. 'I'm not well.'

'Not well?' He shrugged, affecting uninterest — but she could tell he was stung. She'd always been able to read him.

'I'm dying,' she said, surprised how easy it was to say the words.

'What?' Tom gasped behind her. 'Auntie Brenda?'

She ignored him and kept her eyes on Gavin, who'd stopped his frenzied work and was standing stock-still, eyes down.

'You don't have to say anything,' she told him quietly. 'It's a shock, isn't it? But I wanted you to know, and to hear it from me.'

Still nothing. He took a deep breath and held it.

'Auntie Brenda, you never said!'

'I know. But it's my news to share. Gavin had to hear it first.'

'What do you want?' Gavin asked her, peering at her from under his brows.

'Nothing at all. I just wanted you to know. The rest is up to you. If you don't want to see me again, then I'll understand.'

He muttered something, hands reaching for his papers again.

'What's that?' she asked.

'I said, I can't believe you'd do this to me.'

'Do what, son?'

'Turn up and land this on me,' he barked. 'It's just like you. I bet you were thrilled when you found out. I bet that was your first thought, wasn't it — I can use this as an excuse to see Gavin and fuck with his head.'

'Not that,' she said quietly.

'I think we should go, Auntie Brenda,' Tom said.

She began to answer him when sirens outside made them all start.

'*Shit.*' Gavin looked at the door in panic.

'Oh God,' Tom groaned.

'I should have been away from here by now,' Gavin said, grabbing his phone and a jacket, licking his lips as he examined the windows at the back of the Portakabin.

'Talk to them,' Brenda said helplessly. 'Explain! Tell them you did nothing wrong.'

'Fuck that,' Gavin said, and threw himself shoulder first at the reinforced window, making the whole wall shudder.

More sirens now, from multiple vehicles. Voices too.

Tom had his hand on her shoulder and was pulling her, pleading with her to leave. Gavin threw himself at the window again, dislodging the frame and splintering wood.

Tom manhandled her outside. There were cars, flashing lights and police officers everywhere.

'Gavin MacQuoid?' a female officer demanded of Tom.

'No!' he cried. 'My name's Tom. Gav's—'

'There's no one called Gavin here,' Brenda said firmly. 'Just us. It's a false alarm.'

'*Auntie Brenda!*' Tom hissed in her ear.

'It's you!' a man shouted.

It was the big scruffy detective again. Izatt. She locked eyes with him and lifted her chin, ready to take him on.

'You again,' he snarled.

'I've nothing to say to you,' Brenda said.

They were past her and Tom and into the Portakabin, but swarmed back out seconds later. Which meant Gavin had got away. *Thank God!*

'Where is he?' Izatt demanded, looming in her face.

An unseen car revved and tyres screeched. Heads turned. A black BMW lurched out from behind the Portakabin, throwing up dirt as it turned. Its windows were tinted, but she knew who was driving.

It pointed at the gates, but police cars blocked the way.

The BMW revved, brakes on, tyres spinning wildly, sending mud and gravel flying. Police officers dragged at door handles on either side. Izatt beat at the driver's window. An officer approached with a heavy-looking instrument and angled it at the glass. The BMW tore forward, scattering the officers, and smashed into the nearest police car, sending it whirling back into the car behind it.

The BMW reversed, revved, juddering on its brakes, then cannoned forward again. The police cars jumped under the impact, angled in a V that might just open. The BMW came back again for another assault.

The officer with the hammer ran for the tinted driver's window. A single jab and it shattered. Gavin's arm came up to protect his face, then he sent the BMW ahead once more. The police cars were nearly parted now, but had become wedged between the metal gate posts.

Two officers scrambled through the broken window, arms reaching down for the handle. Brenda ran and threw herself on them, screaming, 'Let him go, *let him go!*'

Izatt grabbed her forearms, lifted them and squeezed, hurting her. 'Cuff her,' he yelled over her shoulder.

Brenda struggled on, and all the time Gav revved the BMW's engine and smashed again and again into the cars that formed the barrier.

Hands took her shoulders, but she managed to free one wrist, and struck Izatt in the face, making him flinch and release the other wrist.

She twisted, facing the female officer who had cuffs out now, screaming, '*Leave me alone!*'

Something seemed to shift in her hip and she screamed in pain this time, and she felt herself falling.

It seemed to happen so slowly: the pain, the falling, the BMW's tyre spinning, kicking up dirt so close to her face, catching her hair; then raised, panicked voices . . .

CHAPTER EIGHTY-THREE

6.09 p.m.

Kirstie drove them to Parry's place, while Lola studied Google Maps. Parry had given his address as Little Street in Finnieston, but according to the map the street was closer to Anderston, and in spitting distance of Anderston Quay on the north bank of the river. From the end of the Little Street, Parry would be able to cross the Expressway using a foot tunnel and cut down the side of wasteland to one of his two killing grounds. An attack carried out, he could return through an area of little or no streetlighting and be home and dry in minutes.

Kirstie turned off West Nile Street into St Vincent Street and Lola realised something was bothering the constable.

'What's wrong?' she asked.

'We're being followed,' Kirstie said, eyes on the rear-view mirror.

Lola turned in her seat. 'You sure?'

'Blue Mercedes. It was parked up in Milton Street and did a U-turn after we passed. I've been keeping an eye on it.'

'Try to put a little distance between us,' Lola said, still twisted in her seat, and Kirstie moved ahead a little — enough for Lola to get a glimpse of the registration plate.

She called the control room and asked them to do a PNC check on the number.

'Blue Mercedes-Maybach S-Class, registered in 2021,' the woman on the other end of the line told her. 'Owner is a Caleb Munn.' She gave Munn's Ayrshire address. Lola didn't need it so said thanks and hung up.

'It's Munn,' she told Kirstie, half laughing. 'My God, he really is insane, isn't he?'

'Want me to stop?'

'No,' Lola said. 'Let him follow us. Park on Argyle Street. If he parks up, I'll have a few words for him.'

'You sure, boss?'

'He doesn't frighten me.'

Her personal phone began to ring. It was Tom. She didn't have time for it. He'd have to wait.

* * *

6.24 p.m.

Kirstie pulled in behind one of the police vans already parked up on Argyle Street at the end of Little Street. Lola watched as the Mercedes slowed then swerved past them and disappeared, heading west.

'Weirdo,' she muttered.

A quick discussion with the most senior uniformed officer to plan their approach, then Lola led the way down Little Street.

Parry's address — or rather the address he'd given them — was for a modern, end-of-terrace townhouse at the south end of the street. Lola noted a footbridge only metres away that spanned the Expressway, leading to wasteland and, beyond it, the riverside.

The house was in darkness. Uniformed officers massed behind her while Kirstie led three more officers to the back of the property.

Lola rang the bell and knocked loudly, then shouted, 'Ivan Parry, it's the police. Open up!'

No response. She tried again. Nothing.

She gave the signal to the officer carrying an enforcer — the heavy battering ram that was a match for the strongest doors.

Two thrusts and the doors burst open and they were inside, officers throwing on lights, swarming into rooms and up the stairs. Within five minutes they knew he wasn't there. Lola found papers in a drawer in Parry's name. And, creepily, a stash of 'Hallowe'en Eyes' — coloured single-use contact lenses in the bathroom in a number of styles, but mostly ones labelled 'Dead Eyes' which appeared to be opaque white.

'This place is a treasure trove of evidence,' Lola said to Kirstie. She turned to the senior uniformed officer. 'Secure the property. Two-officer locus.'

* * *

6.51 p.m.

She and Kirstie made their way quickly back up the street, through a growing crowd of onlookers.

She phoned Anna, who was at the river with Cammy Leavey.

'No sign of Parry at home,' she told her. 'We're heading back to base to make a public call. How's Cammy?'

'He's all right. Pumped up, if anything. Talking about wanting some dry clothes so he can go after the guy who threw him in. Obviously *that* won't be happening — not while I'm here anyway! He knew him, boss. He'd seen him the other night with Brenda Cheney, but he said that guy was old and had a stick. Sounds like it was definitely Parry. But Parry was with Brenda Cheney when they saw the Pusher, so how . . . ?'

'I've an idea about that,' Lola said.

'Boss,' Kirstie interrupted her, eyes on her phone. 'Report of a man in a hood and face mask on top of the Kingston Bridge, beside the railings. Several drivers called it in. Uniforms are there and they've closed the bridge in both directions.'

CHAPTER EIGHTY-FOUR

7.03 p.m.

'That blue Merc's behind us again,' Kirstie said, eyes on the rear-view mirror as they reached the cordon at the westbound slip road that lifted traffic from the Expressway onto the Kingston Bridge. Traffic was gridlocked because of the closed bridge and they'd had to use the hard shoulder. The Merc had followed their lead.

Kirstie wound down her window and spoke to the young male officer at the temporary barrier. She showed her badge. Lola leaned across to show hers and said, 'See that blue Mercedes? Don't let him through. Arrest him if you have to.'

'On what charge?' the officer asked.

'Stalking,' she told him, 'or being a prick.' She gestured for Kirstie to drive up the ramp and onto the bridge.

The Kingston Bridge, where the M8 crossed the river, was normally hoaching at this time, with vehicles constantly changing lanes trying to squeeze through jams. Tonight it was empty and eerily quiet. The traffic was held back by cordons at each end.

Police cars and a van were parked against the railings by the side of the westbound lanes, lights flashing but sirens quiet. Kirstie drove carefully forward. A huddle of officers stood beside the furthermost car, and beyond them, at the apex of the bridge's arc, Lola could see a hooded man at the railings, facing east towards the river. A little way beyond the man, an empty Nissan Micra was parked close against the railings. The man stood very still, and seemed serenely unaware of the police presence.

Kirstie stopped the car and they got out into the freezing night. The sound of car horns came up from the gridlocked streets below. A helicopter whirred to the south of the bridge. Police or media? At this distance, Lola couldn't tell. She approached the group of officers.

The most senior uniformed officer, an inspector, identified himself.

'Thanks for waiting for us,' Lola said.

'Is it the Pusher?' the officer said.

'Could be. The car?'

'We think it's his.'

'I'll talk to him.'

She caught Kirstie's worried eye. 'I know what I'm doing — and I'm not going to do anything heroic. Promise.'

She took a few tentative steps towards the man at the parapet. 'Hello again, Ivan,' she said, voice raised over the horns and the helicopter.

He didn't move. Was it definitely him? Yes, there was something about his posture, the set of his shoulders.

'It's DCI Lola Harris. Remember me? Didn't think we'd be seeing you again so soon.'

Still nothing.

She swallowed and came closer still, only three or four metres away from him.

It seemed even colder up here on the bridge, high over the water, the city spread below them. Lola's breath billowed before her. She watched similar puffs seep from under the man's hood, and tried to imagine what he was thinking.

'We know everything,' she said affably. 'I'm not going to make you go over it all — not tonight. Why don't you just give it up and come for a ride with me? I'll get you a cup of tea and something to eat in the warm and we can have a chat.'

Still nothing. Just white clouds of breath rising into the frozen night.

'I expect it's a relief in a way,' she said. 'All this time, all this secrecy. Time to get it off your chest.'

At last he turned his head slowly towards her and she saw his face. The mask was down, hooked under his chin. But his eyes made her start. They were bone white but for the pupils and they made Lola's skin crawl.

'Those contact lenses are effective, eh?' she said, making light of her own fright.

'I knew it would end one day,' Ivan said, conversationally. 'All good things do.'

'Why up here, Ivan?'

'I like it.'

He turned back to the view so that she could no longer see his face, just his breath dispersing in the air.

'What is it about the river?' she asked. 'I mean, why do you throw them in here?'

'It's my place, isn't it?'

'Not sure I follow you.'

He hunched his shoulders inside his jacket, as if feeling the cold for the first time. The twitch of discomfort was interesting.

'You came to the river when something happened to you, is that it? A while ago?'

He nodded, still facing the river.

'And what was that?' she pushed.

'It was after Lynnie, my wife, died. I was free to . . . try new things.' He paused, struggling to find the words, she thought. 'I went on one of those dating apps. Someone came to the house. Turned out . . . turned out he knew me. He recognised me. One of his friends had been a client when I was still working. By then we'd done things. Exchanged pictures. He wasn't very nice. He mocked me. Said he was going to show the photos to people. I even offered him money, but it wasn't that. He enjoyed torturing me. He said he'd given the pictures to his friend — the one who'd been my client. I . . . I was so scared. I was . . . *humiliated*.'

'I can imagine.'

All the time he'd been talking she'd been inching closer, until she was within a metre of him. She could reach out now and grip his shoulder. If she moved now she could get him under control and take him forcibly to one of the waiting vans. She was scared he would jump. From this height the chances weren't great that he'd survive. She needed him to surrender. It would make everyone's lives easier. Also, he seemed happy to talk. It might be her — and his victims' families' — only chance to really understand why he'd done what he'd done.

'I walked for miles that night. I thought about ending it all. Throwing myself into the river. I ended up at the Albert Bridge at one in the morning. I was wondering how to do it. The tide was in so the water was deep just then. You know the river's tidal as far as Glasgow Green? I thought about weighing myself down, like Virginia Woolf did. She filled her pockets with stones and walked into a river. And then something happened. I was standing there feeling such *misery*, when a young man came along. He was gay. I could tell by looking at him. He was singing to himself and sort of *dancing along*.' He spat the words. 'And I thought, "Here's one of them and he's so *happy*. Who gave him the right to behave with such abandon, while I'm here on the bridge contemplating killing myself?" And then I knew what I had to do to make myself feel better. To take away some of the despair. I waited until he'd passed by, this . . . *camp* individual. I lifted a block of stone that had come loose from the bridge. I ran up behind him and hit him. He fell against the parapet, and I reached for him and lifted him and tipped him over the side into the water. It was so, so easy.'

'That was Ricky Linton. Someone's son. Someone's nephew.'

'That was him.' A satisfied nod. 'I ran off. I was frightened. Anyone could have seen, but it was so late and there was no one about. Then I became paranoid about the CCTV cameras. They're everywhere. A few days later I remembered a young man who'd had a payback order. I supervised him. He worked at the main CCTV centre. And so I paid him a visit.'

'Quilan MacDonald,' Lola said.

'I told him a story about a friend being mugged on the bridge and got him to check the video from that night. He bought my story and checked. Nothing had been picked up. I started to ask him to do favours for me — to avert a particular camera now and then. He was suspicious but I managed to . . . persuade him.'

'You blackmailed him, didn't you? And in the end, you killed him.'

He nodded.

'The night you and Brenda Cheney saw the Pusher on Clyde Street,' Lola said. 'That was MacDonald, wasn't it?'

'A piece of theatre, if you will. A neat distraction. I made him wear a visor so Brenda wouldn't see his eyes. But that was Quilan.'

'Why did you carry on after the first death?' she asked.

'It was so *satisfying*. It was something I thought about for months afterwards. I wouldn't expect you to understand. In time, my need grew. I suppose it became a sort of compulsion. I used a dating app to draw them out at first, but then realised I was making myself vulnerable if someone managed to track the data. After that I relied on my ability to spot a target.'

'Well, I'm afraid your "ability" was a bit off. Not all of your victims were gay. One was straight. Another living with his girlfriend though he was bisexual.'

Parry gave a light shrug. 'Collateral damage.'

She bit her tongue and said, 'Tell me about Cameron Leavey. Did you see him the night you killed J.P. McCrae?'

'He ran, but I'd already recognised him. He was one of Brenda's friends. She'd had me take an armchair to his flat one time. I went to the flat in the daytime, but he spotted me and ran off. So I went there again after it got dark. Those kids never close the security doors. I got in and hid in the stairwell. Then he left the flat's door open when he took the bin out. I slipped into the flat and waited. He went to bed, the lazy good-for-nothing. I crept into his room and cut his throat. I don't think he knew a thing!'

'Except it wasn't Cameron Leavey you killed.'

'So I discovered! Bit of a shock, that. Still, never mind. I got another chance this evening. You'll find his body in the river at some point over the next few days, I'm sure.'

'But you're wrong about that,' Lola said. 'He survived. He's safe.'

Silence as Parry took it in. Lola took advantage of the pause to ask a question that was on her mind.

'Was it you who drove at the green Jaguar, killing the driver?'

'Not me, no.'

'Quilan MacDonald then — doing your bidding?'

'I very much doubt it. I'm fairly sure Quilan couldn't drive.'

She put that to one side, to contemplate later.

'Do you regret it at all, Ivan?' she asked. 'All the misery and destruction you caused?'

He turned to face her, and this time lowered the hood with gloved hands. His lips curled into a humourless smile, and those strange milky eyes gleamed. 'Not a bit,' he said. 'My only regret is that I can't carry on.'

A disturbance caught Lola's attention: a vehicle speeding onto the bridge from one of the ramps.

'I won't let you take me,' Parry told Lola, and stepped closer to the parapet — in reality just three low railings.

'Ivan,' Lola said sharply, 'you don't need to do this.'

The approaching car had come to a halt beyond the cordon. Lola stole a glance. It was Caleb Munn's blue Mercedes. Cops were surrounding it.

She turned back to Parry and saw he'd climbed the parapet and stood balanced on the top rail, facing east up the river.

'Ivan, listen,' Lola began, and she heard Munn's voice in the distance, raised in shrill protest, and a woman's voice with it. Melda?

Away from the noise, Lola felt she was quite alone up here above the river.

'Ivan, take my hand,' she said.

'Put me with Lynnie,' Parry said. 'I loved her so much. That's all I ask.'

He lifted his arms, then, stretching them out like Christ the Redeemer, he fell into the air, tilting his body so that he plunged head first towards the black and deadly river below.

Lola gripped the parapet, her body heaving with despair at her failure.

Then voices sounded close behind her. Munn had broken through, his white hair undone from its ponytail, teeth bared in a rictus. Brodick was running after him.

'I hope you're happy,' Lola said icily to him. 'That man who fell? He just admitted to a series of murders you were only too happy to ignore.'

She didn't add, *your son among them.*

Munn stared at her, his face twisted, as he absorbed what she had said.

'Turns out Glasgow isn't so "safe and sound", after all,' she said.

CHAPTER EIGHTY-FIVE

Tuesday 21 February
11.13 a.m.

They waited half the morning outside the gates of the construction site — Cammy pacing, Larissa perched on a low wall, smoking and yawning, forcing her eyes open — but finally someone came. It was the handsome one, the one who looked a bit like Warren but younger and stockier — his brother, whose name was Patrick, according to the news. He arrived in an open-backed truck and set about unlocking the chains that bound the gates.

Cammy skipped lightly over to him and called out, 'All right?' making him jump.

'It's you,' Patrick said, eyes wide and scared.

'Yeah. Cammy. Wa — *David*'s friend.'

'What do you want?'

'To talk to you.'

'Nothing to say.' The man lifted a second padlock and fumbled for the right key.

'I get it,' Cammy said. 'I'll go see your folks instead, then, shall I? Up at Inchallan. Fancy name for a house, that.'

Patrick stopped, eyes on his hands, breathing hard.

'Or maybe I could go see that fiancée of his. Tell her what was going on. I've got photos, text messages, even a video.'

He'd broken through, he could tell.

'Okay,' Patrick said, pushing the gate open. 'We can talk in the office.'

'Only if I can bring my friend,' he said, waving over to where Larissa sat, watching them.

'Okay.'

'I only want what's due to me,' he said, once they were in the site office.

And Patrick — if that was his name, because he never actually told him — folded fast. Well, semi-folded. Cammy asked for ten thousand, but got five. He made Patrick do the transfer there and then on his phone, and waited to check it on the app on his own phone, trying not to giggle with excitement when the total in his bank account went from double digits to four digits in the blink of an eye.

'Now leave,' Patrick told him and Larissa. 'And don't come back, or I'll call the police and you'll be done for blackmail.'

'It's no' blackmail, though, is it?' Larissa pointed out. 'It's his entitlement as a bereaved partner.'

'Piss off,' Patrick told her.

They went for lunch after that, to a fancy steakhouse on a corner, and ate what they wanted and drank themselves silly.

And then Cammy got the call.

CHAPTER EIGHTY-SIX

1.47 p.m.

'How was he?' Tom asked, sitting anxiously on the edge of one of his mid-century armchairs.

'Not good,' Lola said, putting her phone away. 'He was very upset. He loved her.'

'So did lots of people,' Tom said. 'Even when she was trying her hardest to alienate them and drive them up the wall.' He began to laugh but the laughter turned quickly to tears.

Beside him on the settee in his living room, Sorcha rubbed his arm. Ella was there too, biting her lip and looking traumatised. She was young and Lola suspected violent death was entirely new to her. But Tom had wanted her here, and so she'd come.

Cammy had been distraught at the news, but had thanked Lola for telling him herself, saying it would have been awful to see it on the news. Lola remained worried about him, not knowing whether he had a place to stay. She'd text him later and maybe go and see him.

'I keep asking myself,' Tom said now, 'if she went there *hoping* for something like this to happen. I mean, she knew she was dying, even if nobody else did. The way she threw herself on your colleagues like that — it was as if she was trying to make it happen.'

Brenda had died at the scene, before paramedics even got there, her son Gavin, under arrest and cuffed, at her side. Whether she'd been aware he was with her, they'd never know.

As for Parry, Brenda's old friend, he'd hit the water from an estimated height of twenty-two metres, and probably died on impact. The body boat had already been circling under the bridge, in case it was needed. It fished Parry's body from the river while onlookers in their hundreds watched, many holding up phones to record it.

'I saw you on the news,' Sorcha said. 'You talk very well on camera. You're very factual but empathetic.'

'Am I? Oh well, that's good. I had about three minutes to prepare a statement and I winged the answers to the questions. To be honest, I was so tired I just went into autopilot.'

'Barry saw you,' Sorcha added. 'He asked me to pass on his good wishes.'

She managed not to roll her eyes. 'Tell him "thanks",' she said. 'You can give him my good wishes in return. And tell him . . . tell him I'm sorry it didn't work out. It's just not the right time.'

Sorcha looked disappointed.

'*You* go out with him if he's so wonderful,' Lola snapped, then saw Sorcha's face and suddenly understood. 'Oh . . .'

'It's okay,' Sorcha said. 'He's not your type and I'm not his, apparently.'

'Me and my big mouth,' Lola said.

Tom asked, changing the subject, 'Do you think I should try and help the kid? It's what Brenda would want, don't you think?'

'You're under no obligation,' Lola said.

'Do you mean give him money?' Sorcha asked. 'Dangerous move, if you ask me.'

'I think he wants to make something of himself,' Lola said, trying not to sound overly protective. 'He wants to be a chef, except he's been put on a business administration course. He's feisty. He'd do well with a steer.' She saw Sorcha was on the verge of saying something. 'What are you thinking?'

'Do you think he'd mind starting at the bottom, like in a catering business?'

'Working for your sister, do you mean?'

'I'd have to speak to her, obviously, and he'd need to perform. Jill has high standards, but she's *always* needing people. The young ones go off to university or find other jobs.'

'Want me to ask him if he's interested?'

'Why don't you? I'll speak to Jill. No promises, though.'

CHAPTER EIGHTY-SEVEN

3.12 p.m.

Superintendent Angus Wilde was going to be tied up for another fifteen minutes at least, so Lola headed up to the canteen. Anna, Kirstie and Janey were already in a corner and waved for her to join them.

She queued for an Americano and was making her way across the canteen when Lachlan Gray stepped into her path, lips thin and pale eyes gleaming. She eyeballed him, ready.

'It wasn't my fault,' he said quietly.

'What wasn't?' she asked.

'What happened. The management of the case. I only did what I was asked to.'

'What? Fobbing bereaved families off? Taking half-arsed statements? Blinding yourself to reality? Letting a murderer continue murdering?'

His eyes widened and he began to tremble. 'It wasn't like that! Mr Munn picked me specially.'

'Mr Munn, the disgraced councillor and possible sociopath? *That* Mr Munn?'

'You can't hold me accountable for him! It isn't fair.'

'Oh, I think it's fair,' Lola said. 'Munn gave you power and you took it. I expect you enjoyed it too. You had the power to control and silence people — and I know others helped you, by looking the other way or by egging you on. People like Melda, who I understand was suspended by the council this morning.' She wondered briefly if she was being too harsh, but then remembered the story Dougie had told, of how Gray had intimidated and threatened Mark Brodie's elderly mother into silence. 'You *knew* what you were doing, and I expect you even understood *why* you'd been given the task. Because you're amenable and corrupt and utterly amoral.'

His mouth opened and closed and he gave an impotent shake of his head.

'Nothing to say?' she enquired. 'Well, I expect you'll get your chance when they start picking over the bones of the cover-up.' She enjoyed the expression on his face when he heard that. 'Oh, didn't you know? Reid's planning to commission a public inquiry into the whole "scandalous episode". His words, DS Gray, not mine. Good morning to you.'

And she walked to the table, and her waiting colleagues — ones she was pleased to see.

CHAPTER EIGHTY-EIGHT

3.45 p.m.

'I was talking to the ACC,' Superintendent Angus Wilde said, to explain his delay in meeting her. 'He passes on his good wishes. I expect he might be in touch directly over the next few days. He thinks very highly of you, but I think you know that.'

'Nice of you to say, sir.'

He slumped in his chair and took his time before speaking.

'I wanted to apologise to you, personally. The truth is, I resented your involvement. If I'm honest, I probably feared it more than resented it. It's frighteningly easy to turn away from reality and choose not to see certain indications.'

'Sir.' She wasn't about to sympathise or even try to understand. 'I saw Councillor Munn has gone on "extended leave",' she said now. 'What do you think will happen to him?'

'I have no idea. He'll need to resign from the council, but other than that, probably nothing.' He paused. 'He made a fool of me and several other people, DCI Harris. He and that . . . that girlfriend of his.'

'He and Melda are an "item", then?'

'I believe so. It's grotesque, isn't it?'

'I just hope the council drops that horrible slogan,' Lola said. 'Why can't they use something more honest — like "Glasgow's okay really" or "Watch yourself on a Friday or Saturday night and you'll be fine."'

He laughed and she joined him.

'I heard Gavin MacQuoid talked,' she said now, recalling a conversation she'd heard reported second-hand.

'Oh yes. I hear he wants to cut a deal by shopping Jamie McGregor.'

'Has he admitted to running over Kevin Millar?'

'He has. At McGregor's instruction. Says he was scared of McGregor, though I find that hard to believe.'

'Kevin Millar was a bag of nerves when I interviewed him, sir. Has MacQuoid said how he enticed him out of his flat so early in the morning?'

'He texted Millar from a burner phone, saying he had written evidence of McGregor's guilt in the fire-raising. That he'd be pleased to hand it over, and then Millar wouldn't have to go on record with what he'd heard in the pub.'

'And he bought it?'

Wilde nodded, then he frowned when he saw Lola's distracted face. 'What are you thinking?'

'There's something else we don't know, sir. Parry said he wasn't the one who drove into and killed David Warren Maxwell. He said Quilan MacDonald couldn't drive — something I've checked, and found to be true.'

'And?'

'I'm just wondering, that's all . . .'

'Whether it was MacQuoid driving?'

'I need to think about it some more.'

He nodded and seemed to relax.

'DCI Harris, you ought to know that I've decided to retire,' he said now, eyes down, recomposing himself. 'Cynthia . . . well, her health is getting worse, and I want to be with her. It's best for everybody. I'll leave with immediate effect at the end of this week.'

'I'm sorry,' Lola said, referring to Wilde's wife, but realising it could sound like regret at his leaving the force.

'Not as sorry as I am, DCI Harris. One last thing I wanted to say to you. You acted very bravely, at some personal and reputational risk.'

'Thank you, sir.'

'You fought for what you believed was right, and you followed through. I admire that very much.'

CHAPTER EIGHTY-NINE

Wednesday 22 February
11.13 a.m.

Lola went alone to the temporary offices of Maxwell Land and Buildings, on the south bank of the Clyde, and asked to see Patrick Maxwell.

'I think you know who killed your brother,' she said to the broken man sitting opposite her in his office. She added gently, 'You might feel better if you tell me about it.'

He eyed her, blinking, then his lower lip began to tremble.

'Just tell me, then we can decide what to do.'

Patrick Maxwell cleared his throat. 'You've already got him,' he said.

'Is that right?'

He nodded. 'Unless you've let him go. It was Gavin MacQuoid.'

'Why did he do it, do you know?'

Another nod, eyes down.

'He worked for us. He knew about explosives. We used him for demolitions. We knew he worked for other people too, McGregor included. But then when those warehouses down at Scotstoun went on fire, David got suspicious. You see, a load of explosive materials we keep here had gone walkabout a few days before. He accused Gavin and Gavin got nasty. David said he was going to go and talk to your lot. That was the day he died.

'I knew Gavin had done it. But I was . . .' He licked his dry lips. 'I was too scared to do anything about it. Has he admitted it?'

'No.'

Graeme Izatt had offered Lola the chance of an interview with MacQuoid the day before, a malicious light gleaming in his eyes. He knew full well what he was doing, taunting her with the fact MacQuoid had taken her out on a date.

She wasn't having it. 'No, you put it to him. Ask him direct: did he follow David Warren Maxwell's car and then flatten the man? And if so, why?'

Izatt had asked the question, in the presence of MacQuoid's solicitor, and got a blank denial.

'In that case, maybe I can help you,' Patrick Maxwell said now.

'Oh?'

He opened a laptop and tapped away at it, then swivelled the machine so she could see the screen. A video began to play. It was grainy, but clear enough. It showed Gavin MacQuoid moving something from a box into a backpack, then zipping the backpack and slinging it over one shoulder. He then replaced the box in a cupboard, locked it up and glanced around guiltily. The film cut to show him crossing a yard and getting into a car.

'This was recorded three days before the warehouses were set on fire. In all, he took twelve sticks of explosives.'

'Enough to bring down the roofs of three warehouses?'

'Plenty.'

'Where was this taken?' Lola asked.

'Here at the yard. I can show you the location of the cameras. We'd only just had them installed. They're discreet. Gavin wouldn't have known they were there. Is it enough, do you think?'

She thought about it, then nodded. 'I think it's a start, Mr Maxwell,' she said.

'I hope it buries him,' Maxwell said.

Lola didn't say as much, but she rather hoped so too.

CHAPTER NINETY

Thursday 23 February
8.56 p.m.

There were nine of them and they'd arrived in cars in twos and threes and parked up in the gravel car park. They'd changed in the car park, shivering from the cold, Lola taking Anna's lead as she got into her wetsuit — borrowed from her sister, Frankie — and prepared herself mentally to enter the water.

'You have to be single-minded,' Anna had told her as they'd driven here. 'You're here because you mean to go into the water and nothing — neither the cold nor the fear — will stop you. You'll walk steadily in until you're waist deep, then you let your body fall forward until your shoulders are under. Don't let your head go under, though. Then swim, just a short way the first time. And come out before you feel you're ready.'

Anna had brought a floating flashlight and a tow-float, both of which she attached to Lola's arm. 'Just in case,' she said cheerfully.

Then, wearing plastic shoes, again borrowed from her sister, she stepped cautiously down to the water's edge, trying not to let her mind dwell on the cracked ice frosting the edge.

The loch spread out to the west and south, a perfectly still black mirror reflecting stars. The others, whom Anna knew to differing degrees, and to whom Lola hadn't yet been introduced, began to wade calmly into the water all around her, and Lola's heart raced with panic. What if she couldn't bear it and made a fool of herself? Or worse: what if the shock of the cold stopped her heart and killed her dead?

'Take my hand,' Anna's sweetly smiling voice said to her. Lola took it.

Her feet felt as if they were encased in liquid ice.

'Just keep going,' Anna said.

Up to her calves, then her knees, now her thighs. She gasped and screamed silently inside.

'Go with it. You won't like it when you get to your waist but you'll push through. And then you'll feel the endorphins.'

Anna was right. She didn't like it, and wanted to whimper and run out of the water, but she pushed on regardless, until the glittering water came up and enclosed her — *and she was swimming.*

She stayed in for ten minutes, coming out with a sense of bursting euphoria that made her want to laugh and cry at the same time. She felt as if she'd survived a trial by fire and come out healed, with infinite potential. It was an astonishing feeling. Spiritual.

Anna handed her the spare drying robe she'd brought. She wrapped herself in it, feeling its heavy warmth like a hug.

'And now we drink tea,' Anna said, and unscrewed a thermos.

* * *

9.51 p.m.

Afterwards they drove to a pub in Eaglesham, meeting the others in the bar. Lola felt drugged, but in a good way, fuzzy in her core and all round her edges. A sensation she remembered from being a child, after she'd got out of the bath and was drying in front of the fire on a Sunday evening.

She'd had a text from Sorcha, saying that her sister Jill had met up with Cammy Leavey and liked him a lot. She was going to give him a try-out. *Thought you'd like to know*, she'd texted.

Lola began typing a reply when a voice interrupted her.

'I thought it was you,' a good-looking man said, sitting down on a stool beside her. Anna was still at the bar ordering their soft drinks. He had dark hair, a broad smile but with a gap between the front two upper teeth, and shining dark blue eyes. 'I saw you getting out of the water earlier. I said to myself, I know that face.'

'Sandy?' Lola stared. Sandy Johnson. She hadn't seen him in years.

'You remember me, then!' He grinned, and she found herself smiling along — and felt something flip in her stomach.

'Of course I do. You left the police — what, ten years ago?'

'Aye. Went to work for my brother. Got my own business now. How you doing, anyway? When did you join the club?'

'Oh, I haven't joined. Not yet, anyway. I just came tonight with a friend.' She waved idiotically towards the bar, catching Anna's beadily amused eye and feeling herself redden with pleasurable embarrassment.

'It's so good to see you.' More grinning, as if he really meant it.

'You too, Sandy. And how's — sorry, I can't remember your wife's name. Began with a G, didn't it?'

'Geraldine. I guess she's fine. Only we're not together anymore.'

'Right. I see.' She bit her lip.

Anna came back with their drinks and Sandy made to move. 'Don't go on my account,' Anna told him. 'You two know each other?'

'Just a bit,' Sandy said, then smirked and began to giggle with embarrassment.

Anna turned an enquiring eye on Lola, who smirked herself. 'Actually,' Anna said, 'I might just go have a catch-up with Joan over there. I'll leave you two to it.'

'Nice one,' Sandy said, cheeky as ever, and moved onto the bench beside Lola.

She told him in outline about Joe and what had happened. That they were no longer in touch. He told her about Geraldine. She told him about work, and about the Pusher. He knew some of the story, but not that she'd caught the man. He told her about his business, a private investigations agency, which she was keen to know more about.

At one point, unable to help herself, she yawned.

'It's getting late,' he told her, and she saw it was after ten thirty. 'You look all in.'

'I am,' she said.

'Let me take you to dinner and we can take our time. If . . . it's not retreading too much old ground, that is.'

'I'd love that,' she said, trying not to sound too eager, though at the same time not particularly caring if she did.

'Then let me give you my number.'

Numbers exchanged, she got up and waved to Anna.

She was quiet driving home, and Anna didn't pry. Dropping her at home, Anna said, 'You'll sleep tonight, for sure.'

Lola smiled. 'Do you know?' she said, retrieving the bagged soggy wetsuit from Anna's boot. 'I think I will.'

The Gouger, *Friday 17 March, p. 1*

*PUSHER HERO COOKS UP NEW
CAREER AS CHEF*

by Dougie Latimer and Jack Everett

A young man who was attacked by the Clyde Pusher in February is cooking up a bright new future as an apprentice chef.

Cameron Leavey was attacked by the Pusher and thrown into the Clyde from the Victoria Bridge the same night the attacker was exposed and jumped to his death from the Kingston Bridge.

The Pusher, real identity Ivan Parry, a retired social worker, is thought to have killed at least ten men in Glasgow in the past seven years. His reign of terror will be the subject of an enquiry commencing this summer.

Since the attack, Leavey, 19, has been hired by Jill Monkman, owner of Finer Foods, a catering business in the city that specialises in exclusive parties and events.

'Cammy impressed me straight away with his enthusiasm and willingness to learn, and with his skills as a chef,' Ms Monkman says. 'His savoury petit fours are to die for.'

'I'm really happy,' Cammy told the Gouger this week. 'That night I thought I was going to die, but I didn't, so I reckon it was meant to be. I'm excited about working for Jill and I'm looking forward to going to college to study properly.'

Cammy, who grew up in care, has just moved into a new flat with his friend Finlay. 'I feel like I finally have a future in front of me,' he said.

Continues on p.2

THE END

ACKNOWLEDGEMENTS

A big thank you to Chief Inspector Kirsty Lawie of Police Scotland for, once again, answering a million questions and for generally keeping me in line. It was Kirsty who prompted me to think about the role of CCTV in the plot.

Kirsty introduced me to David Shannon at West Dunbartonshire Council, who kindly explained the uses and ethics of public CCTV and answered my questions.

Thank you to William Sinclair at Safedem Ltd for giving me information about explosives, and to Mark Willshaw for assistance with scenes relating to large fires.

Chris Burrows from Glasgow City Council provided me with information about the river and its depth at various points in the city centre. Fascinating. Thanks to Kathryn Connor for putting us in touch.

All of these people were generous in sharing their professional knowledge and skills. It's all the more important, therefore, to stress that I often employ 'poetic licence' to help make the story work; any deviations from reality are mine.

I want to acknowledge the support of the late Hon. Lord McEwan for checking the legal aspects of the story, for helpful feedback, and for me as well as providing me with some fascinating insights into Scotland's legal landscape — some of which may feature in future stories.

Thanks to Lynn Sheridan for explaining criminal justice social work, and for introducing me to RoseAnn Cameron at Routes Out. RoseAnn and her colleague Emma Howard were very generous with their time. Lynn and RoseAnn read a draft of the book for me and gave me much-needed reassurance.

Thanks also to Ben Crawford for taking me out on the Glasgow scene and for making me feel like a granddad; also for his help with 'youth speak'. Blame Ben if it's not on trend.

Sarah Neely invited me to talk to the Glasgow Feminist Book Group. It was here that Alenka Jelen told me about the legend of the Manchester Canal Pusher and planted a seed that grew into this story. Thanks to Alenka for that. The same night I learned about the 'Covid Divorce Club' and realised Lola might enjoy joining such a group, so invented a parallel version for her.

Thank you to Heather Reid for her generosity in hosting the launch of the second Lola Harris book in June 2023.

A shout out to Simon and Chris for once again letting me stay at their cottage in Kintyre to write bits of the book. Thanks, too, to the Perch Café in Garelochhead, the Park Pavilion Café in Helensburgh and Skoosh Café in Drymen, for letting me type in corners — and to the Perch for selling so many signed copies of the books!

Big thanks to writer friends for their ongoing support, which ranges from technical help to sanity checks: in particular Sally-Anne Martyn (my 'Blackpool wife') and Linda Mather.

Clare O'Donnell and Fiona Macdonald helped me with character names, after mocking some of my choices.

Tom and Kay Dingwall generously bought copies of my books for half of Helensburgh. I really do appreciate the support.

I asked a number of people to read the book for me in draft, which was reassuring when my confidence was lacking.

Thank you to my mum, Julie, and to my partner, Gordon Munro. Also to Alison Winch, Allan Radcliffe, Astrid Reid, Fiona Macdonald, Janice Fraser, Joanne Welding, John Gregory, Katharine Bradbury, Laura Hamilton, Linda Mather, Martin Rennie, Phil Milverton and Rowena Gregory (who gets a gold star for the most incisive analysis, comments and suggestions this time!).

Emma Grundy Haigh and all at Joffe Books are so great to work with. I'm grateful for their enthusiasm for Lola and her exploits.

I'm very grateful to my agent Francesca Riccardi for her ongoing support, pep talks and encouragement.

Last but not least, a special thank you to Margaret Murphy for her wisdom, technical advice and ongoing support and friendship. I wouldn't be doing this without her.

THE JOFFE BOOKS STORY

We began in 2014 when Jasper agreed to publish his mum's much-rejected romance novel and it became a bestseller.

Since then we've grown into the largest independent publisher in the UK. We're extremely proud to publish some of the very best writers in the world, including Joy Ellis, Faith Martin, Caro Ramsay, Helen Forrester, Simon Brett and Robert Goddard. Everyone at Joffe Books loves reading and we never forget that it all begins with the magic of an author telling a story.

We are proud to publish talented first-time authors, as well as established writers whose books we love introducing to a new generation of readers.

We won Trade Publisher of the Year at the Independent Publishing Awards in 2023. We have been shortlisted for Independent Publisher of the Year at the British Book Awards for the last four years, and were shortlisted for the Diversity and Inclusivity Award at the 2022 Independent Publishing Awards. In 2023 we were shortlisted for Publisher of the Year at the RNA Industry Awards.

We built this company with your help, and we love to hear from you, so please email us about absolutely anything bookish at: feedback@joffebooks.com.

If you want to receive free books every Friday and hear about all our new releases, join our mailing list: www.joffebooks.com/contact

And when you tell your friends about us, just remember: it's pronounced Joffe as in coffee or toffee!

ALSO BY DANIEL SELLERS

DCI LOLA HARRIS SERIES
Book 1: MURDER IN THE GALLOWGATE
Book 2: MURDER IN LOVERS' LANE
Book 3: MURDER ON THE CLYDE

Milton Keynes UK
Ingram Content Group UK Ltd.
UKHW050731160424
441246UK00004B/129

9 781835 264980